By Ian Douglas

Star Corpsman
BLOODSTAR
ABYSS DEEP

Star Carrier
EARTH STRIKE
CENTER OF GRAVITY
SINGULARITY
DEEP SPACE
DARK MATTER

The Galactic Marines Saga

The Heritage Trilogy
SEMPER MARS
LUNA MARINE
EUROPA STRIKE

The Legacy Trilogy
STAR CORPS
BATTLESPACE
STAR MARINES

The Inheritance Trilogy
STAR STRIKE
GALACTIC CORPS
SEMPER HUMAN

DARK MATTER
STAR CARRIER
BOOK FIVE

IAN DOUGLAS

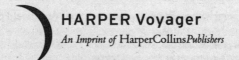

HARPER Voyager
An Imprint of HarperCollinsPublishers

HARPER Voyager
An Imprint of HarperCollins*Publishers*
195 Broadway
New York, New York 10007

Copyright © 2014 by William H. Keith, Jr.
Cover art by Gregory Bridges
ISBN 978-0-06-218399-6
www.harpervoyagerbooks.com

First Harper Voyager mass market printing: June 2014

Harper Voyager and) is a trademark of HCP LLC.

Printed in the U.S.A.

10 9 8 7 6 5 4 3 2 1

As always,
throughout the multiverse,
worlds without end,
for Brea

DARK MATTER

Prologue

They called themselves the *Consciousness*.

Following the faint but telltale leakage of gravity from one universe to another, they'd detected the circle of whirling masses as they opened a passageway between the 'branes, emerging in a four-dimensional space subtly different from other, known realities. They were working now to create a permanent gateway between universes, creating girders and connectors spanning light years, coaxing solid light from the vacuum energy itself, anchoring suns, mining starcores, imbedding the structural components within the fabric of spacetime itself.

At this point, the scope of the Consciousness spanned a number of universes. A metamind, a hive mentality, it was an emergent epiphenomenon arising from the interplay of some hundreds of quadrillions of individual minds, extending across separate realities and billions of years of time. The oldest individuals among them had outlived the universes of their birth, existing now in a kind of nomadic existence as they moved from reality to parallel reality.

The Consciousness was powerful to the point of truly godlike creativity, omnipotence, and omniscience. It was aware of events across vast scales in size and time, from quantum fluctuations in the vacuum energies that formed the base state of reality up to the gravitational interactions within galactic clusters. Their senses extended across multiple dimensions, allowing them to peer inside the cores of stars as they mined them, and they could manipulate time in subtle and surprising ways.

Unfortunately, some phenomena simply were . . . not too *small*, exactly, since they could perceive the dance of individual atoms, but too inconsequential, too unimportant to register clearly within the metamind's awareness without a special act of focus.

Phenomena such as the squadron of USNA naval vessels now entering the construction field . . .

Chapter One

20 January 2425

Recon Flight Shadow-One
Omega Centauri
1010 hours, TFT

"And three . . . and two . . . and one . . . *launch*!"

Acceleration slammed Lieutenant Louis Walton back in his seat as his CP-240 Shadowstar hurtled down the long and narrow tunnel, riding the magnetic launch rail, vision dimming . . . and then he emerged into open space, the pressure of 7 gravities replaced in an instant by the blessed, stomach-dropping relief of zero-G. Astern, the vast gray disk of *America*'s forward shield cap fell away, dwindling to a star, then to invisibility in moments. He was traveling now at better than 600 kilometers per hour.

Ahead was twisted, enigmatic light . . . and sheerest wonder.

"*America* Primary Flight Control, this is Shadow One," he called over his in-head. "I'm clear and in the open."

"Copy, Shadow One," a voice replied. "Come to one-five-one by two-seven-zero by zero-three-two. You be careful out there, okay?"

"That is a very large affirmative," Walton replied. "You

just happen to be talking to the ship library's downloaded image of *careful*."

"Lou," the voice in Prifly said, "if that were true, you wouldn't have volunteered for this run in the first place."

True enough. But Walton wouldn't have missed this for the world. For *several* worlds . . .

The panorama ahead was being fed by the Shadowstar's imaging system directly into his brain. From his perspective, he *was* the reconnaissance fighter, hurtling into strangeness.

He was hurtling through the depths of a globular star cluster, a vast, teeming beehive of stars called Omega Centauri, some sixteen thousand years from Sol. But the cluster was . . . changed from what it once had been.

Across the whole, vast, star-crowded sky, hundreds of thousands of suns were gone, leaving dark streaks like daggers piercing the cluster's heart. Stars had deliberately been merged with stars, creating a central blue giant blazing at the cluster's core, filling a spherical region almost two light months across with hazy, blue light.

And stretching out from that central sun was a structure of some kind. *Stellarchitecture*, they'd dubbed it, back in the labyrinths of *America*'s intelligence department. An unimaginably vast tangle of beams and platforms and spheres and connectors and sweeping curves, some of the structures apparently solid, but the larger ones apparently consisting of blue mist. Following some of those beams with your eye was not a good idea. They were . . . *bent*, somehow, twisted in disturbing ways suggesting that dimensions other than the normal three spatial ones were being employed here.

Most disturbing of all was the fact that time was being twisted through strange dimensions as well. None of this had been here when the deep-space research survey vessel *Endeavor* had arrived in the Omega Centauri cluster four months earlier. Now, the sky was filled with structures that appeared to span *light years* . . . and yet, portions of stellar-architecture more than four light months across were plainly visible. The light from the far ends of those things simply couldn't have traveled this far in the intervening time.

And yet, there it was, defying what Walton and *America*'s science department were pleased to call the inviolable laws of physics. There were beams, like gossamer threads glittering in the light of 10 million cluster stars, somehow anchored within the central sun and stretching out and out and out until they were masked by the cluster's massed suns. Space and time both were not what they seemed here.

The effect was eerily and indescribably beautiful, an abstract painted in myriad shades and hues of blue and violet light, with deep, rich reds in those eye-watering places where structures vanished from normal spacetime.

"*America* CIC, this is Shadow One," Walton said. "Handing off from PriFly."

"Copy, Shadow One," a different voice replied from *America*'s Combat Information Center. "Primary Flight Control confirms handoff to CIC. You are clear for maneuver."

"Accelerating in three . . . two . . . one . . . *engage*!"

At 50,000 gravities, the Shadowstar hurtled deeper into the cluster.

USNA CVS America
The Black Rosette
Omega Centauri
1016 hours, TFT

"I wish I knew what the hell we were looking at."

Rear Admiral Trevor "Sandy" Gray stared at the deck-to-overhead viewall in *America*'s officers' lounge. He'd been staring into the cosmic panorama every chance he got for three days, now, and was no closer to understanding what he was seeing than he'd been when the task force arrived.

It was, he thought, unimaginably, sublimely beautiful.

It was also utterly mysterious, quite possibly completely and forever beyond human understanding.

The Omega Centauri globular star cluster was the largest such known within the Milky Way galaxy. Some 230 light years across, that teeming, crowded sphere of 10 million closely packed stars was known to be the stripped-down core of a small, irregular galaxy cannibalized by the Milky Way perhaps 800 million years before. That long ago, Earth had been inhabited solely by single-celled microorganisms that were just on the point of discovering sex, but a highly advanced collective of numerous technic species had already been stellarforming their galaxy. Among other things, they'd created a rosette of six supergiant stars, each forty times the mass of Earth's sun, rotating them about a common center of gravity in a way—it was now believed— that had opened pathways to other places in space . . . and almost certainly other times as well.

That galaxy, called the N'gai Cloud by its inhabitants, had been devoured and shredded, its inhabited worlds scattered. At about the same time, the N'gai's starfaring cultures, collectively called the ur-Sh'daar, had undergone a technological singularity . . . a technic metamorphosis that had transformed them far beyond the ken of those left behind.

The remnant left had, with the passage of 876 million years, become the Sh'daar, mysterious galactic recluses who dominated some thousands of technic species across the galaxy, and who'd become the enemies of Humankind.

That much, at least, had been learned by *America*'s battlegroup under the command of Admiral Koenig, which had used an ancient, artificial singularity generator, a massive, fast-spinning cylinder a kilometer across called a TRGA, to travel into the remote past and confront the

Sh'daar within their home galaxy. Communications of a sort had been established, a kind of truce declared; electric downloads had revealed the ur-Sh'daar, and the fear-crippled, broken relics that eventually had become the modern Sh'daar.

That had been almost twenty years ago. Gray, at the time, had been a Navy lieutenant and a fighter pilot. Before that he'd been a monogie prim—the words were *not* compliments—from the half-sunken ruins of Manhat.

God, he'd come a long way since then.

Captain Sara Gutierrez was one of two black-uniformed women standing next to Gray in the officers' lounge. "It's so *terrible*."

"Terrible? In what way?"

"You can see where they've destroyed whole swaths of the cluster. Destroyed the *stars*. What kind of monsters are we dealing with here?"

"Very, very powerful ones," the other woman observed. She was Commander Laurie Taggart, *America*'s chief weapons officer.

The Omega Centauri cluster had been partially disassembled. Needle-slender, impossibly long black streaks could be seen now, stretching out from that artificial central sun, gaps and swaths among the cluster's tightly packed stars where hundreds of thousands of suns had been moved or destroyed.

The sky at the cluster's center was dominated by a vast and hazy field of blue-violet light, by enigmatic structures that themselves seemed to be made of light, by impossibly vast constructs of beams and platforms and spheres and connectors of pale, blue mist. Many of those structures appeared bent in disturbing ways that hurt the eye. Like a lithograph by M. C. Escher, many of those shapes did not appear to obey the usual laws of three-dimensional geometry. In the distance, an artificial sun, a star fifty times more massive than Sol created by dragging a number of the cluster's stars together and merging them, illuminated the central reaches of Omega Centauri with a harshly actinic glare.

"I think they must be adding on to the Rosette," Gray said. "We may learn more when our recon probe gets in closer."

What was the name of the VQ-7 Shadowstar pilot they'd just launched? Walton, that was it. His in-head provided the name and service record access. Young kid, twenty-five . . . four years in the Navy, two wives and a husband back in Omaha . . .

And he was hurtling now into the very heart of strangeness.

Deep within Omega Centauri's core was the enigmatic Black Rosette, an obviously artificial arrangement of six black holes, each some forty times the mass of Sol, all orbiting their common center of gravity in a tight, tight gravitational embrace. If you were close enough to see them, the individual black holes blurred into an indistinct, smoky ring by the speed of their orbit—something like 26,000 kilometers per second.

Eight hundred seventy-six million years ago, the Rosette had been the Six Suns, six blue supergiant stars in a gravitationally balanced circle apparently created by the vanished ur-Sh'daar. But stars with forty times Sol's mass don't live for long on the cosmic scale of things . . . a few tens of millions of years at most. Long ago, the Six Suns had exploded, their cores collapsing into black holes, point sources of incredibly powerful gravitational forces. Now, they were the Black Rosette. As they circled their common center, their movement through space and their combined gravitational fields sharply distorted spacetime, creating a kind of stargate, one far larger and far more powerful than the enigmatic TRGA cylinders that had been discovered elsewhere in the galaxy.

The truly chilling import of what he was seeing, Gray thought, wasn't so much the destruction of so many suns as it was the fact that the Rosette Aliens, whatever they were, appeared to be building their colossal stellarchetecture in time as well as in space.

The light from those changes in the starfield could not possibly have reached this point in space yet.

Somehow, the Rosette Aliens were disassembling the cluster and weaving their structures through time as well as space. The best guess the physics team on board *America* had been able to come up with so far was that the aliens had so distorted the local spacetime continuum that they'd actually changed Omega Centauri's history. Those black swaths and gaps now visible among the stars had not been created within the past four months . . . but as of now had been there for well over a century, long enough for the light recording those changes to have traveled this far.

And that fact alone spoke volumes about the Builders' power.

"I wonder if any of those stars they destroyed had worlds?" Gutierrez said. "*Inhabited* worlds?"

"Not likely," Gray replied. "These are stars from an ancient galactic core, remember. Population Two, most of them. That means they're metal poor, almost entirely hydrogen, and very, very old. No heavy stuff—no iron or silicon or anything else—for building planets."

"It still seems . . . arrogant," Taggart observed. "Just pop in out of nowhere and start taking apart a star cluster! Like they own the place!"

"Like the stargods?" Gray said, smiling gently.

"Fuck you," Taggart said, then added, "*Sir.*"

Gray accepted the vulgar familiarity with a chuckle. He *had* deserved it. Laurie Taggart was an AAC, an Ancient Alien Creationist, a follower of a religion that boasted perhaps 20 million official adherents Earthside, and millions more who believed the basic dogma without belonging to the church. The AACs held that Earth had been visited in the remote past by technologically advanced aliens who, among other things, had tinkered with the genome of certain native bipeds to create *Homo sapiens*.

Gray couldn't buy that himself. The AAC mythology painted the Ancient Aliens as interstellar busybodies who were so . . . so *human*, building pyramids here, creating alien-human hybrids there, nuking Sodom and Gomorrah or whipping up a planetary flood to drown the human population out of existence when they got pissed off.

If there were stargods, Gray thought, they would be more like those Builders out there, annihilating stars without a second thought, rewriting the time line of an entire galactic cluster, and those were beings so advanced that they might not even notice mere Humankind. He and Taggart had discussed the idea more than once, and he enjoyed lightly tweaking her about it now and again.

But the encounter with these cluster-reshaping beings during the past few days had profoundly shaken her, he knew. It might be a good idea not to tease her about her religion.

In any case, that sort of thing nowadays was considered socially unacceptable. The White Covenant, a set of international agreements in place since the late twenty-first century, mandated only that you weren't allowed to proselytize or forcefully convert others when it came to religion . . . but after three and a half centuries most people took that to mean a prohibition on *any* discussion of religious belief or disbelief. At the very least, such a discussion was considered rude. Bull sessions among friends were okay, sure . . . but in a professional setting like this . . . not so much.

That alien vista outside of *America*, Gray knew, was wearing at everyone in the squadron. *Gnawing* at them. The worst of it was knowing that the aliens had already destroyed the research ship RSV *Endeavor* and two escorting destroyers, *Miller* and *Herrera*, killing over fifteen hundred personnel on board. They'd been obliterated in an instant, four months ago, when something had come through the Rosette from . . . somewhere else. The destruction had been captured on video taken by an HVK-724 high-velocity scout-courier robot, which had subsequently returned the images to Earth.

Gray and his staff had spent a lot of hours studying those images. The alien vessels, if that's what they were, appeared to be featureless, mirror-polished silver ovoids ranging in size from a few meters to nearly a kilometer in length. There was no sign of them now, though . . . only those enigmatic and impossible structures of light.

"As for what we're looking at, sir," Taggart continued quietly, "I think we have to assume that they're using the Rosette as a transit gate from wherever they came from. We know that there are many possible paths through the space-time opening."

"One octillion," Gray said. "Ten to the twenty-seven distinct spacetime pathways. Assuming that the Black Rosette is the same as the Six Sun rosette built eight hundred seventy-six million years ago."

"The number may be very much larger now," a voice said in their heads, speaking through their in-head circuitry. The AI that ran *America* was always there, listening, and very occasionally putting in a word or two.

"Why is that?" Gutierrez asked.

"The black holes of the Rosette in Omega Tee-Prime distort spacetime between them to a far greater degree than was true for the Six Suns of Tee-Sub. The actual number of distinct spacetime pathways through Tee-Prime may exceed one centillion—or ten to the three hundred third power—essentially, and for all intents and purposes, nearly infinite."

And *that* was a sobering thought.

Omega Tee-Prime was the shorthand term for the Omega Centauri cluster today, time now, in the year 2425. *Omega Tee-Sub*, on the other hand, was shorthand for the unwieldy $T_{-0.876gy}$, a clumsy term pronounced "Tee sub minus zero point eight seven six gigayear" and identifying the N'gai Cloud of the ur-Sh'daar, 876 million years in the past.

If the Rosette Aliens were busily rewriting the cluster's immediate past, Gray thought glumly, it might be necessary to come up with some new spacial-temporal terminology as well. Time travel made everything so damnably *complicated*.

And yet, the ability to reshape time was an obvious follow-on to the ability to warp space. Ever since Einstein, physicists had known that space and time were not distinct entities, but dimensional aspects of each other, of *space-time*. Human ships used projected, artificial gravitational singularities to move themselves through space; in theory, it should be possible to do the same to move through time, though that would require a *lot* of energy—more energy than even a star carrier's quantum power tap could supply. In another few centuries, perhaps . . .

But the Black Rosette Aliens were doing it *now*.

From *America*'s current position, the Black Rosette was made invisible by distance, but close-up passes by the *Endeavor* before her destruction had shown tantalizing glimpses of alien scenes, alien starfields peeking out through the lumen of that hazy circle of rotating singularities.

What, Gray wondered yet again, were the Rosette Aliens up to? Who were they? Where—*when*—did they come from? Were they Sh'daar? Transformed and transfigured ur-Sh'daar? Or someone, some*thing* utterly and completely different?

The stargods? It was as good a name as any . . . though the term *Rosette Aliens*, for now, carried less emotional baggage for the merely human observers on board *America* and her consorts.

Gray checked the time. Walton's Shadowstar should be approaching the Rosette fairly soon, now. And if Walton survived the flight, they just might learn something more about exactly what the Rosette Aliens were up to.

Recon Flight Shadow-One
Omega Centauri
1118 hours, TFT

Lieutenant Walton was decelerating now, his Shadowstar flipped end for end so that he was slowing from very nearly the speed of light. He needed to be moving at a more sedate pace if he and the ship's AI were actually to see and record anything as they made their close passage of the Rosette. He couldn't see much at all right now. He'd reshaped the drive singularity forward to extend a stealth sheath aft over his fighter. From most angles, now, his Shadowstar was invisible, the light coming from space around him sliding around the craft without ever quite reaching it. As camouflage, it was moderately effective, though instruments and organic eyeballs might still see a distortion of the background stars as he slid past—and the rapidly flickering gravity well of his drive singularity was, as always, a dead giveaway.

So far, though, the Rosette Aliens hadn't appeared to notice him. That . . . or they didn't *care.*

He found the thought disturbing, akin to the thought of humans paying no attention to an ant crossing the path in front of them.

But if one of those humans chose to bring his foot down just so . . .

"I recommend dropping the sheath," his AI told him. "We are approaching our objective."

"Do it," Walton said. "Let's see what we have."

He braced himself . . . and just in time. The sheath fell away as the artificial intelligence running the Shadowstar reconfigured the drive singularity, and the dazzling light of the heart of a globular cluster flooded in.

Millions of stars crowded one another across the spherical interior of that radiant sky. Streaks of blackness showed where the Rosette Aliens had been busy at their enigmatic work of demolition and construction. Visible, too, was the tangle of structures created over the past few months by the aliens, an incredibly vast spider's web of pale blue light apparently anchored on and within the encircling stars.

Ahead and to starboard, a cluster of spheres hung adrift in space, each gleaming silver and as reflective as liquid mercury. And to port: the Black Rosette.

Whirling about their common center of gravity at 26,000 kilometers per second, the six black holes themselves were little more than a circular blur. Gas and dust streamed in from surrounding space, encircled the Rosette in a tight spiral radiating far into the short end of the electromagnetic spectrum and filling the sky with actinic blue-violet light. Hard radiation glared from the annihilation of infalling dust. This was, Walton thought, an extremely dangerous place to be. His ship's shields would hold off the radiation for a time, but not indefinitely.

Walton's Shadowstar was drifting rapidly across the face of that spiral, 100,000 kilometers away from the central maw. The expanse of space haloed by the rotating singularities revealed a starscape beyond, but not the vista of the Omega Centauri cluster.

He glimpsed a starfield . . . but one far thinner and poorer than that of the interior of the cluster. That scene was replaced in an instant by utter strangeness, by twisted and entangled streamers of red and gold and blue, the heart, possibly, of a nebula . . . or just possibly something else entirely, something beyond human experience. After that, more starfields, coming in rapid succession, and then a vast and mottled expanse of deep red-orange glare . . . the surface, he thought, of a red sun, a red dwarf, possibly, seen at close range. More starfields . . . and a panorama that seemed to show a spiral galaxy tilted sharply on end . . . and then a blast of blue light and hard radiation—a supernova, perhaps—or, again, something for which human astrophysics had no name.

Walton had the distinct impression that the scenes revealed within the Rosette changed as his angle of sight changed. There were myriad distinct paths through that gravitationally tortured gateway . . . that rip in the fabric of spacetime itself, and he was glimpsing hundreds of them as his Shadowstar fell across the Rosette's maw. So fascinated was he by the succession of alien vistas that his AI had to give him the warning.

"We have elicited a response from the Rosette Aliens," the Shadowstar's artificial intelligence announced, its mental voice as calm and dispassionate as a netfeed announcement of next week's weather over Omaha. "Directly ahead."

Walton jerked his attention from the Black Rosette, and turned it instead to a bright silver star moving now into his recon ship's path. He enhanced the magnification, zooming in on a perfectly reflective sphere that did not register on radar or any of his other sensors, save those recording the visible portion of the electromagnetic spectrum. He couldn't even guess at the range or size of the thing. It might have been a meter across and a hundred meters away, or a kilometer across and much, much farther away. Since it was visible, a laser pulse would have given him a precise range . . . but a laser pulse might be interpreted as an attack.

Walton's orders were specific: Do *not* provoke the aliens; do *not* initiate a hostile exchange.

He wished the aliens themselves had received those orders. According to the guys and gals in *America*'s intelligence department, they'd vaporized an unarmed survey vessel a few months ago, along with two escorting destroyers. That sounded like a pretty solid initiation of hostilities to *him*.

But the scale and scope of the stellarchitecture visible now around the Rosette gave some pretty convincing testimony about the aliens' technological abilities, suggesting that nothing the human squadron could do would pose a particular threat to them.

The target ahead was growing steadily brighter. Since the thing appeared to be reflecting ambient light from the surrounding stars rather than glowing with its own, that suggested that he was closing with it.

"Engage drive," he told the AI. "Let's end for end and scoot."

"That is not possible," the AI replied.

"Why the hell not?"

"Unknown. Attempts to initiate singularity projection have failed. The Rosette Aliens may be manipulating local space in such a way as to damp out such attempts."

"Shit! What about the power tap?"

The Shadowstar's power plant was a scaled-down version of the power taps on board *America* and all other human starships. Microscopic artificial black holes rotated around one another on a subatomic scale, liberating a fraction of the zero-point energy available in hard vacuum at a quantum level. If the aliens had damped out his drive singularity, his power plant would have been affected too.

And yet, his in-head instrumentation showed a steady flow of energy.

"Ship power tap is functioning at optimum," the AI told him.

"Can you explain that?"

"No . . . other than to suggest that the Rosette Aliens are damping out a very small and very specific volume of space immediately ahead of the ship."

Walton had no idea how such a thing could be accomplished. An old, old phrase from the literature of some centuries before came to mind, a phrase suddenly sharply relevant. *"Any sufficiently advanced technology is indistinguishable from magic."* He didn't remember where the quote was from, and didn't have the time now to look it up. He planned to do so once he got back to the *America*.

If he got back to the *America*. The silver sphere ahead was now rapidly growing larger, approaching him at high speed. His AI flashed a full update back to the carrier group.

And then the sphere, the encircling walls of brilliant stars, the mysterious and bizarrely twisted alien structures, the gaping maw of the Rosette, everything *smeared* halfway around the sky before winking into blackness. . . .

Chapter Two

Recon Flight Shadow-One
Omega Centauri
1122 hours, TFT

. . . and then exploded into visibility once more.

Walton blinked. *America* hung in space 10 kilometers directly ahead. An instant before, he'd been almost 50 astronomical units away from the carrier . . . a distance of 7.5 *billion* kilometers, drifting at a velocity of a kilometer per second. Now he was traveling at the same speed, but his course had changed 180 degrees, and somehow he'd leaped across 50 AUs in an instant, and *without* accelerating to near *c*.

He remembered the way the sky had smeared around him, as though the space through which he'd been traveling had been bent through 180 degrees. And an instantaneous jump of 50 AUs? That was simply flat-out impossible. Even at close to the speed of light and subject to relativistic time dilation, he would have experienced *some* time making a passage that long . . . and fighters were too small by far to mount the drive projectors necessary for the faster-than-light Alcubierre Drive.

Alien magic. . . .

Working through his AI, which with a machine's tight focus seemed unsurprised by any of this, Walton decelerated, drifting into *America*'s inner defense zone. "*America*!" he called. "*America*, this is *Shadow One*!"

There was a real danger that the carrier's automated defense systems would target the incoming fighter and destroy it. The Shadowstar's IFF *should* have flagged him as friendly on *America*'s scanners . . . but Walton found himself nursing a profound mistrust of the technology. Right now, the universe didn't appear to be functioning the way it should.

And the recon fighter should not have been able to simply drop inside *America*'s defensive perimeter that way. It not only violated the rules and regs of combat operations . . . but it violated the laws of physics as well.

"Shadow One, *America*!" the voice of the ship's CIC called. "What the hell are you doing *there*?"

"I . . . I'm not entirely sure, *America*. One second I was at the Black Rosette. The next . . ."

There was a long pause from the carrier, as though they were waiting for Walton to finish the thought. "Very well, Shadow One," CIC replied after a moment. "You are cleared for approach and trap. C'mon in."

"Copy. Accelerating."

He didn't trust himself to say more.

USNA CVS America
Omega Centauri
1205 hours, TFT

"So, we're left knowing even less than we knew before," Gray said. "Super-powerful aliens are dismantling a star cluster . . . and when one of our recon ships gets too close they teleport it across fifty AUs without even breaking a sweat. Recommendations?"

Gray was in *America*'s main briefing room with his command staff and department heads. Half were there physically; the rest had linked in from other parts of the ship. One entire bulkhead had been turned into a viewall, which was displaying video of Walton's flyby of the Rosette. At the moment, it was showing the alien structures, looming vast and shadowy across the backdrop of stars.

"What . . . what they did to our recon fighter," Lieutenant Commander Philip Bryant said slowly, shaking his head, "is flat-out impossible according to all of the laws of physics we understand." He was the *America*'s chief stardrive engineer, and arguably the ship's officer most conversant with her Alcubierre Drive and the essential *malleability* of empty space in the presence of powerful gravitational fields.

"The sheer *power* . . ." That was *America*'s other senior engineering officer, Commander Richard Halverson, the newly promoted head of the ship's engineering department, and an expert on power taps and vacuum energy.

"Yeah. How the hell are we supposed to fight something like *that*?" Commander Dean Mallory was *America*'s chief tactical officer. "They could swat us like a bug if they wanted."

"I don't think the admiral was suggesting we *fight*," Captain Connie Fletcher said. She was *America*'s CAG, an old acronym identifying a carrier's Commander Air Group from back in the days of wet-Navy ships and aircraft. "That would be pretty pointless, right?"

"It would be more like fucking suicide," Commander Victor Blakeslee, *America*'s senior navigation officer, said, scowling. "Recommendations? Hell, *my* recommendation is that we chart a course for home and high-tail it."

"Assuming they let us go," the voice of Acting Captain Gutierrez added. She was on *America*'s bridge, but telepresencing the planning session through her in-head. "It might not be that easy."

"We have no reason yet to assume hostile intent on the part

of the Rosette Aliens." Lieutenant Commander Samantha Kline was the head of *America*'s xenobiology department— "X-Dep," for short. "They could have vaporized Lieutenant Walton. Instead, they bent space to drop him back here."

"I would remind you," Halverson said slowly, "that those . . . those things out there *did* vaporize the *Endeavor*, the *Herrera*, and the *Miller.* If that's not a hostile act, what the hell is?"

"The vid returned by the HVK robot is . . . open to interpretation, sir," Kline replied. "That might have been an accident. Or a mistake . . ."

"A mistake by beings that powerful?" Fletcher said. "Beings that much like . . . like *gods*? That's a pretty scary thought all by itself."

"They *are* powerful," Gray said. He wanted to redirect the session away from the aliens' godlike aspect, however. He didn't want his staff demoralized before they even encountered the Rosette Aliens directly. "But they're not gods. If they *did* make a mistake when they destroyed the *Endeavor*, that would pretty much prove it, don't you think?"

"More likely," Dr. George Truitt said, "it simply means they don't *care.* Keep in mind, people, that we could be dealing with a K-3 civilization here."

Truitt was a civilian specialist assigned to *America*, and he was something of a wunderkind. He was a xenosophontologist, studying nonhuman minds and ways of thinking, and therefore worked in X-Dep under LCDR Kline.

Gray frowned at Truitt. In November, just two months ago, the man had been instrumental behind the scenes in devising a bit of offensive propaganda that had secured a Terran victory at Osiris—70 Ophiuchi A II—a colony world conquered by a Sh'daar client race called the Slan. By carefully analyzing communications with the Slan commander and what had been gleaned about their biology, Truitt and his xenosoph people had extrapolated a likely model of Slan psychology, one showing that they would be horrified at the idea of attacking their own community, an unthinkable act of barbarism . . . an act of *animals*. By beaming a message to the Slan suggesting that humans thought the same way Slan did, that humans actually shared the Slan collective-based psychology, Gray had forced the technologically superior Slan fleet to break off and retreat . . . a singular, *spectacular* victory.

And Truitt was the instrument of that victory.

It was too bad, Gray thought, that Truitt was also an egoistic grandstander, pompous, and possessing of social graces approximately on a par with wolverines.

"What the hell," Mallory asked, "is a K-3 civilization?"

"Christ, you don't know what Kardashev classification is?" Truitt said, glaring at Mallory. "I hope you understand tactics, Commander, better than you do technic sophontology."

"Kardashev was a Russian astronomer," Gray put in, "who developed a means of classifying planetary or interstellar civilizations based on how much energy they use. A K-3 civilization would use roughly as much energy as is emitted by all the stars of an entire galaxy."

"That is a gross oversimplification," Truitt said. "In point of fact—"

"*If* you please, Doctor," Gray said sharply, interrupting, "we're not here to argue definitions or sophontology. The Rosette Aliens have demonstrated the ability to rework an entire globular cluster, millions of stars—which, on the Kardashev scale, makes them at least a high K-2, and quite possibly a K-3. Human technology currently stands at . . . what is it, Doctor? K-1.2?"

"Approximately that," Truitt said, "yes. But—"

"The point is that our industrious friends out there, as a civilization, routinely wield something like one hundred quintillion times more power than we can. I agree with Commander Blakeslee. There's little we can do here, except establish automated monitoring stations."

"Again, assuming they let us leave," Captain Guiterrez said. "We are deep, *deep* inside their operational area."

Gray opened a new channel within his in-head circuitry, and the bulkhead opposite the view of the cluster's heart flowed and shimmered and then lit up with a schematic of the star cluster. The stars themselves were ghosted; otherwise, points of interest at the very center, including the position of *America*'s task force, would have been completely hidden.

With a thoughtclick, the view zoomed in on Omega Centauri's heart. The entire cluster was a tightly packed ball of suns about 230 light years across, but the Black Rosette—and the majority of the alien constructs—was at the very center, and *America* and the other Earth ships were only 50 AUs away—no distance at all in interstellar terms. One AU was defined as the distance between Earth and her sun—150,000,000 kilometers, on average. A single light year was roughly equal to about *64,000* Astronomical Units.

It was interesting, Gray thought, not to mention quite worrying, that the aliens, whoever and whatever they were, had taken no apparent notice whatsoever of *America* and the ships with her. Carrier Battlegroup 40 consisted of the star carrier *America*; one cruiser, the *Edmonton*; three destroyers, the *Ramirez*, the *John Young*, and the *Spruance*; plus the provisioning ship *Shenandoah*. Though small as naval task forces went, the squadron represented a great deal of firepower, and yet the aliens had simply ignored them when they dropped out of their Alcubierre metaspace bubbles on the doorstep of . . . whatever the hell it was that they were building here.

But they'd moved Walton's recon ship when it drifted in front of the Black Rosette. Maybe they *did* care about humans . . . that or else human activity actually could inconvenience them or somehow pose a threat to their operations.

Which was it? And how could the task force answer that question?

"How would X-Dep suggest we communicate with these . . . people?" Gray asked.

"We can't," Truitt said.

"We might try various Sh'daar languages," Kline added. "The Agletsch trade pidgins."

"Whoever the Rosette Aliens are," Truitt said, "they likely come from a *long* way off. I doubt they've ever heard of the Sh'daar Collective *or* the Agletsch."

The Agletsch were a galactic spacefaring species well known as traders of information. Two had been on board *America* until her last swing past Earth, when they'd disembarked for an extended chat with naval intelligence Earthside. The Agletsch were known to carry minute artificial intelligences within them, called Seeds, that communicated with the Sh'daar when they were within range. Having them on board a military vessel was always a risk, since the Sh'daar Seed might well compromise the ship's security . . . but they were also incredibly useful as allies. Agletsch knowledge spanned a large fraction of the Sh'daar Collective, and their knowledge of artificial trade languages, developed to allow diverse members of the Collective to communicate with one another, had more than once proven vital.

"I'm not so sure about that," Gray said. "We know the Rosette started off as the Six Suns, almost a billion years ago. We know that the Builders left TRGA cylinders scattered across the galaxy, and that those artifacts allow at least a limited form of time travel. The Rosette Aliens might be the Builders . . . and if so, they've had contact with the Collective . . . or at least with the Sh'daar of over eight hundred million years ago."

The TRGA cylinder at Texaghu Resch had provided access to the Sh'daar inhabiting the N'gai Cloud 876 million years ago. It was generally believed, however, that the civilization that had constructed the TRGA cylinders was far older, and far more advanced, than even the now-vanished ur-Sh'daar.

"We have no evidence that these aliens are the Builders,"

Truitt snapped. "The Builders in any case are probably long extinct."

"I wonder?" Kline said. "A K-3 civilization might well be beyond threats of extinction. At the very least, they likely possess what for all practical intents and purposes amounts to both individual and cultural immortality."

"Don't you think that a true galaxy-wide civilization, a K-3," Gray said, "would be aware of other K-3 level civilizations nearby? That they would be able to communicate with one another?"

"Some of the electronic Agletsch pidgins might be ideal for that," Kline said. "They were designed for sapient species that have little or nothing in the way of biological similarities."

"But we've already transmitted messages of friendship and requests for open communications channels," Commander Pamela Wilson said. Like Gutierrez, she was on the bridge at the moment, but linked in to the briefing session electronically. "In *Drukrhu*, and in four other Agletsch pidgins."

The languages had been loaded into *America*'s AI, so the Agletsch themselves weren't necessary for translations. Gray wished the spidery little aliens were still on board, however. He would have liked to ask them if they'd ever encountered anything like the Rosette Aliens.

But then again, the Agletsch traded in information, and rarely gave away anything for free. That particular bit of data might well be priced beyond Gray's reach.

He would have some questions for them, though, once *America* made it back to Earth.

"Very well," he said. He focused his concentration for a moment, composing a new message. "Transmit this, Commander Wilson, broadband and in all known Sh'daar languages.

"Commander Blakeslee? Give us a course out of the cluster. We're going to head for home."

Emergency Presidential Command Post
Toronto
United States of North America
1435 hours, EST

"What the hell is going on over there, Marcus?"

Marcus Whitney, the president's chief of staff, spread his hands. "Damned if I know, Mr. President. Intelligence doesn't have a clear picture right now."

"Do we now what's happened to President Roettgen?"

"No, sir. Presumably, she was in the Ad Astra Complex when the rebel forces overran the place. She may be a prisoner; she may be dead."

Alexander Koenig, president of the United States of North America, stared at the viewall news feed and wondered if this would be the end of the war. Facts were sketchy, less than trustworthy, and often contradictory.

But it did appear that the Terran Confederation government was on the point of collapse.

The United States of North America had been a part of the Terran Confederation since 2133 and the creation of the Pax Confeoderata. That union had become increasingly strained, however, until open warfare had broken out.

The causes of war were varied, but chief among them was a fundamental disagreement over how to prosecute the Sh'daar War. The USNA was committed to continuing the fight. The Confederation government wanted to accept the Sh'daar Ultimatum and become a part of the Sh'daar Collective. Disagreement in extrasolar policy—together with lesser issues such as rights of self-determination and rights to abandoned coastal areas like Manhattan, Baltimore, and Washington, D.C.—had led first to skirmishes in space, then to all-out war. Geneva's forces had attacked the flooded ruins of D.C. and attempted to capture the Tsiolkovsky Array, the hyperintelligent AI computer complex on the lunar far side. Both attempts had been beaten off . . . but then the unthinkable had taken place.

On 15 November, 2424, Confederation ships had struck the USNA capital at Columbus from space with a nano-deconstructor warhead, chewing a hole three kilometers wide and half a kilometer deep down into the heart of the city in an attempt to decapitate the North American leadership—meaning Koenig himself, as well as the USNA's Earth-based command and control assets.

The attack had failed—though the city had been destroyed and millions of people killed. The heavily shielded presidential command bunker had been two kilometers down . . . and Koenig and his staff had been able to escape by high-speed maglev train through a deep, evacuated rail tunnel connecting to the city of Toronto. And from the emergency command center set up in and beneath Toronto's York Civic Complex, the USNA government had continued the war.

Now, two months later, it appeared that the Confederation effort was collapsing.

Appeared. That was the operative word. It won't do, Koenig thought, to become overconfident now, or to drop your guard. The devastating nano-D attack on Columbus, an atrocity in contravention of any number of treaties and protocols, had triggered defections from the Confederation ranks. Russia and North India both had seceded from the Confederation and allied with the USNA. Two powerful independent powers had entered the war as well—the Chinese Hegemony and the Islamic Theocracy, both long excluded from the Confederation, both siding with the USNA in exchange for promises of inclusion in any new Earth government.

But the Confederation had been scoring victories as well. Besides annihilating Columbus, they'd destroyed a number of USNA orbital assets, were effectively in control of the SupraQuito space elevator, and had brought together a large fleet with which they were effectively dominating solar space. Mexico and Honduras had seceded from the USNA and invaded South California, Texas, and two other districts. Pan-European forces had occupied the Manhat Ruins and parts of the Virginia and Carolina Periphery coastlines. The USNA military was badly stretched, outnumbered, and just hanging on. Even with Hegemony and Theocracy help, the issue was in doubt.

"Maybe Konstantin has some information," Koenig said.

Whitney grinned. "The Great Konstantin sees all . . . knows all . . ."

It was a running joke within the emergency command post. The computer array in Tsiolkovsky on the moon had been instrumental in a number of successes in the war so far—not least of which had been opening negotiations with the Theocracy and with the Chinese.

"Sometimes I'm afraid that it *does* all," Koenig replied.

But he opened the channel anyway.

The artificial intelligence known as Konstantin was very much an enigma, and one that many—perhaps *most*—humans did not entirely trust. Computer AIs had surpassed the commonly accepted measures of human intelligence four centuries ago, and the Konstantin Array was a fifth-generation AIP running within a network of DS-8940 Digital Sentience computers. AIP stood for *artificial intelligence programmed*. Humans hadn't programmed Konstantin; *machines* had, by copying large chunks of code and weaving them together in ways that often surprised their human overseers.

Theoretically, computer minds programmed by computers still carried the same constraints as their human-programmed counterparts. While Konstantin was theoretically 10^{10} times more powerful in terms of synaptic complexity than a human, he still possessed what was comfortingly known as *limited purview*. He was very good at processing data and he could follow orders quite well, but computers weren't supposed to be able to make decisions independently of humans, nor were they supposed to demonstrate what was theoretically a purely human trait: *creativity*.

And yet, Koenig knew, Konstantin had displayed remarkable creativity several times already, most notably when he'd quietly opened negotiations with the Theocracy and the Hegemony. No human had directed him to do so.

The fact that he had might well mean victory for the USNA.

Koenig gave a wry smile. He was used to calling AIs "it," . . . but over the past few months, Konstantin for him had definitely become a *he*.

After a delay of a few moments, a window opened in Koenig's mind. A balding and white-haired man in old-fashioned clothing and gold pince-nez looked at him from behind a book with its title in Cyrillic letters. Behind him were the anachronistic screens of a circular workstation complete with floating monitor displays and free-floating transparent control panels. "Ah, Mr. President," the AI's electronic avatar said. "I've been expecting you."

The original Konstantin Tsiolkovsky had been a Russian schoolteacher in the early 20th century, a hermit who'd seemed strange, even bizarre, to his neighbors, but who'd been convinced that one day Humankind would spread out to the stars. With Oberth, Goddard, and Korolyov, he'd become known as one of the fathers of modern spaceflight . . . *the* father, in fact, since he'd predated the others.

"I assume you've been watching the situation in Geneva," Koenig said.

As always, there was an awkward two-and-a-half-second pause as Koenig's words crawled up to the moon, and the AI's reply crawled back.

"Of course. We expected something of the sort, of course, but events appear to be moving with unexpected speed."

"You *expected* a revolution?"

"There has been considerable public outcry over the destruction of Columbus, particularly in Europe," Konstantin replied. On the screens behind him, European soldiers were fighting in the ravaged streets of Geneva. It was night over there, the sky reflecting the light of a burning city. In the background of one monitor, Koenig recognized the sprawl of the Plaza of Light in Geneva's heart, dominated by the immense statue *Ascent of Man*. Hover tanks were moving toward the Confederation's Ad Astra Government Complex.

"Too," Konstantin continued, "the war has been dragging on without significant victories for two months. Anticipation for an early and easy victory has given way to doubts about the morality or legality of the war."

"This could be the end of it, then," Koenig said.

"Do not assume a USNA victory yet, Mr. President. The rebels appear to be a faction under General Janos Matonyi Korosi, formerly a hard-liner within the Confederation Senate. He has wanted President Roettgen's job and power for some time, now, and he may see this coup as a means not only of defeating you, but to opening negotiations with the Sh'daar directly, ending the Sh'daar War, and presenting himself as Earth's savior. There is also a personal aspect."

"What aspect?"

"His brother was Karl Mihaly Korosi, executive officer of the destroyer *Mölder*."

"Ah."

Mölder had been one of the Pan-European warships that launched the deadly nano-disassembler attack on Columbus. She'd been destroyed by a spread of nukes fired from the *Missouri*. Moments later, the bombardment vessel *Estremadura* had fired six nano-D warheads. Five had been intercepted out in space by the frigate *John Paul Jones*, but the sixth had destroyed Columbus, D.C.

Koenig recalled that Ilse Roettgen, the president of the Confederation Senate, had seemed shocked when she learned that Columbus had been hit by nano-D. He was as sure as he could be that she'd not been putting on an act—and that suggested that rogue elements within her own government or military forces had been operating on their own, behind her back. And if Korosi's brother had been killed on the *Mölder* . . .

That connection, tenuous as it was, suggested that the hard-liners in the Geneva government had planned and carried out the attack on Columbus, and now were using the situation to seize power. Lovely.

"You think General Korosi is out for revenge, then?"

"Unknown. I am simply relying on Big Data to build up a comprehensive picture of what is going on over there. I have been unable to penetrate Pan-European electronic security."

That, of course, would have been one of the first things Konstantin tried, and the Europeans would have expected that, and have had their electronic defenses in place. In fact, one of the causes of the war had been their attempt to capture the Konstantin Array, deploying an armored force across the lunar surface from the Confederation base at Giordano Bruno. They'd been stopped on the north rim of Tsiolkovsky Crater by a small force of USNA Marines, but it had been a close-run thing. Koenig had gathered through his daily security briefings that the Confederation had been trying to electronically compromise Konstantin ever since, trying and failing.

So far . . .

Curious, Koenig glanced at the book Tsiolkovsky's image was holding. He neither spoke nor read Russian, but a translation program riding within his cerebral implant overlaid his mental view with the book's title in English.

The Will of the Universe: The Unknown Intelligence, by Konstantin Tsiolkovsky, Kaluga, 1928.

Koenig had never heard of it, but wondered if Konstantin was allowing him to see that title for some specific reason. The AI array could be remarkably subtle at times.

"So, do you have any recommendations?" Koenig asked. If others mistrusted the giant AI array, even if he, Koenig, still had misgivings, he nevertheless had been relying more and more on the powerful AI's advice. Konstantin could mine what was called Big Data, pulling tens of thousands of minute, often unrelated facts from a vast sea of information floating Out There in the electronic ether of Global Net and the various smaller, local news and communications networks. He could piece together disparate data and reveal connections, conclusions and intelligence of which no human observer could have been aware.

"I have been tracking Confederation communications exchanges, and conclude that the rogue component of their government is staging their operation from here."

One of the screens shifted from the streets of Geneva to a scene in deep space, the vast, ringed glory of Saturn in the distance, a small rock-and-ice moon in the foreground. Koenig read the information scrolling up the side of the screen. "Enceladus? What's at Enceladus?"

"Evidently, the renegade faction's headquarters. The evidence suggests that they have been planning this for a very long time. I suggest a Navy-Marine task force tasked with capturing the surface base and any senior personnel stationed there."

"That may not be easy," Koenig said. "We're stretched damned tight right now."

"I am aware of this. The USNA may need to disengage at several points—retreat—in order to free forces for the strike. Some of the slack might be taken up by Chinese and Russian forces in Asia."

"We'll need ships. And right now, most of what we have is protecting the space elevator . . . or in low orbit High Guard, waiting to block another nano-D strike."

"I do not need to tell you, President Koenig, that a purely defensive stance will, ultimately, fail. Your best chance lies in going over to the offensive. And speed is of the essence."

"Eh? Why? What else have you heard?"

"Nothing definite. But some of my data mining has revealed an unsettling possibility."

Koenig sighed. "Okay. What is it?"

"It is possible that the renegade Confederation government has been in direct contact with the Sh'daar, and they may be on their way here."

The words hit Koenig like a hammer blow. "Christ! The Sh'daar? *Here?*"

"It may be a good idea," Konstantin said, "to attempt the destruction of your *human* enemies before having to face something considerably more exotic . . . and dangerous."

And Koenig could only nod in dumb agreement.

Chapter Three

USNA CVS America
Omega Centauri
1750 hours, TFT

The Rosette Aliens were letting them go.

Gray scarcely allowed himself to believe it at first . . . but when a number of those bright silver eggs took up positions around the task force, a few thousand kilometers out and escorted them toward their Alcubierre jump point, effortlessly matching their acceleration, he had to admit that that was the case.

"I just wish we'd been able to open a comm channel with them," Gray said. He was on the flag bridge, now, sitting at his partially enclosed workstation above and behind the captain's chair.

"I think," the CAG said quietly in his mind, "that we *have* been in communication with them."

"What do you mean?"

"They turned our recon pilot around and dropped him back alongside the *America*," Connie Fletcher said. "*Without* harming him . . . and that's important. Kind of like shooing a curious kitten away from the power outlet."

"We began accelerating out-system, and they paced us," Acting Captain Gutierrez pointed out. "Seems like pretty clear communications to me. 'Here's your hat, what's your hurry? Don't let the door slam your ass on the way out.' "

"I think you're right. No specific response on the messages we sent them. I think it possible that they simply aren't interested in us."

"Well, Admiral . . . a K-3 civilization might not find a K-1.2 all that interesting."

"Coming up on our jump point, sir," the Helm reported. "Twenty seconds."

The view of the stars outside of the *America* was weirdly distorted by the carrier's velocity, now just a hair less than the speed of light itself. The entire universe, the light of all the stars in the Omega Centauri cluster, had been squeezed into a bright ring of light forward. The seconds dwindled away . . .

. . . and then *America*'s AI pulled the already tightly distorted space around the carrier in, creating a tight bubble that was not, strictly speaking, a part of normal space. *Metaspace*, the physicists called it . . . and the nonmathematical explanation declared that while a material object such as an atom or a star carrier could not travel faster than light—or, indeed, even *reach* light speed—there was nothing preventing the space within which it rested from doing so. The Mexican physicist Miguel Alcubierre had worked out the theory in 1994, and the first FTL transit had occurred less than a century and a half later.

At maximum drive, now, *America* hurtled through metaspace for home.

Gray willed himself to relax. He'd not realized how tense, how *stressed* he'd been at the prospect of confronting the Rosette Aliens. Sh'daar client species—those encountered so far by Humankind, at any rate—tended to be somewhat more advanced than humans. Higher technology translated as greater power, faster ships, and more deadly weaponry, and staying ahead of such an enemy, meeting him and out-fighting him despite his technological lead, was a dangerous and uncertain game.

The Rosette Aliens were far more advanced than any species yet encountered by Earth. A technological difference representing tens of thousands or even millions of years instead of a century or two could not be overcome by grit, cleverness, or determination.

Gray leaned back in his command chair and opened a series of data links. He wanted to see what there was in *America*'s memory about Kardashev classifications.

He was wondering if the Rosette Aliens might be induced to ally with Earth against the Sh'daar . . . or if Earth would one day have to fight them.

America Data Files
Extant Galactic Civilizations
Classification: Green-Delta

KARDASHEV CLASSIFICATION: First proposed by astronomer Nikolai Kardashev in 1964 as a means of classifying hypothetical galactic civilizations in terms of the amount of energy they use. In its original form, it stated that a Type I civilization utilizes all of the available energy resources of its home planet; while a Type II uses the energy of its entire star system, and a Type III uses the resources of an entire galaxy. Lacking useful fine detail, this early scale was later refined and expanded.

Currently, galactic civilizations, both observed and hypothetical, can be assigned a more precise Kardashev number using the formula $K = \log_{10} MW/10$, where K is the Kardashev level, and *MW* is the energy, in megawatts, used by the civilization in one year.

Type 0: Established as a baseline, a K-0 civilization utilizes roughly 1 million watts (1 MW) of energy. Energy and raw materials are extracted from crude, organic-based sources such as wood or fossil fuels. Earth's civilization during the late twentieth century when the Kardashev scale was first proposed, utilizing roughly 15 terawatts globally, would have been defined as approximately K-0.71.

Type 1: A civilization utilizing all energy available on a planetary scale. For Humankind, this would be an energy capability equivalent to Earth's insolation, the radiation it receives from the sun, or around 10^{16} watts. It is capable of interplanetary and possibly limited interstellar travel and colonization, of planetary engineering, and can utilize a variety of energy sources, including but not limited to fission, fusion, antimatter, and zero-point energy. Earth's interstellar civilization in 2425 utilizes an estimated 10^{18} watts, and therefore has a Kardashev level of approximately 1.2.

Type 2: Sol has a luminosity of about 4×10^{26} watts, and this would be the energy usage typical of a Type 2 civilization. The ancient ur-Sh'daar, who manipulated entire stars to create hyperdimensional gateways, are estimated to have utilized around 10^{34} watts, and would have been considered to be Kardashev 2.7 at the time they entered their technological singularity 876 million years ago. Such a civilization would be capable of interstellar and possibly local intergalactic travel, as well as stellar-forming projects such as Dyson spheres, Dyson swarms, and star mining.

Type 3: The Milky Way galaxy has a total luminosity of about 4×10^{37} watts. While capturing the totality of a galaxy's radiation output is problematic, a civilization generating and utilizing energy on this scale would be considered to be Type 3. The ancient civilization or civilizations variously known as the Builders, the Starborn, or the Stargods, who are believed to have been capable of time travel and of large-scale stellarforming, are almost certainly at least Type 3.0. Such cultures would be capable of extragalactic travel and to perform stellar engineering on a galactic scale.

Type 4: This is the designation for a purely speculative category of cultures able to use energies on the scale of galactic superclusters, or approximately 10^{42} watts.

Type 5: Also speculative, a K-5 civilization would utilize energy equivalent to the output of the visible universe, or very roughly 10^{49} watts.

Type 6: Even more speculative. Type 6 civilizations would span a number of parallel universes, and might engage in " 'brane forming" activities such as creating or manipulating entire universes. Since this scale clearly surpasses concepts based on current scientific understanding, no data on energy usage or predictions as to a Type 6 culture's technological capabilities are possible.

When the Kardashev scale was first introduced, the underlying concept suggested that galactic civilizations might literally use all of the energy available from their local star or galaxy. The Dyson sphere, proposed by Freeman Dyson four years earlier, might represent an attempt to trap all available stellar energy, allowing Earth to detect a K-2 civilization by modifications to its light output, or by recognizing the radiated infrared emissions of that civilization's industrial processes. The development of zero-point energy obviates the need to efficiently trap the star's light, however, since the energy drawn from hard vacuum represents a far more abundant source of power than stellar fusion. Nevertheless, the overall amount of energy utilized by the civilization, can still be quantified as the amount available from a world, a star, or a galaxy, no matter what the actual source of that energy might be.

Obviously, the breakdown presented here is extremely rough—a guide only—and can make no predictions of the specifics of a given advanced culture's technologies, or of its motivations, philosophies, or attitudes toward other species.

Where, Gray wondered as he finished the download and closed the channel, did the modern Sh'daar fall on this scale? The data specifically mentioned the ur-Sh'daar, the empire or collective of mutually alien species that had inhabited a small, irregular galaxy devoured by the Milky Way 876 million years ago. At that time, shortly before the smaller galaxy had been torn apart by intergalactic tidal forces and the empire disrupted, the ur-Sh'daar had entered its version of what was commonly called the Technological Singularity. Also known as the Vinge Singularity, after the mathematician and author Vernor Vinge, who first popularized the idea in the late twentieth century, the singularity was broadly seen as that point in a civilization's development where organic intelligence merged with artificial intelligence in ways that utterly transformed the meanings of words like *life* and *intelligence*. For humans, the so-called GRIN technologies were seen as the drivers of this change: Genetics, Robotics, Information systems, and Nanotechnology.

Twenty years ago, Gray and *America*'s battlegroup, under the command of Admiral Alexander Koenig, had used one of the enigmatic TRGA cylinders to cross a very great deal of both space and time to reach the doomed galaxy—known to its inhabitants as the N'gai Cloud. There, they'd learned about the *Schjaa Hok*, the Transcending or Time of Change, when the highly advanced species of the ur-Sh'daar had entered a period of transcendence, vanishing from the ken of minds still firmly anchored in what they thought of as Reality. Gray had seen downloaded records of that event almost 900 million years in the past, and was still shaken by it. Of particular interest was the fact that not all members of that long-ago civilization had transcended. Called *Refusers*—those who had refused the augmentation and the advances in genetics and computer enhancement of an artificially directed evolution—the remnant species had rebuilt a shattered civilization from scratch . . . the civilization Humankind knew now as the Sh'daar.

Traumatized as a collective of intelligent species by the Time of Change, the Sh'daar had eventually recovered, spreading not only into the much larger galaxy that was devouring the N'gai Cloud, but ultimately through time as well, at least in a limited sense. Within the current epoch of the Milky Way, they'd established themselves as a dominant, apparently electronic civilization that had first appeared a few million years ago, creating a network of client races, the *va Sh'daar*. They seemed dedicated to the active suppression of higher technologies among their clients—in particular the GRIN drivers of the singularity that had wrecked their culture ages before. Newly encountered species were given the opportunity to join the Sh'daar Collective freely. If the offer was rejected, the new species were forced; Humankind had received the Sh'daar Ultimatum, as it was known, in 2367, through the recently contacted Agletsch. A steady, grinding series of wars had been waged with various *va Sh'daar* races for the following thirty-eight years.

Then, twenty years ago, the Sh'daar were beaten . . . or, at least, so it had appeared. *America*'s battlegroup had passed through a TRGA cylinder and emerged at the heart of the N'gai Cloud 876 million years in the past—a temporal end run that seemed to have panicked the Sh'daar more than the possibility of a new technic singularity. The resulting truce engineered by Admiral Koenig had promised an end to hostilities, and had actually held for two decades. But recently,

Sh'daar client species had been testing human resolve once again. The Confederation insisted that Humankind could not long hold out against superior alien technology and numbers; better to surrender *now*, Geneva insisted, before Earth was obliterated.

The difference in cultural philosophies between Old World and New, differences between two alternative and mutually contradictory views of Humankind's future in the galaxy, had, along with other more mundane problems, resulted in the current civil war back home.

"The Alcubierre bubble is stable," Captain Gutierrez reported, jerking Gray's full awareness back to *America*'s flag bridge. "We are currently 'cubing at five point three. We should reach the local TRGA in eight hours."

"Very well," Gray replied, and he smiled. *'Cubing* was naval slang for traveling under Alcubierre Drive. The number was how many light years *America* was now crossing in a day.

The Sh'daar, with their distinct advantages in technology over what humans were capable of right now, had obviously missed an important point. That series of wars between their clients and Humankind had put considerable pressure on the Confederation for more than half a century . . . but what the Sh'daar seemed to have missed was the fact that human technology tended to advance *much* more rapidly during times of war than during peace. Intelligence believed that they were avoiding launching an all-out attack that might easily drive humanity into extinction; they wanted another pliant and cooperative *va Sh'daar* client, not a glassed-over cinder that once had been an inhabited world. Obviously, a galactic culture capable of merging old stars to create new would have no trouble at all annihilating Sol if they so chose. Forcing a stubborn *Homo sapiens* to accept Sh'daar dictates on permissible levels of technology, evidently, was a lot harder.

When forced to fight, however, Humankind was always

tinkering, trying to come up with a better hand ax . . . a better spear . . . a better high-energy laser. The Alcubierre Drive was a case in point. Theoretically, there was no upper limit to a starship's pseudovelocity, but in practical terms everything depended on how much energy a starship could generate and direct to the artificial singularities that served to pull space in on itself. When *Columbia*, the first human starship, had 'cubed to Alpha Centauri in 2138, she'd managed the passage in six and a half months . . . a pseudovelocity of 0.095 light years per day. Until recently, most naval vessels had managed an Alcubierre rate of around 1.8 light years per day, though high-velocity message couriers could manage better than 5 light years per day.

Late in 2424, new developments in the quantum power taps used on board starships had greatly boosted the energy available for FTL transitions, drastically cutting travel times between the stars. Moving as swiftly as the old HAMP-20 Sleipnir-class mail packets, and by taking advantage of the shortcut afforded by the TRGA gate at Texaghu Resh, *America* and her entourage could cross the 16,000 light years from Omega Centauri to Sol in just forty-four days.

Of course, the march of technological advancement involved other measures of progress than mere speed, and implementing some of those changes—the introduction of new and more powerful weapons, for instance—could take time. *Engineering* was not the same as mere technological understanding. The important thing was that human military technology was in an all-out race, now, to develop faster ships and more potent weapons before the Sh'daar could overwhelm Earth's interstellar polity.

It was, he thought, the one bright side of the human tragedy of war. In-head circuitry had begun as high-tech communications devices for elite troops—Marines and Special Forces. Global Net had evolved from the old Internet, itself an outgrowth of the Defense Advanced Research Projects Agency Network, or DARPANET. Singularity generators, used now both to generate zero-point energy and to warp space for high-velocity travel, had started off as microscopic black holes projected into enemy ships or structures as a weapon.

Gray just wished that Humankind could get occasional stretches of peace in which to enjoy the non-military benefits of those advances.

But that golden era, if it was even possible in the first place, would have to wait a while longer. The Sh'daar . . . the Confederation . . . and now, just possibly, if things went *very* wrong, the Rosette Aliens . . .

Humankind was going to have some scrambling to do to catch up.

And if they failed, the consequences might well be the *final* peace, the peace that would come with the extinction of the human species.

York Plaza
Toronto
United States of North America
1953 hours, EST

President Koenig, too, had been thinking about the threat presented by the Sh'daar. Just how had humans been able to hold off the onslaught of the Sh'daar client species for so long, despite the fact that human technology couldn't match that of the H'rulka, the Turusch, the Slan, or any of the other enemies encountered so far?

And he thought that he just might know the answer.

"You guys are busted," he said, his voice mild. He took a sip from his drink. "I think I know why your masters can't get their act together."

"You mean the Sh'daar, yes-no?" one of the two small beings in front of him said through the small, silver-badge translation device adhering to her leathery skin just beneath her four weirdly stalked eyes. "We no longer refer to them as *masters*. . . ."

Koenig was standing with the two Agletsch representatives within a mostly human crowd filling Toronto's outdoor York Plaza. Thousands of people were in attendance, and many thousands more were present virtually, linked in from home through small robotic drones or teleoperated androids. The function was a diplomatic reception for the Hegemony and Theocracy ambassadors and their staffs, a grand celebration of the new alliance. The Office of Presidential Security had just about gone hyperbolic with collective fits when they'd heard; what, his security chief had demanded, was to stop the Confederation from launching another nano-D strike? If they hit Toronto tonight, they could vaporize most of the USNA government leadership with one precisely placed shot.

The answer had been to redouble both space and atmospheric patrols over North America to make sure nothing got in. USNA High Guard ships were positioned as far out as Lunar Orbit, and Marines were manning long-range planetary defense batteries up at SupraQuito. This reception tonight was *important*, a means of showing the entire planet that the USNA's refusal to bow to Confederation tyranny was shared by a majority of Humankind—that it was not simply the squeak of a small and disgruntled minority.

Besides, global popular reaction to the Confederation's nano strike on Columbus had been overwhelmingly negative. There was a reason weapons of mass destruction had been banned by the Geneva Protocols of 2150, and nano-dissassemblers were especially nasty, taking apart *everything* they touched—buildings, dirt, trees, children—literally molecule by molecule, then atom by atom. Another nano-D strike by the Europeans might cause wholesale defections from the Confederation.

The Agletsch, Koenig was glad to see, appeared to have sided with the USNA cause . . . though it was always difficult figuring out what the spidery aliens were actually thinking.

"I still don't understand that, Gru'mulkisch," Koenig said. "You both carry Sh'daar Seeds. Seems to me that means you're working for them . . . at least some of the time."

After twenty years, Koenig was only just beginning to be able to tell one of the two liaisons from the other—or to pronounce their names. The other one was Dra'ethde.

Known popularly as "spiders" or "bugs," the Agletsch were actually very little like either. Each possessed an un-segmented oval body a bit more than a meter across, supported by sixteen jointed limbs like slender sticks. The rear legs were shorter than those in the front, the bottom-most pair little more than sucker-tipped stubs, while the upper limbs serving both as legs and as manipulators were long enough to hold the body semi-upright, so that the tiny head was a meter and a half off the ground. When she wanted to move, she could do so quickly, tipping her forebody forward to lift the hind leg-stubs off the ground. The rotund body was covered by tough, flexible skin, not chitin. The reddish skin was covered with gold and blue reticulated markings and by the Agletsch equivalent of tattoos—swirls and curlicues picked out in gold and silver. The four stalked eyes were gorgeous—black Y-shaped pupils set in rich gold.

Both of the Agletsch speaking with Koenig were female, of course. The males of the species were small, brainless tadpoles attached like leeches to the female's face.

And somewhere within those flat, ovoid bodies, Koenig knew, were minute electronic implants that stored the Agletsch's sensory impressions, and beamed them to a receiver when the range was short enough—probably a few hundred thousand kilometers. Sh'daar Seeds, as these poorly understood devices were called, also apparently allowed the Sh'daar to talk with their minions—and served as the glue that bound the Sh'daar Collective together, making the whole vast, sprawling thing work.

"As we have stated in times past," Dra'ethde pointed out, "the Seeds do not work in the manner in which you seem to believe. Some of us work within the Collective, yes-no? Others do not . . . even if we by chance carry within our bodies the Masters' . . . the Sh'daar Seeds."

"If no Sh'daar are nearby," Gru'mulkisch added, "the Seeds are useless to them."

Koenig considered a sharp reply, but decided to drop the issue. Humans tended to think in terms more black and white than did the Agletsch, who traded in information among hundreds of galactic species and seemed able to at least comprehend the psychologies of myriad alien world-views. They seemed friendly and agreeable . . . but sometimes it was obvious that they simply didn't think the same way as humans. The fact that they referred to the Sh'daar as *Masters* tended to make humans suspicious, and the various human intelligence agencies looked at them with something approaching xenophobic paranoia.

"Many of us believe," Koenig said carefully, "that those Seeds are what tie together the Sh'daar Empire."

He was being deliberately provocative. For years, in fact, Alexander Koenig had argued against the popular notion of a Sh'daar *empire*, holding that the word suggested far more cohesion and organization than was apparent through scattered encounters with Sh'daar clients over the past few decades. Koenig understood the Sh'daar threat, understood it quite possibly better than any other human alive. He'd been the admiral in command of the battlegroup that threatened the Sh'daar homeworlds in 2405. And he believed that he understood their one fundamental, crippling weakness, the flaw that had let human forces beat their forces time after time.

The Sh'daar Collective was, to be blunt, just too freaking big. *That* was the secret.

"The Sh'daar do collect information . . . what you call military intelligence through their Seeds," Dra'ethde admitted. "But . . . your ambassadors and diplomatic staffs, they do the same within the nation-states in which they are stationed, yes-no?"

"Any intelligence which the Seeds provide the Sh'daar," Gru'mulkisch said, "is quite minor. After all, the Agletsch charge for major pieces of data."

Koenig realized that the spidery alien had just made a *joke* . . . and quite a human one at that. He was impressed. Humor was quite a difficult concept for many nonhuman species to understand, much less master.

"What then have you discovered?" Dra'ethde asked. "What about the together act of the Sh'daar?"

"Quid pro quo?" Koenig asked. It was a term that the Agletsch loved, and which fit well with their trade in information. *This for that.*

"Of course. What do you want to know?"

Koenig had been giving a lot of thought to what question he could ask. It had to be relatively low level in terms of import . . . what they called first-level compensation. More critical information—eighth level, say—could be quite expensive.

"Will the Sh'daar use you or another client species as their representatives when they come to Earth? Or will they come to Earth themselves?"

"Almost certainly they will send servant representatives," Dra'ethde told him. "The Sh'daar have not been seen . . . *in the flesh*, I believe is your term, for many tens of thousands of your years. However, those representatives will no doubt have a direct communications link with their Masters."

"That's good, because if they came themselves, we'd need to lock up our friend Gru'mulkisch, here, to keep her Seed from dumping."

It had happened once before, when the star carrier *America* had passed close to a *va Sh'daar* base at Alchameth, a gas giant in the Arcturan system, and data stored in Gru'mulkisch's Seed had been transmitted to the enemy.

That was the reason human intelligence services were so cautious when it came to Agletsch in human space.

Dra'ethde and Gru'mulkisch both had been carefully scanned, and their Sh'daar technoparasites identified. A scrambler had been designed and placed into the translator units they wore to block the receipt and transmission of any state secrets. In general, however, it was wiser simply not to discuss state secrets in their presence.

In any case, it was possible that a hotline to the Sh'daar might someday be useful.

"And your information in exchange?" Gru'mulkisch asked him.

"The Sh'daar have trouble dominating the galaxy," Koenig said, "because the galaxy is far too large. Too many worlds, too many sapient species. Interstellar empires, as such, simply can't exist . . . not when the amount of information needed to manage them is so vast. And that's where we humans have an advantage. Interior lines of communication."

"I do not understand your use of *interior*," Gru'mulkisch said. "The Sh'daar do not surround you."

Score, Koenig thought. Until that moment, the Earth Confederation had not been sure how extensive Sh'daar space was. Most contacts with their clients had been in toward the galactic core, in the constellations of Sagittarius, Ophiuchus, Libra, and others in that general direction.

Earth needs allies, Koenig thought to himself. *Technic species not yet under the Sh'daar thrall. We just might find them in the opposite direction from the core. Orion, Taurus . . . out toward the rim.*

"I meant the word figuratively," Koenig told the Agletsch. "With a much smaller volume of space to defend, and fewer worlds with which we have to be concerned, we can move from one to another more quickly, react more quickly to a threat than can the Sh'daar, with their much larger domain. When we make a decision, when Fleet HQ gives an order, it can be disseminated among all of our forces and put into effect much more swiftly than is possible for the enemy."

"Quite true," Gru'mulkisch said. "Of course, you currently have the singular disadvantage of being . . . I believe one of your politicians called it 'a house divided.' "

"The quote originally was from one of our sacred texts," Koenig said. He tried to find a way to give a positive response, to turn it around and dismiss the implied threat, but could not. "And . . . no. You're quite right."

He looked away from the two aliens, letting his gaze drift across the glittering crowd of humans filling the plaza. Most were in formal attire—evening dress, diplomatic cloaks, designer gowns and dinner jackets. Numerous others were stylishly nude, some with luminous jewelry or skin adornment . . . or wearing holographic projections that flowed and rippled like liquid light. You would never guess, looking at that throng of civilians, that the nation currently was at war both with the unseen alien puppet masters dominating much of the galaxy and with other humans.

He turned back to the two Agletsch data traders. "You're right . . . and we're going to have to do something about that."

Chapter Four

Squadron Briefing Room
USNA CVS America
In transit
0950 hours, TFT

By now, Omega Centauri was far behind. *America* and her escorts had threaded their way through the TRGA cylinder at Omega Centauri—one of seven discovered so far in that star-packed volume of space—and emerged again at the original Sh'daar Node cylinder from which the acronym was taken . . . the Texaghu Resch Gravitational Anomaly.

"Funny name," a young Starhawk driver with lieutenant's rank tabs at his throat said. " 'Texaghu.' Does that have anything to do with Texas?"

America's fighter squadron pilots had been gathering on the carrier's briefing-room deck for the past ten minutes, now, and the place was already pretty crowded.

"Nah," Lieutenant Donald Gregory said. "But you're new, right? Just came aboard a couple of months ago?"

"That's right." The pilot extended his hand and Gregory took it. "Lieutenant Jamis Anderson. Late of the great state of Texas, and now with the Merry Reapers."

"Don Gregory." He slapped the VFA-96 squadron patch on his shoulder. "Black Demons." He turned to introduce the attractive woman with him. "And this here is Meg Connor."

"*Very* pleased to meet you, ma'am," Anderson said, a broad grin spreading across his face. "I downloaded your report about you and your run-in with the Slan!"

Connor, formerly of VFA-140, the Dracos, had been captured by the highly advanced alien Slan in an operation at 36 Ophiuchi two months ago, but been rescued by the Marines shortly after. Her observations of her captors had helped Naval Intelligence put together a strategy to deal with the *va* Sh'daar aliens . . . and led to Admiral Gray's unexpected victory over them a few days later at 70 Ophiuchi. Since then, her own squadron lost in the Slan attack, she'd been transferred to the Black Demons.

"Texaghu Resch," Gregory told him, "is *Drukrhu*—that's the principal Agetsch trade pidgin—for a star originally catalogued by the Turusch, another Sh'daar client species. Means 'the Eye of Resch.' Actually, it's a transliteration from the language of a species called the Chelk."

"Never heard of 'em."

"They're extinct," Connor told him. "Apparently, the star was seen as the eye of a mythic god or hero in their culture, a being called Resch."

"And they're extinct?"

Gregory nodded. Whoever or whatever Resch had been, he'd not been powerful enough to save the Chelk. Like Humankind, they'd chosen to fight the Sh'daar rather than have their technologies restricted. "Humans haven't been there, but according to the Agletsch, the Chelk homeworld is now a lifeless, airless, glassed-over ball of charred and blasted rock. Seems like they didn't get the Sh'daar memo about no technic singularities."

"Damn . . ."

"It's all written up in *America*'s archives," Connor

pointed out. "Interesting reading . . . and it helps you kind of stay focused on what we're fighting for."

"Better living through higher technology," Anderson said, still grinning. The catchphrase was currently a popular one, and expression of North America's determination to continue Humankind's exponential increase in GRIN technologies.

"May I have your attention, please," another voice said over the pilots' in-head circuitry. They turned to face the front of the briefing room, where Captain Fletcher, *America*'s CAG, stood on a low stage. "Please grow your seats and link in. We have the visuals from the recon flyby yesterday."

Chairs began emerging from the deck in neatly ordered rows, and the crowd—more than two hundred strong—began taking seats. *America* carried six fighter and strike squadrons, one recon squadron, and two search and rescues . . . fifteen hundred people if you included the support, intelligence, logistics, and maintenance personnel. But the meeting this morning had been called just for the pilots and flight officers—the pointed end of *America*'s very big and powerful stick.

With a rustle of motion and dwindling conversation, the crowd of men and women sat down and began linking in. The briefing would be carried out through *America*'s primary AI, and consisted of a download of information acquired by the recon squadron—VQ-7, the Sneaky Peaks. Commander James Henry Peak, who'd given his name to the group twenty-some years ago, had long since been promoted to captain, rotated Earthside to Naval Intelligence, and eventually retired, but his old squadron had kept the punning name. VQ-7's current CO was Commander Thom McCabe, who was on the stage now with the CAG.

"Good morning," McCabe said. "I'm sure you're all eager to see the results of our close recon pass of the Black Rosette yesterday. What Lieutenant Walton saw was . . . interesting. . . ."

Data flowed into Gregory's in-head, and he opened an inner window to view it. He saw again the crowded inner reaches of the Omega Centauri cluster, millions of brilliant stars filling the sky, and, ahead, the blurred and eerie doughnut of blue light and gas, turned almost edge-on, set in an infalling swirl of hot dust and tortured hydrogen atoms. Shadowy, vast structures hung in the distance, made indistinct by the dust . . . the stellarchitecture of the Rosette Aliens. *America*'s fighter squadrons had flown CAP over the past several days—the term was from *combat air patrol*, an anachronistic holdover from the days of wet navies and atmospheric fighters—but never approached the Rosette. It would be kind of nice, Gregory thought, to actually see up close what all of the fuss and scuttlebutt was about.

The blurred disk grew larger, and the angle shifted as Walton's ship approached, giving them a line of sight into the Rosette's interior. Gregory saw scattered stars . . . a black and empty night sky . . .

"We've slowed down the images by a factor of ten," McCabe told the audience. "Lieutenant Walton was only over the Rosette for a few seconds, but by slowing down the feed we can see details that are not, at first, apparent. What we're looking at here, obviously, is deep space . . . but you can see that it's not the space within the cluster. The stars are few and far between. This particular line of sight, we think, lets us look through to a region out on the galactic rim."

One by one, the other spaces recorded during Walton's passage came into view, each replacing the one that had gone before. The heart of a nebula . . . various starfields . . . the mottled, close-up surface of a red sun . . . a scattering of distant galaxies . . .

The final scene was of a searing field of radiant blue light, as though the line of sight was plunging into the heart of an exploding sun.

McCabe froze the image there. A new window opened to one side, one showing the familiar blurred cylinder of a

TRGA. The two images floated next to each other in Gregory's mind at identical angles, allowing a close comparison.

"Despite the obvious physical differences," Commander McCabe went on, "the Rosette is a transport mechanism quite similar to the TRGAs, except for the size, of course. A TRGA, we now know, is a kind of everted Tipler machine. The original device—the theory, rather—was developed in 1974 by a physicist named Frank J. Tipler. According to him, a cylinder of extremely dense matter rotating at near-light velocity would drag the spacetime fabric around it in a way that would permit what physicists call closed, timelike curves, creating gateways or portals across vast distances of both space and time. Two decades later, physicist Stephen Hawking demonstrated that closed, timelike curves were impossible, as was time travel.

"Evidently, the TRGA Builders did not read Hawking. Instead, they seem to have turned the idea inside out, creating a hollow cylinder about a kilometer across, with solar-sized masses rotating around the cylinder's axis within the walls. A number of distinct paths through the interior of the cylinder result in spacial displacements of, in one case, several tens of thousands of light years—and a temporal displacement of eight hundred seventy-six million years. The Agletsch refer to the TRGAs as Sh'daar Nodes. However, we know that the Builders were not the modern Sh'daar, but instead they were, hundreds of millions of years ago, the *ur*-Sh'daar, the ancient community of highly advanced civilizations inhabiting the small, irregular galaxy called the N'gai Cloud.

"Which, of course, brings us to the Black Rosette."

The TRGA image vanished, and the in-head image expanded slightly, closing in on the Rosette's eldritch maw. Harsh blue light glared from the opening.

"The Rosette," McCabe continued, "appears to be an expansion of TRGA technology . . . but on a far vaster scale. Six black holes, each fifty times the mass of Sol, rotating about a common center of gravity at high speed, creating a gateway nearly one hundred thousand kilometers across."

A second window opened once again, this time showing a perfect circle of six brilliant, sapphire-blue suns—the Six Suns, encountered by *America*'s task force in the N'gai Cloud in the remote past.

"The Rosette is at least nine hundred million years old," McCabe said, "and obviously artificial. The original members of the Six Suns were balanced in a rotating hexagon one hundred astronomical units across. The stars themselves seem to have been artificially enhanced or rejuvenated by merging smaller stars together . . . but as is well understood, hot, bright, blue stars like these have lifetimes measured in, at best, a few tens of millions of years. When they ultimately burn up their reserves of nuclear fuel, they collapse into black holes, such as what we see in the Rosette today. We do not as yet know whether the distances between the member stars of the Rosette were deliberately manipulated—shrunken from about fifty astronomical units, in the remote past, down to a few tens of thousands of kilometers—or if this represents a natural evolution of the system over hundreds of millions of years. . . ."

As McCabe's voice continued downloading into Gregory's head, he stared into the blue glare. *America*'s AI was stopping the light down by a good 80 percent to keep the image from being washed out completely—or more likely the dimming had first taken place within the recon fighter to keep from blinding Lieutenant Walton.

Gregory had heard scuttlebutt to the effect that the "blue-light gateway" represented a pathway into the heart of a star or, just possibly, was looking at an exploding star, a nova or supernova, at close range. He could make out a kind of texture in there, a variation in tone and brightness—the light was not at all flat or uniform in its intensity. That seemed to rule out a star core, a supernova, or some other stellar disruption, but he couldn't guess what it might be instead.

"We're not at all sure what we're looking at in this image," McCabe was saying, echoing Gregory's own thoughts, "but the physics department thinks that this particular line of sight *may* be a glimpse into an altogether different universe . . . a parallel universe to our own somewhere within the Bulk, and quite possibly an alien universe with completely different physical laws, environments, geometries, and characteristics than our own. . . ."

Funny name, Gregory thought, *the Bulk*. He knew the theory, of course: that there were other universes, a near infinity of them, side by side in a hyperdimensional way, like the pages of a book, but arrayed in a non-spacial otherness called the Bulk. All of the universes taken together were termed the *metaverse*. The nature of those other universes was still in doubt; they might host wildly differing natural laws and physical properties . . . or they might be alternate variations of one plan, spawned by the trillion in response to alternative solutions to collapsing quantum wave equations.

The blue-lit space within the Rosette apparently represented a space with different physics . . . where *pi* was equal to *exactly* three point one four, perhaps . . . or where gravity was stronger than it was here . . . or where sigma, the strength of the strong nuclear force, was strong enough to overwhelm the repulsion between electrons and protons.

So far as Gregory was concerned, however, this one universe he was inhabiting now was more than big enough—more than *strange* enough—for him.

"We estimate," McCabe told his audience, "that the Rosette opens up a *very* large number of spacetime pathways . . . as many, the physics boys think, as ten to the twenty-seventh power. That number, one *octillion*, is so large as to be all but infinite for any practical purposes.

"So . . . are there any questions?"

Several hands rose. McCabe pointed at one.

"Sir," Lieutenant Wes Fargo said. "Our ships can't stand

up to technology like that! Just what in hell are we supposed to *do* about these . . . people?"

"Unknown, as yet," McCabe replied. He sounded grim, and Gregory realized that he didn't have any answers, and that the lack of answers worried him. "All we know is that the Rosette Aliens, as we call them, are coming in through a crack in space, quite possibly from an entirely different universe. They may be a million years in advance of us . . . they may be much more. They may be so far beyond us that meaningful communication between their species and ours is impossible.

"And intelligence believes that their emergence only sixteen thousand light years from Sol is a matter of extremely serious concern. . . ."

And Gregory was forced to agree.

Emergency Presidential Command Post
Toronto
United States of North America
1322 hours, EST

"Recombinant Memetics," Konstantin said, "may offer you your best hope for defeating the Confederation relatively quickly. Speed is, of course, essential if you are to have a chance of an alliance between Geneva and the Sh'daar."

President Koenig studied the system's schoolteacher avatar in his inner window and wondered about the AI's programming. How did Konstantin pull off that kind of magic, anyway?

Not that the carefully crafted image conversing with him inside his head would yield any clues. The lunar computer network had not been directly programmed by humans; Konstantin, he knew, was an artificial intelligence-programmed machine, an AIP. Given that, how much could Konstantin possibly know—or guess—of human behavior?

"I notice," Koenig said carefully, "that you tend to emphasize the fact that you are not human. When you're speaking with me, you always say '*your* war,' '*your* nation,' as if you're not one of us."

"A fact that should be self-evident," Konstantin replied. "I am *not* human. This is not my war. And while, technically, this facility was funded primarily by the United States of North America, I was intended, I remind you, to work on problems affecting all of Humankind. War is the single most wasteful, tragic, and senseless of human activities, and is not within my purview."

"But you *have* been helping us." Konstantin had been instrumental in formulating strategies against the Confederation, and in using its data-mining capabilities to gather intelligence from the Global Net.

"I have," the system replied. "My function—my higher purpose, a human might say—is to gather, assess, and provide information. It is up to human agencies such as your government to determine what to do with that information."

Konstantin's mandate was to provide information useful for all of humanity, or at least so ran the claim. So far as Koenig was aware, though, Konstantin had been providing intelligence to the United States of North America and *not* to the Confederation. Was that because Konstantin had been designed and funded primarily by the USNA government, and by USNA-based corporations like Bluetel and Simmons-AI? Or were there other, deeper motives . . . perhaps motives not even remotely comprehensible to brains of mere blood and tissue?

"And the Confederation government? Do you provide them with information as well?"

"I maintain covert links with certain Confederation communications and AI networks, of course. Doing so requires that I provide certain information, yes. IP eddresses and DNS registration, for instance, as well as synchronization pingpackets."

"Okay, Konstantin," Koenig said after a moment. He knew better than to try to get the hyperintelligent AI network to say *anything* it was not prepared to divulge. "But how are you planning on using memetics?"

That was the *real* question, he thought—how well could a silicon-based intelligence understand the complexities of recombinant memetics? A machine figuring out the most effective buttons to push, to change human cultures, to reshape Humankind . . .

That, Koenig decided, was a truly chilling concept. . . .

If you had enough small and disparate bits of information, if you could conduct Big Data mining on a large-enough scale, could you accurately and consistently predict human behavior?

Koenig knew the *official* answer, of course. Predicting the actions of a handful of people or, worse, of an individual, was possible only in fairly limited situations—if the subject was a sociopath, for instance, and following the dictates of his disease, and even then, predictions could all too easily be lost in the randomness of background noise.

Large groups of people, however, were another matter altogether. As with large numbers of atoms or molecules acting within the rules laid down by quantum dynamics and basic chemistry, the actions of large populations were more predictable.

And where actions were predictable, it was possible—if you were both careful enough and skillful enough—to guide them, to change the shape and course of those actions to achieve a desired outcome. The science was called recombinant memetics, the science of using one set of memeplexes to alter another. In much the same way that recombinant DNA can change genetic structures and give rise to whole new types of life, it was possible to identify particular memes within a social unit and change them into something else entirely.

But identifying and targeting key memes within a given

culture could be tricky, requiring data mining on a scale only possible for an AI as complex and as perceptive as Konstantin.

And changing them was trickier still, requiring selective manipulation of memes within the target culture.

The word *meme* had been coined four centuries before by Richard Dawkins, the evolutionary biologist who first suggested them as units transmitting cultural practices, ideas and concepts, or as symbols passed from mind to mind through writing, speech, rituals, mass entertainment, or imitation. Like genes, memes spread from person to person, and like genes they compete, vary, select, mutate, and attempt to ensure their own survival. Put another way, a meme is like a virus, propagating through a population, infecting individuals, and spreading by means of the behaviors it generates in its hosts.

The question in Koenig's mind was how a computer network, no matter how complex, could understand how memes worked, how memes could infect and affect human populations without possessing a key human ingredient—*emotion*.

And if a silicon mind like Konstantin's could understand memetics, it gave AI systems an absolutely incredible power with which to manipulate human civilization.

"Several possibilities present themselves," Konstantin replied. "I could foment revolution within the Confederation by building upon the impetus already generated by the defections from the Confederation's ranks—Russia and North India. Or I could create a new religion . . . one that would require Geneva to embrace peace."

That statement rocked Koenig back on his figurative heels. A *religion*?

A cluster of related memes working together and supporting one another was a *memeplex*; religion was the perfect example. Religions evolve, spawn new and different offspring, become set or rigid in their ways, or they mutate under cultural pressures which are themselves memeplexes.

"I see. And how are you going to get around the White Covenant?"

"The White Covenant prohibits attempts to proselytize," Konstantin replied, "and it directly prohibits the use or the threat of force to effect conversions as a basic violation of human rights. It does not prohibit the establishment of a new faith."

Centuries before, late in the twenty-first century, a particularly nasty war between the West and radical Islam had ended . . . in part because Western psyops programs had created the White Covenant, a gentlemen's agreement among the winners that proselytizing in *any* form was a violation of basic human rights to believe and to worship according to one's own conscience. Ultimately, full membership in the newborn Earth Confederation for any nation had depended upon acceptance of the Covenant.

And at the same time, an early application of recombinant memetics, then in its infancy, had made proselytizing, the fear of hell or judgment, and even the very idea of fundamentalist acceptance of sacred writings as God's literal word . . . *embarrassing*. Passé. Even insulting. Populations that rejected the Covenant were encouraged to practice their beliefs . . . *elsewhere*, in deep space colonies out beyond Pluto, or even on the worlds of distant suns. Mufrid, at Eta Boötis, had been one such colony, until its destruction twenty years ago by the Turusch.

What the hell did Konstantin have in mind?

"Good luck with that," Koenig said. "People tend to take their religions seriously."

"Some do, though for many it is more a matter of convenience. Very often, religion is an accident of where a person was born, or when."

"True. But there's going to be a lot of back-blast and noise when you launch it."

"Secrecy will be essential," Konstantin observed.

Konstantin had pulled off some miracles lately in its

dealing with the Confederation, but Koenig thought that this time the system might have bitten off more than it could process. Propaganda always ran into the basic problem of knee-jerk rejection by the target society—called *back-blast* in RM terminology—and, more, there often were so many competing voices out there in the memetic ether that it was impossible for any one message to be heard over the noise. Basic commercial advertising starting back in the twentieth century had been a primitive form of RM, using jingles and product placement and sexy spokespersons to sell, say, a certain brand of ground car. But when a dozen other companies were countering with jingles and ads dripping with sex of their own, the result was . . . noise, and lots of it, enough to render such ads largely ineffective.

There were also defenses, AI agents that patrolled cyberspace in search of potentially dangerous memes, like antibodies.

The best way to get a memetic virus through the noise and the defenses was to do so without the target being aware.

"It is imperative that we end the civil war within the Confederation as swiftly as possible," Konstantin went on. "A recombinant memetic attack on the Geneva leadership gives us a good chance of uniting Humankind before the Sh'daar or the unknown alien threat at Omega Centauri can act."

"But we still don't have a clue as to how to defeat the Sh'daar," Koenig said. "And we know even less about the Rosette Aliens." He hesitated, thoughtful. "It's the time-travel aspect that bothers me, Konstantin," he said at last. "With that one factor alone, they ought to be able to walk all over us."

The Sh'daar Collective was a truly formidable enemy. No human knew just how big the Collective actually was. At the very least, it included within its far-flung embrace well over a thousand distinct star-faring species scattered across perhaps a quarter of the galaxy, and controlled the resources of thousands more that for one reason or another had never ventured into space.

The discovery that at least one TRGA cylinder gave direct access from the Milky Way at time *now* to the N'gai Cloud some 876 million years in the past added the dimension of time to the problem. What passed for a Sh'daar galactic government appeared to be based in what Confederation intelligence called Omega Centauri $T_{-0.876gy}$, the designation for the N'gai Cloud as it was almost 0.9 of a gigayear before time *now*, but it evidently had spread through time as well as space. How such a possibility could be made to work without endless complications from temporal paradox remained one of the great unsolved mysteries of galactic history.

And with that kind of strategic advantage, one would think that the Sh'daar could have intervened at any point in Humankind's history or even prehistory and written humanity out of existence. Suppose a Sh'daar battlefleet had showed up over the Earth of 876 million years ago, when terrestrial life—still limited to bacteria and protists and blue-green alga—was confined to the sea. They could have glassed over the Earth, boiled away the ocean, bombarded what was left with high-energy neutrons . . .

Exterminated the life in those ancient terrestrial seas and Humankind would never have appeared.

The fact that the Sh'daar had *not* eradicated all life on Earth by rewriting history suggested that there was more to the problem than was immediately obvious.

The problem, Koenig thought, likely had to do with a key aspect of what it meant for species to be mutually alien. The Turusch, the H'rulka, the Nungiirtok, the Slan . . . all were client species of the Collective and all, at one time or another, technic species that had attacked human forces in T_{prime}, meaning time *now*, captured human interstellar colonies, and even launched assaults on Earth herself. And while there'd been attempts at joint operations—the Nungiirtok were specialists in ground warfare, for example, and had invaded the colony on Osiris in conjunction with Turusch fleet elements—the different Sh'daar clients were so different from one another—in physiology, yes, but especially in *psychology*—that they apparently had trouble coordinating military operations with one another. The Sh'daar guided their clients, or tried to, through the Seeds . . . but either the distances were too vast or the number of Seeds sending back data was too large. Whichever it was—and it might well be both—the Sh'daar Empire was not particularly efficient in the ways it dealt with ambitious upstarts like Humankind.

Humankind, Koenig believed, possessed one vital advantage in its struggle with the Sh'daar, something he privately thought of as the *Greek advantage*. Koenig was a thoroughgoing student of history, and was among other things fascinated by the spectacular victories of the ancient Greeks over the far larger and more diverse Persian armies at Marathon, at Plataea, and, later, by Alexander the Great over Darius. Like the Greek city states of 2900 years earlier, modern Earth was far from united . . . but the member species of the Sh'daar Collective had so little in common with one another that communications—even facilitated by Agletsch pidgins—must be very nearly impossible.

So far, Humankind had managed to use that essential disunity, beating Sh'daar client species in turn rather than en masse. The question, though, was whether the enemy would learn from those defeats and get their collective act together. If they did, *when* they did, humanity would be in very serious trouble indeed.

Somehow, Earth needed to unite, and then end the Sh'daar threat once and for all. If Konstantin could pull that off with memegeneering, well and good. If he could not, then Humankind's long-term survival was very much in doubt.

And so far as Koenig could tell, Humankind was running out of useful options.

Chapter Five

12 February 2425

Washington, D.C.
USNA Periphery
1220 hours, EST

"Damn it, Lieutenant, we need trained pilots! Lots of them! You were one of our best! It's your *duty* to volunteer!"

Shay Ashton looked the small, gray man up and down, almost openly sneering. "If service is mandatory, how the hell can I volunteer?" she said. "You can go to hell!"

"Lieutenant Ryan—"

"It's *Ashton*, not Ryan," she snapped. She'd married after she'd returned to the D.C. Ruins, though Fred had been killed ten years later by marauders from across the broad and tide-swollen Potomac. This USNA government agent wouldn't understand. To him, taking the name of the person you married was *quaint*, a holdover from a long-gone era . . . or, worse, that she was a filthy "monogie"—a pervert who dared to believe in monogamous marriage.

She saw emotion flicker across the man's face—disdain, possibly disgust. But in the lawless territories of the Periphery, cast off centuries ago by the rest of the country, monogamy had carried a certain survival value . . . two people so closely bonded that each could watch the back of the other in a way not possible for complicated line marriages, poly-amories, or *ménages a politique*.

Behind her, a city, at once ancient and newly born, was growing skyward from mangrove swamp and muck. The relentless global rising of the oceans four centuries ago had finally flooded the low-lying regions along the U.S. coast, forcing their evacuation. But not everyone had been willing to leave their home. . . .

For centuries since then, the stay-behinds, the "swampies," had inhabited the former capital of the old United States, fish-farming among the tangled mangrove swamps now growing along what once had been the Washington Mall. When the US had reorganized itself as the United States of North America and as a founding member of the Earth Confederation, the Periphery—including low-lying and flooded coastal areas like Manhattan, Boston, and Washington, D.C.—had been abandoned by a government unable to afford the massive costs and effort of beating back the encroaching sea. The people still living in those areas had adapted, as people do, living in the ruins without modern technology or medical care, making their own law, and becoming fiercely independent in the process.

The Periphery had become a major political issue, however, when Geneva had attempted to seize those regions, to take them over as a trust. The inhabitants had fought back an assault three months ago; the massive, broken shell of a Confederation Jotun troop flier still lay on its side in the shallow waters of the Washington Mall, partially obscured by the enthusiastic tangle of mangroves around it. Ashton had somehow found herself in command of the ragged band that had defended the Ruins, holding out until USNA aerospace forces had arrived to turn the tide decisively in the defenders' favor.

Since then, USNA troops and equipment had been pouring into the areas around both D.C. and Baltimore, and reportedly up in the Manhattan Ruins too. Ashton was grateful for the help . . . but gratitude did have its limits. She hadn't *asked* for the government's help.

"Whether you like it or not," the government man said, "the USNA has taken over direct control of the Peripheries. You *are* citizens of the USNA now, and as such you have both rights and responsibilities. That is *especially* true of former military personnel such as yourself."

She held a middle finger up under his nose. "See this, Government Man?" she snapped. "Sit and rotate!"

"Lieutenant Ashton—"

"I retired, damn it! I put in my time, and I *retired*, okay? You do *not* own me!"

The man nodded toward the downed Jotun. "Looks like you've been doing a pretty good job of it since your retirement."

In fact, that troop flier had been brought down by a flight of USNA Starhawk fighters. But she wasn't going to mention *that*.

"This is my home, okay? I have a right to defend it."

"Granted. And we're offering you a chance to make sure the Confederation doesn't try to grab your home from you again."

"You can fight your own damned war. I'm not playing."

The man sighed. "Well, I'm not going to force you. USNA jurisdiction is still . . . a bit fuzzy out here in the Periphery, and will be until we formally re-annex it. I will ask you why you won't help us, though. You were an outstanding Starhawk pilot. Excellent record . . ."

"Like I said . . . I put in my time. And they need me *here*. This is . . . home."

"Okay. Let's leave it at this." He focused a thought, sending Ashton a mind-to-mind eddress, which her in-head circuitry dutifully recorded and logged. "We want you to volunteer for an electronic incursion into Geneva. It's a no-risk op; you'll go in clean and virtual. Your fighter skills are very much needed in this operation, and if you succeed, you will ensure Washington's freedom from the Confederation. If you can see clear to changing your mind, give me a yell. Fair enough?"

She nodded, but reluctantly. "Ain't gonna happen, though."

"The USNA is taking back the Periphery, Lieutenant," the agent said. "Sooner or later, all of this will be under our control, our *full* control, again. Since the destruction of Columbus, there's even been . . . talk of bringing the nation's capital back here. Like it was a few centuries ago. It'll mean unprecedented prosperity for your people . . . medical coverage . . . full access to the Global Net. There *are* some major advantages for you in this deal."

"There're advantages in staying independent, too."

"Indeed. *If* you can keep that independence." He didn't add that to win independence, Ashton and her neighbors would have to fight against the USNA.

He didn't need to.

As he walked away, Ashton wondered if he'd really meant that last unspoken thought as a threat. As far as she was concerned, there wasn't a decidollar's difference between the United States of North America and the Earth Confederation. She'd served both when the USNA had been a part of Geneva's global hegemony, and her loyalties had been to the other members of her squadron and to her shipmates on board the *America*, not to such abstract concepts as duty, country, or even freedom.

Hell, what had the USNA done for her or her fellow swampies of late?

Well, other than showing up at the last possible second and helping to drive off the Confederation invasion three months ago. . . .

And it was true that the government—the *USNA* government, not the ragged committee of swampies who'd been making decisions here for the past few centuries—*had* been

sending a lot of high-tech help after the precipitous depar-
ture of the Confeds. The old Capitol dome had been freed
from the enveloping shrouds of kudzu and tropical vines,
water levels were down so far that most of the Mall was now
dry land, and three-meter dikes had been grown along the
ancient shores of the Potomac, allowing the standing water
to the east to be pumped out. There was even a detachment
of USNA Marines in place across the river, now, guarding
what to them was a sacred site . . . the ancient Iwo Jima
Memorial, which now flew, not the flag of the USNA, but
the old U.S. flag under which the Marines once had fought
during centuries past. As a side benefit of that deployment,
there'd been no more marauder raids on the D.C. Ruin set-
tlements from the Virginia side of the river. Ten years ago,
Ashton had led an armed team across the river to avenge
Fred's death, and had wiped out one nest of those snakes, but
new marauder clans had shown up during the past few years.

Maybe there were advantages to having the USNA government renew its claims along the coast after all.

Angrily, she shook off the thought. The government was
the proverbial camel with its nose worming in under the side
of the tent. Let it in just a little, and pretty soon the whole
damned camel was in there, shouldering you out into the
desert cold.

No. . . .

Blue Seven, VF-910
Saturn Space
1315 hours, TFT

Lieutenant Frank Gallagher accelerated at nearly 10,000 Gs,
streaking up from the tiny white, icy moon and into open
space. Above him, Saturn hung huge and vast and beautiful, filling half the sky, her rings a diamond-hard and ruler-
straight white scratch across all of heaven.

"Enceladus Base!" he called. "Blue One clear and accelerating!"

"Copy, Blue One," the voice of Enceladus Flight Control replied in his head.

"Joining formation." The three other Starfighters of Blue Flight drifted in open formation a few thousand kilometers ahead and he moved to join them. "Okay, Blues," he said. "Keep it tight."

"Blue Two, affirmative." That was Lieutenant Karyl Joyce.

"Blue Four, ready to boost." Lieutenant Dwayne Tanner.

"Blue Three, ready." Lieutenant Victor Truini.

"Blue Flight formed up and ready for formation intercept," Gallagher announced.

"Copy, Blue Flight. Unknowns now bearing at one-seven-three plus twelve, range two-niner-five thousand. Unknowns have fired on Red Flight, and are confirmed hostile. You have weapons free, I say again, weapons free."

"Copy weapons free. Coming to one-seven-three plus one-two."

"Go get 'em, Frank."

"No prob, Salad Bowl. Keep the coffee warm for us back there."

"Will do." The voice hesitated. "We're reading the hostiles now as twelve Krag-sixties. Range now two-five-zero thousand. The big boys are moving in, range one-point-seven-seven million."

Not good. "Copy."

The Pan-European Krag-sixties—KRG-60 Todtadlers, or Death Eagles—were as fast, as maneuverable, and as heavily armed as modern USNA Velociraptors, which meant that they were much better than Blue Flight's older Starhawks, especially at long range.

They would have to get in tight to make a difference.

But *twelve* of them! Blue Flight consisted of four Starhawks, and Red Flight of four more, assuming they were all still operational. The USNA defensive contingent at Enceladus was going to be badly outclassed in this engagement—and there were still the "big boys," the Confederation capital ships, to contend with.

"Blue Flight, engage sperm mode," Gallagher ordered. The external hulls of the SG-92 Starhawks softened and flowed, morphing into their high-velocity configuration—a rounded body with a long, slender spike at the tail. Streamlining wasn't normally a factor in spaceflight—at least, not at normal planetary velocities. But minute flecks of debris—stray hydrogen atoms, for the most part—were definitely a consideration at higher velocities.

And, more to the point, the region of space close to Enceladus was not hard vacuum. The dazzlingly white moon was imbedded inside the thickest part of Saturn's E ring; in fact, specks of frozen water streaming out from Enceladus were responsible for creating the E Ring, and for keeping it in existence. Though local space was still hard vacuum by terrestrial standards, flying through that blizzard of ice particles at high-G accelerations would be like plowing through an atmosphere of molasses.

"On my mark, boys and girl," Gallagher told his flight. "Fifty-kay gees in three . . . and two . . . and one . . . and *boost*!"

Powerful, tightly wrapped balls of warped space flickered into existence off each Starhawk's bow. In existence for only a tiny fraction of a second, each microsingularity lasted just long enough to bend space ahead, allowing the fighter to fall forward. By continuing to flicker on and off, the drive allowed the craft to bootstrap itself to higher and higher velocities . . . and since the fighter was in freefall, following the local curvature of space itself, there were none of the unpleasant side effects of acceleration—like having the pilot smeared across his acceleration couch in a thin, red stain. At 50,000 gravities, a Starhawk could nudge up against the speed of light in about ten minutes. They wouldn't be boosting for that long, however. The idea was to engage the incoming enemy, not blow right past him at a high percentage of *c*. The fighters' AIs cut off acceleration when the closing velocity was up to 5,000 kilometers per second, and the enemy was thirty seconds away.

"Prepare to engage," Gallagher called. "Arm Kraits. Spread for area effect . . . but watch out for our Red Flight. Blue Four, hold yours in reserve."

"Copy, Blue Leader."

Kraits were nuke-tipped VG-10 antiship missiles. They were particularly effective against capital ships, but a near miss would fry a fighter's circuitry and the expanding plasma sphere might shred hull matrix if the detonation was close enough. They weren't as powerful or as long-ranged as the newer Boomslangs or Taipans, but they could do the job well enough with good tactics.

Gallagher watched the red points of light representing the enemy fighters drift across an in-head window, each accompanied by a small block of text describing the target's mass, direction, speed, and acceleration. The friendlies out there were in full retreat . . . three of them dropping back toward Enceladus at high-G. A white sphere of light blossomed . . . and then there were *two* friendlies left. The hostiles kept closing.

Damn it, they should have ordered Red Flight to open up on the unknowns as soon as they'd become visible. Who the hell else had the Salad Bowl—the squadron's pet slang name for Enceladus Station—been expecting out here?

He selected four Kraits, marked detonation points on his in-head to create a spread across the expected paths of the Confederation fighters, and triggered the release. "Fox One!" he announced. "Blue One, missiles away!"

"Blue Three! Fox One!"

"Blue Two! Fox One!"

Fox One was the code phrase indicating the launch of smart missiles—fire-and-forget warheads equipped with

AIs to guide them to their targets. Released from the fighters' bellies, the missile drives switched on an instant after they were clear to avoid changing the fighters' vectors, sending them streaking into darkness. One vanished two seconds later, wiped from the sky by a Todtadler's particle beam, but the others detonated in a pulsing one-two-three blossoming of white light. The enemy fighters had scattered off their path as soon as they'd detected the launch . . . but the spreads launched by Truini and Joyce had been placed to box the Todtadlers in, and as additional fireballs flared in the distance, two of the enemy fighters vanished, while a third, torn by an expanding plasma fireball, tumbled helplessly out of control.

But there were missiles incoming now, answering Blue Flight's volley. Gallagher's AI pegged the designation as AM/AS-9, which carried the USNA code name Black Mamba. The AM/AS designation stood for antimatter/antiship; rather than a nuclear warhead, it packed several grams of antimatter in a magnetic containment capsule, enough to generate a multi-megaton blast laced with deadly X-ray and gamma radiation. There were eight of them, pushing a 100,000 Gs. The Pan-Europeans, it appeared, were out for blood.

"Blue Four!" Gallagher called. "Try to block those Mambas!"

"Copy, Blue Leader! Fox One . . ."

For several endless seconds, two sets of artificial intelligences vied with each other tactically, each trying to outguess the other, feinting, dodging, putting on sudden bursts of acceleration, or decelerating sharply to spoof its opposite numbers. Then nuclear flashes erupted against the black of space, deathly silent, and half of the Mambas vanished in the blasts.

Four kept coming, their AIs seeking out the formation of USNA Starhawks for the kill.

"Blue Flight, go to E-and-E!" Gallagher yelled, breaking

hard high and to port. E and E—Evasion and Escape. It was time to get the hell out of Dodge.

Sharp turns with a singularity fighter were always dicey, requiring the drive to anchor the gravity ball and allow the fighter to whip around it into the new desired course. The tricky part was keeping the fighter smoothly riding the gravity well's sides without slipping in close enough to be caught in the microsingularity's tidal effects. Maneuvering in a singularity fighter was completely unlike flying an atmospheric wing. Rather than banking and turning on air, it was space itself that was being twisted, allowing one vector to be shifted to another in a 90-degree turn, or even through a full one-eighty. Do it right and you slid around the artificial black hole smoothly, the sky wheeling past your head and you didn't even feel the turn because you were still in free fall. Do it wrong and in an instant your fighter would be shredded into metallic confetti . . . a process technically known as spaghettification.

Jinking in three dimensions, Gallagher worked to keep the enemy warheads guessing, letting his ship's AI handle the math, but guiding the process with his organic brain to keep the maneuverings as random and as unpredictable as possible. One of the antimatter warheads detonated several thousand kilometers to starboard, the flash wiping out the sky for a light-dazzled couple of seconds. A blue icon winked out of existence with the flash. Blue Four, Dwayne Tanner . . . and the end had come so quickly he'd not even realized he was dying.

"Blue Leader, Blue Two!" Joyce screamed. "I've got two on my tail! Can't shake them!"

On the in-head, Gallagher could see Blue Two twisting hard to escape a pair of Todtadlers closing on her six, but he was too far . . . *too far.* . . .

"I'm on it, Karyl," Truini called back. "Going to guns. Target lock . . . and *fire!*"

Blue Three swung into perfect line with the two Death

Eagles at close range, spraying kinetic-kill Gatling rounds into their path. First one, then the other of the KRG-60s flared into savage smears of white-and-orange light, the wreckage twisting wildly into the fighter's own drive singularity and vanishing in an instant.

"Good shot!" Gallagher told Truini, but then he had some serious problems of his own: a Black Mamba settling in on his own six and accelerating fast.

Cutting acceleration, Gallagher spun his Starhawk end for end, so that he now was facing the oncoming Mamba, traveling stern-first. He selected two AS-78 AMSO rounds. The acronymn stood for anti-missile shield ordnance, but they were better known as sandcasters—unguided warheads packed with several kilos of lead spherules, each as small as a grain of sand.

"Fox Two!" he called—the launch alert for unguided munitions, and he sent the AMSO warheads hurtling toward the Mamba. They detonated an instant later, firing sand clouds like shotgun bursts directly in the Mamba's path. Before the Black Mamba's AI could correct or dodge, the missile had hit the sand cloud at a velocity so high that the missile flared and disintegrated . . . then erupted in a savage burst of matter-antimatter annihilation.

The blast was close . . . very nearly *too* close. The expanding plasma wall nudged Gallagher's Starhawk as it unfolded at close to the speed of light, putting him into a rough, tumbling spin. For the next several seconds he was extremely busy, trying to balance his Starhawk's attitude controls to bring him out of the tumble.

Then he had the nimble little ship back under control, with tiny Enceladus and, beyond, the looming bulk of Saturn filling the forward sky. Red icons were scattering rapidly past and around him, he saw; those were the enemy fighters. Farther off, still a million kilometers away, a small knot of red icons marked an incoming continent of Confederation capital ships. The big boys were decelerating now, closing on Enceladus and leaving the mop-up of the defending USNA squadron to their own fighters.

And Gallagher didn't see any way he could stop them, or even to get close. The last of Red Flight was gone, now, and the three remaining fighters of Blue Flight weren't going to be able to do a damned thing about those heavies. His AI's warbook was busily cataloguing the enemy fleet . . . two heavy cruisers, a light carrier, half a dozen destroyers, a couple of monitor gun platforms, a heavy transport . . .

Jesus! What did they think the USNA had deployed out here on this damned little iceball? Salad Bowl was a civilian research station, nothing more, an exobiology outpost hunting for alien life in the salty deep-ocean pockets beneath the Enceladean ice. The Starhawk squadron had been placed here to protect against minor Pan-European raids . . . but what he was seeing here was a large-scale invasion. That transport was almost certainly a troop ship.

They might yet manage to do some damage. "Listen up, team," he called. "We're on a vector that will take us within ten thousand kilometers of that transport. I think it's probably a troop ship, okay? Hit that baby, and we might be able to throw a major wrench into the Pannies' plans."

A troop ship meant troops, which meant the Pan-Europeans were here to occupy Enceladus or some other body in the Saturn subsystem . . . Titan, possibly, or the Huygens ERRF observatory in Saturn orbit. Destroy or damage it badly enough, and those invasion plans would have to be scrubbed. Gallagher had two Kraits left in his armament bays; he would shoot one and save the other as a just-in-case.

"That's gonna really stir up a hornet's nest," Joyce said.

"Yeah, boss," Truini added. "And what's the point, anyway? We have to surrender. We've freakin' *lost*!"

Gallagher considered the question. Out here on the cold, empty ass-edge of the system, concepts like duty and honor just didn't count for as much as they might back in more civilized areas. Here, you fought for your buddies.

Or, in this case, the other members of the squadron back in the Salad Bowl, the loaders, manglers, technicians, and all of the other support and logistics personnel that made a squadron work. Not to mention some six hundred scientists, technicians, and support personnel stationed at the Bowl.

"Yeah, and how are we supposed to do that, True?" Gallagher replied. Another antimatter warhead detonated in the distance, flooding the area with a harsh and deadly light. Surrender was not a matter of simply contacting the enemy . . . not when their electronic defenses were up to prevent attempts to hack into fighter control systems or AIs. "If the Bowl tells us to stand down, we stand down. Until then, we fight, damn it!"

There was no response . . . and Gallagher realized with a sudden cold impact that Truini's fighter had vanished from the display with that last detonation. It was down to Gallagher and Joyce.

"Blue Two calling Fox One!" Joyce announced. "Missiles away!"

Gallagher programmed the shot and triggered it. "Fox One!"

"Their fighters are trying to cut us off!"

"I see them." He considered their options . . . which were few and not good. He considered ducking in Saturn's rings and immediately discarded the idea. The thicker portions of the rings were too distant—the outer reaches of the massive and brilliant B Ring orbited over 120,000 kilometers farther in from Enceladus, more than a third the distance between Earth and Luna.

But damn it, they needed *cover*.

Nuclear fireballs flared and blossomed in the distance. The enemy transport was still there . . . but it was no longer decelerating. Maybe they'd done some damage. *Maybe* . . .

Something about the data coming up on the alien transport didn't add up. The ship was longer than a French Orcelle-class transport—nearly 700 meters—and its power curve was closer to that of a battle cruiser than a troop ship. Gallagher called up a magnified image . . . and he stifled a sharp, bitter exclamation.

He didn't know what that . . . that *thing* was, but it wasn't a troop ship.

No time for analyses now. He would store the data and hope he lived to transmit it.

"Okay! Make a run for Enceladus, Karyl. Close pass . . . crater hop if you have to. We'll see if we can lose 'em in the ice!"

"Right behind you, Frank."

The problem with being so badly outnumbered was the openness out here, with enemy fighters and capital ships now moving in from all sides. If they could get down on the deck of Enceladus, half the encircling sky would be blocked, and the radar and laser signatures of the fighters themselves might be masked by the ice skimming beneath their keels.

"Enceladus Base, this is Blue Leader!" he called over the tactical channel. "We're down to two fighters! I think we managed to ding their troop ship, but they're trying to swarm us! What are your instructions?"

"Blue Flight, Enceladus Base. You've done what you can, Frank. Get the hell clear of battlespace. RTB when you can."

"Copy." RTB—Return to base—when they could, *if* they could. More Black Mambas were streaking toward them, now. If things had been bad before, they were worse now. The enemy fighters were furious at the attack on the Confederation capital ship. Gallagher launched several more sand-caster rounds, then put on a burst of raw, hard acceleration that sent him hurtling toward the fast-swelling white disk of the moon. He was aware of the crater-pocked surface grow-ing swiftly larger, of the dazzle from a distance-weakened sun glinting from the ice plains below . . . and then he was twisting around his drive singularity, fighting to shift his vector to one a little closer to parallel to the moon's surface. Enceladus was so near now that its bulk blocked out the far vaster loom of giant Saturn.

Three enemy fighters were following him down. Where were the rest?

Where was Karyl?

He didn't know. The three bandits on his six were closing fast, though. It looked like they were lining up for a gun attack rather than another volley of antimatter warheads. Maybe their missile rails had gone empty. Maybe . . . maybe . . .

A nuclear fireball blossomed to port, the detonation rapidly lost astern. They were popping nukes at him then . . . and one had just impacted the surface. He swerved to starboard, angling toward the tiny moon's south polar region, still accelerating.

His fighter shuddered, and he heard the rapid-fire banging of small high-velocity pellets against his hull. He cut back on his speed . . . then cut back again as the shuddering increased in strength and decibel level.

A shimmering, hazy wall rose against the black of space from the horizon ahead.

Shit! In the excitement, Gallagher had forgotten about the moon's south pole . . . and the tiger stripes.

Cassini, an early robotic probe exploring the Saturn system, had discovered the mysterious jets streaming out from the moon's south polar region in 2005. The constant tug-of war between Saturn and Enceladus created tidal heating and heavy tectonic activity, generating titanic cryovolcanoes erupting from four parallel fractures—deep cracks in the icy crust popularly known as "tiger stripes" for their dark color. Geysers of water emerged at high pressures from the vents and froze almost instantly, creating plumes extending as far as 500 kilometers up and out into space.

Much of this ice drifted back to the surface of Enceladus as snow, carpeting the moon's southern regions to create a brighter, whiter surface much younger than existed in the north. The rest drifted clear of the satellite and formed the broad, highly diffuse E ring of Saturn, a 2,000-kilometer-thick belt circling the planet all the way from the orbit of Mimas, an inner moon of the planet, out to Rhea.

Those cryovolcanic plumes had been the first evidence that Enceladus might harbor a liquid-water ocean beneath the ice . . . and possibly life as well. Enceladus base had been established a century and a half earlier to search for that life—a far more difficult task than on Jupiter's Europa. While the subsurface ocean had a temperature close to 0° centigrade, the surface of the ice was a numbing 240 degrees colder, just 33 degrees above absolute zero. And unlike Europa, the internal ocean seemed to exist in pockets, limiting the areas where the xenobiology people could drill.

The effort had been worth it, however. Life had been discovered beneath the Enceladean ice . . . very, very *strange* life, life based on hydrogen-germanium chemistry—on organometallic semiconductors rather than on carbon chains.

Exactly how an ice ball like Enceladus had acquired enough germanium—a relatively rare element on Earth—to evolve life based on the stuff was a mystery; how it *worked* was a bigger mystery still. Simply identifying the flecks of organometallics exchanging photons with one another in the Enceladean oceans as being *alive* had taken the better part of a century . . . and a near-total rewrite of the definition of the word *life*.

Enceladus Station, located in the permanent blizzard 100 kilometers from the terminus of one of the tiger stripes, was a xenobiological outpost maintained as a joint venture by Phoenix University of Arizona and the Universidade de Brasília. With Brazil siding with the Confederation against the North American rebels, there'd been some understandable political stresses at Enceladus. VF-910 had been dispatched to the moon to keep the peace . . . and the scientific neutrality of the base.

Obviously, it hadn't worked out as planned. The Confederation had dispatched a naval squadron to seize Enceladus and to isolate North America from the rest of Earth's scientific community.

None of this was of particular interest to Gallagher at the moment, as he skimmed above the polar ice toward a misty wall, which, at his current velocity, would have nearly the same effect on his ship as a cliff of solid ice. He gave orders to his AI, nudging the fighter into a slightly different path. Those tiger stripes each were about 35 kilometers apart. It would be like threading a needle, but he might slip between the plumes if he could maintain a low-enough altitude.

The Pan-European fighters were still behind him, following him in.

Hurtling between two towering plumes that filled the sky with misty light, Gallagher flipped his fighter end for end again, hurtling tail-first and head-down, meters above the roiled and jaggedly broken icy surface. He had one Krait remaining. He rolled back to keel-down, giving orders to his AI in brief, staccato bursts of thought.

"Fox One!"

His last Krait dropped from his keel, ignited, streaked aft . . . and detonated on the ice. The flare was blinding . . . and an instant later a fresh and violent plume of freezing water geysered into space above the hole he'd punched into the surface, directly in the path of the trailing enemy fighters.

Unfortunately, the expanding plasma shock wave from his missile caught the Starhawk and nudged it to one side, nudged it enough to send it skimming through the fringes of one of the other plumes. Gallagher felt a savage shock, saw pieces of his fighter ripping free . . .

. . . and then the jolt of deceleration slammed against him, sending him hurtling into blackness as he lost consciousness. . . .

Chapter Six

4 March 2425

Emergency Presidential Command Post
Toronto
United States of North America
1640 hours, EST

"The President of the Confederation Senate is on the link for you, Mr. President," Marcus Whitney, the Chief of Staff, said. "The *new* President, I should say."

President Koenig glanced at the others in the room—Pamela Sharpe, the Secretary of State. Lawrence Vandenberg, the Secretary of Defense. Dr. Neil Eskow, the Secretary of Science. All maintained facial expressions of careful neutrality.

"You have the security issues worked out already, I presume?"

"Of course, sir."

The security problem was far more difficult than merely one of virus control. A direct data link between Geneva and the emergency USNA capital in Toronto could easily serve as a conduit for a variety of electronic attacks—viruses, worms, or brute-force virtual assaults aimed at downloading confidential data or knocking out the American communications network. Powerful e-security AIs would be monitoring the exchange on both sides of the Atlantic, making sure that *only* the video and sound being exchanged between the two government leaders would pass the firewalls.

There was also the question of e-psych attacks, which would amount to a direct assassination attempt. Koenig and his Confederation counterpart carried sophisticated nanochelated circuitry inside their brains, cerebral implants that let them interface directly with computers, vehicle control systems, medical scans, the Global Net, and, of course, mind-to-mind communications links. It was possible to hack another person's implants, either to steal data or—more viciously—to infiltrate personal RAM and distort the victim's perception of reality. Such an attack could leave a victim hopelessly insane . . . or so distort his reality that he *acted* as though he were schizophrenic.

The virtual agents resident within implant hardware—Koenig's personal in-head secretary, for instance—were designed to screen out such attacks . . . if only to block unauthorized attempts at communication, or the transfer of electronic advertising. The ICEware carried by Koenig and other government leaders was several orders of magnitude more powerful and comprehensive than what was available to average citizens, and should be proof against any possible electronic attack.

There was always the chance that the other side had come up with something new, however. The electronic battleground was constantly evolving, constantly growing more complex, more subtle, and more dangerous.

The secretary of defense broke the uncomfortable silence first. "Sir," Vandenberg said, "I *really* don't think that taking this call is a good idea."

"Why is that?"

"Simple. It's likely to be a plot to get at you. They might have something new that our ICE can't handle. Something dangerous."

ICE, an old acronym for intrusion countermeasures electronics, was the catchall term for electronic software defenses, some of it artificially intelligent, some not.

"Konstantin says they do not," Dr. Eskow said with a shrug. "And Konstantin should know. It monitors the Global Net closely, and would be aware of any such new developments."

"I don't see Konstantin running our antiviral software," Vandenberg said.

"Of course not," Koenig said. "The time lag from the moon and back is too long. God knows what could sneak through in three seconds."

In fact, clones of Konstantin were already running on several USNA networks on Earth, though they were more closely circumscribed in operational procedures and restrictions than was the hyperintelligent AI on the moon's far side. Most humans still didn't fully trust AIs that were *too* intelligent . . . or too independent.

And Koenig didn't fully trust any AI networks that might already have been compromised by Confederation hacks.

Still, there were times when you needed to take a chance. If you sat inside a sealed box doing nothing because someone out there might be trying to get *you*, you would never get anywhere.

"I'm going to take the call," Koenig said, deciding. "I'm sick of working in the dark against these people. Maybe he'll let something slip."

"Stay behind your avatar, Mr. President," Eskow said. "He'll certainly be staying behind his."

Avatar was the term given to a computer-created simulation based on the real person. With a decent AI behind it, it could even mimic the organic personality so closely that people linking in on the Net could not tell whether they were talking to the person or to their electronic secretary. Avatars could be a convenience or they could be a kind of personality fashion statement. They also could be designed to create a certain psychological impact. What Eskow was suggesting was that Koenig remain electronically masked by his avatar in the conversation. If the Confederation did manage to slip a nasty worm through the link, it would hit the electronic presence first, and, with luck and some very fast electronic reactions, be stopped there.

But that would also mean that Koenig would be isolated from the discussion, experiencing it secondhand and with little opportunity to guide it. He shook his head.

"I'll be careful, Doctor. But there's no point in my being here if I'm going to let an electronic puppet do my talking for me." He looked at his SecState. "Pam? What's the global lineup right now? Has anything changed I should know about?"

"Nothing substantial has changed since this morning's PICKL, Mr. President," she said. The PICKL was the President's Intelligence ChecK-List, a data download prepared by the various USNA intelligence services for his review first thing each morning. "We have feelers out to Brasilia. They may pull out of the war over the Columbus atrocity, though they probably will stay with the Confederation. If they stay with the Confederation, Argentina may pull out. Those two are still at each other's throats."

"Russian Federation? North India?"

"They're both solidly with us, now. But we're not yet sure how much *practical* use those alliances might provide."

"And Mexico?"

"Still solidly against us, sir. Confederation agents have been promising them the return of the old U.S. Southwest."

"Aztlan," Koenig said, frowning and nodding. "I know. Old news. Okay, let's do this. Marcus?"

"The link is ready, sir. He's waiting. Or his avatar is."

"Right." Koenig sank back in his chair, which responded to his thoughts, opening up, opening back, letting him lie back in a reclining position. He closed his eyes, and an inner window opened. A face formed out of static, and in Koenig's mind's eye, he was seated now in a large conference room, across an expensive mahogany table from President Christian Denoix de Saint Marc.

He was surprised at first that he wasn't sitting opposite General Janos Matonyi Korosi who, according to USNA Intelligence, was currently the real head of both Pan-Europe and the Confederation. But Denoix's presence was not, perhaps, all that surprising. The Confederation would be scrambling to put a legitimate face on their war—and that meant a civilian leader, not a military one. Denoix might well be little more than a figurehead. It would be good to keep that in mind.

The wallscreen behind the Confederation leader looked down on the Plaza of Light and, in the distance, beyond the skyward sweep of modernist buildings, the gray sheen of Lake Geneva.

"President Koenig," the man said through a craggy and unyielding scowl. "It is good to meet with you at last."

Koenig had little patience for political amenities. Figurehead or not, this was the enemy, for Christ's sake, and one of the men responsible for the atrocity at Columbus. Better, he thought, to go on the offensive immediately, perhaps nudge his opposite number off-balance.

"What has happened," Koenig demanded of the stern image in his head, "to President Roettgen?"

The scowl on the image's face grew deeper. "We have done nothing to . . . the lady. She appears to have fled . . . with a great deal of the treasury's money, I might add. We *will* find her, and her accomplices, I assure you. In the meantime, *I* have been appointed as Confederation Senate president until general elections can be held in two months' time."

Koenig studied the face. There was no way to read another person's emotional state through an in-head link, since the image was meticulously crafted by an AI. All he had to go on was the man's on-line bio . . . and on guesses as to why the other side was presenting this psychology, this attitude.

According to the download, Christian Denoix de Saint Marc was French. His principal residence was on the Channel Coast in the ultra-wealthy Boulogne-Billancourt suburb of Ile-de-France, just west of the seaside Parisian Dome, but he'd lived many years in Germany, Italy, and Poland, as well, and he had a second working home, of course, in Geneva, the Pan-European capital. His English was fair, but by prior common agreement, the AI connection was doing the actual work of translation, just to be certain that there were no critical misunderstandings.

That avatar face, Koenig knew, was designed to give away nothing.

Fair enough. In his office, Koenig himself was wearing nano-grown utilities, as close, as light, as comfortable, as informal as his own skin, but Denoix would be seeing him through the link in his formal black-and-gray admiral's full dress uniform from fifteen years earlier. The uniform was a deliberate reminder, on Koenig's part, that he'd been a military man before being elected to public office. Once Navy, *always* Navy, ran the old saying, and it was particularly true of Koenig.

The clear message was that he'd beaten the Pan-Europeans before, and he would do it again if they didn't back down.

"I don't believe you, you know," Koenig said. "People don't just disappear. Not these days."

Well, he thought to himself . . . *not unless they were willing to disable their in-head circuitry and go live in some godforsaken periphery region without modern technology.* Most of the world's population now was so wired in that anyone could be found and tracked anywhere on or near the planet . . . one of the advantages—and curses—of modern personal nanoelectronics.

And that was most especially true of heads of state.

Koenig knew that he was *always* under the electronic eyes of his own security apparatus, as was every man, woman, and robot within the Toronto emergency CP.

"It doesn't much matter what you believe, President Koenig," Denoix said with a nicely crafted shrug of his shoulders. "The truth of the matter is that you must now deal with me . . . and with my party."

On the in-head, the Pan-European leader was wearing an elegant scarlet cloak over black skintights. Koenig wondered what he was really wearing.

Hell, it was even possible that the image was being run by an AI—that Denoix was doing office work or off on holiday with his mistresses and leaving this call to his personal AI secretary. There was no way to tell, really, though there were supposed to be electronic tags indicating that an avatar's image was being worn by a flesh-and-blood human, or by an AI.

" 'My party?' " Koenig repeated. "That would be *Tout le Monde*?"

"Of course."

Tout le Monde—All the World—was Europe's major opposition party to President Roettgen's Globalist party. Both were leftist/socialist in economic outlook—the Mondes a bit further left than the Globalists—and both had called for peace with the Sh'daar. The big difference between the two, Koenig had decided, was in how far each group was willing to go in pursuit of their goals. USNA Intelliegence was more than half convinced that the destruction of Columbus, D.C., had been carried out by a pro-Monde cabal within the Pan-European government, and Koenig was inclined to agree. The Globalists, generally, advocated wearing down the opposition with talk along with *some* military pressure . . . not committing large-scale atrocities in order to force compliance with the world order. The fact that Roettgen had seemed genuinely surprised by the nano-annihilation of Columbus a few months ago suggested that it had been carried out by rogue elements of her own government.

That surprise might have been a ruse on her part, of course, but Koenig didn't think so. Her disappearance from the world stage suggested that this was much more than politics as usual.

So . . . why have you called me?" Koenig asked. "Do you wish to surrender? We can offer generous terms—"

"Most amusing. I am calling, President Koenig, to inform you *personally* that a Sh'daar delegation is arriving in-system in two weeks' time. We are welcoming them . . . and if you wish to have any role at all in deciding the content . . . the *shape* of the peace, you will agree to an armistice at once and make arrangements to attend the meeting."

"In person?" Koenig asked, with an ironic lift to an eyebrow. Showing up in person at a designated conference site would be a great opportunity for the Confederation to take Koenig, the leader of the rebel opposition, prisoner. They would just *love* that. . . .

"Of course not." The voice oozed scorn, coupled with a bitingly aristocratic disdain. "Virtual. We will provide the link-in data and eddresses."

It occurred to Koenig that Denoix would be as careful about being set up by the other side as was Koenig. With a virtual conference, however, just as with this one between Toronto and Geneva, there was no need for the participants to be in the same room . . . or even on the same continent.

"And what would be the purpose of this meeting?" Koenig asked.

"Peace, of course, and open communion with the Sh'daar Collective before they squash us like insects. Even you must see and understand that continued human resistance against the long-time rulers of this galaxy can only lead to Humankind's extinction."

There'd been a time, Koenig knew, centuries before,

when the government leaders of two countries at war with each other could not possibly have talked directly like this, virtual face to virtual face. Messages, peace feelers, requests for formal negotiations all would have been relegated to back channels, to the embassies of neutral nations, and to the efforts of third parties, or, in a few notorious cases, to teletype, telephone, or Internet hotlines. Koenig liked to believe that free and open communication, leading to better mutual understanding, was the best hope Humankind had for peace.

There were times, however, such as now, when he was convinced that he was wrong. Too often, good communication led simply to more and bigger opportunities for misunderstanding. Christian Denoix de Saint Marc sounded arrogant and firmly convinced of the rightness of his own cause.

"I take it, then," Koenig said carefully, "that you've already been in touch with Sh'daar agents. Who? The Agletsch?"

"That is not your concern, President Koenig. Suffice to say that the Sh'daar are willing, in principle, to forego their proxy campaigns against us in return for our . . . cooperation."

" 'Peace in our time,' eh?"

"I beg your pardon?" The image in Koenig's mind hesitated, no doubt as the Pan-European leader downloaded the reference. "Ah. Neville Chamberlain, 1938 . . ."

The fact that the European leader of the Earth Confederation had not known that historical datum offhand was . . . disturbing. Koenig was immediately reminded of another ancient quote. "Those who cannot remember the past are condemned to repeat it." The Santayana quote was usually taken out of context, with the assumption that it applied to history rather than to the way a man, an *individual*, learned from experience and memory, but it still was apt. As Koenig listened to the Confederation president, another line from

Santayana came to mind: "Fanaticism consists in redoubling your efforts when you have forgotten your aim."

Ilse Roettgen and Koenig might not have agreed on much politically, but she was *not* a fanatic. He wasn't so sure about this arrogant aristocrat, however. And if his guess was right that it was the Karosi-Denoix faction that had ordered the horrific destruction of Columbus, then the man was the worst possible type of fanatic—utterly dedicated to his own twisted view of right and wrong, and willing to go to *any* lengths to preserve and advance it no matter how many died in the process.

"I'm not here to discuss ancient history with you, Koenig," Denoix told him. "This . . . this petty rebellion of yours needlessly squanders lives and resources. Fighting the Sh'daar Collective is futility itself—you must see this! Fighting such a power is hopeless, useless, and doomed to draw down the full and inescapable wrath of the rulers of this galaxy, a civilization that is *millennia* beyond us in terms of its technology—quite possibly more. The Sh'daar have their roots within a technic civilization that stretches back in time nearly a billion years! We *must* make peace and join their collective. It is the only sane course of action for our species, especially now that the Rosette Aliens have shown themselves to be hostile."

"I suggest that we await the return of the *America* task force," Koenig told him. "The Rosette Aliens destroyed the *Endeavor* and her escorts, yes, but it's possible that the destruction was an accident."

"Three of your ships obliterated, Koenig! How do you reconcile that with an *accident*?"

"Quite simple, actually. When we drop the programmed nanosubstrate onto a patch of ground and start growing a structure, converting dirt and rock and whatever else might be there into the walls and floors of a new building, the ants and earthworms and mice and anything else that might be living there are all just shit out of luck, aren't they?"

"Humans—and humans on board starships, no less—are *not* ants! They are manifestly of a *far* higher order of intelligence, reason, and capability!"

"And I submit, sir, that the difference between you or me and an ant may simply be completely beneath the notice of a technic species that may be a million—or a *billion*—years ahead of us! They might not even have known that the *Endeavor* was there."

Denoix gestured with his hand, a dismissive wave. "Nonsense. According to my sources, it is far more likely that what has emerged from the Black Rosette is the ur-Sh'daar, which the modern Sh'daar have ample reason to fear. *They* are the reason for the Collective's emphasis on limiting technology. I strongly suspect that such limitations will be lifted indefinitely if we join the modern Sh'daar in the defense of this galaxy against their ancient . . . ah . . . selves."

"And what are your sources, monsieur? The Sh'daar themselves? Or one of their client races?"

"That, sir, is none of your business. I say only that the Sh'daar may well find that they need our help . . . and that it may be particularly advantageous for us if we give it. But they will not be inclined to accept our offer if we as a species are divided by civil war."

"I see. And you would offer the United States of North America . . . what, exactly, to elicit our cooperation?"

"To begin with, we might not need to obliterate you utterly!"

Koenig shook his had. "There has to be more than that, Chris. All in all, I'd say we've been holding our own pretty well. Washington and Manhattan? Dushanbe? Atlantica? And off world . . . there's Tsiolkovsky."

"Minor setbacks at worst. And I remind you that there have been Confederation victories lately as well: Venus, Bangkok . . . and Enceladus, of course. The Earth Confederation's forces, you must admit, are in the ascendant."

It was true. The Confederation had scored some significant victories lately, and the USNA was feeling the pinch as her forces were stretched to their very limit, and well beyond. Confederation raids against Deimos had forced the USNA to group the majority of her naval forces around Mars, to protect the USNA's military command center there—HQMILCOM. If the Pan-Europeans made a determined push in that direction, Koenig wasn't sure how he was going to block it.

Ship losses had been heavy of late too; he wished now that he'd not dispatched the *America* and her escorts to Omega Centauri, because he could have used the carrier battlegroup to strike the Confederation's orbital base at LEO, or to put Marines down at their space naval headquarters at Copernicus, on the moon.

But immediately after the USNA victory at Tsiolkovsky last year—followed by the spectacular win over the Slan va-Sh'daar at Osiris—it had seemed like a reasonable bet. Damn it, the war had been going well! To use the quaint and ancient term drawn from an old and particularly barbaric blood sport, it had looked like the Confederation was on the ropes!

Koenig knew all too well that in war *nothing* is certain except the grief and loss, the destruction, and the dread. He hated war, as only a war veteran could hate it. Bad enough that Humankind was locked in this struggle with the alien Sh'daar; Denoix was absolutely right about one thing: the civil war between North America and the Confederation *was* a needless waste of lives and resources. People were dying by the thousands, by the *tens* of thousands, in this three-month-old conflict stretching from across the face of the Earth to the moons of Jupiter to extrasolar colonies tens of light years distant. The Confederation was still in the fight, and evidently Geneva was not as convinced that they were losing as was Koenig.

"As a mark of good faith," Koenig said, "you might for-

mally renounce your claim over the USNA Peripheries."
That had been the other proximate cause of this war: Geneva's insistence that they could and should annex North
America's coastal areas—in particular the cities and lands
from Nova Scotia to Mexico partially submerged by the
global climate change of four centuries back. Boston . . .
New York City . . . Philadelphia . . . Baltimore . . . those all
were *American* cities, not part of the Confederation's global
trust. They were slowly being reclaimed from the sea and
from the salt marshes, reclaimed and rebuilt, and the USNA
didn't need Pan-European help to restore them, or to take
them over as wards of the global state.

"The United States of North America," Denoix replied,
"formally renounced those lands long ago. It is the Confederation's legal responsibility—it is our *right*—to take control of failed states and restore both law and productivity."

"Then I don't see that we have much to talk about, monsieur. We're taking back the Periphery. And we're not going
to let you *or* the Sh'daar bully us into giving up the technology that ensures our survival."

It was an old and bitter argument. With the collapse of
America's economic base in the twenty-second century,
the country hadn't been able to save the rapidly submerg-
ing coastal cities. The Periphery had been abandoned, save
for those few rugged individualists who'd insisted on staying behind, staying with their homes. Of course, Geneva
hadn't shown much interest in the Periphery either . . . at
least not until *now*, as the USNA began to drain the swamps
and regrow the buildings, restoring the lost cities to better
than before.

As for the technology issue, the Sh'daar Ultimatum of
2367 had demanded that Humankind restrict the growth of
those key technologies—the "GRIN" technologies—that
were believed to be the gateway to the Vinge Singularity.

But GRIN technologies were also vital to the survival
and the continued growth of humanity, to its transforma-

tion from a juvenile species to maturity. Obeying the Sh'daar command would mean lowering humanity's defenses, leaving the Earth vulnerable to an all-out offensive by the Sh'daar's clients. Nor did Koenig want to be the USNA leader who'd surrendered to the alien demands after almost seven decades.

Damn it, twenty years ago the Sh'daar had been *terrified* of the human battlegroup when it had dropped into their pint-sized galaxy 800 million years in the past. Their consternation had led to a ceasefire that had lasted nearly twenty years.

Earth needed to learn just what the Sh'daar were afraid of, and find a way to take advantage of it.

They would get nowhere, though, if they let the Pan-Europeans take the lead.

"A pity," Denoix said. "North America will find itself facing both the rest of Earth *and* our new galactic allies. How long do you think America can hold out against such odds?"

"Long enough for you to recognize our independence."

"*That*, my dear Koenig, will never happen. Earth must be united if she is to take her rightful place within the Collective." He gave an expressive, Gallic shrug. "Well, I had to give you the chance. There's nothing more I can do for you now. The United States of North America will be brought into the Earth Confederation, which in turn will be absorbed by the Sh'daar Collective. A pity so many must die to satisfy your ego."

My ego? Koenig almost laughed at that. Instead, he decided to try to nudge Denoix into divulging a little more information. "Does that mean you're planning on melting more cities?"

"The historical record, Koenig, will prove that *you* ordered the destruction of Columbus in an attempt to paint the Earth Confederation as the perpetrators of atrocities. It is possible that *several* American cities will be dissolved in clouds of nano-D. I do truly hope that this will not be the case. . . ."

And the virtual image vanished, the connection broken.

Koenig was back in his office, blinking in the harsh light. "Son of a bitch," he said, with considerable feeling. "Son of a *bitch* . . ."

Chapter Seven

USNA CVS America
Emergence, Outer Sol System
0620 hours, TFT

Emergence . . . and the tightly warped bubble of metaspace surrounding the star carrier *America* collapsed in a burst of raw light. The ship drifted Solward, nearly 20 astronomical units from a pale and distance-shrunken sun. Around her, the other ships of the battlegroup dropped into normal space, shedding their pseudovelocity in blasts of raw photons: the *John Young* and the *Ramirez* first, followed—as the light announcing their arrival crawled across intervening space to reach *America*'s sensors—by the *Edmonton*, the *Spruance* and the lumbering *Shenandoah*.

Gray let out a pent-up breath of heartfelt relief. He was an admiral only provisionally, on sufferance, and probably quite temporarily. President Koenig had bumped him up to flag rank so that he could command the entire six-ship formation of CBG-40. He didn't have nearly enough time as an O-6—a Navy captain—to justify that big a jump in command authority, and he fully expected to resume his role as *America*'s captain under a new admiral once he returned Earthside.

But it was good to be returning with his entire tiny command intact. Quite apart from the loss of life and the failure of the mission, if he'd lost any ships out there at Omega Centauri, the moment he returned to Earth he'd have been called on the carpet to explain himself. No matter how the inquiry went, his chances of another promotion down the line—or even of holding a captain's command—would have become slim to nonexistent.

So far as Gray was concerned, though, the important thing was that he'd not lost anyone on the mission—not even Lieutenant Walton, the young pilot who'd volunteered to make the up-close flyby of the Rosette wormhole. The data he'd brought back would keep the physics people on Earth happily busy for years . . . and might yet provide a clue or two about the identity of the Rosette Aliens.

"All task-force vessels accounted for, Admiral," Commander Wilson told him.

"So I see. Inform all vessels to close up on *America*, and prepare to accelerate in-system."

"Aye, aye, sir." There was a hesitation. "Admiral?"

"What is it?"

"I'm also picking up a SAR beacon. Range . . . six AUs, low and just off the starboard bow. The signal is very weak. . . ."

Gray opened a three-D navigational plot in his mind. Black space surrounded him, the tiny yellow glare of the sun ahead . . . with five green stars scattered around the carrier at varying distances. Ahead, circling the sun, the orbital paths of planets, major asteroids, and deep-space colonies and facilities were picked out in primary colors; nearest was the orbit of Saturn, with the planet itself a tiny, ringed toy 7 AUs ahead.

And yes . . . there it was. Weak, as Wilson had said, a minute orange pinpoint winking on and off just this side of Saturn. *America*'s AI filled in navigational data as he requested it; the target was a disabled USNA fighter—a Starhawk—and it was on an outbound drift from the immediate vicinity of Saturn . . . about 1AU—150,000,000 kilometers—from the planet, and drifting at a quarter million kilometers per hour.

The encrypted fleet tag ID'd the fighter as a Starhawk with VF-910, a squadron currently based at Enceladus. The pilot was listed as Lieutenant Frank Gallagher, life support was minimal, and the craft had been adrift for . . . *gods*! Twenty-two days! There *were* life signs, though, faint and slow.

"Medical department," Gray said.

"Yes, Admiral." It was the voice of Dr. Haynes, *America*'s senior medical officer.

"Are you getting these readings? From the streaker up ahead?" *Streaker* was the term used for fighters disabled in a fight, sent drifting at high speed across space.

"I am, yes. Low heart, low respiration. Minimal brain-wave activity. It looks like he's been put into nanomedical suspension."

"Warm up a treatment bed, Doctor. I'm sending out a SAR."

The DinoSARs, one of *America*'s two Search and Rescue squadrons, was tasked with tracking down streakers and rescuing the pilots. The question here, Gray thought, was why no one had come after Lieutenant Gallagher from Enceladus Station. *Twenty-two days* . . .

The guy had only survived thanks to nanomedical suspension. Once he'd realized no one was coming out after him, he would have ordered his fighter's AI to inject him with a variety of nanobots programmed for survival intervention. Freitas respirocytes would have provided him with oxygen over the long haul, while cleansing the blood of carbon dioxide and other wastes. Some 'bots would have moved into his medulla oblongata, drastically slowing his heart rate, respiration, and maintaining his blood pressure. Others coursed through his circulatory system by the billions, maintaining his blood chemistry almost literally molecule by molecule. Perhaps most critical, others were programmed to migrate to his hypothalamus and suppress certain key nerve centers, putting him into a coma. Asleep, he wouldn't go crazy locked up in a tiny cockpit for day upon day upon claustrophobic day.

His AI, meanwhile, would be watching for friendly ships. It would be another fifty minutes before the light announcing *America*'s arrival in-system reached the derelict and could be seen by the fighter's sensor arrays. By that time, a SAR tug would be closing on the fighter, and the battlegroup would be close enough behind to learn what the hell had happened out here.

But Gray had a nasty feeling that he already knew. There were several bases in Saturn space—Titan, Enceladus, the Huygens Ringstation. They wouldn't have been heavily defended, and the Confederation might well have decided that they were easy targets. That drifting Starhawk might be part of a USNA squadron dispatched to Saturn space to protect American assets out here.

And if a SAR tug hadn't recovered him, it suggested that the base or bases had fallen.

"Pryfly, Bridge," Gray said. "What do we have ready to go?"

"The Demons and the Knights are on ready-one, Admiral," said the voice of Captain Connie Fletcher, *America*'s CAG in Primary Flight Control. "That's ready for launch in one minute, on your word."

VFA-96, the Black Demons, was one of *America*'s six fighter/strike squadrons—twelve of the older SG-92 Starhawk fighters. VFA-215, The Black Knights, consisted of twelve of the much newer and more modern SG-101 Velociraptors. Two squadrons were always up on "ready-one," meaning they could be launched within one minute, each time the battlegroup emerged from metaspace, a precaution in case the carrier emerged into enemy-controlled space.

There was a very good chance that that had just happened.

"Launch both squadrons," Gray said. "Clear me a path into Saturn space. Bring the other strike squadrons up to ready alert. And put a SAR tug on that Starhawk adrift six AUs ahead."

"Aye, aye, Admiral." There was a pause. "Initiating fighter launch sequence now. . . ."

VFA-96, Black Demons
Saturn Space
0625 hours, TFT

"Bay doors are open," the voice of PriFly said in her head. "VFA-96, you are clear for launch."

Lieutenant Megan Connor made a final check of her ship's systems. Everything showed green, green and *go*. It was, she decided, about damned time she saw some action. Being on ready-one meant sitting out the hours already suited up and linked in to your fighter . . . just waiting.

"Copy, *America*," Commander Luther Mackey's voice replied. "Okay, Demons. On my command! In five . . . four . . . three . . . two . . . one . . . *drop*!"

Connor's feeling of weight vanished. She'd been dangling in her harness, facedown, watching unwinking stars sweep past the opening below her, subject to the artificial gravity of the hab module rotating steadily about *America*'s spine. As the launch bay magnetics switched off, however, she went into free fall, dropping out and down and into a sudden, yawning immensity of space. Hurtling out from the carrier's central axis, she cleared the curving, deep-shadowed loom of *America*'s shield cap. To her left, Saturn showed as a dazzlingly bright golden star close beside a small but brilliant Sol emerging from behind the planet in a dazzling burst of light.

Ahead, the green icons marking the Velociraptors of VFA-215 were spread out in the shape of a Y, four fighters to each arm of the formation. They were already accelerating. Connor swung her ship sharply through ninety degrees, then engaged her drive singularity, falling toward the planet six astronomical units ahead. She flashed past the vast, dark curve of *America*'s bow cap.

Astern, a lone SAR tug emerged from one of the side-by-side spinal launch tubes, flashing past the Starhawks and on after the now distant Black Knight Velociraptors.

"*America* CIC, this is Demon One," Commander Mackey said on the tactical channel. "Handing off from PryFly. All Demons clear of the ship and formed up."

"Copy, Demon One," a new voice replied from *America*'s Combat Information Center. "Primary Flight Control confirms handoff to CIC. You are clear for maneuver."

"Keep a nice, tight formation, now, Demons," Mackey's voice ordered, switched now to the squadron channel. "Let's not let the damned Velocicrappers show us up! Everybody set?"

One by one, the voices of the other Starhawk pilots came in over the channel.

"Demon Five, ready to go."

"Demon Seven, ready for acceleration."

"Demon Eight, go."

"Demon Six," Connor said. "All green."

The voices continued, filling out the Black Demons' roster. Connor couldn't help but think about one uncomfortable fact. After the Battle of Osiris, out at 70 Ophiuchi just four months ago, the Black Demons had been reduced to five pilots, including her . . . and she'd been the newbie, having been transferred to VFA-96 after her rescue from the Slan at Arianrhod. Lieutenants Don Gregory, Ted Nichols, and Joseph Kemper, plus the squadron CO, Luther Mackey. The other seven pilots all were newbs, replacements fresh out of pilot training at Oceana. They'd reported on board in time for *America*'s deployment to Omega Centauri, and in three months' time had seen no action whatsoever.

It was a hell of a note when "Happy" Kemper—a bully and a bigot who rode Gregory incessantly for being a colonial and Connor for being an immigrant from the independent city of Atlantica—was more trusted, more of a *friend* than any of these kids. She didn't like Kemper at all . . . but she would trust him to cover her tail in a furball anytime.

She couldn't say that about Rodriguez or Stuart or the others. Combat veterans tended to hold the newcomers, the FNGs, at arm's length for a time, until they'd had the chance to prove themselves. They seemed to be pretty sharp, but the only way for them to prove it was to mix it up in a furball.

No matter. It looked like they were going to get their chance today.

"CIC, Demon One," Mackey said. "Black Demons ready for acceleration. On five . . . and four . . . and three . . . and two . . . and one . . . *punch it!*"

And the sky ahead grew strange.

Virtual Combat Center
Colorado Springs, USNA
0810 hours, CST

"Welcome to Vee-Double-Cee, people. I'm Major Corbett, and we call this facility Mindwar Mountain. Make yourselves comfortable."

Shay Ashton looked around, then grew herself a chair out of the deck's nanomatrix. Forty-some other military personnel had entered the cavernous room with her and were making seats for themselves. During the past week, she'd gotten to know a few of them . . . but none yet were what she could think of as *friends*. Not yet. Most were from the USNA and had the usual disdain for Prims from the Periphery. A few—Mustoll and Cabot and Dewitt—were from the

Periphery, like her, but like most people from the various coastal ruins, they mistrusted strangers—and usually with damned good reason. It would take a while to break down the barriers and get to know them. And Ashton wasn't sure yet that the effort would be worth it.

She was still questioning why she'd changed her mind and reported to the recruiting center in Pittsburgh. She was already regretting the decision and wondering if there was a way to back out. Not bloody likely, she thought, looking around at the unyielding ferrocrete walls of the underground command center. She'd thoughtclicked her acceptance of a dozen different security forms before she'd even begun her training; this place was so secret it did not officially exist . . . though the chances were good that the enemy knew all about it.

With the Global Net's massive interconnectivity, there were few real secrets anymore.

"Ladies and gentlemen," Major Corbett said as the crowd murmurs and rustlings died away, "your training commences now. Starting today, and for the next two weeks, you are going to be hammered with a great deal of heavy DD."

DD—data downloads. Most military training nowadays began with a download program. The real work came after, with the integration and the physical practice.

"Virtual warfare," Corbett continued, "is unlike regular combat, and you will need to develop new reflexes, new attitudes, new ways of thinking in order to be successful. I want you all to relax and get comfortable, then thoughtclick the new link that you'll find riding your in-heads."

Ashton did as she was told, using her cranial implants to soften her chair and stretch it back. A new icon winked at her from within her mind and she thoughtclicked it. Data began to flow.

Much of military training was now a matter of downloading information, storing it first within in-head RAM, and eventually transferring it to organic memory. Physical skills had to be physically practiced; muscle memory was more than stored information. But virtual combat, as it was being explained through these downloads, was far less physical than it was mental.

In fact, virtual combat was very much like the virtual reality games that had been so popular for the last several centuries. A scene—a kind of virtual landscape—was created by the AI moderating the operation, and the virtual warriors maneuvered through in-head terrain to disable electronic defenses and hack into enemy networks. Fighter pilots were favored for this type of engagement because they already had the necessary physical reflexes . . . and because they wouldn't be disconcerted by holding on target, corkscrewing into an inverted loop.

Unlike most of her classmates from the wealthier and more e-connected inland cities of North America, Shay Ashton had never played virtual war games, but she was a damned good fighter pilot, and that seemed to count for something with the brass.

She gritted her teeth and pushed ahead into the unfolding mass of technical data.

USNA CVS America
Saturn Space
0916 hours, TFT

"So, how's our guest doing?" Gray asked. He was in *America*'s sick bay, in the office just outside the ward. His exec was there as well, but virtually, watching in-head from the command chair on the bridge.

"He'll make it, Admiral," Dr. Joseph Haynes told him. "We're maintaining the coma while we bring his blood chemistry fully back on-line."

"When can we talk to him?" Sara Gutierrez asked,

speaking inside both Gray's and Haynes' heads. "It's . . . important."

"Give the boy some time," Haynes told her. "We need to bring him up gradually to avoid major psychochemical trauma. I'd say . . . six hours."

"Hell, we'll be at Enceladus by that time," Gutierrez grumbled.

"Let me know when he's conscious, Doctor," Gray said. He directed a thought at his XO. "We have the Agletsch database in our network, Number One. We should be able to identify the new bandit there."

"*If* the spiders have had contact with them," Gutierrez said. "It's a big galaxy. Even they haven't met everyone in it."

Some time ago, the USNA had purchased from the Agletsch data traders a portion of an extensive database listing thirty-five sapient species currently within the Sh'daar-dominated portions of the galaxy. This *Encyclopedia Galactica*, as it was popularly known, was by no means complete. There might be four or five thousand technical, star-faring species within the Sh'daar Collective alone, and in the entire galaxy there were an estimated fifty *million* intelligent or parasapient species in all.

Those thirty-five *va*-Sh'daar races included all of the starfaring species Humankind had encountered and battled in the past seven decades—the Turusch; the H'rulka; the Nungiirtok and their odd little Kobold symbiotes, the Slan; and several other lesser-known races. The rest were known only by means of the data purchased from the Agletsch, and there'd as yet been no way to confirm the information.

But the AI on Gallagher's fighter had recorded a high-mag image of an alien ship of some sort—a flattened, 800-meter egg shape, deep scarlet in color, covered with lumpy protrusions that gave it a distinctly organic look. There was nothing like it in either the USNA or Confederation warbooks . . . so what the hell was it doing with that Confed squadron Gallagher had encountered en route to Enceladus?

"Admiral Gray, Comm," a voice said in his head. "We have a reply coming through from Earth."

He checked the time: 1015. Damn, that was pretty fast. *America* and her consorts had emerged from metaspace at 0620, immediately sending an AI alert back to Earth. With the current layout of the Sol System's planets, Earth was 15.7 astronomical units distant . . . about 126 light-minutes. Gray had dispatched a fuller, burst-encoded message ten minutes later, giving USNA Fleet HQ a brief but detailed report on what had happened out at Omega Centauri, plus a rundown on what was planned next: the rescue of a streaker 1 AU out from Saturn. Headquarters would have received that message about 126 minutes later—call it 0836, Terran Fleet time—but during that time *America* had accelerated toward Saturn, picked up the SAR tug and the fighter pilot, and decelerated on into Saturn space. If Earth had responded instantly, that reply would have reached *America*—now 10 AUs from Earth—80 minutes later . . . call it 1000 TFT, just 15 minutes ago.

Fifteen minutes' turnaround was remarkably quick for the Naval HQ staff, which, in Gray's experience, tended to discuss things to death rather than actually *doing* anything.

"Put it through," he said. "Route it to all task-force department heads and senior staff."

"Aye, aye, sir."

A new window opened in Gray's mind, static-filled at first but swiftly clearing, to show the craggy face of Fleet Admiral Michael Diaz of USNA Military Command. "Admiral Gray," he said. "Welcome home. I wish it could be under happier circumstances."

"Your emergence so close to Saturn space is . . . fortuitous, however. We have a problem."

America's arrival just 6 AUs from Saturn had been purely by chance. Until relatively recently, of course, starships had not been able to emerge closer to a star of Sol's mass than about 40 astronomical units—some 6 billion kilometers, or about the mean distance of Pluto from the sun in its long, dark orbit through the Kuiper Belt. But the powerful AIs at the Navy Bureau of Engineering were constantly working to refine the capabilities of singularity drives, as well as all of the other technologies required in modern ship design and weaponry. Capital ships could now emerge from their Alcubierre warp bubbles 12 to 15 AUs out from a sunlike star. But the fact that Saturn, 9.5 AUs out from Sol, had happened to be at that part of its orbit around the sun, had been sheerest happenstance.

"Twenty-two days ago, on February twelfth, a Confederation task force took over USNA facilities in Saturn space, including bases on Enceladus, on Titan, and in the rings. There were reports, as yet unconfirmed, that spacecraft of unknown but alien origin accompanied the enemy fleet. . . ."

"Comm," Gray said. "Get confirmation of the alien sighting off to SpaCom. Include the vid Gallagher grabbed during the battle."

"Aye, aye, Admiral."

Diaz continued talking, describing the latest Confederation offensive. Geneva appeared to have established a stronghold in Saturn space. Exactly *why* they'd done so was as yet unknown.

"The Confeds claim that they are allied with the Sh'daar now," Diaz went on. "It's possible that the alien forces with them at Saturn are Sh'daar . . . or Sh'daar clients, like the Turusch and the Slan. . . ."

Gray was willing to bet on a Sh'daar client race. So far as was known, no human had ever seen an actual Sh'daar in all the decades of war with them.

"Admiral, this is asking a lot of you and your people, I know," Diaz went on, "but we're badly stretched here in the Sol System. Right now, *America* is the only operational star carrier we have in-system, so we're damned glad to see you. *Constitution* is protecting the Chiron colony at Alpha Centauri, *Intrepid* has deployed out to Vulcan on deep recon, and *Constellation, Independence,* and *Saratoga* are all undergoing extensive refits or repair at SupraQuito. Those are the closest other carriers in service we have.

"We want you to make a close reconnoiter of the Saturn system—especially of Enceladus, which appears to be the Confed's main target out there. Get an idea of their strength, and, in particular, see if you can get more data on the alien bandit. We need to know where it's from, what he hell it's doing here, and if it's actively helping the Confederation.

"We are deploying what we can from Earth High Guard to Saturn to support you . . . the *California,* the *Inchon,* and five destroyers. Sorry it can't be more.

"Sorry to delay your happy homecoming, Sandy. Do a good job with this, and those admiral's stars might become permanent. HQMILCOM, out."

Damn *the man,* Gray thought, angry. He wasn't here to earn his stars. They'd needed someone with command experience—specifically command experience at Omega Centauri, either the Tee-Prime of today or the Tee-Sub of hundreds of millions of years ago . . . and Gray had been it. He'd volunteered, and he'd taken the strictly temporary bump up in rank because it wasn't *proper,* according to the hoary perspective of Navy tradition, for a mere captain to command a squadron of capital ships. Koenig had understood that when he'd offered Gray the job.

He would be happy to get back to being a captain again. But in the meantime, he would do what he had to. *Duty. Honor.*

There was nothing at all in that litany about *rank.*

He pushed the thought aside and called up an in-head tactical display. "Where are our fighters?" he wanted to know.

"Coming up on Enceladus now, Admiral," Connie Fletcher told him. *America* and her consorts were 70 million kilometers out from Saturn now—just less than half an AU—and the golden planet showed as a slender sickle curving away from the shrunken sun. Its rings were a straight, needle-thin slash across the crescent, giving it the look of an arrow drawn back on a bow. The giant moon Titan was a bright orange star off to one side.

"Good. Launch the rest of the fighters in support."

"Yes, Admiral."

"Tactical!"

Commander Dean Mallory was in the link. "Aye, sir."

"You heard Admiral Diaz?"

"Yes, sir."

"We need an operations plan and we need it *now*. One squadron on CAP, protecting the task force. The others will swarm Enceladus—that's the primary objective—but I also want to check out both Titan and the ring facility. It'll be recon, but be prepared to engage the enemy if he comes out. Put an opplan together and send it out through the taclink. You have fifteen minutes."

"Yes, *sir*."

Fifteen minutes, Gray reflected, was not enough time to come up with a working opplan from scratch, or to test it through AI modeling and simulation. He was counting on the Tactical department's ROP, the Ready-Op Cascade—an ongoing series of operational plans running and evolving constantly within *America*'s primary AI. As *America* moved from objective point to objective point, thousands of plans based on the current tactical and logistical situation were created, amended, evolved, or discarded, based on the best current tactical data. Commander Mallory and his team would be pulling up a handful of the best current opplans, plugging in Gray's tactical and strategic requirements, and making a final determination. That plan, then, could be transmitted directly to the fighters already en route to their objectives, with very little time lost.

Red geometric icons were beginning to emerge from Enceladus within Gray's in-head view . . . Confederation fighters deploying to meet *America*'s approach. *It's about time*, he thought. *Where've you guys been?* The enemy should have had pickets out . . . and possibly some capital ships on patrol to cut off or block a USNA attack. So far, it looked like about two squadrons' worth of fighters . . . KRG-60 Todtadlers, it looked like. That wasn't good. *America* had only two squadrons of modern SG-101 Velociraptors, which were a reasonable match in combat for the Death Eagles. *America*'s older Starhawks would be at a distinct disadvantage with the newer and more technologically sophisticated Pan-European fighters.

Gray had long campaigned with HQMILCOM for a high-tech upgrade for the USNA Navy's fighters. It *should* have been a simple-enough program. Logistics vessels routinely grew replacement fighters using raw materials and nanoassemblers in a matter of hours, even while on deployment, after all—so why not simply grow all Velociraptors and not the older, slower Starhawks?

But even with the most advanced military technology, things are rarely that simple. . . .

While it was true that with the right programming, nanoassemblers could take masses of raw material mined from asteroids—carbon, hydrogen, oxygen, iron, titanium, and dozens of other elements—and literally grow a working fighter on the spot. The same was true for the implants nanotechnically grown inside the brains of military pilots, implants that intimately connected them with the software running their fighters, merging human and machine into a single, integrated cybernetic organism.

More difficult, however—more difficult by far—were the *organic* components of this man-machine hybrid. Human fighter pilots were trained by downloading vast amounts of data into their implants, but to make use of this material there had to be downloads into the organic component as well. Pilots trained long and hard to learn how to use the fighter-control software, how to interface with their craft, how to exchange information with the fighter's AI seamlessly and automatically, how literally to become a part of their fighter.

There were significant differences between the newer Velociraptors and the older Starhawks, especially in the way data were stored on the organic side of the equation. Retraining a Starhawk driver required extensive reprogramming—essentially going in and wiping old training in order to make room for new. A pilot carrying both sets of wetware programming was a disaster waiting to happen, especially considering that much of that programming would be expressed at a pre-cerebral level, meaning before the neural impulses had time to reach the brain or to be considered on a conscious level. A pilot making a tight turn, for instance, by whipping his fighter around the flickering death zone of its own drive singularity without getting spaghettified by the tidal forces, demanded absolute agreement and precision between the organic and inorganic components.

So while the inorganic mass of an advanced, high-tech singularity fighter was easy to grow, retraining the pilots was hard and it was involved. Far easier to train new pilots for the new squadrons than to try to retrain the old ones.

Gray had been trained twenty-four years ago with what had then been the relatively new SG-92 Starhawk. He'd heard about the bells and whistles on the SG-101s and knew he wouldn't care to try strapping one on himself. *That* was something for a younger, newer generation of pilots.

And so, USNA carriers continued to fly squadrons of both. The SG-92s tended to be deployed against capital ships and planetary targets but *not* against top-of-the-line fighters like the Franco-German Todtadlers . . . not unless there was a way to win a *very* clear numerical advantage in a dogfight.

Going up against a Todtadler in a Starhawk one-to-one was a perfect recipe for suicide.

And the USNA Navy, conservative to begin with, tended to resist efforts to dump the old tech in favor of the new.

That, Gray thought, might be a form of suicide as well—national suicide—but so far the powers that be had not been able to bring themselves to the point where they could sign off on a massive restructuring of USNA military training programs.

It *should* have been as simple, Gray thought, as not training any more Starhawk pilots, while accelerating the training programs for Velociraptors and some of the newer, still as yet unnamed fighters that would be coming on-line over the course of the next year or so—the XSG-420 or the absolutely astonishing XSG-500.

But, no, HQMILCOM Mars would rather keep cranking out obsolete pilots than spending the money on a complete retooling of the military's spaceflight training centers, and that meant that logistics vessels like the *Shenandoah* had to keep growing obsolete fighters as well.

Gray watched the Confederation Death Eagles spreading out across his tactical in-head, and prayed that obsolete fighters—and pilots—would be enough.

Chapter Eight

VFA-96, Black Demons
Saturn Space
0918 hours, CST

Three hours after launch, the Demons were plunging deep into Saturn space. Ahead, Connor could see the golden arc of Saturn stretched across half the sky, the thread-slender slash of the gas giant's rings, and the small but brilliant glare of Sol off to the side, a dazzling burst of light.

The approach had been a torturous one, an insertion dictated by the opplan downloaded from *America*'s tactical department, which was bringing them in toward Enceladus from the dark side of Saturn. By skimming just beneath the plane of Saturn's rings and coming in from the planet's day side, they might be able to delay the moment when the enemy spotted them.

That part of the plan, however, hadn't worked out . . . not at all. Nearly ten minutes ago, flights of Confederation Todtadlers had boosted from both Enceladus and Titan and deployed toward Saturn's night side, spreading out to block the American fighters' approach. According to the opplan, VFA-215's 'Raptors would engage any European fighters trying to block the Enceladean approach, allowing the Starhawks to pass through to the objective.

"Okay, Demons," Mackey's voice said. "We'll go in through a barrage of nukes and AMSOs. Weapons free!"

By laying down a wall of exploding nukes, the American fighters would momentarily scramble the enemy's sensors, and clouds of high-velocity antimissile sand would both detonate incoming enemy warheads and might do significant damage to the Confederation fighters.

The problem was that while Enceladus was directly ahead, on the far side of Saturn, there were also enemy fighters deploying from Titan, off to the right, and from the orbital base within Saturn's rings, to the left and currently masked by the vast loom of the planet itself. No doubt the base orbiting Titan had been responsible for spotting the incoming USNA fighters and for giving the alarm. Other squadrons off the *America* were angling toward those other fighter groups. First contact would be within another few seconds.

The slash of the rings expanded . . . expanded . . . and then Connor's fighter was skimming a sea of gold and opalescent light, seemingly so close she could imagine reaching out and touching it.

"Demon Three," Gregory called, "*Fox One!* Missiles away!"

Connor had already thoughtclicked a target lock, a region of empty space that would shield her approach beneath the rings when it became filled with an opening blossom of white-hot plasma. "Demon Six! Fox One!"

The other Black Demon fighters loosed their missiles. Nuclear detonations strobed and pulsed against black space ahead. Connor glanced up at the smear of ringlight a scant few kilometers above her fighter's dorsal hull.

The particles in the main rings, she knew, were myriad fragments ranging in size from around a centimeter up to perhaps ten meters and almost entirely composed of water ice. Backlit by the sun, the rings were spectacularly gorgeous, giving the impression of millions of individual rings as slender and as delicate as the threads of a spider's web, each nestled close between its neighbors, but the impression of narrow ringlets separated by even narrower gaps was an illusion. True gaps in the rings were relatively rare—circles of black emptiness swept clean by tiny "shepherd moons," or by gravitational interactions with somewhat larger moons, the way Mimas cleared the broad gap between the A and B rings known as the Cassini Division. In fact, the rings were more like a single, annular disk etched by countless grooves where the ring particles were of low density, alternating with bumps of high density and brightness. *Like the grooves in an old-fashioned phonograph record* was the comparison Connor had heard . . . though she had no idea what a "phonograph record" might be.

Whatever the simile, the scene was unimaginably beautiful, serenely spectacular, eerily surreal. Even the Cassini Division glowed slightly with scattered sunlight when backlit this way.

She was hurtling past Saturn now at 8,000 kilometers per second; at that speed, she cut a chord across the arc of the immense B Ring in less than seven seconds. Silent explosions flared ahead and to either side. The blasts seemed . . . unimpressive, unremarkable when staged against the backdrop of Saturn's luminous rings.

Connor felt a bump as her AI corrected the fighter's course. The rings in this portion of circum-Saturn space were thin—only about ten kilometers thick, but there were numerous ice chunks above or below the ring planes, put there by collisions or gravitational jostlings, and her Starhawk had to constantly shift her course to avoid collisions.

And then it was a wild and swirling free-for-all as fighter swarm penetrated fighter swarm . . . and the carefully crafted opplan went to hell.

USNA CVS America
Saturn Space
0925 hours, TFT

"Trouble, Admiral."

"I see them, Mr. Mallory."

Gray sat on *America*'s flag bridge, perched on the edge of his seat and staring down into the tactical tank. Red icons marking enemy ships streamed out from Enceladus, a cloud of fighters moving to block, then to engulf the fighters off of *America*. There were hundreds of them.

"The enemy fighters are of an unknown design, Admiral. I think they may be from Gallagher's bogie."

"If they are, the Confeds have just escalated to the next level," Gray said. "Where are those High Guard ships?"

"Still three AUs out, and decelerating, sir," Gutierrez told him. "ETA thirty-five minutes."

Gray scowled at that piece of unwelcome news. Half an hour was an agony of time in combat . . . long enough for the battle to unfold, come to a climax, and be lost long before the reinforcements could join the fight.

But the implacable laws of physics dictated that there could be no turning back. *America*'s fighter squadrons were already engaging the enemy, and the ships of the carrier battlegroup were hurtling into the heart of the battle, decelerating to combat velocities—and with no time left for acceleration enough for escape.

What, he wondered, were the capabilities of those alien fighters? What surprises might they be able to inflict on the incoming USNA ships?

Gray selected one of the red fighter cons and opened up a detailed image within his in-head, the data relayed back from the star carrier's fighters ahead, and from an expanding cloud of robotic battlespace drones spreading now through the Saturn system. The enemy fighter had an organic feel to it, lumpy and uneven, with no attempt at symmetry or streamlining. Streamlining, of course, was not normally required for operations in the vacuum of space . . . but could be important for fighters accelerating to a high fraction of the speed of light. At even 10 percent of c, the density of dust motes and stray atoms of hydrogen within solar space could acquire the character of a thin atmosphere. Either those alien fighters didn't maneuver at high speeds . . . or they had power to spare, power enough not to be concerned with such mundane considerations as friction or high-energy particulate radiation.

With alien technology it was always best to expect the unexpected . . . and in combat it helped to expect the worst.

"All ships," he said, using the battlegroup's tactical link. "Stay tight, stick together. CAG, have the fighter screen expand to cover everyone. Captain Richards . . . you tuck the *Shenny* in close on *America*'s ass. Don't let them separate you from the herd."

Gray was concerned about the provisioning ship *Shenandoah*—Captain Jennine Richards commanding. When they'd begun this run, the mission specs had called for a reconnaissance of possible enemy positions in Saturn space, and it wasn't until they'd picked up Lieutenant Gallagher that they'd realized that a formidable threat faced them up ahead. By then, it was too late to detach the *Shenandoah* and pack her off to someplace safe. The bulky logistics vessel *did* have weapons—mostly laser batteries for close-in missile and fighter defense—but she would add little to CBG-40's overall massing of firepower. *America* did have some major firepower, however, and might be able to cover the *Shenandoah* if things got tight.

Might. . . .

There were no guarantees in combat, none at all, and if the star carrier became too hard-pressed in the coming battle, she would have to focus on defending herself, leaving the *Shenandoah* on her own. Gray hated that kind of decision, about who lived, who died . . . but it came down to the necessities of command.

Sometimes there simply *were* no good choices. . . .

VFA-96, Black Demons
Saturn Space
0926 hours, CST

Megan Connor twisted in her seat, trying to see behind her
. . . then spun her Starhawk end for end to get a better view.
Her in-head showed her detailed imagery across the entire
sphere of view as if her fighter were invisible, but it was still
possible to forget about your six, the area of space directly
astern, where you generally weren't looking. Her AI would
give her alerts to approaching threats, but she liked to be
able to try thinking ahead of the enemy before that threat
unfolded. That, after all, was why space fighters still had
human pilots, and were not crewed solely by electronics.

A number of the unknowns had spread out as the Black
Demons approached, and were now boosting to move
around behind the USNA fighters, to cut them off from the
lumbering capital ships coming up astern. The alien ships'
capabilities—both those of the alien fighters ahead and of
the 700-meter thing Lieutenant Gallagher had glimpsed
weeks ago—were still very much large and troubling unknowns. The human pilots were going to have to treat them
with extreme caution until they showed their hand . . . or
whatever other manipulatory organ they might possess.

There was no time to do anything about the alien fighters
surrounding them . . . not when Confed Death Eagles were
whipping in from ahead and from the right, plasma beams
snapping out to spear USNA ships. Spinning again, Connor
loosed a spread of VG-10s, rapidly targeting as many of the
nearer Confed fighters as she could.

Blinding detonations pulsed and strobed across the sky,
nuclear warheads deployed to carve a path through the
enemy fighter wall. One of the Demon newbies, Groeller,
tried to change course to avoid a suddenly erupting cloud of
plasma in his path, but in the next instant a beam of star-hot
energy nicked his fighter and sent it into a death spin, blur-

ring as it whipped around its own drive singularity so close and tight and hard that the fighter literally disintegrated, coming apart in a cloud of glittering debris.

"Jink, Demons!" Mackey called. "Don't let the bastards get a fucking lock!"

If singularity fighters had one special strength, it was their maneuverability. With the onboard AI juggling the wildly shifting forces and accelerations, a fighter could decelerate at tens of thousands of gravities, change direction at right angles or even through a full one-eighty, accelerate again on a new vector, all within a fraction of a second. Such maneuvers, if carried out both at high velocity and with a high degree of randomness, could prevent the enemy from getting a solid target lock—and that meant precious extra seconds of survival in the hellstorm of close fighter combat.

"Podeski!" Mackey's voice yelled over the tactical link. "Watch the ring plane!"

"I've got it, Skipper!" Lieutenant (j.g.) Podeski called back. "I've got it!"

Podeski, another of the newbs, in trying to lose an enemy fighter that had dropped onto his tail, was attempting the spectacularly dangerous tactic of scraping his pursuer off by skimming close past the rings. The Death Eagle fired and Podeski swerved sharply . . .

. . . and then his ship plunged into the gauzy veil of Saturn's B Ring and instantly exploded, torn to white-hot shreds as it slammed into a blizzard of ice particles and shards just 15 meters thick at a thousand kilometers per hour. A ripple of disturbance spread out through the ring material from the impact—spread, faded, and vanished.

Connor was already jinking wildly, maintaining a forward velocity of at least a thousand kilometers per second, but throwing in new vectors side to side or up and down, and varying her forward velocity from between 1,000 to 10,000 kph. She was feeling hemmed in, now, unable to jink toward the hazy gleam of Saturn's rings without risking Podeski's fate at these speeds. Depending on the attitude of her fighter, the rings appeared now as a ceiling overhead . . . now as a solid floor of glittering ice . . . now as a deadly, speed-blurred wall to left or right. A missile detonated within the rings just a hundred kilometers to port, and she had an instant glimpse of ripples spreading out through the plane. The rings looked solid at a distance; up close they had a gauzy translucence through which stars and the minute orbs of distant moons were visible . . . but to enter that thin layer of ice particles would be to enter a maelstrom of debris, from dust to pebbles to randomly scattered house-sized boulders, and not even her Starhawk's AI would be able to dodge them all.

A Confed Death Eagle dropped in out of nowhere directly ahead, firing its primary beam weapon. Connor jinked to starboard and loosed a VG-10 Krait . . . a mistake, because the enemy fighter was gone by the time the Krait had accelerated across the intervening 2,000 kilometers and detonated in a white-hot blossom of light and hot plasma. *God*, those things were fast!

She allowed her fighter's AI to guide her. . . .

She became a part of her fighter, her mind so tightly interwoven with the craft's intelligent software that distinguishing one from the other was impossible.

Centuries before, psychologists and neural physiologists had discovered that decision making happens consciously as much as several seconds *after* the decision is made *unconsciously*. Those experiments had actually threatened to undermine the whole concept of free will; did humans make choices through conscious reasoning . . . or were they rubber-stamping decisions already made by the subconscious, which, in effect, was reducing them to puppets on strings?

The debate still raged in academic neuroscience circles four hundred years later, though the default position held that it was a constantly shifting gestalt of conscious and unconscious thought that let humans decide everything from the color and pattern of today's skin suit to whether or not to join the military, to get married, or to deliberately put their lives in terrible danger. At the moment, her decision making—augmented in both speed and scope by AI software—was focused on choosing targets, locking on, and firing, a complex dance of maneuver, fire, and maneuver again, unfolding at superhuman speed.

Her AI, with senses far quicker and more penetrating than hers, could spot and identify incoming threats. Her mind, however—her thoughts—meshed closely with the software, selecting specific threats, often relying more on instinct than on reason or calculation. A thought, a mental nudge, would send her Starhawk whipping around its flickering drive singularity and onto a new course.

The idea at any given instant was to be where the enemy or his weapons were not.

Reacting to a warning from her AI, she spun fast and fired her primary weapon just as a Todtadler flashed in close—less than 300 kilometers. Her Starhawk's Blue Lightning PBP-2 particle beam projector, a "pee-beep" in the lexicon of fighter pilots, loosed a tightly focused stream of high-energy protons, which erupted in a coruscating flare of blue-white light across the enemy fighter's hull and chewed deep into its inner structure.

That's one . . .

She spun again, locked onto a second Death Eagle at 500 kilometers, and burned off a chunk of the enemy fighter's port side. Pieces spun off into space . . . and then suddenly the imbalance in the distribution of the Death Eagle's mass nudged the craft into a tight spin around its own drive singularity, shredding it into a wildly expanding spray of sparkling debris.

Two . . .

Then there was no time for counting, no time for thought as she whirled, shifted, and dodged through the enemy formations. Move and fire . . . move and fire . . . and all the while she was aware that there were fewer and fewer fighters remaining in her own squadron, which was scattering across the whole sky. Chuck Taylor's Starhawk exploded, vaporized in a direct hit. Jayli Adrian's fighter crumpled a moment later, its atoms smashed down into a sub-microscopic point as she lost control of her drive.

VFA-96 was down to seven fighters, now, and though they were scoring victories, the enemy fighters kept coming and coming, waves of them sweeping in from two different directions. One of the egg-shaped alien fighters slipped onto Connor's six, 800 kilometers astern. She spun end over end, hurtling tail-first now across the shimmering, translucent blur of Saturn's rings as she locked and fired her primary weapon.

The enemy fired as well, an eye-searing bolt of violet-blue energy that crisped some of her external hull's nano-matrix as she rolled away from it. Connor's AI identified the radiation as an X-ray laser: coherent radiation at a wavelength of 1.8 exahertz and with energies approaching 80 terajoules—as much energy as the detonation of a 20-kiloton nuke. The visible light wasn't x-rays, of course, which were invisible . . . but appeared to be part of the excitation process that generated the alien weapon's charge.

Connor's plasma bolt struck the enemy fighter full on . . . but that lumpy, scarlet hull appeared to drink in the energy, with no damage that the sensors could detect. That just wasn't *possible*.

She was expecting a second bolt from the alien, but her AI whispered in her thoughts that it appeared to be recharging. Power levels were at 40 percent . . . at 60 . . .

She locked on with a VG-10 and let the shipkiller drop from her Starhawk's weapons bay. Its drive triggered as soon as it was clear and the missile streaked aft toward the alien. Seconds later, the Krait's warhead detonated in a searing, silent flash, and as the sphere of expanding plasma cleared, the enemy fighter drifted slowly to one side, a charred and burned-out husk. Whatever those things were made of, they were *not* invulnerable.

"Skipper!" Connor called. "Demon Six! Those new alien fighters slurp down pee-beeps like soda! But I killed one with a Krait. . . ."

"Copy that, Six. Good work! I'll pass that along."

VFA-215 was heavily involved in a dogfight up ahead, drawing enemy fighters away from the Black Demons, at least for the moment. The Velociraptors had taken heavy casualties, Connor saw . . . but as word of her kill began rippling through the various USNA squadrons, more and more nuclear detonations pulsed and flashed against the night.

And the USNA fighters began breaking through.

Her discovery put some sharp constraints on the fighters. They would have to save their PBP-2 primary weapons for the human-piloted ships, and use nuke-tipped Kraits on the scarlet aliens. In the heat of combat, it was easy to lose track of who was who, even with AI help in sorting out the targets and IDing them.

The worst problem was that there were a *lot* of the aliens—her AI was currently counting over two hundred sixty of them—and the USNA fighters were limited in how many VG-10s they could carry in a warload. Depending on how many larger projectile weapons they carried—missiles like VG-44c Fer-de-lance ship-killers—Starhawks could mount between twelve and forty-eight VG-10s, enough to use cascade volleys to tear through enemy defenses and fire patterns. She'd expended half of her load of thirty-six already . . . and it griped her to use her precious Kraits against fighters instead of the far more valuable capital ships.

But there appeared to be no other way to tag the scarlet-painted alien fighters. Beam weapons were useless, or nearly so. Kemper announced that he'd killed one with combined pee-beep and laser fire—his store of VG-10s was exhausted—but only by hammering the enemy with six or eight shots in rapid succession. Apparently, the aliens had a limit on how much plasma energy they could absorb . . . but that limit was still uncomfortably high.

Connor hurtled clear of the main rings and into open space, with Saturn an immense, gold-ocher globe astern, bisected perfectly by the paper-thin, knife-edge slash of the rings.

In fact, she was still well within the planet's ring system. Beyond the edge of bright, well-defined A Ring lay a broad gap known as the Roche Limit, extending all the way out to the F Ring . . . but in fact, this gap was occupied by a tenuous sheet of debris. Three thousand kilometers beyond the A Ring lay the F Ring, the outermost discrete ring in the system, narrow, twisted, knotted in places, teased by passing moonlets until it formed a central core ring with a more slender spiral of material encircling it.

Beyond that, 180,000 kilometers from Saturn's cloud tops, was the orbit of Enceladus, and that tiny moon was imbedded in the E Ring, which it had created and continually renewed with cryovolcanic material spewed from its south polar vents. Unlike the inner rings, the E Ring was more of a debris cloud than a plane, its individual ice particles microscopic in size. Ring particles out here were more dispersed, too; there was less of a chance of a direct collision with a rock big enough to inflict serous damage.

But at the same time, flying through this zone was like pushing through a blizzard. Connor could hear the steady hiss and crackle of particles sleeting across her Starhawk's outer hull, and her in-head instrument feeds showed her that she was losing nanomatrix to a steady, high-velocity sandblasting effect that would strip her hull down to the support struts in minutes if she kept up this speed.

Ahead, Enceladus showed as a hard, diamond-brilliant, and tiny crescent bowed away from the shrunken sun. With much of its surface constantly being renewed by ice particles dropping back to its surface, Enceladus was the brightest reflective body in the entire solar system, its sunlit portions reflecting better than 99 percent of the light that hit it. The moon, barely 500 kilometers across at its longest, gleamed like a minute, brilliant jewel.

Closer, between Connor's ship and Enceladus, the Black Knights of VFA-215 were engaging individual enemy fighters, both human and alien. There were six Velociraptors remaining of the Knights—half of their original contingent—and they were up against a couple of dozen enemy ships. Not good. . . .

Astern, more squadrons off the *America* were funneling through the hole the Demons and the Knights had punched through the enemy fighter defenses. Off to starboard, VFA-224 had reached Titan and was scattering a small enemy contingent there; and to port, and back closer to Saturn, inside the Cassini Division, between the A and B Rings, the Starhawks of VFA-99 were clearing out a gathering of Pan-European fighters at the Huygens Station. Pulses of brilliant light flashed and flickered, casting oddly shifting bursts of hard illumination across the vast sweep of the rings.

Silent explosions were erupting to port as well, where enemy ships were trying to flank the incoming USNA squadrons.

The greatest concentration of enemy forces, however, appeared to be up ahead, at small and brilliant Enceladus. Why that should be was unknown . . . but it certainly wasn't up to Connor to figure out that part of the enemy's motivations.

"Form up on me, Demons," said Mackey. "We're going to help out the Knights."

"Shit," Kemper's sour voice put in, "when did the damned Velocicrappers ever take any help from us?"

It was an old rivalry—the gleaming new-tech of the Velociraptors versus the near obsolete Starhawks.

None of that mattered now in the least. Those were fellow pilots out there . . . *shipmates.*

And they were outnumbered and needed help.

USNA CVS America
Saturn Space
0946 hours, TFT

"How long?" Gray demanded.

His tactical officer stared into the highly detailed, 3-D projection tank, his face eerily stage lit from below. "An hour twenty minutes before we can engage, Admiral," Mallory told him. "We can't push too hard or we'll ablate ourselves in the rings."

Gray let more data through his conscious mind, data revealing the ship's status, the coherence of the ceramic-plastic composites covering *America*'s shield cap, of power drain, of rising temperatures on the ship's leading surfaces as friction clawed at them.

The star carrier *America* was shaped like a colossal mushroom, a pencil-slender stalk trailing behind a 500-meter shield cap. That cap was, in fact, an enormous water storage tank holding some 27 billion liters, the water serving both as radiation shielding when the carrier was plowing through supposedly empty space at near-c velocities, and as a store of reaction mass for her plasma maneuvering thrusters. Of the two, the radiation shielding was actually the more important; individual hydrogen atoms or stray protons adrift in hard vacuum were perceived as hard radiation when they were encountered at relativistic speeds.

Here, just beneath the plane of Saturn's spectacular rings, the particles *America* was encountering were considerably larger than protons. The carrier's shield cap was slamming through a cloud of particles—mostly flecks of ice—that ranged from microscopic in size up through occasional chunks a meter or more across. The largest could be vaporized by the automated point-defense lasers mounted around the shield-cap rim, but there was simply no way to clear out all of the debris floating in *America*'s path. The carrier had been forced to slow sharply to avoid

vaporizing herself in the storm of minute ice crystals and
debris.

"What's the tacsit on our fighters up ahead?" Gray demanded.

"They've all suffered pretty heavy casualties, Admiral. VFA-99 is down to three fighters left, plus a couple of
streakers. Most of the action right now is centered around
Enceladus. Mackey's squadron reports that they've punched
through the main enemy defenses, but they're outnumbered
and beginning to run low on expendable ordnance."

"Meaning nukes." Gray had received the report earlier
about the alien fighters and their resistance to beam weapons. For a time, space ahead had been bright with the flaring blossoms of nuclear detonations, as *America*'s fighters
had hunted down the swarming aliens, but they would be
running low on missiles by now. Even their stores of small
and efficiently compact Kraits wouldn't last forever in a fight
like this.

"Any sign of planetary defenses?" Gray asked.

Mallory shook his head. "No, sir. Not yet."

"Capital ships?"

"A few, in orbit around Enceladus. A couple of monitors protecting that big alien ship, plus two cruisers, a light
carrier, some destroyers. We're reading some destroyers at
Titan, too. They may be preparing to break orbit and join
the main force." Mallory hesitated. "The biggest question
right now is the alien capital ship. It's in close orbit around
the moon, but has not opened fire on our fighters as yet. It
may not be armed."

"It carried those fighters," Gray said. "That makes it a
warship."

But did it, really? The aliens were still a complete unknown . . . and that meant that their psychology, their way
of looking at the universe, their motivations, their essential
codes of morality or ethics were still unknown as well. The
aliens might see nothing wrong at all with bringing space

fighters into the system on board the equivalent of a hospital ship or a diplomatic courier. What humans considered to be violations of the rules of war might be completely unfathomable to another species.

Gray pushed the uncomfortable thought aside. The aliens obviously had had contact with Confederation representatives, and were working closely with them. They'd stepped into the middle of a major civil war . . . and Gray intended to show them exactly what that meant.

"Here's what we're going to do, Commander," he told Mallory. "We're going to start putting out AMSOs, a lot of them . . . and we're going to sweep ourselves a tunnel from here to Enceladus."

Mallory looked worried. "You think that will work, sir?"

"We'll find out. I want this task force to be over Enceladus in ten minutes or less. Now *move!*"

And *America*'s tactical officer began issuing orders.

Chapter Nine

USNA CVS America
Saturn Space
0957 hours, TFT

Braking hard, *America*'s carrier battlegroup plowed into and through the Confederation fleet at 10,000 kilometers per second—just over 3 percent of the speed of light. It was a daring, even reckless approach this deep within a planetary subsystem, burning through walls and veils of drifting ice specks that comprised Saturn's rings.

But they were coming in behind clouds of high-velocity sand, coming in tightly clustered around and behind the giant mushroom shape of the carrier *America*, coming in behind a steady barrage of AMSO rounds that continually replenished the sand clouds ahead, sweeping clear the CBG's path.

Admiral Gray sat on *America*'s flag bridge, studying the virtual tactical tank before him, his mouth set in grim determination. The main portion of the enemy fleet lay directly ahead . . . a light carrier that *America*'s warbook had identified as the *São Paulo*, a Brazilian vessel of about 95,000 tons, plus two heavy cruisers of roughly the *Edmonton*'s

class, and three destroyers. Two more Confederation destroyers were at Titan now, and a sixth at the Huygens facility in the Cassini Division of the rings.

The big unknown, still, was the 700-meter alien ship,
which appeared to be closely guarded by two monitor gunships, both German—the *Rostok* and the *Emden*. Meant for
defensive operations in orbit, they were massive, slow, and
clumsy vessels each massing over half a million tons, but
they were heavily armored and bristling with heavy-weapons
turrets. They were by far the most dangerous warships in the
enemy squadron, and they would be the principal targets of
CBG-40 in the coming bloody minutes.

The task force had entered battlespace behind the expanding, fast-moving clouds of sand grains launched from hundreds of AS-78 anti-missile shield ordnance rounds at high
velocity. *America* was releasing AMSO clusters through its
two spinal railgun mounts every few seconds, as quickly as
the magnetics could recycle. Already traveling at a few percent of the speed of light, the AMSO rounds accelerated for
a few seconds at 50,000 gravities, and when they released
the several kilos' worth of sand-grain-sized lead spherules
in their warheads, each grain was traveling at nearly 10 percent of the speed of light.

Those grains carried kinetic energy enough to vaporize
ice fragments, sweeping clear a tunnel through which the
USNA ships were traveling at high speed. There weren't
enough lead spherules to get *all* of the debris, especially
within a few kilometers of the visible surface of the rings
where the ice cloud was thickest, of course. *America*, in the
lead, got most of the rest, plowing through the remaining
particles and wisps of hydrogen and oxygen and vaporizing
anything solid still in their path.

The leading surface of *America*'s shield cap had been
polished clean, the enormous letters spelling out her name
and hull number sandblasted away by billions of ice chips
that had escaped the sand clouds. As the carrier continued

to close on the enemy, her shield cap began to get hotter . . . then hotter . . . then hotter still, as the alloyed metals and ceramics covering the water storage tank boiled away.

"The water tank won't take much more, Admiral," Captain Gutierrez told him. She sounded worried. "We're going to get wet."

An exaggeration, that. Gallows humor. If *America*'s shield cap ruptured, billions of liters of water inside would instantly and simultaneously boil and freeze in hard vacuum. The ship might well not survive as her leading structures were torn apart.

Even more worrying was the loss of *America*'s forward gravitic projectors, a forest of antennae a few centimeters high that bent space around the ship's hull. They were important in establishing and balancing the Alcubierre warp field around the entire ship . . . and in combat they bent space enough to deflect incoming lasers and particle beams, providing a measure of protection.

That protection was gone now, ablated away by temperatures high enough to make *America*'s shield cap glow a dull red in places.

But the trick with the sandcasters appeared to have worked well enough that *America* had survived the passage, so far, at least.

"Everyone still with us?" Gray asked.

"The *John Young* and the *Ramirez* report minor damage, Admiral," Mallory told him.

The destroyers had been out on the flanks, outside of the protective cone swept by *America*'s disintegrating shield cap.

But none of the CBG vessels would have made it without the AMSO sandcasters. Years before, as a raw, young fighter pilot, Gray had earned the nickname "Sandy" when he'd used AMSO rounds as antiship missiles. AMSOs were primarily intended as anti-missile defense systems, to detonate incoming warheads well away from friendly ships as well as to scatter beams of radiation, but it turned out that grains of lead sand traveling at close to *c* were a damned effective weapon against enemy fighters, against capital ships . . . and even planetary bases and defense systems.

So the "Sandy" handle had stuck with him through the years. He had a feeling he was going to be hearing more of it in the future.

Assuming they survived the next few minutes, of course. Using AMSO rounds to clear out an approach corridor allowed CBG-40 to maintain a high-velocity approach. Now, though, they would have to use that velocity to good effect against an enemy fleet that outnumbered them—and that represented some serious unknowns in the capabilities of the alien capital ship and its fighters.

"We're reading high temperatures on some of the enemy ships, Admiral," Captain Gutierrez reported. "I think some of the sand that got through the ring particles must have scoured the Confed ships. Not enough to destroy them, but . . ." Her mental voice trailed away.

"Every little bit helps, Captain," Gray replied.

At 9,000 kps, the battlegroup swept out from beneath Saturn's glowing rings, and in an instant, Enceladus loomed ahead, a brilliant white crescent swiftly growing larger. Decelerating sharply, *America*'s battlegroup slashed its forward velocity, and the tiny moon's swift growth slowed.

Enceladus was only about 500 kilometers across, a frozen flyspeck all but lost in emptiness. As the crescent expanded, however, and just for an instant, Gray could clearly see those enigmatic ice and water geysers at its south pole, backlit and glowing in the light of the distant sun. Pinpoint flashes sparkled across local space as fighter battled fighter in the near distance . . . and hammered away at Confederation warships orbiting the moon.

"Any time you're ready, Commander," Gray told *America*'s weapons officer.

Taggart's mental command snapped out an instant later. "All weapons, when you bear . . . *fire!*"

The other ships in the squadron opened up a second or two later. *America*'s weapons were relatively light—mostly lasers and plasma weapons for close-in point defense, though she did have the paired spinal-mount rail guns that could accelerate multi-ton kinetic-kill warheads to high velocities. The other capital ships, though, possessed heavier and longer-ranged weapons—the cruiser *Edmonton* especially. She was slamming high-velocity KK warheads into the nearer of the two monitors, the Pan-European *Rostok*.

The *Rostok* returned the fire, her massive quad turrets pivoting to track the fast-passing cruiser, but her target acquisition antennae had been damaged by the scouring effect of incoming sand moments before, and she was having trouble locking on. *Edmonton*'s shield cap took several solid hits, and she was trailing bits of glittering wreckage and the telltale bleed of ice crystals escaping from her punctured tank, but she was still in the fight and giving much more than she was taking. The *Rostok* staggered under a trio of heavy KK projectiles that punched through weakened gravitic shields and thick armor. Atmosphere spilled into space, an expanding silver fog as air and water boiled . . . then froze.

The big alien ship opened fire in the next instant, dozens of high-energy X-ray lasers stabbing out through the night, slamming into the *Edmonton*. Part of her shield cap exploded in a dazzling spray of freezing water.

"The alien has opened fire, Admiral," Dean Mallory said.

"I see it. He's declared himself as a combatant. Return fire."

America was pivoting as she passed, targeting the alien, slamming a pair of depleted uranium shells into the huge craft at thousands of kilometers per second . . . the velocity of the magnetically accelerated rounds plus the forward velocity of the star carrier. Those rounds struck at hundreds of kilometers per second, but had a sideways vector equal to *America*'s current velocity, and so they ripped through hull metal like savage can openers, doing horrific damage.

As *America* hurtled close to the icy moon, Gray strained for a glimpse of the alien, magnified and projected on one of the flag bridge tactical displays . . . but then *America* was past Enceladus and hurtling on out into open space, away from Saturn.

The sun lay directly ahead, shrunken by a billion kilometers.

America continued her turn. When she was pointed back at the receding Enceladus she engaged her singularity drive again, slowing her outbound passage, then slowly building up speed back toward the moon. The other ships of CBG-40 matched the maneuver; enemy fighters closed on the USNA ships, hungry for blood, but the point defenses of the cruiser and three destroyers burned them down like moths in a candle flame.

"Order our fighters to close with us," Gray told Mallory.

"Aye, aye, Admiral."

"*Rostok* is breaking up!" Gutierrez called. "She's had it!"

A flare of antimatter annihilation seared across the sky. "What the hell was that?" Gray asked.

"That was the *Spruance*, sir," Taggart told him. "X-ray burst from the alien . . ."

Damn . . .

There'd been three hundred in the destroyer's complement. Her skipper, Commander Craig Yashimoto, had been a friend.

But right now, Gray's principal concern was for more than five thousand people on board the *America*. She was . . . struggling.

The space-warping shields that protected a starship in combat were created by gravitic projectors extending out from the vessel's hull just a few centimeters. They could be melted away by a nearby thermonuclear blast—or by the sandblasting from a high-velocity AMSO round—and when that happened, that section of shield would fail, exposing the ship's hull to incoming missiles or radiation.

As the battle continued to drag itself out through Saturn space, the ships of CBG-40 were taking more and more damage—light stuff, at first . . . but the more gravity shield projectors that were damaged by ice or nearby nuclear detonations, the more hard stuff began leaking through. Gray felt *America*'s deck shudder as something big slammed into the ship. Something struck the side of his face, then spun through the air . . . an electric clipboard adrift in the microgravity of the flag bridge. The blast had dislodged it from a magnetic clip.

"Secure that!" Gray barked at an enlisted rating manning a workstation behind him. Bits of insulation were filling the air as well, hammered out of the bulkheads by the steady vibration of shuddering, incoming hits. *America* lurched and shuddered again as she took a direct hit from a particle beam, which punched a small, tight hole straight through the shield cap in a spray of debris and freezing water. The ship wouldn't be able to stand up to this kind of pounding for very much longer.

"Fire!" Taggart yelled over the tactical link, and two more massive kinetic warheads hurtled from the launch tubes and slammed, seconds later, into the monitor gunship *Emden*. On the main tactical display forward, the monitor began to crumple, falling into its own onboard black hole arrays. A cheer went up on the flag bridge as the collapse accelerated . . . and then the Confederation ship, what was left of it, exploded in a blinding flare of silent light.

Nearby, the scarlet, misshapen egg of the alien transport or whatever it was began picking up speed, looping low over the icy limb of the frozen moon, fleeing for the safety of deep space.

"The bastard's running!" Taggart yelled.

"Stop the alien!" Gray snapped. "Hit him! *Hard!*"

America shifted her orientation slightly, tracking the enemy, and Taggart yelled, "Fire!" Two more KK projectiles hurtled after the receding ship.

The destroyer *John Young* broke off from the battlegroup formation, pursuing the alien. Beams were all but useless, but the destroyer was loosing clouds of nuke-tipped missiles, including a couple of VG-44c Fer-de-lance shipkillers and one VG-120 Boomslang, a missile usually reserved for space-to-ground bombardment, with heavy shielding and a superb onboard AI.

Gray watched as the alien's X-ray laser snapped across the two KK warheads and vaporized them. One of the Fer-de-lances went next, flashed into hot plasma by the searing breath of that beam.

But the second Fer-de-lance detonated an instant later, well short of the fleeing alien vessel, but close enough, perhaps, to scramble its shields and electronic sensors.

When the Boomslang exploded, it lit up the entire sky close to the curve of Enceladus . . . and then the alien ship was tumbling . . . tumbling . . . falling out of Saturn space and into the blackness beyond.

"Target appears neutralized, Admiral," Taggart told him.

"Send *Ramirez* and *Young* to secure that hulk," Gray said.

He wanted to know who—what—was on board that alien vessel.

And what they were doing working with the Confederation.

Emergency Presidential Command Post
Toronto
United States of North America
1140 hours, EST

"It appears, Mr. President, that we're winning."

Koenig looked up at his aide and acknowledged the

news with a curt nod. "That's good, Marcus," he said. He felt no elation . . . not even an expected sense of relief. Instead, he felt . . . drained. "Do we have any word yet on losses?"

"The *Spruance* has been destroyed, sir," Whitney replied. "And the *Edmonton* is badly damaged. They may lose her. The *Shenandoah* and *America* both took damage as well, but nothing their onboard damage repair systems can't handle."

Again, Koenig nodded. He knew too well the terror, the uncertainty, the sheer determination that would be unfolding out there now. A billion kilometers away, a ship was dying, her crew struggling to save her.

"There have also been heavy fighter losses, Mr. President," Whitney told him. "Perhaps as high as fifty percent. We'll know better once they've rounded up the streakers."

"What about the aliens?"

"They did fire on our ships, and *America* shot back. Their fighters are scattering, but the large ship has been disabled. *America* is going to try to intercept it and board."

"And the enemy? The *human* enemy?"

"In full retreat, sir. Our relief force is deploying to intercept them. We don't yet know if they'll succeed."

It hardly mattered. So long as USNA bases and personnel out in Saturn space were safe.

The larger question remained, though. Why had the Confederation been trying to seize those bases? They were too far from Earth to be useful as strike or logistical positions.

And perhaps even more pressing were two other, related questions.

Who were the aliens who'd allied with the Confederation?

And why had they done so?

"Sorry, people," Major Corbett's voice said above the murmur and tumble of incoming data. "We have to interrupt your DL."

Shay Ashton blinked as the immense viewwall within her head winked out, taking with it the cascade of raw data that had been flooding into her brain. God . . . how long had she been under? She checked her internal clock and was surprised to see that less than four hours had passed.

Around her, her classmates were looking up and looking around, some stretching, others blinking or rubbing their eyes. All looked exhausted and drawn.

"Hey, it's time for lunch anyway," one of the students said, raising his voice above the growing murmur from the class. "Man, I'm starved!"

"We'll go to chow in a moment, Akerly," Corbett said. "Right now, I need to give you all an update . . . and we're going to ask for volunteers."

That got their attention. The room went death silent.

"A few hours ago," Corbett told them, "CBG-40, a star carrier task force, entered Saturn space and engaged Confederation forces at Titan and at Enceladus. At last report, our people had the upper hand. The Confeds appear to have broken, and are either surrendering or in retreat."

Ashton felt a shiver of excitement at that. CBG-40 was *America* and her escorts . . . her old ship.

Corbett continued with the briefing. "This presents us with a unique and singular strategic opportunity. Konstantin, our super-AI at Tsiolkovsky, has been closely monitoring computer and communications traffic within the Confederation. It reports that the Confederation government is, for the moment at least, completely preoccupied with events out at Saturn."

A virtual screen opened behind Corbett, stretching almost deck to overhead and spanning the room. On it, the camera perspective drew back from Sol to show the orbits of, first, the inner planets, then, as the distance increased, of Jupiter and then Saturn. Numerous curving paths were picked out in either red or green, showing the movements of the space fleets well over a billion kilometers out in space.

"The current time lag between Saturn and Earth is just over seventy-six minutes," Corbett went on. "The Confeds appear to be scrambling to pull together additional ships in order to counterattack our forces. And Konstantin has suggested that this represents an ideal moment for an RM insertion."

The murmurs picked up again, a low-voiced buzz of conversation. "Sir," one woman said, raising her hand. "Are you talking about *us*?"

"We just started dee-elling this shit this morning, Major!" another student said. "We don't know what the hell we're doing yet!"

Corbett pursed his lips, then nodded, reluctantly it seemed to Ashton. "If we wait, we'll lose the opportunity to take the Confeds by surprise. It's not as bad as you might be thinking right now."

Ashton wasn't sure she saw how it could be worse. The schedule called for two weeks of training before going out virtual-hot. She and the other students all knew how to pilot fighters . . . but from everything she'd heard, virtual incursions were an entirely different breed of cat.

"The usual rule of thumb," Corbett told them, "is twelve hours of download to twelve *days* of practice. You've all taken about thirty percent of the program . . . the nuts-and-bolts hard data you'll need to operate in vir-sim. We can give you the rest this afternoon. What you'll be lacking is *experience*—actually being able to practice the skills you're learning. And"—he hesitated, looking unhappy—"we won't have time to inoculate you against ICEscream."

Again, the room was silent. They'd all heard of ICE-scream, of course . . . a black-humor, even laughable term referring to the darker side of virtual combat.

Intrusion countermeasures electronics generally did their work in a purely defensive posture, detecting outside attempts to break into a network and blocking or isolating the threat. The nature of countermeasures, however, suggested something more direct, something stronger— the ability to strike back at an intruder to cause serious injury, insanity, or even death.

ICEscream indeed . . .

Virtual simulations were generally regarded as being completely safe. After all, they were the most popular form of public entertainment by far, an industry worth hundreds of billions. Vir-sim recreation ranged from exploring dangerous environments to experiencing mind-bending hallucinations or dreams to having virtual orgies with sex-play stars . . . and just about everything else imaginable. Docuinteractives allowed a person to be an active part of a lecture, meeting with simulated historical personalities, asking questions, and experiencing a full spectrum of sensation in computer-generated environments as diverse as the bottom of the Jovian atmosphere or the Battle of Hastings or the surface of the sun. Draminteractives let people become a part of a fictional story, anything from role-playing in the distant past to science-fiction tales set in the remote future. Teleoperation let workers operate equipment in deadly environments—like the heart of a fusion reactor or the event horizon of a microsingularity—as if they were physically present. A person linked in to the computer network and experienced in-head the simulated or the remotely transmitted realms of other worlds, separated from the action by multiple buffering layers of electronics and the superhuman speed and watchfulness of the moderating AI software.

The important thing to remember with the technology, though, was that a vir-sim operator's mind—his awareness—might be hurtling through artificially created electronic vistas, but his body and—most important—his *brain* were safely back in the virtual combat center.

At least, that was supposed to be the idea.

In practice, however, it wasn't smart to put too much reliance on this promise of invulnerability. Commercial inhead dramas had built-in safeguards and generally were *not* trying to kill you. But most military networks and many government systems were protected by ICE software, usually through AI guardians watching for deliberate incursion attempts.

And some were quite heavily armed.

It took some seriously fussy programming, but it was possible to open a communications channel from the guardian to the intruder's system and have it look like a normal data channel from the target computer. Rather than data, that channel could guide the equivalent of a small lightning bolt back to the intruder. Normally, this would result in the meltdown of the intruder's system if his AI couldn't disconnect in time, but it wouldn't reach the system's *organic* components.

But a truly sophisticated ICEscream AI could overwhelm and subvert the intruder's software, hijack his hardware, and deliver a few million volts directly to his cerebral cortex. Such systems were illegal under international law, of course, but the simple threat that they might be out there—a threat encouraged by rumor and deliberately planted misinformation—was enough to forestall most attempts by organic hackers to penetrate secure systems.

But there was another threat flesh-and-blood hackers faced that was, if not as violent, more common . . . and ultimately nearly as dangerous, and that was the threat of PNS.

Perceptual neural shock was an effect experienced by people immersed in a virtual world who faced something sudden and life-threatening while in simulation. Their bodies might be quite safe and well protected, but in their minds they died. The shock could trigger a massive heart attack, stroke, traumatic apnea, or even a general shutdown of the conscious mind that left the person in a coma.

Perhaps even worse, at least to Shay's way of thinking, was the danger of being left insane. The brain could do some astonishing things to protect itself, and by far the most extreme was to withdraw from reality entirely.

And yet modern virtual simulation was an extremely popular recreation, as well as a vital tool for dangerous or unpleasant work requiring a human presence . . . or telepresence. People linked in to NTEs—non-terrestrial environmental robots, or "Noters"—exploring the hellish surfaces of Venus or Triton or Pluto, or enduring the crushing depths of the ocean abysses of Earth or Europa, experienced sim-death all the time. Too, there were entertainment centers that offered customers the thrill of virtually falling to Earth from orbit or engaging in combat with other gamers, and they were at risk as well.

The best way to protect such explorers—or paying customers looking for a thrill, for that matter—was to *inoculate* them, a process that let them face life-threatening situations in progressively stronger and stronger doses over a period of time. That allowed their brains to cope, to adjust and come to terms with the realization that they were *safe* and that they weren't going to die when they smacked into the pavement at hundreds of kilometers per hour.

Most of what a virtual combat warrior needed to know in terms of mere data could be downloaded in a day or two. But working with that data, both integrating raw information and learning how to control your fight-or-flight reflexes when confronted with what looked and felt like certain death, took longer—generally a couple of weeks at least.

But now it looked like the class wasn't going to get any practice time at all.

"How many here," Major Corbett went on, speaking into

the shocked silence, "have experience with Class One virtual threats?"

Class Ones were the most dangerous type of simulation, the sort of perceived threat that could kill a person, or leave her comatose or insane. Two hands went up, and Ashton heard their voices over her in-head, *"Yo!"* and "Here." Senior Chief Raymond Blaine had been a deep-sea construction worker on Atlantica before his enlistment in the Navy. And Major John Aldridge was a Marine officer, a fact that all by itself said a lot about his experience.

"Okay," Corbett said. "Major Aldridge, you'll be team leader. Blaine, you're his Number One. You two will help coordinate this afternoon's training . . . and you'll be leading the team in when we attack Geneva.

"The assault will be initiated tomorrow morning, at 0900 hours."

Ashton felt a whisper of dread at that.

She *knew* she wasn't ready. . . .

Chapter Ten

USNA CVS America
Enceladus orbit
Saturn space
0810 hours, TFT

In Admiral Gray's mind, he was drifting down a broad internal passageway with a low overhead, a Marine in full combat armor to either side. Ahead, two more Marines stood guard at a closed doorway of squat design. Light panels suffused the corridor with bloody glow. The door dilated open, and Gray moved through.

He was floating a meter and a half off the deck on a pair of grav-impellers, drifting along at a man's pace with a tiny hum in his ears. Gray's telepresence was being conveyed by an ATD-90 robot drone, a sophisticated device that was feeding everything he was seeing, hearing, and feeling back to his organic brain, which was still back on board *America*. Both Colonel Harold Martin, his security officer, and Captain Gutierrez had *strongly* recommended that he not go on board the captured alien vessel or meet with the nonhuman prisoners in person. The admiral commanding CBG-40 was too valuable an asset to risk, Martin had told him, while

Sara Gutierrez had simply looked him up and down and said, "Admiral, with respect, are you fucking *crazy*?"

And so Gray had allowed them to convince him to use a telepresence robot to make the crossing from *America* to the captured alien vessel. In fact, the technology was good enough that it was tough to tell that he wasn't actually on board the captured vessel. It *felt* as though he was right there, in the hovering robot's metal and plastic shell. After all, in the human body, the optic nerves are several inches long, extending from the eyes to the visual cortex at the back of the brain, and sensations of hot, cold, touch, pressure, and pain travel as much as a meter or two, but the mind is blissfully unaware of the distance. With the signals relayed back to *America*'s primary AI, and with the two ships close enough to each other that there was no noticeable time lag, the incoming sensory data bypassed Gray's normal sensory processes and fed directly into his brain. His body was lying comatose, strapped to a couch in sick bay; his mind, as near as he could tell, was in the small, grav-floating robot navigating the bowels of an alien starship.

Every now and then, someone in the government back home would submit a scheme to have all naval warships—especially the fighters—be teleoperated in order to preserve the lives of their crews. What those schemes couldn't address, however, what they didn't seem to understand, was the fact that space combat tended to sprawl across a very large volume of space. The speed-of-light delay between *America*'s sick bay and the captured alien ship was, at the moment, something on the order of 3×10^{-5}, or .00003, of a second—the time it took for any speed-of-light signal to cross one kilometer. There was a slight additional delay as the signal was processed by *America*'s comm suite and vetted by her AI, but the actual time delay was far shorter than any human mind could perceive. A typical distance for combat between starships was on the order of three to four hundred thousand kilometers—about the distance between

Earth and Earth's moon—which meant a time lag of over a second. That *was* noticeable to the human mind—and insurmountable if you were trying to pilot a fighter across that distance in combat.

"You ready for this, Admiral?" one of the Marines asked him. He was Captain James Kornbluth, from *America*'s detachment of Marines. "These things are pretty ugly!"

"Let's have a look, Captain."

"Doc Hallowell is already inside, sir." He touched the center of the door, which dilated open, and for the first time Gray saw one of the aliens.

There were two more armored Marines inside the compartment, plus another human in a standard environmental suit. The blond head inside the fishbowl helmet turned as he drifted in, and Gray felt her ping his ID.

"Oh, good morning, Admiral! I wasn't expecting *you*. . . ."

Gray checked her ID. Tara Hallowell was a civilian, one of the scientists with *America*'s xenosophontology department. He wondered why *she* was here, and not the head of xenosoph, George Truitt.

"Carry on with what you're doing, Doctor," he told her. "Forgive me for not coming in person. I just wanted to see this thing up close. Well . . . as close as they'd let me get, anyway."

She smiled. "According to some of the human prisoners we've talked to, they call themselves *Grdoch*." She gave the final *ch* the German rasp, as in *Bach*. "At least that's as close as we've been able to shape the sound in our speech. Isn't it magnificent?"

Magnificent was not quite the word Gray would have used. It *was* large . . . and it was utterly inhuman, unlike any life form he'd ever seen.

What struck him first was how it resembled the starship itself. He'd heard a description of the things when the Marines had first boarded the alien warship, but words simply hadn't prepared him for the full, direct shock of the thing. The Grdoch was soft-bodied and surprisingly imposing, perhaps two meters tall when at rest, but able to puff itself up to three meters high or more when it was alert or surprised, as seemed to be the case now. Varying between egg-shaped and a fleshy mound wider than it was high, its deep scarlet surface was covered by hundreds of fleshy tubes, like short elephant's trunks, attached to the body at one end, and with toothed suckers or mouth openings at the other, alternately gaping and puckering like the heads of so many blood-sucking lampreys. The skin was wrinkled and convoluted, and looked quite soft.

Three evenly spaced, jointed limbs stuck a meter out from the center of that pulsing mass—legs or arms, Gray couldn't tell—each ending in three splayed, clawed digits. Those appeared to be tougher, covered with scales or plates of something resembling an insect's chitin, black and shiny. As he entered the compartment, the creature flailed those legs wildly, scrabbling against the deck, and the body rolled back a couple of meters. It came up against a bulkhead and stopped there, quivering. Was it afraid? What was it *feeling*?

There were no eyes or other sense organs visible, no other features at all that he could see. How did the being perceive him? *What* did it perceive?

Gray thought about the alien Slan, another Sh'daar client race, beings that possessed eyes, but which relied more on tightly focused beams of sound to examine their surroundings, like the dolphins of Earth's seas. "Is this another damned sonar race?" he asked aloud.

"We're not sure yet, Admiral," Hallowell replied. "We've been recording all of the sounds in this compartment, and while it's making a lot of noise, none of it is at frequencies that would be useful for sound imaging."

Gray was aware of sounds coming from the creature. He boosted his audio gain, listening. Squeaks . . . chirps . . . whistles . . . pops . . . a kind of background wail or groan

. . . but all at audible frequencies. Sound had to be up in the ultrasonic range, with short, short wavelengths—as for dolphins or terrestrial bats—in order to carry echoes with enough detail to be useful in a visual sense.

And yet Gray had the distinct impression that the creature was *studying* him, and closely. He also had the feeling that it was frightened . . . something about the way it was trembling, as though it were terrified.

Of what? Of *him*? The being was larger and more massive than any human—even than one of the Marines clad in massive combat armor. And at the moment, Gray was a rather unprepossessing black-and silver sphere the size of a basketball, perhaps, with various slender metallic appendages and lenses for seeing.

"The Confeds must have been communicating with them," Gray said. "What have you learned . . . anything?"

"We have AIs going through the Enceladus Station computer system," she told him. "It looks like they released a worm into the base network, trying to destroy the translator program, but our people are working to reconstruct it now. And G-2 is looking for records of human interaction that might help us."

That made sense. Gray didn't know when the Confederation had first made contact with the Grdoch, but they would have kept meticulous records of each meeting since, and copies of those records—some of them, at least—would have been stored within Confed networks. Even such basic information as the planetary environment the Grdoch had evolved in could be tremendously useful in acquiring a basic understanding of them . . . their language, their culture, the way they saw the universe around them, both physically and emotionally.

"Does it have eyes?" Gray asked, bemused. Clearly, the thing could sense him somehow—was reacting to his presence—but there was nothing like a face or obvious organs of sight.

"Those appendages," Hallowell told him. "It has about a thousand of them growing all over its body. Most are . . . mouths, though it seems to use them as manipulators too. They apply suction to pick things up, you know? But we think about five percent of those tubes absorb EM radiation at various wavelengths. That's our working theory, anyway, until we can put some nanoprobes into its body and take a closer look at its nervous sysem."

"You're saying it has over nine hundred *mouths*? What the hell does it eat?"

"Unknown, sir. The . . . bodily fluids of some kind of prey animal is our best guess."

"There must be food for it on board this ship," Gray said.

"Yes, sir. We're looking. It's a damned big ship."

"How many Grdoch are there?"

"We've found twenty-three so far. They're being kept under close watch, in separate compartments like this one."

"Any trouble from them?"

"Negative, Admiral," Kornbluth replied. "I think they know their only hope of seeing home again is to cooperate with us. Wherever the hell *home* is . . ."

Twenty-three individuals wasn't much of a crew for a ship 700 meters long—not unless they'd elevated robotics and automated control systems to a remarkable degree. Gray wondered about the alien fighters. Were those robots? Or were they crewed? At last report, there'd been about a hundred of the red fighters remaining. Most had fled with the Confederation ships; a few were still in orbit around Saturn or Enceladus, either shut down or . . . waiting.

The Grdoch, Gray realized, *did* look like something he'd seen before. Certain marine sponges in Earth's oceans had that same rugose surface and bodies comprising multiple tubes through which they filtered seawater. Sponges, however, had no nervous systems and were not exactly promising candidates for building starships . . . or even fire. The similarity, he thought, likely was a product of parallel evolution—a case of dolphins looking like sharks even though they were not related.

He drifted closer, hoping for a better look, and the creature erupted in a series of chirps, chitters, and squeaks, together with an oddly harmonious blend of separate voices from a number of those pulsing mouths, a kind of wailing that sounded like a human vocal choir.

"They don't like it when we get too close," Hallowell warned. "And I don't think they like machines, either. Your Noter . . ."

"Understood," Gray said, letting the NTE robot drift back again. The creature quieted somewhat. "You know, we may get more information from the human prisoners. They've been working with these things for a while, obviously."

Hallowell nodded inside her helmet. "I agree, sir. We're working on the idea that they must speak LG."

LG—*Lingua Galactica*—was an artificial language, one of several, in fact, created by the nonhuman Agletsch during their explorations of the galaxy. "The Agletsch," he replied.

"Well, if they're working for the Sh'daar, then the Agletsch probably know them."

"I'm curious, Doctor. Have you scanned yet for a Seed?"

"Yes, sir. Nothing, not even way down deep."

Interesting. It didn't confirm that the Grdoch were not a Sh'daar client species, part of their immense and far-flung empire, but it didn't rule it out, either. Sh'daar Seeds were minute—about the size of a BB pellet—but humans had learned how to detect them using non-intrusive microwave scans. What to *do* about them, especially in the case of friendly ETs like the Agletsch, was still an open—and extremely worrisome—question.

"We need to get these . . . these people to the XRD at Crisium," Gray said. "President Koenig is just going to *love* this. . . ."

The xenosophontological research department, occupying a vast subsurface facility in the Mare Crisium on Earth's moon, was Humankind's premier scientific facility for the study of nonhuman intelligences. They had a number of Nungiirtok POWs there, along with their odd little Kobold symbiotes. They had Slan as well . . . and a colony of several thousand Turusch. Technically, Earth was currently at war only with the Nungiirtok, since armistice pacts had been hammered out with the others.

At least, they were armistices from Humankind's perspective. What they thought of them was still open to question.

Because of the uncertainty, many in both the USNA's government and military disliked having that many nonhumans so close to Earth, especially since many carried the Sh'daar Seeds. Koenig wasn't concerned about any danger the aliens might represent, but he did have to deal with senators, district congressional representatives, and generals who were.

In fact, now that the civil war with the Confederation had turned decidedly *un*civil, and with Geneva actively seeking an alliance with the Sh'daar, the Crisium facility was probably a Confed target for liberation. Something to think about.

Fortunately, that was Koenig's problem now, Gray thought. In war, knowing your enemy was of supreme importance. Sun Tzu had stated that deceptively simple fact almost three thousand years ago. When the enemy wasn't even human, when he didn't think in human terms and didn't react to emotional stimuli like humans might, the problem became much, *much* worse. That was why the Crisium facility was so vital—to learn how ETs like the Slan or the Turusch looked at the cosmos, to find out what motivated them, and why.

Of course, the other half of Sun Tzu's famous dictum was just as important: *know yourself.*

Gray had the distinct feeling that humans would remain a mystery to other humans long after they understood perfectly what motivated the Turusch with their three-part consciousness . . . or the hulking, belligerent Nungiirtok.

But there was nothing more he could learn here. "Good luck, Doctor," he told Hallowell. "Let me know if I can direct any assets, anything at all you might need, in your direction."

"Yes, sir. And we'll call you if we learn anything important."

"Do that."

Anything important. Like what the Grdoch were getting out of an alliance with the Confederation. Surely they had enough in common with humans that they wouldn't have offered their military help without an expectation of something in return.

But what was it?

His inner clock told him it was past 0930 hours. Time to compose an update for HQMILCOM Mars.

And maybe a personal report for the president as well . . .

Virtual Combat Center
Colorado Springs, USNA
1310 hours, CST

"New orders, people," Major Aldridge told his team. They were gathered again in the VCC's briefing center, deep within the heart of Cheyenne Mountain. "Or . . . I should say . . . an *addition* to our orders. Just what we all wanted."

Several in the group groaned—those with hard-core military experience, and Shay Ashton was one of them. In any military operation, the key was *keep it simple* . . . and attempts by the brass to add on extra bells and whistles, extra objectives, extra constraints, or new complications were just about guaranteed to royally fuck things up.

"Yesterday," Aldridge went on, "Carrier Battlegroup 40 won a significant battle at Enceladus. In the process, they captured a ship belonging to an unknown alien species . . . critters that call themselves the *Grdoch*. Apparently, Geneva has climbed into bed with these things, and is working with them, at least to some degree."

In-head windows opened for each of them, and they looked at a vid clip of one of the aliens—bright red, covered with questing, pulsing tubes of a soft and fleshy material. Ashton had never seen anything at all like it.

"The carrier *America* will be bringing some of these things back for study," Aldridge told them. "In the meantime, though, it's important to find out what the hell the Confederation knows about them. While most of the information is probably highly classified, there's a good likelihood that at least some has been circulating through Confederation IS networks. Some of their AIs may know about it. Some of their senators might have files. Their intelligence services certainly do.

"Our primary objective is the same: infiltrate Confederation computer networks and initiate a recombinant memetic attack. But I want two of you . . . Cabot . . . and you, Ashton, to volunteer for something a little extra."

Never volunteer was a standard piece of advice for military personnel that probably went back to Sargon the Great, but it was different when your CO pointed at you and said *you* . . . you just volunteered. It could have been worse, possibly. Lieutenant Commander Newton Cabot was a good guy . . . a fellow Navy Starhawk driver and a combat veteran.

He was also a fellow Prim—a Primitive from the periphery zone inland from the sunken wreck of Old Boston. A confirmed monogamist like many Prims, he'd encountered a lot of prejudice in the hidebound aristocracy of the Navy, and had eventually resigned his commission when he'd been passed over for promotion to full commander.

He was back in military harness again, however. And he was going to be her partner.

"You two," Aldridge continued, "will be sniffing around for any hint of data on the Grdoch. If you find it, you'll slap a siphon onto it and shoot it back here. You won't have to worry about staying covert, or about deniability. We don't care if Geneva knows we got the goods or not. Just get in, get the information, and get out."

Of course, unspoken was the knowledge that if Ashton and Cabot managed to set off the alarm bells when they reached Geneva's electronic safeguards, there would be a full load of ICEscream thundering down on their virtual avatars, and it would *not* be pleasant.

"The rest of you," Aldridge said, "will plant your RM worms, then cover Cabot and Ashton as they complete their op and pull out." He looked at the two of them in turn. "You will both carry RM worms as well, of course, and place them wherever you think they might do the most good. Questions?"

There was one, from Cabot. "If the RM attack works, Major," he said, "we'll just be able to *ask* them for that information, won't we?"

"If it works, sure," Aldridge replied. "And keep in mind that we're dealing with an entire culture and government ideology here. Even if the RM insertion works perfectly, it might be months before we see any changes. Changing a government's belief set takes time . . . and time is something we're a little short of right at the moment."

The earliest, most primitive forms of recombinant memetics had been simple military or nationalist propaganda, an ancient science developed more fully in the late twentieth century as military psyops programs. Do you need to unite your population against an enemy? Do you need to convince an enemy population that they should change sides and support you? Nothing simpler. You bombard the target audience with words, music, images, and ideas designed to nudge them around to your way of thinking.

Four centuries before, that sort of thing had been all hit or miss. With enough data, however, plus the computational power and a delicate touch, it was possible to subvert entire populations. Global Net sampling and data mining, the manipulation of databases, and the precise, electronic subversion of entertainment and news media to introduce new memes to a social equation . . . some argued that these now were the most fundamental weapons in the human arsenal.

As new memes and new memeplexes took root and grew, they could change old and well-established memeplexes. By carefully balancing crafted meme against meme, a good RM team could convince a target audience that left was right, right was wrong, and blue was green.

At least, that was the claim. Ashton hadn't seen any evidence of major memetic rewrites . . . not since the social engineering that had led to the White Covenant in the late 2100s.

The trouble was that this level of social manipulation took *time*, as well as incredible computing power and direct access to the target's information systems. RM manipulation could not promise a rapid end to the war.

And if the Confederation was already on the lookout for an RM penetration, they might have counter-memetics ready to de-fang any attempted ideological assault—might even have offensive memes ready for an attack of their own.

"Other questions?" Aldridge asked. There were none. He nodded. "Good. H-hour has been set for 2030 hours this evening . . . that will be 0230 Geneva time, the middle of the night for them.

"Let's just see if we can wake the bastards up out of a sound sleep."

Emergency Presidential Command Post
Toronto,
United States of North America
1425 hours, EST

"Tonight?" Koenig asked.

"That's right, sir," Admiral Armitage said. "We're calling it Operation Luther."

"*Martin* Luther?"

Armitage looked uncomfortable. "That's right, sir. We're starting a new religious movement, after all."

They were in the Presidential Command Post's Operations Center, deep beneath the York Civic Plaza in downtown Toronto, the emergency USNA presidential headquarters since the nano-D annihilation of the city of Columbus. Admiral Eugene Armitage was head of the USNA Joint Chiefs of Staff. With him were Phillip Caldwell, the National Security Council director; Secretary of Defense Lawrence Vandenberg; Dr. Mara Delmonico, the head of the Department of Cybersecurity; Thomas McFarlane, Director of Central Intelligence; and Dr. Horace Lee, an expert in Recombinant Memetics; plus his Chief of Staff, Marcus Whitney, and a small army of other aides, assistants, and human secretaries. The room, with its large central conference table, was almost claustrophobically crowded.

"I still find this whole idea . . . unlikely in the extreme," Vandenberg said. His tone of voice sounded like he found the operation *distasteful* rather than unrealistic.

Vandenberg and Caldwell both had opposed the RM program almost from the start. Both men had strong personal religious beliefs, Koenig knew. Were they resisting Operation Luther because of the idea of introducing a new—and therefore false—religion to an unsuspecting planet? Or was it that they technically would be violating the White Covenant?

"Mr. President, we have absolutely no proof that something on this scale is going to work," Caldwell said. "A religion, *any* religion, is an extremely powerful memeplex. Memeplexes like that are extremely resilient . . . and they have built-in defenses. Very strong defenses."

"Dr. Lee?" Koenig said. He'd not met the diminutive RM expert before, but knew him by reputation. His e-file listed him as a memetics consultant on Delmonico's staff, but he also held a position as senior chair of the memetics program at the University of Chicago. "What do you have to say about it?"

"Well, an entrenched memeplex does have defenses," Lee said. "One of the defining characteristics of a memeplex, of an association of interrelated memes or sociocultural ideas, is the idea that—like genes—memes evolve through natural selection, and do so in order to protect and strengthen themselves from outside pressures. Successful memes became extremely stable, and resist any attempts to change them."

"I don't understand how a meme can protect itself," Koenig said. "A meme is just . . . an idea, isn't it?"

"Oh, it's an idea, Mr. President, to be sure. But human nature makes it more. A *lot* more.

"Take the idea that you *must* convert others to your religion out of duty or altruism. That injunction has long been one meme within the larger memeplex of certain religions—most notably radical Islam and some of the noisier fundamentalist sects within Christianity. The entire memeplex works together to protect individual memes within the system.

"For example, a meme that values *faith* over *reason* serves to protect the overall memeplex from attack by societal or cultural forces outside of that belief set. So does the meme stating that this particular faith is the *only* way to reach heaven. People infected by those memes tend to close ranks against any and all others, *outsiders*, who are not infected by those memes. Arguments based on reason or science are automatically rejected since they don't come from faith. Suggestions that other faiths might be acceptable to God are rejected because clearly *my* interpretation of the Bible or the Quran or the Book of Mormon is right. If it's not, *then I am wrong.*

"And being wrong is an unthinkable paradox, one leaving the disappointed believer vulnerable and adrift. He'll cling to the original memeplex, and all of the internally consistent internal memes, at all costs, against all arguments, against all reason, even, rather than admit he was wrong."

"I see. Thank you." Koenig reflected that in some ways, the White Covenant had sidestepped such issues by making any discussion or comparison of religions wrong . . . or, at the very least, an unconscionably bad breach of manners. Don't attack another's religious faith. Don't try to convert him. Don't attack him because he doesn't believe what *you* believe. No matter what he believes in, he has an absolute and unalienable right to that belief . . . so long as he doesn't try to harm others. For the majority of humans on the planet, the White Covenant had pushed religion into the background . . . something you believed or did but which you did *not* discuss with others not of your faith.

But even after more than three centuries of enforcing a truce among competing religious memes, attacking a religion head-on was still almost unthinkably difficult. Lee was claiming that people who were immersed within their religion, no matter what it was, were shielded by that religion's defensive memes, defenses that rendered true believers blind to logical fallacies, to mistaken assumptions, to bad research or impossible history, to *any* argument that denied or even questioned the rationality or the reality of that faith.

What they were going to try to do with Operation Luther, however, wasn't quite as head-on direct as attacking another religion. Instead, Konstantin had crafted a spiritual-humanistic movement called, variously, *lumière des étoiles* or *Sternenlicht* . . . in English, "Starlight."

Koenig still wondered if Konstantin understood humans or the way they thought well enough to create what amounted to a new religion, but the Starlight Movement was going to cause a stir, of that much he was certain.

Assuming, of course, that Starlight worms could be

planted within the Pan-European AI networks in the first place.

"I don't think it will work, Mr. President," Caldwell said. "People's beliefs . . . they're just too strong to be taken apart overnight by advertising. This Starlight movement of Konstantin's is going to be squelched from the very beginning."

"Do you agree, Dr. Lee?"

The man shrugged. "Recombinant memetics is nowhere even remotely close to being an exact science, Mr. President. Predictions are impossible. But, given time, and good placement, there's a chance. . . ."

"It's not perfect, Phil," Koenig said after a long moment, replying to Caldwell's blunt statement. "We don't know if it will work. We *can't*. But it's the best weapon we have right now to reach inside the Confed government and grab them where it hurts.

"Operation Luther will go as planned . . . tonight."

USNA CVS America
Enceladus orbit
Saturn space
1640 hours, TFT

"Admiral Gray? We have a . . . situation."

He checked the caller ID—and saw it was Dr. Tara Hallowell, calling him in-head. "Go ahead, Dr. Hallowell. Make it quick."

Gray was on the flag bridge, going through the seemingly endless checklist required by regulations before breaking orbit and boosting for Earth. Of particular concern was *America*'s water tank, holed in numerous places during the battle. And besides that, as admiral of the battegroup, he had to make decisions about the readiness of every ship under his command. He didn't really have time for civilians at the moment.

"Sorry to bother you, sir, but we've found more Grdoch."

He sighed, exasperated. "Then put them under guard and file a report. I don't need to be notified about every—"

"Sir, it's what they're . . . what they're *doing*. I think you should see."

He was about to chew her a new one . . . but something about the tone in her voice made him hold back. She sounded . . . not frightened, exactly. But she was stressed and she was worried. It almost sounded as though she was fighting back tears.

"Do I need to fire up my Noter?"

"No, sir. I can feed you vid straight from here. I'm afraid it's not very pleasant. . . ."

Now he was curious. "Do it."

"We only just found this compartment, Admiral," she told him. "This ship is—is *big*!"

An in-head window opened, and he saw . . . what the hell *was* it?

It took him a few seconds to make sense of what he was seeing. Hallowell evidently was in a large, open compartment on board the alien vessel. A line of armored Marines partly blocked his view, but they also added a sense of scale to the life form rising in the background.

The thing was . . . immense. It towered above the Marines at least fifteen meters away, and might have been ten or twelve meters tall and twenty long. At first glimpse, it was almost featureless, a blob, but it was alive. Things like stubby, useless flippers, three of them around that flabby mess of a body, waved and stretched, flapping helplessly against the air. It took Gray a moment to identify what might have been a face . . . puckered mouth . . . widely spaced, flaring openings that might have been for breathing . . . a circle of eight tiny, disturbingly human eyes that rolled and shifted in pain or terror or, quite likely, both. The skin appeared rubbery and gray green . . . except where it had been gashed open and was leaking gray liquid and yellow-white froth.

The mouth split open, and the thing screamed, a thunderous roar torn by agony.

"Hallowell!" Gray snapped. "What the devil—"

"It's a *food* animal, Admiral! They're eating it! They're eating it *alive*!"

He saw them, then, perhaps a dozen of the scarlet Grdoch wallowing and rolling inside the far larger creature's wounds, or swarming up its sides. He watched as one extended a three-clawed limb and ripped at the huge beast's flank. Others crawled up or clung to the screaming beast's flesh as it shuddered and rolled, slashing to open ways inside. Once the wounds were open, the Grdoch used their limbs to peel the flaps of wound back, brace it wide open and squeeze themselves inside. Those hundreds of fleshy mouths or trunks fastened to glistening, weeping tissue and *pulsed* as they fed.

"My God. . . ."

"We—we think the food animal is either an artificially created genetic life form, or it's something that's been genetically manipulated. But the Grdoch . . . it's like a feeding frenzy!"

Gray had attended training seminars and downloads for military officers, designed to hammer home the lesson that alien cultures, customs, and biologies, while different from humans, were nonetheless valid for those alien species. Concepts like good and evil were human constructs, and should not be applied to beings that had evolved on other worlds, under radically different conditions, in alien environments and with alien cultures.

But Gray was having a great deal of trouble remembering that as he watched the Grdoch consume the living animal literally from the inside.

"Damn it," Gray said, suddenly angry. "Can't you put that creature out of its misery?"

"*No*, sir!" Hallowell shot back. "The Grdoch clearly evolved as hunters on their home world . . . and they may *need* their prey to be alive!"

Gray checked the list of people on that channel. Captain Kornbluth was there. Good.

"Captain Kornbluth!"

"Yes, sir!"

"Kill that large creature. Burn it down!"

"Aye, *aye*, sir!"

"Admiral! No!"

"That thing is *suffering*, Doctor."

Kornbluth gave an order, and laser light flared off the food animal's head . . . if that's what it was. The huge animal continued bellowing with agony-laced thunder.

"I don't think it keeps its brains in its head, Admiral!" Kornbluth told him.

Great . . . just great. Gray realized he'd just made the situation worse.

"Those things are riled, Captain!" a Marine yelled. "They're gonna rush us!"

Within the window, Gray could see more and more of the Grdoch emerging from the food animal's bulk, wet and dripping. The one he'd seen earlier had seemed skittish, afraid . . . even cowardly. These appeared to be very, *very* angry, and fearless.

Several in the front of the pack rushed the Marines, and the Marines opened fire. As Gray watched through the vid link, he saw the marines firing bolt after bolt of laser and plasma energy into the oncoming mass of rugose scarlet. *Damn*, but those things were hard to kill! One took five or six direct hits before it collapsed, shuddering, on the deck.

And as the Marines covered the technicians backing out through the door, others began to collapse as well. Smoke boiled through the compartment. Dying Grdoch chittered and shrieked.

"Kornbluth!" Gray shouted. "Get your people out of there!"

"Aye, aye, sir! You heard the Admiral, Marines! Fall back! Fall back!"

"Seal the doors," Gray ordered as the last Marine reached safety. The door slid shut . . . and then Gray heard a massive thud as something heavy hit it on the other side. "Keep them locked up in there until we get them back to Luna."

And *still* the prey-beast thundered beyond the door. . . .

Chapter Eleven

Virtual Reality
0230 hours, Geneva Time

Her body was back in Colorado Springs, but Shay Ashton's mind hurtled through an alien landscape that scrolled beneath her in a speed-blurred rush. From her inner perspective, she was in her old SG-92 Starhawk, flying wingtip to wingtip with Newton Cabot's ship. Both had morphed into sperm mode for the sake of greater speed and maneuverability.

There was something about that which struck Ashton as just a little silly; it wasn't as though they were flying through a real planetary atmosphere where they had to worry about lift or drag or friction. They weren't even maneuvering through interplanetary space, where near-c impacts with dust grains and stray molecules of gas could generate enough radiation to cook you. Virtual combat took place in your *mind*, within a shared reality generated and moderated by a powerful AI.

But *belief* was an important factor in the generation of that reality, and the more realistic the simulation, the more completely the sim-warriors could buy in to the visual and tactile in-head story being woven by the AI. The intruding cyberforce needed speed to trace its way through the Confederation's computer networks, through their outer shells of defense and access, and so the Starhawks in Ashton's mind were in sperm mode. It helped the illusion.

And the illusion, Ashton thought, was pretty damned good. It was night, starless and black above, but with the ground below showing as a vast and sprawling landscape of geometric patterns picked out in light. Skyscrapers marked junction routers, major server clusters, and shared distributed processing loci, and circuit networks were vast fields of straight-line highways, while logic gates and ports to external interfaces looked like tunnels or like literal gates outlined in light and vanishing toward a distant horizon of blackness and blue-white light. Data traffic on the Confederation network appeared as other aircraft flying from point to point across that landscape . . . or as luminous monorails or mag-lev travel pods swiftly zipping from node to node below.

In fact, the Starhawks themselves were software, as was Ashton's viewpoint from the cockpit of one of them. Very complex software, to be sure, created and supported by the super-AI Konstantin on the moon, but software nonetheless. It wasn't like it was *real*. . . .

It certainly *felt* real. Skimming above a bundle of circuit lanes, feeling the flow of electrons and photons within the dynamic matrix, she could not tell that she wasn't actually piloting her Starhawk through alien wonder, that she—or her body, rather—was actually back beneath Cheyenne Mountain.

The other Starhawks in the flight were branching off, vanishing into other gateways, other ports. She and Cabot continued hurtling through vistas of pure light.

By glancing at individual buildings as she approached, then passed, and by focusing a part of her awareness, she could see ID tags pop into view, identifying the structure in question. She was searching for a particular physical repository of system firmware—the EPROM holding the BIOS, or basic input/output system. From her current vantage point, she was looking down on a variety of computer architectures, a vast and complex forest of interlinked computers and advanced AI.

First, though, she had to find the right computer network, then the right set of servers. There were so *many* of them. . . .

PANEURO.GOV 83723-669-945 . . .
GENEVA.GOV 83736-444-735 . . .
GENEVA.ADMIN 84736-839-335 . . .

Network defenses spread across the sky, a blue-black cloud, like an onrushing thunderhead, seeking to drag them down. Ashton triggered her own countermeasures . . . answering clouds of viral antisoftware eating through the ICE like acid.

As she penetrated the network, she was bringing with her the cold and vast intellect of the Tsiolkovsky AI, Konstantin. Excluded from standard access to the Pan-European networks by firewalls and physical barriers, Konstantin could use the swift-moving software fighters as a back door to piggyback itself into the system, penetrating, exploring, revealing . . . and changing.

"They know we're here," Cabot's voice said over their private link. "The alarm is spreading."

"I see it." One after another, systems around them were releasing countermeasures . . . or else going dark as the physical connections between networks were broken. More thunderheads gathered in the distance . . . searching . . . questing. . . .

"Releasing RM," Cabot announced.

"Copy." She wanted to hold on for a few more moments,

wait until they were deeper inside, before releasing her own viral warhead.

Ah! *There* it was. That was what they were looking for. *OERE.ADMIN 89749-783-003* . . .

Thunderheads, dozens of them, guarded the portal.

The *Organisation Européenne pour la Recherche Extraterrestrienne* had been spawned by the much earlier European Council for Nuclear Research, better known by the acronym CERN. The modern OERE had been designed to study both extraterrestrial cultures and biologies as they were encountered. The port yawned below them as Ashton and Cabot peeled off and accelerated. Light blurred past them, their illusion of velocities too great to properly measure. In fact, their brains were in drug-induced and implant-manipulated overdrive, with nanoseconds passing for them like seconds. There would otherwise be no way for human awareness and perception to experience the light-speed interactions among computer networks online.

The target system opened around them, a bewildering maze of three-dimensional towers and lattices and geometric frameworks of dazzling light. Twisting sharply, the two Starhawks sped deeper into the labyrinth. A tunnel yawned—a major virtual-memory array. Thunderstorms reached for them, lightning jabbing and exploding across a black sky, but the two fighters dodged and wheeled, their own countermeasure software engaging the enemy ICE, holding it at bay, sometimes distracting it, sometimes melting it away . . . or even convincing it that there was no threat all.

They were inside.

Konstantin, invisible but ever present, led them in, questing ahead for metadata tags of interest. Code numbers and file names flickered and rippled around Ashton. Several flashed brightly, highlighted in red . . .

Grdoch ...
La Connaisance d'étrangere ...
L'Affaire Vulcan ...
40 Eridani A II ...

This was why *human* minds were necessary in this sort of virtual assault. AIs were very good at following orders, and perhaps one as powerful as Konstantin could have made its own decisions about which data to tag, what to ignore. "Grdoch" was self-evident, so much so that it was quite possibly a false front, something placed there to distract virtual raiders. Konstantin would be examining that very closely indeed, searching for signs of viral land mines. Same for a file labeled, in French, "Alien Contact."

Others, though, tugged at Ashton's intuition. "Vulcan," for instance, was the name of an Earthlike planet only 16.5 light years from Sol, the location of an important German-Argentinean colony, while "40 Eridani" was the name of Vulcan's star. Somehow, they called to her, so she tagged those as well.

Keid ...
La Massacrer ...
Le Rapport d'Gouverneur Delgado de Vulcan ...

She had no idea what those were, but they seemed important. She could see the hyperlinks, channels of light, connecting those with the other more obvious data structures.

As she tagged each highlighted data structure with a thought, Konstantin was able to open each file and siphon off the contents, shunting them via a high-speed Global Net pipeline back to Cheyenne Mountain, to USNA Intelligence headquarters, to USNA Naval headquarters on Mars, and to its own data banks at Tsiolkovsky, on the far side of the moon. Within seconds, the data would be backed up in so many different secure locations that there would be no chance of having it tracked and destroyed by Confederation counterintelligence.

"Let's get the hell out of here!" Ashton called.

"Rog! Just a sec . . ."

Ashton still had her own software bomb. An immense building loomed to her left and below: *OERE7746.gov.com*, a massive cluster of quantum encryption servers. Thought-clicking the structure, she released her worm. "Missile away!" she cried. "Okay, Newt! Let's unjack."

Withdrawing from the Pan-European network should have been as simple as cutting the connection, but with their minds heavily invested in the fantasy of flying in a particular three-dimensional space, it was better—safer—to extract gradually, following the trail they'd blazed deep into the core of the OERE network. It didn't take long . . . no more than a few seconds of perceived time . . .

But Newt screamed in her ear.

She glanced right just in time to see an amorphous blue-gray cloud, a thunderhead shot through with flickers of lightning and the dark gray shadow of rain as it engulfed Cabot's fighter. There was a flicker . . . and Cabot was *gone*.

Ashton felt a shudder run through her body . . . and then she was lying on her back, strapped down in an acceleration couch in the Ops Room at the Virtual Warfare Center. Cabot was in the couch next to hers, screaming, shrieking in an unholy mix of terror, rage, and agony as white-gowned technicians tried to restrain him.

"Are you okay, Lieutenant?" It was Aldridge, standing next to her couch.

"Y-yeah. Fine. What happened to—"

"ICEscream. Poor devil . . ."

She tried to rise, clawing at the safety straps.

"Stay put, Lieutenant," Aldridge told her. "Stay still. We need to check you out."

But there were other people screaming in the room as well, a shrill cacophony of horror and madness.

"Get them off me! Get them off me!" Cabot was screaming, going on and on.

And Shay Ashton wondered if she was going mad as well.

Admiral's Quarters, USNA CVS America
En Route, Enceladus to Sol
0425 hours, TFT

"Admiral Gray. Please wake up."

Gray blinked himself awake out of a deep sleep. "Whazzat?"

"Admiral Gray, I have an incoming communication for you. Comm department."

He checked his internal clock. Almost zero four thirty. Beside him, Laurie Taggart stirred, then reached for him, her hand gliding up his chest. His in-head personal assistant rarely spoke to him directly, but when it did there was good reason.

"Okay," he said in his head. "Put it through."

An in-head window opened, and he saw the face of Lieutenant Gary Kepner, one of *America*'s communications officers. "Sorry to wake you, Admiral," Kepner said, "but we have an incoming laser com, marked urgent and personal for you."

"Who from?"

"Uh . . . It's flagged Office of the CIC, sir."

Meaning President Koenig. Zero four thirty . . . damn! The star carrier was on Eastern time, same as the president. Didn't the guy ever sleep? A quick check on ship's status showed him that *America* was currently accelerating at 0.7 gravities, boosting toward Earth . . . and was currently approaching the halfway point, just over 500 million kilometers out. The time delay on the incoming message would be about half an hour.

"Put it through."

"The message requires a security release, Admiral. Blue-Two."

Ah. Gray swung his legs out of bed and sat up. Laurie stirred, but didn't wake. Good. As the message window opened in his head, he got up and padded naked to the small office adjoining his sleeping quarters so that he could take the call without waking Laurie.

He'd not been getting much sleep anyway. The sight . . . the sound of that alien food animal being devoured by that pack of Grdoch haunted him, banishing sleep. He might as well get up and be productive.

In his office, he sat down at his workstation and touched a contact, raising a retinal scanner from its recess in the desktop. *America*'s AI knew who he was and where he was on board the ship at all times, of course. It could tell from his brain waves that he was who he claimed to be, but the ancient amenities still had to be observed. "Gray, Trevor, Admiral, one-nine-six-six-five-one-eight-zero-three Bravo," he said.

"Identity confirmed, Admiral," the voice of the ship's network said in his head. "Incoming message released."

"Admiral Gray, this is President Koenig."

Gray didn't reply. It would take half an hour for any response to get back to Koenig. If necessary, computers could edit two halves of a conversation together for the records later.

"I've been following your progress out there with great interest, Admiral," Koenig went on. "Congratulations on your victory at Enceladus. Well done. Very well done indeed."

You didn't call me in the middle of the night to congratulate me for *that*, though, Gray thought. Was he in for a reprimand over trying to kill the Grdoch food animal? He'd

sent that report off hours ago, just before the moment when
America broke orbit over Enceladus and started boosting for
Earth.

"Crisium XRD is looking forward to meeting your prisoners," Koenig went on. "Have the *Shenandoah* take the
captured alien directly to Luna. A cargo heavy-lift hauler
will be there in orbit waiting to help get it down to the surface."

That made sense. The controls on the alien vessel were
utterly beyond human comprehension—spongy cabinets
large enough to hold a single Grdoch in a claustrophobic
embrace; possibly they used their flexible, trunklike mouths
to control the ship . . . or it was possible that they used some
sort of direct neural linkage, as with human fighter pilots.
Either way, there was no way for humans to control the captured alien transport independently, so the *Shenandoah* had
taken the vessel under tow. Hallowell and two platoons of
Marines were still on board, making certain the captured
aliens stayed under lockdown. Once at the xenosophontological research department base beneath the dusty, crater-
pocked plain of the Mare Crisium, the XRD staff would
be able to address the problem of communicating with the
Grdoch, and they'd be able to bring many more tools to bear
on the problem than were available to *America*'s overworked
xenosoph department.

Better them than him. Gray thought again about those
scarlet creatures rolling and squirming inside the living
food animal and shuddered. He wanted no part of them.

"In the meantime, we've come into possession of some
new intelligence. I needn't remind you that this is classified
at Blue-Two. No discussion of this stuff even with your staff
until either I personally or CO-HQMILCOM Mars gives
you direct clearance, okay?"

That was interesting. What the hell was going down?

"A few hours ago," Koenig went on, "we carried out a
virtual military assault on the Pan-European computer net.

The primary purpose of the raid was to plant recombinant memetic worms throughout the network, with the goal of undermining support for the war within the Confederation, and driving wedges between the various member states. It will take some time before we see the results of that action, of course . . . but the secondary goal of the raid has already born fruit. The raiders were able to tap into certain computer files in the Geneva Cloud, and steal top secret data on a recent ET contact—the Grdoch."

Well, well. Interesting indeed. Maybe they wouldn't need to start from square one in learning how to communicate with the things.

"What is of particular interest is that the Grdoch are *not* Grdoch va-Sh'daar, *not* members of the Sh'daar Collective. The Confederation apparently ran into them a year ago at Vulcan, made contact . . . and cut some sort of a deal with them. We're . . . still studying the records we brought back from the Geneva Cloud. We're not certain, but our analysts believe Geneva *may* have just turned over one of their extrasolar colonies to the Grdoch, and that that colony was destroyed."

God! Gray felt an unpleasant twist in his stomach. What would the Grdoch *do* with a human colony . . . with thousands of men, women, and children?

He'd seen the hellish things eat, and he didn't like the place where the thought was taking him.

"The carrier *Intrepid*, Captain Glover, was deployed to Vulcan two weeks ago along with three destroyers . . . and all four ships are now overdue and presumed destroyed.

"I don't need to tell you, Sandy, that we—the USNA, I mean—need allies. Badly. We may be able to break up the Confederation if this RM plan succeeds . . . but we still need to stop the Sh'daar . . . and after that we have the Rosette Aliens out at Omega Centauri to worry about. The Grdoch offer us an enormous opportunity. I can't stress this enough. They may be our one hope of survival, *if* we can pry them away from the Confederation and *if* we can enlist their help against the Sh'daar."

"Oh, is *that* all?" Gray said out loud. Aliens were, by simple definition, *alien*. Their motivations, their goals, their very worldview all were unknown to the USNA, and might well be unknown or even *unknowable* to the Pan-Europeans and to the Confederation as a whole.

For a start . . . were the Grdoch helping the Confederation against North America in order to make peace with the Sh'daar, as Geneva wished? Were the Grdoch even aware of the Sh'daar . . . and would they be willing to ally with the United States against them?

"I have issued orders," Koenig told him, "to assemble an expeditionary force to travel to 40 Eridani and make contact with the Grdoch fleet that has assembled there. I want you and *America* to lead it.

"Yes, I know *America*'s battlegroup is pretty badly dinged up," Koenig said, and it felt like he was reading Gray's mind across 3 AUs. "*Edmonton* and *Spruance* are destroyed . . . and *America* is badly damaged, with significant damage to the *Shenandoah*, the *Young*, and the *Ramirez*.

"But HQMILCOM Mars is assembling a new force—we're calling it Task Force Eridani. Besides the *America*, it will include the carrier *Saratoga* and, if we can get her back here from Chiron in time, the *Constitution* as well. Your operational orders will direct you to proceed to 40 Eridani and there investigate the disappearance of the *Intrepid* battle-group, but you'll also be working under a set of secret orders . . . to make contact with the Grdoch and, for a start, enlist their aid against the Confederation. After that, we'll see if they'll help us against the Sh'daar.

"Time, obviously, is absolutely of the essence. You will bring *America, Young,* and *Ramirez* back to the dockyards at SupraQuito, where we will perform as much of a nano-refit as is possible, complete the refits on the *Sara* and on the *Indie* . . . and wait for the *Connie* to make it back from

Chiron. HQ-Mars will release as many support vessels as they can—the *Long Island*, the *Calgary*, the *California*, and the *Maine*, at the very least. We also expect to bring in a Russian task force . . . and possibly smaller battlegroups from North India, China, and the Theocracy as well. Altogether, we hope to be able to deploy as many as twenty major warships.

"You will command the USNA contingent, of course. The others will be under their own national commanders, but I have every confidence that you will be able to get them all to pull together and work with you. To give you the leverage you will need, I am granting you a *provisional* promotion to full admiral. Congratulations."

"What the *fuck*?" Gray shouted.

"Yes, I know how you feel," Koenig went on, again appearing to read Gray's thoughts across half a billion kilometers of emptiness. "There are plenty of other four-star admirals running around here . . . Matthews, for a start. And Bennington. And Kinkaid. And not a damned one of them has your level of experience when it comes to First Contact. You'll need to pull at *least* an Oh-ten if you're going to be on an equal footing with the likes of Ulyukayev or Gao or Singh. I don't want one of them calling the shots out at 40 Eridani." He grinned at Gray from inside the window. "Call it the president's prerogative."

"*Damn* you," Gray said, groaning. "How to win friends and influence people." Damn it, president or not, Koenig couldn't do this to him!

"I'll need to see you here as soon as you get to Supra-Quito. Be sure to file your engineering, damage control, and expendables reports with the orbital dock, so we can bring your contingent up to full strength. And . . . one thing more. I'm attaching a classified file to this message under the header *Starlight*. I want you to review it before you get here. It may have a bearing on your communications with the other fleet commanders.

"I know I'm asking a lot of you, Sandy. Of you *and* your crew. But I also know that if anyone can pull this off, it's you.

"Koenig . . . out."

The president's face winked off, and Gray blinked at the top of his desk.

"Sandy? Are you okay? I heard you yell . . ."

He turned in his chair. Laurie stood in the office entryway, naked, looking worried.

"Sorry I woke you, dear," he told her. "I got some . . . unexpected news."

"What is it?"

Gray frowned. How secret was the news? Well . . . the fact of the promotion would be published soon, might already have been published, if Koenig was on the ball. He couldn't talk about the upcoming mission yet, but he could tell about *this* lunacy.

"I've just been bumped up to four stars," he said, angry. "By Koenig. Provisionally, of course. Presidential prerogative, he calls it. But it's not like I *deserve* it."

Taggart appeared to relax a bit, looking relieved. "Oh, *well* . . . do I bow in your presence? Or just kiss your ring?"

"It's not funny, Laurie."

"I thought you were having a nightmare."

"This *is* a nightmare! And I can't wake up! Damn it, I don't deserve the provisional rank I have now . . . and the son-of-a-bitch is jumping me up by two pay grades!"

"Did he give you a reason?"

"Yes." Gray hesitated . . . then decided that this would be common news soon as well. "He's putting me in command of a joint fleet. USNA, Russian, Chinese, Indian. And he wants me to have enough mass to run the show."

"Makes perfect sense, if he doesn't want the fleet commanded by a Russian."

"Ron Kinkaid is the man," Gray said. "CO of CNHQ,

Mars. Thirty years in the Navy, five of them as a full admiral."

"Yes. And how many alien civilizations has he made First Contact with?"

Gray gave her a hard look. "What does First Contact have to do with anything?"

She sighed. "It's kind of obvious, isn't it? You were with Koenig when *America* went back in time and met the ur-Sh'daar on their home ground. And last year you made First Contact with the Slan. First Contact, *and* you made them break off in their campaign against us!"

"My *people* did that. Lieutenant Connor. Dr. Truitt. Not me."

"Exactly. *Your* people. They reported to you, and were guided by your decisions. And that's what Koenig is looking for: experience in making key decisions in a first-contact situation. You're the best person for the job. Koenig is just making sure you can *do* that job."

Yeah, that he was. And by jumping outside the regular ladder of command and promoting him over how many thousands of rear and vice admirals, what was he doing to the Navy hierarchy—tradition-bound, aristocratic, and so weighed down by layers of seniority and flag-rank officers that promotion generally meant that someone above you had died? There would be insane jealousy just for a start, and that meant trouble just working with the men and women responsible for getting him the ships, repairs, and supplies he needed. There would be a perception of favoritism, with Gray cast in the role of teacher's pet, and with it criticism of Koenig that he was playing favorites and interfering with military good order and discipline. Gray was already viewed as an outsider and as a maverick. His Prim background, the fact that he'd been a "squattie" in the swamps of the Manhattan Ruins until he'd been forced to seek medical attention for his wife—that would be held against him as well. He didn't play the game, didn't play well with others

. . . and any naval officer with an anti-Prim prejudice—and that was most of them—would see him as a security risk, as immoral, even as a foreigner.

And there were the political issues as well. A sizeable fraction of the American population favored peace, both with the Confederation and with the Sh'daar. Not a majority, certainly . . . perhaps 40 percent, but enough to make trouble, to make themselves heard, maybe even to shake things up with a public renunciation of Koenig, his policies, and those close to him.

If enough passed-over admirals or issue-hunting asshole politicians complained, there would be an investigation . . . and just possibly a call for the USNA Senate to do something about it—like institute impeachment proceedings. If anything happened to Koenig, his patron, Gray would be left twisting in the breeze. He would be lucky if they let him retire, and didn't charge him with grave crimes and misdemeanors against the state just for being in Koenig's good favor.

Gray despised politics.

Damn the man!

"I don't want the job, Laurie," he said. He wanted to say more, wanted to explain . . . but he was just feeling too overwhelmed at the moment to put one word after another.

"Well, it sounds like you've got it," she told him. She came closer, slipped behind the desk, then sat on his lap, her arms encircling his neck. "You've got it, want it or not. And if anyone can pull success out of his ass against impossible odds, it's going to be Sandy Gray."

They kissed. Gray wanted to argue, to tell her how foolish, how impossible the whole thing was . . . but there really wasn't any point. Like she said, the job was his, want it or not. He supposed he *could* tell Koenig where to get off . . . but refusing a direct order from the president of the United States of North America would not exactly be a good career move.

And Gray damned well wasn't ready to retire from the Navy *yet*.

Laurie broke the kiss, grinned mischievously, and wiggled her bottom against his lap. "Well! Feels like you're not *entirely* ready to give up! You want to take me back to bed? Or do you want me right here?"

As it happened, he chose both.

Eventually.

Chapter Twelve

USNA CVS America
Naval Dockyard, SupraQuito
0825 hours, TFT

Star carrier *America* pulled into the space dock at SupraQuito the next day, at the end of a largely uneventful run. Toward the end, there were reports of Confederation lurkers—lean, needle-slender ships with heavy stealth shielding and a couple of nuclear shipkillers on board. Like the submarines of warfare on and under Earth's oceans centuries before, lurkers posed a serious threat, especially for ships coming into or leaving port.

The *Ramirez* and the *Young*, however, fired salvos of high-yield nukes into the seemingly empty area of space where *America*'s scanner and deep space sensor operators had thought they'd detected an echo. If there'd been anything there, it never showed itself . . . and no nuclear fireballs blossomed among the incoming USNA ships.

SupraQuito was a sprawling terminus at the synchorbital point on the Quito space elevator, almost 35,000 kilometers above the ice-clad top of Mt. Cayambe, in Ecuador. Since 2120, the space elevator had been Humankind's key to space, providing swift and inexpensive access to geostationary orbit. SupraQuito now consisted of some hundreds of habitats, factories, and orbital structures, including several hotels, an enormous spaceport with docking facilities, a naval base, a long-obsolete solar power station that still provided electricity for the immense microgravity hydrophonics farms, and a permanent population of more than 150,000.

Travel up and down the woven buckyfiber cable was by magnetically accelerated travel pods; a trip from synchorbit down to Earth still took hours, however, even with constant acceleration for the first half of the trip and deceleration for the rest. Gray elected to take *America*'s gig, which would get him to Toronto's spaceport in just over an hour.

He made the journey with his senior staff—Captain Gutierrez and Captain Fletcher, of course, as well as Commander Dean Mallory, heading up tactical-ops; Commander Roger Hadley, chief of Intelligence; Commander Harriman Vonnegut, the fleet logistics officer; and Dr. George Truitt, head of Xenosoph. Now that he was getting bumped up to four stars, he wondered if he would be getting a larger and fleet-dedicated staff. All five of the military personnel on the shuttle were wearing two hats at least, and all were part of *America*'s senior staff. Gutierrez was *America*'s skipper but served as Gray's flag captain as well, *and* as his fleet exec. Mallory was head of *America*'s tactical department but was also filling in as fleet operations officer. In a similar vein, Hadley and Vonnegut both were department heads on board *America*, but had also stepped up to oversee Intelligence and Logistics for the entire battlegroup. It was a juggling act possible only with thanks to implant technology, in-head links, and massive AI, but it still meant a high-stress workload for all concerned.

Gray had already made the decision that he was going to demand a full staff. If they were going to stick him with a full-admiral's title and responsibilities, then by God, they could give him a decent staff as well. Gutierrez, Mallory, and the rest had been working their asses off since 36 Ophiuchi, and they damned well deserved a sane workload.

Or, at the very least, *one* insane workload apiece, instead of two or more.

The one civilian member of the flag team, Dr. Truitt, wore only a single hat. Even at that, it was damned tough getting any useful information out of the guy when he got into one of his grandstanding moods. Gray wondered if it might be possible to promote him out of the battlegroup—maybe send him with the captured Grdoch to Crisium, and promote someone else to take his place as director of XS.

Hallowell, maybe.

"Dr. Truitt," Gray said. "Has your department made any progress with the prisoners?"

"You mean a language breakthrough?" he growled. "No. Thanks to *someone* giving orders to open fire on them in their mess hall!"

"I would have done the same," Gutierrez put in. She visibly shuddered. "I've seen the vids."

"We've provisionally named the food animals *Praedambestiari truitti* . . . praedams for short," Truitt went on in a conversational manner, ignoring her. "We performed a detailed hand-scanner examination of one of them . . . there are fifteen locked into separate compartments on board that ship."

Gray noted the man's use of the word *we* . . . even though he'd been on board *America* the whole time, and not with Hallowell and other staff members on the alien ship.

"I saw the report, Doctor," Gray replied.

"Yes, well, you know, the interesting thing about the praedams is that they have a massively distributed and noncentralized nervous system . . . several hundred neural nodes scattered throughout their bodies *instead* of a single brain. Your Marines, Admiral, would have had to stand there shooting at the thing all day before they actually killed it. A *very* bad call, I'm afraid."

"I screwed up, Dr. Truitt," Gray said. He made a dismissive gesture with his hand. "It happens."

"Ah . . . yes, well . . ."

Gray's simple admission appeared to have derailed the xenosophontologist. He didn't know how to respond.

"So we need to go on from here, and leave the recriminations to MILCOM. Do you agree?"

"Yes, of course. As you say."

"Your report says that these praedams are most likely genengineered?"

"Yes, Admiral. Clearly, the Grdoch have bred the praedams into a form that would not survive in the wild. Those three flippers, for instance: useless. They may have originally been a large marine creature on the Grdoch home planet—something like the extinct whales of Earth—but they have been bred to produce meat and fat—a *lot* of it, and very quickly. They also appear to heal quickly. It's possible that the Grdoch can keep one alive for *months* while continuing to feed off of it every few days—"

"God, Doctor," Vonnegut said, *"enough!"* He looked like he was going to be sick.

" 'Nature red in tooth and claw,' " the xenosophontologist quoted with a shrug. "It's not our place to judge the ways in which alien species have evolved, or their cultural mores."

"Keep working on the language problem, Doctor," Gray told him. "The Confeds were talking with them, certainly."

"The Confeds must already have the translation software up and running," Hadley pointed out. "That virtual raid on Geneva brought back a lot of hard intel. Maybe the Grdoch language is part of the package."

America's intelligence department, Gray knew, had received its own reports from MILCOMINT since the Geneva raid. So far, though, USNA Intelligence hadn't shared much of what they'd learned.

The news that *America* and an allied fleet were to be deployed to Vulcan was still a closely guarded secret, apparently, and none of the others on board the shuttle knew about that. Speculation—and scuttlebutt—about *America*'s next deployment had been rife ever since she'd broken out of Enceladus orbit and departed Saturn space.

The hyper-compartmentalization of military intelligence could be infuriating and, given the interpersonal connections of modern information systems and links, was more often than not an exercise in futility. If you could communicate with anyone on the planet with a thought, secrets became much harder to keep.

But there were limits, boundaries often set by common sense. Keeping secrets from your own people so that an enemy didn't know what you were going to do was one thing. Tying yourself up in knots keeping secrets from yourself was something else entirely.

Hell, if his people weren't fully briefed today, Gray thought, he was going to brief them himself. They *deserved* to know.

As the others continued to discuss the Grdoch and what might be learned from them, Gray leaned back in his cabin seat, closed his eyes, and opened the download on Vulcan, the battlegroup's next destination.

Planetary Data Download
Vulcan

PLANET: 40 Eridani A II

NAME: Vulcan

COORDINATES: RA 04h 15m 16.32s, Dec -07° 39' 10.34", distance 16.45 ly

TYPE: Terrestrial/rocky; oxygen-nitrogen atmosphere

MEAN ORBITAL RADIUS: 0.68 AU; **ORBITAL PERIOD:** 223d 2h 07m

Inclination: 04.1° 15' 10.1"; **Rotational period:** 25h 17m 15s

Mass: 1.05 Earth; **Equatorial Diameter:** 12,883 km = 1.001 Earth

Mean planetary density: 5.63 g/cc = 1.02 Earth

Surface Gravity: 1.0 G; **Escape Velocity:** 11.2 km/sec

Hydrosphere percentage: 47.4%; **Cloud Cover:** 30%; **Albedo:** 0.39

Surface temperature range: ~-10° C — 40° C.

Surface atmospheric pressure: ~900 millibars = 0.89 atmospheres

Percentage composition: N_2 81.8; O_2 18.1; Ar 0.2; SO_2 < 300 ppm; CO_2 < 300 ppm; others < 200 ppm

Age: 5.6 billion years

Biology: C, N, O, H, S, H_2O, PO_4; Mobile Heterotrophs, photosynthetic autotrophs. Dextrose, levo-amino acids, terrestrial biochemistry.

Colonial History: Among the earliest truly earthlike worlds to be discovered, the Keid Colonial Administration was established in 2270 under auspices of the Confederation Xenoplanetological Directorate. In 2275, the world was opened to full colonization by WeiteWelt, a joint Germano-Argentinean cooperative. Colony cities were established along the west coast of Neubavaria and Las Pampas, the two principal continents, and by 2420, the population totaled more than 80 million....

Vulcan was that rarest of jewels, a genuinely Earthlike world, a near twin of Earth right down to the breathable atmosphere and essentially terrestrial biochemistry. Oceans of liquid water shone gold and purple beneath the K1-type star, which, though smaller than Sol, appeared twenty percent larger in Vulcan's sky than the Sun did from Earth. The other two members of the triple star system, B and C, gleamed in the sky as a pair of bright stars, one ember red, one white and diamond brilliant, some 400 astronomical units away. The main star of the trio was visible from Earth to the naked eye. The Arabs had named it Keid, from their word *qayd*, which had the unlikely meaning of "the broken eggshells," but that ancient name was rarely used now. The star was also known as o2 Eridani.

Gray found the origin of the planet's popular name amusing. *Vulcan*, of course, originally had been the Roman form of the Greek god Hephaestus, the god of the forge, his name the root of the word *volcano*. For a time, during the nineteenth century, astronomers had been convinced that a planet orbited Sol inside the orbit of Mercury, and given the name to that world. Eventually, of course, the oddities in Mercury's orbit blamed on the gravitational effects of an inner planet turned out to be perturbations better explained by Einstein and relativity, and Vulcan had been relegated once again to mythology.

In the middle of the twentieth century, however, the name was revived in a popular science fiction drama broadcast over the two-D entertainment systems of the day, with one of the program's characters being an alien from that world. The writer of some of the print media supporting the broadcast program had suggested the nearby star 40 Eridani as Vulcan's sun, and the show's creator had agreed. Vulcan as a habitable world orbiting 40 Eridani had become canon.

Telescopic evidence in the early twenty-first century had suggested that there in fact *were* several planets orbiting the star; when a robotic probe in the 2120s revealed a desert world with water oceans and a breathable atmosphere, John

Piccard, a virtual actor who specialized in historical dramas and who knew about the old science fiction program, had jokingly suggested Vulcan as the world's name.

Joke or not, the name had stuck.

The real-world Vulcan was not, as it turned out, home to a humanoid race of xenosophs with a penchant for remarkably human logic. Over a billion years older than Earth, Vulcan had evolved its own ecosystem while Sol was still forming its planets. There were tantalizing hints that intelligence had evolved on Vulcan eons ago when the planet was largely covered by oceans, but apparently, like many marine species throughout the galaxy, that culture had never developed fire or a technic civilization. Vulcan was in its long twilight now, its oceans shrinking and becoming steadily more salty, the interiors of its two vast supercontinents turning to desert, its ecology well adapted to current conditions but fighting a steadily losing battle as the planet slowly died.

There was something else about Vulcan that made it a rarity. The local ecology was biochemically similar to Earth's. Specifically, it had evolved right-handed sugars and left-handed amino acids.

Sugars and amino acids each could occur in either "left-" or "right-handed" versions, a reference to the way the atoms of the molecules fit together. A mirror image of a given molecule was called its *isomer*.

There was no guarantee that a world would evolve sugars and amino acids; across billions of worlds there were so many options, so many alternatives. But when it did, there was only a one-in-four chance that the result would include both dextro-sugars and levo-amino acids. Any other combination, and the local biochemistry would be incompatible with that of human colonists. Vulcan had proved to be one of those rare planets where humans could actually eat the local flora and fauna and derive nutrition from it. On other worlds colonized by Humankind, food was either modified or created from scratch in large nanufactories. Without them, humans would starve to death even if they were surrounded by organic bounty; human chemistries simply couldn't derive nourishment from dextro-aminos or levo-sugars.

The Keid Colonial Administration had been created in the late 2200s with the expectation that Vulcan might become a major exporter of food back to Earth. The full impact of the nanotech revolution, however, and the collapse of Earth's economic systems as a result, was only just being realized at that time. When nanagriculture could conjure unlimited supplies of food from the raw materials in carbonaceous chondrites—a type of asteroid rich in carbon, water, and the various elements of biochemistry—there was no need to grow crops on distant worlds and ship them back to Earth. With Earth in economic chaos, Vulcan had become an independent state, still a part of the Confederation, but only nominally tied to either Germany or Argentina.

But now *something* had happened out there, something unexpected. An alien ship had arrived and a deal of some kind had been struck. It was vital that the USNA learn exactly what that agreement had entailed.

The shuttle began shuddering as it plunged into the atmosphere, and Gray felt the sharp tug of deceleration. Through the shuttle's viewwalls, the swiftly expanding planet beneath them had swelled from a globe to a curving horizon, brilliant with sunlight and the swirl of clouds. Their voyage was nearly complete.

He did hope that there were some answers waiting for them when they reached the ground.

Emergency Presidential Command Post
Toronto
United States of North America
0910 hours, EST

"Mr. President," Whitney said. "The morning PICKL just came through."

"Very well."

Koenig finished with what he'd been working on—a speech to be delivered virtually to Congress in another two days. A vitally *important* speech, calling for national unity in the face of both the war with the Confederation and the ongoing fight with the Sh'daar. He hated the need for politics . . . for nudging the opposition along, cajoling them into his camp, instead of simply giving the appropriate orders.

He missed the Navy. Things had been so much simpler then.

Okay, he was ready. Koenig checked the time. The President's Intelligence ChecK-List was supposed to be ready for download first thing in the morning, 0730 at the latest. When it was late, as today, it generally meant there was some important, last-minute intel tucked into the thing. *What the devil are they going to throw at me today?* he wondered.

He leaned back in his seat, closed his eyes, and opened the inner datastream channels with his personal code. Information flooded his brain, taking the form of a particularly vivid and detailed memory . . . a memory that hadn't been there before.

Koenig began processing that memory, then suddenly sat upright, eyes wide open. "Good God!" he said aloud.

"Sir?" Whitney asked, concerned. "Are you okay?"

"Yes, Marcus. But, my God . . . this will change *everything. . . .*"

VCC Military Hospital Complex
Colorado Springs, USNA
1125 hours, CST

"Just tell me whether or not he's going to be okay!"

Shay Ashton felt like they'd been giving her the runaround ever since she'd shown up at the medical center that morning. No one wanted to talk with her, and no one wanted to tell her the truth.

Dr. Patricia Gonzales looked up from the datapad in her hand and gave her a long and, Shay thought, sad look. Gonzales was an ancient, a truly *old* person, with intensely blue eyes that seemed to peer out at Shay from the depths of bone-rimmed sockets beneath a web of wrinkles set in parchment skin. She was by far, Ashton thought, the oldest human she'd ever seen. How old? In her hundreds, certainly. But she was a medical doctor. Was she simply way overdue for her anagathic treatments? Or was she a Purist?

Twenty years before, Ashton had known a member of the Purist sect of the Rapturist Church of Humankind . . . her old CAG on board the star carrier *America*. What was his name? Wizewski, that was it. Captain Barry Wizewski. The Purists believed that you needed to be *fully human* if God was going to save you from hell, and that meant no tinkering with the human genome, no genetic prostheses, no anti-aging treatments. A few rejected any form of medtech tinkering, including cerebral implants, a personal choice that paradoxically left them on the outside of a human society that depended on high-tech modifications to body and brain just to interface with that society. Humans, first and foremost, were tool makers, tool *users*—and by giving up the current available tool set, the Purists, she thought, were making themselves *less* human, not more.

She hoped there was another explanation for Dr. Gonzales's extreme age. Having a doctor who didn't believe in nanomedicine was in her mind one step removed from having a doctor who believed in leeches and incantations.

After a long moment, Gonzales shook her head. "I *can't* tell you that, dear. Commander Cabot's condition is extremely serious. We won't know if the reconstruction is successful for some months, yet."

"Reconstruction? What reconstruction?"

"NNR. Neural network reconstruction. They didn't tell you?"

"Doctor, no one has told me *anything*."

They were standing in the visitors' lounge just outside the medical center's critical ward, the psychiatric version of an ICU. The viewall beside them was set to show Cabot on a hospital bed, his body unnaturally rigid though no restraints were visible. Up the right side of the screen marched a steady, unfolding column of words. The audio from the critical ward had been switched off—the screaming tended to bother visitors—but Cabot was talking, an unending rush of words that *almost* made sense . . . until you tried to parse them out.

" *. . . and God is Goddess I feel You inside my brain when I can't explain the luminous revelation of the transcendent because string theory proves,* proves *the existence of alternate realities that are manifest within the Gaia matrix that transforms our reality in ways that turn base lead into azure skies of radiant blessing that is the sacred marriage with the Divine . . .*"

At least, Ashton thought, he no longer appeared to be convinced that things were crawling on him.

"Religious delusion," Gonzales said, watching Ashton try to make sense of the monologue. "The technical diagnosis is delusional schizophrenia. We call what he's doing there 'word salad,' and it's fairly typical in cases like this."

"He thinks he's talking to God?"

"Possibly. He keeps referencing Gaia . . . but we're not sure if he's talking about the ancient pagan deity of Earth or the common expression of techno-transcendence." Gently, Gonzales reached out and turned Ashton away from the screen. "Don't try to figure it out. There's a—a fault in his brain circuitry that makes it all but impossible for him to communicate sensibly. We record it all to look for clues that might help with the treatment, of course, but mostly it's all scrambled-up garbage."

"What if he really *is* talking to the Goddess?"

Gonzales stared at her for a moment, those blue eyes as penetrating as an X-ray laser. "You're from the Periphery, aren't you, dear?"

That again. She sighed. "Yes. The D.C. swamps."

"Is Lieutenant Commander Cabot your . . . your husband?" She said the word with a hint of distaste. "Or a sex partner, perhaps?"

"No."

How, Ashton wondered, could she explain to a non-Prim? Was there any sense in even trying? Newton Cabot was a fellow Prim and a fellow former Navy pilot, nothing more than that . . . but the fact that they both were outsiders with similar backgrounds within the far larger cultural background matrix of modern society put them in the same foxhole. It gave them something in common, more powerful, more intense even than their shared naval experience. Husband . . . no. But she *did* tend to think of him as a brother.

"I meant no offense, dear," Gonzales told her. "You seem to be . . . deeply attached to him, that's all."

"He's a fellow pilot in my squadron," she said, avoiding the issue of them both being Prims. "That makes us close, yes."

Gonzales nodded, but her expression suggested that she didn't quite believe Ashton.

"Official policy here at the Center is to withhold all patient information from anyone except next of kin, designated marriage partners, or people designated by the patient. Newton listed family in the Boston Periphery . . . but your name wasn't on it."

Ashton came close to exploding. Primitives living marginal existences at the edge of high-tech modern culture tended to bond in pairs . . . a survival mechanism when larger groups tended to be threatened by internal politics, and were harder to feed. Centuries ago, that had been the norm in human culture, at least outside of the Theocracies, but within the context of modern culture, monogamy was seen as . . . a mild perversion.

And *damn* the prudish aristocratic societal traditionalists who passed judgment on anyone who insisted that everyone hold the same beliefs, follow the same cultural mores, and live the same lives!

Gonzales must have seen the storm building behind Ashton's eyes. She held up a hand. "Easy, dear, easy. I was simply explaining Center policy, and why you were having a hard time. I can *tell* you're close, and I'll tell you what I can."

Ashton forced herself to relax. "I'm . . . sorry, Doctor. I feel like I've been slamming my head against plascrete walls all morning."

"I do know the feeling. Essentially . . . the web of neurons inside Newton's cerebral cortex has been . . . partially unwired, partially rewired. This sort of thing happens in cerebrovascular trauma—strokes—or when a feedback effect from a hostile virtual network affects the brain's neuronal net. Fortunately, it wasn't enough to cause major physical damage. But he is insane."

"Permanently?"

"We hope not. There is a treatment plan, though we have to basically start him off at the beginning. We have already injected him with medical nanobots to disassemble his in-head circuitry, to take him down to bare brain, with no technological augmentation. The next step will be to inject his brain with his own stem cells, and use cranial nanosurgery to begin rewiring the neural net within his cerebral cortex. It's called neural network reconstruction, and the idea is to break the connections that formed—re-formed, really—in his neurons when he was hit by the active intrusion countermeasures . . . the . . . what do you call it?"

"ICEscream."

"Funny name. The ICEscream, yes. The . . . the jolt that was fed back to his organic brain while he was in the virtual simulation rewired significant portions of his cerebral cortex. It also fried portions of his implant hardware, which is why we've had to dissolve it. With luck, we'll be able to regrow most of what was lost . . . and disassemble connections that are . . . are interfering with his ability to communicate with the outside world."

"But that means he'll be better, doesn't it?"

Gonzales pressed her lips together, then shook her head. "I wish I could tell you, dear. At best . . . at *best*, he'll be sane . . . but it's possible, even probable that he won't remember people important to him . . . that he'll have lost some of his major skill sets, chunks of his training and experience. He might suffer massive amnesia and have to retrain from the very start, as if he's gone back to a blank slate, like a newborn's."

"And the worst case?"

"He probably won't die. There doesn't seem to be any involvement of his motor cortex or autonomic functions. But he may be . . . in a world of his own. A world that doesn't really relate very well to the world you and I experience." She shrugged bony shoulders. "He *may* just continue talking to the Goddess, and not relate to the rest of us at all."

"And you say it will be months before you know?"

"We'll know the stem cells are replacing damaged neurons successfully within two to three weeks. We won't know how much of his memory has been affected for another six to eight weeks. The retraining, if it becomes necessary, could take a year or more."

"A year?"

Again, a shrug. "How long does it take a baby to learn to be human? Even with downloads, once his implants have been rechelated across his cerebral cortex, it takes time to integrate the training."

"I . . . see. Thank you, Doctor. I appreciate your taking the time to explain."

"Not at all, dear." She turned and looked at the figure on the bed revealed by the ICU viewall. "I wish the news was better . . . but too often we realize that what we're doing here is the art of medicine. We like to think of it as a precise and high-tech science, but it's not. It may never be. Medical science does *not* have all the answers. . . ."

Ashton wanted to ask Gonzales about her beliefs—specifically about why she was so old at a time when most humans lived healthy and relatively youthful lives well into their second or third century, thanks to nanoanagathic life extension.

But if she was avoiding life extension because of religious reasons, she might easily take offense. The White Covenant discouraged *any* questions about a person's religious or spiritual beliefs.

She watched Cabot on the bed for a moment, the column of word-salad nonsense continuing to crawl silently up the screen as he babbled somewhere within the labyrinth of the center's psych ward. Ashton didn't believe in God, not as most people seemed to use the term, but she was familiar with the Gaia hypothesis . . . and with the newer idea of the Gaia matrix.

Centuries before, an environmentalist named James Lovelock had suggested that Earth—or, rather, Earth's tightly interconnected biosphere—might in fact constitute a kind of higher order—self-regulating, internally consistent, an emergent phenomenon arising from the complexity of all life and the way it worked together. He'd called it the Gaia hypothesis, after the Greek goddess of Earth. Some after Lovelock had gone so far as to suggest that the system was self-aware or becoming so, that humans and their electronic communications networks were, in fact, Gaia's nervous system, her means of becoming self-aware.

More recently, believers had pointed out that both human minds and the AIs they worked with tended to link together into higher and higher orders of awareness and consciousness. A crude example might be the tactical link for a fighter squadron, the electronic network tying together all of the pilots and their ship AIs and, when it was close enough, even the main AI back on board the carrier into a kind of physically dispersed but tightly organized single entity. Just as humans were made up of trillions of cells linked together, just as human consciousness could be seen as an emergent epiphenomenon from the neural net of the cerebral cortex, all interconnected humans and artificial intelligences might together comprise a far vaster, far more powerful, far more deeply aware entity called the Gaia matrix.

Ashton had seen no evidence that such an entity existed . . . but, then, was a single cell inside a human liver or in the skin on the tip of the nose or within the glia of the brain itself aware of the whole organism, the person? If it was true, that higher-level organism didn't seem to take much interest in the cells that made up its being, no more than Ashton, most of the time, was aware of the tip of her nose. If Gaia didn't bother her, she wouldn't bother Gaia.

As she looked at the lone figure inside the psych ward, though, she was reminded of a poem, a snippet of verse from centuries ago, which made fun of the then-city of Boston and of the families that made up its rather closely knit aristocracy.

> *And this is good old Boston,*
> *The home of the bean and the cod,*
> *Where the Lowells talk only to Cabots,*
> *And the Cabots talk only to God.*

Ashton didn't know the poem's background. She had no idea what a cod was, or why beans should be exclusively linked to Boston. She did know, however, that old Boston had been long dominated by several old and aristocratic families, the so-called Boston Brahmins, including the Cabots and the Lowells. That had been centuries ago, before rising sea levels and a couple of weapons impacts in the Atlantic— the fall of Wormwood in 2132, and a high-velocity impactor strike during the Turusch attack of 2405—had all but obliterated the low-lying city. The Cabots had included important industrialists, business leaders, politicians, and doctors, hence the joke.

But now Newton really was speaking "only to God."

And Shay wondered again if modern medicine was making an unwarranted assumption here. What if he really was in direct contact with an emergent goddess arising from human electronic networks?

If the doctors managed to break that connection, would he be grateful? Or would he mourn the loss?

She doubted, somehow, that she would ever know the truth.

Chapter Thirteen

York Civic Center
Jefferson Government Complex
Toronto, USNA
1345 hours, TFT

The York Civic Center was a sprawling metropolis in its own right, seated on the banks of Lake Ontario and extending on artificial terrain far out over the waters to the south. The Jefferson Tower rose in sweeping curves above the waterfront, offering an unparalleled view of the city and the lake.

It was, Koenig thought, a relief to be back up and in the light, natural light rather than the glowing light panels of the bunker kilometers below. For months, with only occasional respites on ceremonial occasions, President Koenig and his staff had been squirreled away in the Emergency Presidential Complex far beneath the streets of Toronto, sheltering from the possibility of another Confederation nano-D attack like the one that had vaporized a three-kilometer-wide crater into the heart of downtown Columbus, the former capital of the USNA. His security detail could fuss and fidget; he was going to make the most of this, and had arranged for the staff meeting with Gray and his people in a broad, open briefing room in the sky over a third of a kilometer above Toronto's central business and government center.

There were military units surrounding the city, of course, and on the Atlantic coast, and in orbit, all watching for another attack. If an alarm came through, Koenig and those with him could be in the bunker complex within a few minutes, thanks to dedicated high-velocity mag-rail elevators in the building's spine.

He didn't think it was going to happen. There'd been no repeat of the atrocity, and despite President Denoix's disquieting remarks a few days before—about the possibility of more nano-D attacks—the new Confederation government had been backpedaling on the issue, blaming a cabal or rogue element of some sort within the Confederation military.

Koenig looked down from the Jefferson Building's 194th floor on the crowded expanse of York Plaza and prayed that the Confederation continued to behave . . . continued to abide by the commonly accepted terms and restrictions of *civilized* warfare. Despite Denoix's vague threats, the Confederation seemed to have received enough of a backlash from the rest of the world, even from the nation-states that were still members of the Confederation, to have renounced nano-deconstructor warfare as a weapon.

The whole idea of *civilized* warfare was a colossal oxymoron, of course. War by its very nature couldn't be civilized. Centuries ago, the advent of nuclear weapons had forced certain restrictions on warfare, if only to avoid the unthinkable—a nuclear holocaust on a global scale. Certain lines could not be crossed, certain borders could not be violated even when the enemy was operating freely on both sides. The notion of limited warfare had cost lives and even eventual victory in some of those wars. "There is no substitute for victory" had been a quote by General Douglas MacArthur—but in one way, perhaps, MacArthur was wrong. The human species had survived, after all, when the increasingly deadly weapons of modern warfare had threatened Humankind with utter extinction. If it hadn't been *victory*, at least, it had been an accomplishment more important than mere military or even political success. Extinction is appallingly permanent.

The stakes had become higher since humans had encountered alien civilizations out among the stars . . . and especially since the Sh'daar Ultimatum. It was almost impossible for humans to understand alien motivations or cultural limitations. Worse, when the survival of the entire species was at stake, it made no sense whatsoever to put limits on what could and could not be done in war. The Confederation and the United States of North America had to share the planet, no matter what the outcome of the civil war; the various Sh'daar client species that had attacked Earth over the past decades weren't concerned with such niceties. Presumably, they would save a habitable garden world for their own use if possible . . . but if they had to boil away Earth's oceans and turn the surface into glass they would do so. Koenig remembered the object lesson of a species known to the Agletsch as the Chelk, and suppressed a shudder. Their world, and every living creature on it, had been destroyed twelve thousand years ago by the Sh'daar. The Chelk homeworld's fate might well become Earth's if humans couldn't get their act together and present the Sh'daar with a unified front.

Of one thing he was still certain: simply surrendering to the Sh'daar was not an option. This was especially true now there were two new players on the galactic stage—the Rosette Aliens, enigmatic and transcendently powerful; and the Grdoch. There didn't appear to be any way to communicate with the Rosette Aliens—not yet—but the Grdoch were another matter.

A new carrier task force formed around the *America* might tell them what they needed to know.

And there was also the new information to add to the

mix: the small supernova planted in the morning's intelligence checklist.

"Mr. President," Whitney said in his head, "the naval officers are on their way up."

"Thank you, Marcus. I'll be with the others."

He opened a door in one wall with a thought, and walked
into the main briefing room . . . a large, open area with
transparent walls and an enormous conference table. The
room gave an overwhelming sense of open space—*so* much
better than that damned closet situation room down in the
subbasement. A couple of dozen men and women at the
table stood as he entered: Eskow, McFarlane, and Admiral
Armitage were present physically, along with members of
their staffs. Others—Caldwell, Vandenberg, Sharpe, Lee,
and Delmonico—were virtually present, linked in through
the Jefferson Building's AI and appearing at the table by
means of holographic projectors in the ceiling. One of the
physical attendees was the single nonhuman in the room:
Gru'mulkisch, her Sh'daar Seed carefully screened and
blocked. A special seat had been arranged for her, a kind
of slanted, narrow, padded shelf on which she was resting,
belly-down.

Another person present physically was Congressperson
Julie Valcourt, a Canadian, and the Speaker of the House.
She would bear watching today . . . though Koenig had
issued her a personal invitation to the briefing. Unfortunately, he needed her.

"Sit down, sit down," Koenig said as he strode across the
highly polished floor and took a seat at the head of the table.
"They're on their way up."

"About damned time," Armitage grumbled.

Koenig grinned at him. "They *did* have the farthest to
travel to get here, General."

"They could have telecommuted," the slightly translucent
image of Pamela Sharpe said. "Like some of the rest of us."

"*Not* advisable, Pamela," Delmonico's projection said.

She shot a hard look at the Agletsch. "Not with down links
that might be . . . compromised."

A number of the physical locations and bases now used
by the USNA had started off as Confederation assets, and
were therefore, of course, suspect. Complete cybersecurity
was difficult under the best of conditions; it was damned
near impossible if the other side had ever had access to a
location's infrastructure to the point where they might have
built devices into the physical structure that gave access to
local nets. Electronic devices nearly microscopic in size
could penetrate computer networks, plant viruses, or open
wide the same sort of back door that had admitted the Luther
squadron. Not even quantum encryption could safeguard
computer communications if the hardware at both ends had
been compromised. AI software known as QC, or quantum
crackers, could ferret out clues that could let outsiders listen
in on almost anything.

For that reason, top-secret communications were not held
over channels within structures built or once maintained by
the Confederation. The space elevator and the naval bases
up at Geosynch were a case in point. Though primarily
funded and built by the United States of North America,
those facilities had been used by the Confederation for centuries, and there might easily be QC software residing in the
most innocuous of hiding places.

"I wonder if it might not be too late to worry about that,"
Lawrence Vandenberg said. He, too, was staring at the small
Agletsch at the table. "Mr. President, I still think it was a
mistake to include . . . *outsiders* in this meeting."

There was, of course, a high degree of suspicion among
those present aimed at aliens carrying Sh'daar Seeds, aliens
like Gru'mulkisch. In theory, with the block squirreled away
inside her translator, she couldn't even attempt to release a
network-penetrating virus into the local network without the
deed being detected . . . but no one in the room could be 100
percent assured that the Sh'daar didn't have a technological

wrinkle or three up their collective and nonexistent sleeves that humans didn't know about and couldn't detect.

"It's perfectly safe, Mr. Secretary," Neil Eskow said. "I promise you."

"If we've learned one thing during this conflict," Koenig said, "it's that the Sh'daar are *not* gods. I assume we have no congregationists of the AAC present?"

A polite chuckle rose around the table, and Koenig felt a tiny stab of guilt. The White Covenant prohibited not only proselytizing, but also publically making fun of the religious beliefs of others.

"If there *are* stargods out there, Mr. President," Speaker Valcourt said, "it's all the more reason to end this futile war."

"I honestly don't follow you, there, Madam Speaker," Koenig told her. "The Sh'daar make mistakes. We've found how to nullify certain of the technologies they employ. If there actually *are* godlike beings out there in the galaxy, I submit that the Rosette Aliens are far better candidates. No matter what the AAC says."

There were a number of Ancient Alien Creationists in the fleet. Some—a few, but certainly not all—believed that the Sh'daar were the Stargods of the remote past, super-powerful beings who'd engineered the human species millions of years ago, or mingled with humans and accepted their worship back at the dawn of history. Most of them were in favor of Humankind accepting the Sh'daar Ultimatum and joining their galactic collective. Probably the only reason they didn't make more of a protest against the war was the fact of the White Covenant.

Koenig was perfectly willing to believe that some episodes lost in the darkness of human prehistory had been caused by alien visitors. The human genome showed subtle signs of tampering—and an otherwise inexplicable and sudden increase in brain size between *Homo erectus* and early *Homo sapiens*. And there was a handful of ruins that suggested at least the possibility that Someone Else had been there once, been there and gone: vast stone cities on the seafloor off Japan and Mexico and India that had not been above water since the end of the last ice age, 10,000 years ago; or dry-land sites like Puma Punku and the Nazca plains that simply could not be shoehorned into the acceptable outline of history . . . *maybe* . . .

But for the most part, so far as Koenig was concerned, AAC theories denied the self-evident facts of human creativity, engineering cleverness, and outright genius, and for that reason alone were unconvincing.

And none of that changed Koenig's conviction that whoever those hypothetical alien gods might have been, they were *not* the Sh'daar. The Sh'daar Collective's sole interest in other species appeared to be connected with their technology, *advanced* technology like nanotech and robotics, and not the more basic discoveries like flint-knapping or fire. The multi-specific trauma of the technological singularity suffered by the ancient ur-Sh'daar had left the survivors— the modern Sh'daar—with what amounted to an obsession: detecting civilizations throughout the galaxy that might be approaching their own singularities, and either redirecting them into safer pastimes or obliterating them, as they had the Chelk twelve thousand years ago.

It was distinctly possible that the Sh'daar saw themselves as Galactic benefactors promoting the public good.

But at the same time, their efforts tended to be scattered and often seemed downright ineffectual. Earth had endured attacks by two Sh'daar species at two different times—the Turusch and the H'rulka—while other species—the Slan and the Nungiirtok—had attacked human colonies and research stations on the worlds of other stars. The fact that those attacks had been less than successful suggested either that the collective was deliberately employing a strategy designed to put pressure on Humankind without destroying it . . . or that the collective was less than perfectly coordinated, that its member species were poorly led and inefficiently deployed.

Koenig strongly believed the latter of the two. Waging something as dangerous and as expensive as a war demanded a commitment to *total* war . . . to victory rather than stumbling half measures or political statements.

A number of the men and women in this room, Koenig knew, were not convinced of this. Julie Valcourt, an outspoken member of the Global Union Party, was one—utterly committed to peace at any price. The hell of it was, Koenig agreed with much of what the Globalists said.

The Sh'daar Collective, by some conservative estimates, controlled a third, perhaps even a full half of the galaxy, and might number some millions of intelligent species and all of their teeming resources. If an empire with such overwhelming numbers had not swatted Earth like a bothersome insect in the fifty-eight years since the Sh'daar Ultimatum, they argued, it could *only* be because the Sh'daar puppet masters had wanted humanity to survive.

With an ideology like that, the only reasonable response was surrender—as the Confederation government and the North American Globalists both demanded—before the Sh'daar lost patience and *did* swat humanity into extinction.

For the moment, a majority of North America's voting population appeared to agree with Koenig, but Koenig knew that this state of affairs was strictly temporary and subject to unexpected and largely unpredictable swings in the public mood. The war with the Sh'daar had been a long one, but except for the Turusch and H'rulka attacks twenty years ago, most humans other than those in the armed forces hadn't been impacted much, or even inconvenienced. The ragged state of semi-peace that had existed since Koenig had forced the Sh'daar to agree to a truce two decades ago in the N'gai Cloud of Omega $T_{-0.876gy}$ had actually convinced most people that the threat from the Collective was nonexistent—or, at least, not all that serious. That state of affairs could change very quickly if another Sh'daar client species made it through Sol's defenses and slammed Earth with another high-velocity impactor.

And then—waiting in the wings—there was always Julie Valcourt and her Global Union Party, looking for any opportunity to embarrass Koenig and the American Freedom party.

Koenig looked at Phillip Caldwell, the director of the National Security Council. Sitting next to him was Thomas McFarlane, the director of Central Intelligence. McFarlane, Koenig thought, looked nervous and ill at ease. Generally, presidential intelligence briefings were handled by the DSC. Koenig wondered why Caldwell had dragged him along.

"While we're waiting," Koenig said, "perhaps you gentlemen would care to fill us in on the planetbuster you dropped in the morning's PICKL."

McFarlane looked, if anything, even more uncomfortable. "Mr. President, I must stress that none of this has been confirmed as yet. The data are still . . . quite raw."

"That's okay, Mr. McFarlane. If true, your raw data will have a tremendous effect on the war. The sooner we start looking at it . . . *working* with it, the better."

"Yes, sir. Well . . . as most of you know, we planted more inside the Confederation's electronic networks than the Starlight Worm. There were the generic antinetwork viruses designed to convince Geneva that *that* was the point of the attack. As expected, their ICE and other electronic defenses blocked us from doing any major damage.

"But another subset of the offensive was a set of hackworms designed to give us information channels into the entire Pan-Europaan data net. Since our cyber attack four days ago, Konstantin has been eavesdropping on the Confederation with considerable success."

"That," Delmonico said, interrupting, "is an understatement. We're reading quantum-encrypted stuff over there now almost as though it's in the clear. Even if the religion

thing doesn't pan out, this could win the war for us! At least the *human* part. . . ."

Koenig shot the director of Cybersecurity a hard glance, a gentle warning that she was out of line. "Go on, Mr. Mc-Farlane."

"*This* came through at oh nine thirty hours, GMT," Mc-Farlane said, opening a new window in the group's virtual workspace. "That was at about oh four thirty our time. Konstantin sent it through to Central Intelligence as soon as the data came through."

The message started off with versions in both French and German, then repeated in English. An AI voice accompanied the text, which scrolled through Koenig's inner window.

Lasercom message received via unmanned interstellar message drone,

Type Hermes Mark VII
0127 GMT 09 Mar 2425

Message begins:

Urgent Urgent Urgent

Grdoch elements have attacked civilian population of Vulcan in second incident. Aliens must now be presumed hostile. Motives unknown, but may be related to USNA attack on Enceladus.

[SIGNED] PEILLON, *Amiral d' Flotte*

Message ends

"The message," McFarlane continued, "was being sent from Confederation Fleet Headquarters outside Geneva to Denoix's private Geneva residence."

"It says this is a *second* attack," Valcourt observed. "What was the first?"

"We don't have a good time line yet, Madam Speaker," Caldwell told her, "but two of the files we managed to download during Operation Luther were labeled 'The Massacre,' and 'The Report of Governor Delgado of Vulcan.' We're still studying both documents, of course, but apparently Confederation contact with the Grdoch started off with a particularly nasty and evidently unprovoked attack on the Vulcan colonies. Commodore Becker, commanding the Confederation Fleet at Vulcan, seems to have established a truce with the Grdoch."

"A massacre?" Valcourt asked. "What kind of massacre?"

"We have no details. All we know are that several thousand colonists from the Argentinean side of the fence were either killed or captured and are now presumed dead. Becker reported destroying one of three Grdoch ships. After that, they began talking, negotiating . . . and some sort of peace treaty or truce was put together."

"We can assume," Koenig added, "that communications between humans and the Grdoch are still less than perfect. The alliance was fragile enough that things seem to have broken down since the Battle of Enceladus. Maybe the Grdoch think Confed forces attacked their ship there."

"This might give us our chance to ally with the Grdoch," Secretary Comb said. "We need allies in this business."

"Maybe," Vandenberg said. "Or maybe the Grdoch are so alien they don't understand the idea of a civil war . . . that humans might be divided among themselves. It's a possibility."

"Do we have any idea where the Grdoch come from yet?" Koenig asked. "They're obviously not native to Vulcan."

"Of course not, Mr. President," Eskow said. "There doesn't seem to be any galactic record of these beings. Gru'mulkisch? Do the Agletsch know anything about them?"

"I regret no, Mr. Secretary, Mr. President," the Agletsch representative replied. "They do not appear to be part of the Masters' Collective, and we have no data on them. But the galaxy is excessively vast, yes-no?"

"Yes," Koenig said. "Yes, to be sure."

Even the Sh'daar didn't know, *couldn't* know, every technic civilization among the hundreds of billions of worlds scattered through the galaxy. In a way, that was comforting. The Sh'daar had *limits* . . . and they couldn't know everything.

"That begs an interesting question, though," Eskow pointed out. "Based on reports from the Battle of Enceladus, we estimate that the Grdoch are within a century or two of us in terms of advanced tehcnology. That puts us smack up against the Limited Tech paradox again."

Koenig nodded, thoughtful. He'd already been wondering about that. "It doesn't seem reasonable that the Grdoch are so close to us in technological levels."

"Exactly," Eskow replied. "If the Grdoch were part of the Sh'daar Collective, it would all be part of the same picture. But they're not. And that's a bit of a conundrum."

The universe was 13.7 billion years old. Xenosophontologists generally assumed that the first technological civilizations within the galaxy could not have appeared before, say, 8 billion years ago. While it was possible that intelligent species had arisen earlier—life forms based on organized plasmas within the atmospheres of stars, for instance—civilizations comprehensible to humans—with fire, metallurgy, and spacecraft—could only evolve on the surfaces of rocky planets. Rocky, terrestrial-type planets, in turn, could only form around stars with a high degree of metalicity—that meant, in astronomical terms, they possessed elements heavier than hydrogen and helium—and that meant second- and third-generation stars born after the deaths of the galaxy's first generation of stars. It was those early dying stars that had cooked heavier elements like carbon and oxygen from the primordial hydrogen and helium—everything on the periodic table up through iron, in fact—and exploding supernovae that had created everything heavier. Even life forms arising in the atmospheres of gas giants, like the enormous, free-floating H'rulka, needed elements like carbon, silicon, phosphorous, and iron to give them form and to run their biologies.

So . . . the first intelligent life, the xenosophontologists believed, must have appeared within the galaxy around 4 to 5 billion years ago—or at just about the same time that Sol and Earth were forming out of the dust and gas of their primordial stellar nursery. Four billion years ago, the first starships might have begun exploring the young galaxy, and the first alien colonies were appearing on countless worlds.

If those aliens were still around in any form that humans could recognize, they would possess technologies billions of years in advance of Humankind. *Stargods*. . . .

Such species would have had time to colonize the entire galaxy—every habitable world—many times over. That was the basis of Enrico Fermi's famous paradox: If technological civilizations had begun exploring the galaxy billions of years ago, *where are they now*? Why don't we see evidence of their existence? A technology that advanced might be capable of anything—including reshaping the order and arrangement of the sky itself.

Fermi's paradox had been formulated at the very beginning of Humankind's search for neighbors among the stars. Eventually, a few centuries later, humans had encountered the Agletsch, and from them they'd acquired access to the Encyclopedia Galactica, a nested set of electronic records lising and describing many thousands of alien species scattered across both space and time.

While the E.G. hinted at more-advanced civilizations (the so-called Stargods), however, all of the technologies encountered so far—in particular the Turusch, the H'rulka, the Slan, the Nungiirtok, and the Agletsch themselves—

possessed technologies that were, at most, a handful of centuries in advance of humans.

This was . . . mathematically preposterous. Against just the last billion years of galactic history, every civilization studied so far was within something like .0000005 of 1 percent of modern human technological levels.

And that was generally agreed to be statistically impossible.

Clearly, some unknown, unseen factor was at work constraining technological growth throughout the galaxy—and over the past five decades, the assumption had been that that factor was the Sh'daar. By limiting the technologies available to their client races, they ensured that everyone stayed at roughly the same level, to within a century or two.

Eight hundred million years ago, in the N'gai Cloud, a dwarf galaxy about to be devoured by the Milky Way, the ur-Sh'daar, a civilization consisting of hundreds or perhaps thousands of separate species, had vanished in such a transcendence, leaving behind a remnant unwilling or unable to follow them . . . a remnant that had become the racially traumatized Sh'daar. Entering Humankind's galaxy hundreds of millions of years ago, they'd set about creating their collective, spreading out slowly, conquering world upon world, and suppressing those technologies that might lead to another round of Transcendence.

It made sense. There were no higher technologies—the mysterious Stargods and the Rosette Aliens were the exceptions that proved the rule—because the Sh'daar had enforced their rules against the tech that might lead to technological singularities.

But then . . . why were the Grdoch so close to human tech levels? Their military and spaceflight technologies were somewhat beyond human abilities, to be sure; humans had experimented with X-ray lasers, but problems in focusing and directing them had blocked their deployment. If the Grdoch had never crossed paths with the Sh'daar Collective, the chances that they just happened to be so close to human technology were quite literally something like one in a million, or even less.

"Obviously," Eskow told the group, "there have been other factors at work besides the Sh'daar. Our best guess at the moment is that there've been multiple technological singularities among countless races as they progressed technologically through the course of their histories. Millions of civilizations across the galaxy must have reached technological apotheosis, transcending physical evolution and instrumentality and developing into . . . something else."

"So in other words," Koenig said, "there are no *really* advanced aliens out there, either inside Sh'daar space or beyond it, because the older ones all left to play someplace else."

Which led relentlessly to another, related and very interesting thought. Might it be that technological species tended to enter the Singularity as soon as they reached a roughly human equivalence?

The answer to that question was vital. If the answer was yes, than humans could expect to enter their own singularity very soon, now.

A chime sounded, and a door slid open in the middle of what appeared to be one of the conference room's floor-to-ceiling windows, admitting six naval officers and a single, sour-looking civilian.

"Ah, Admiral Gray!" Koenig said. "Welcome to the briefing. I think you're going to find this . . . interesting. . . ."

Chapter Fourteen

York Civic Center
Jefferson Government Complex
Toronto, USNA
1410 hours, TFT

As he walked into the large, open conference room, Admiral
Gray was a bit taken aback by the crowd in the room, people
both present and virtual. "Mr. President," he said, facing
Koenig. "Sorry to take so long. Building security."

"Understood. My security people are convinced that someone is going to sneak in here with a nuke stuck up their ass."

It was an exaggeration, given the minimum mass of fis-
sionable material necessary for a nuclear device, but only a
small one. There *had* been reports of suicide bombers using
antimatter conversion units a few centimeters long, surgi-
cally implanted inside their stomachs, though that sort of
thing was more a mark of the Rafadeen and the Islamic Theocracy than it was of the Confederation government. The
scanning process in the Jefferson Building's lobby had been
excruciatingly and intimately thorough, including backscat-
ter X-rays, soft-tissue fluoroscopy, and handheld MRI medical imaging scans.

Gray came to rigid attention. "Sir! Command Constellation, CBG- 40, reporting as ordered, sir."

"At ease, Admiral, and shit-can the *kay*-det crap," Koenig said. The President grinned at his discomfiture. "You *are* among friends here."

Gray wasn't quite sure whether to believe him. "If you say so, sir." He looked at the crowd around the table, pinging their electronic IDs one after another. Some he knew, but only from the newsfeeds. God . . . the Secretary of State, the Speaker of the House—what was *she* doing here? And SecSci, SecDef, the DSC *and* the DCI. Others he didn't know . . . Dr. Lee, for instance. But his credentials were impressive. "I just wasn't expecting such . . . such an august assembly."

"Grow yourselves seats and let's get started," Koenig said. "We need to decide how best to apply Task Force Eridani."

Gray and the others found empty spaces around the big table and thoughtclicked chairs out of the carpeted floor.

"Phillip?" Koenig said, addressing the director of the Security Council. "You have something for us?"

"Some background, Mr. President."

A large virtual screen shimmered into visibility at the end opposite Koenig's place, and a world, the illuminated portion of the crescent enticingly blue, white, and orange-gold, swam into view.

"Vulcan," an AI's voice intoned. "A world so Earthlike that humans can actually live and work unprotected on its surface . . ."

Alphanumerics on the lower right-hand corner of the display showed that the image had been shot by the carrier *Intrepid* only a couple of weeks ago, then sent back to Sol by messenger drone. Vulcan's sun, 40 Eridani A, showed in the distance to the right. Far to the left of the screen, almost out of the panorama, two closely paired stars gleamed brightly—one ruby red, the other diamond white.

"At last count," the AI went on, "Vulcan was home to

some eighty million humans, most of either German or Argentinean descent. The capital is the twin city of Himmel-Paradisio, on the southeastern coast of Neubavaria, the principal continent on the planet. . . ."

"Mr. President," Valcourt said, petulant, "do we really need to sit through this . . . this melodramatic travelogue?"

"We need to know what we're stepping into, Madam Speaker. And we all need to be downloading the same page."

Gray suppressed a chuckle. In fact, the presentation, a piece prepared by Central Intelligence and put out over Govnet, *was* somewhat melodramatic, almost embarrassingly so. As the interior voice continued, Gray turned down the volume inside his head. He knew the basic stats of the place, had been studying them now ever since the place had popped in the set of highly confidential advance orders he'd received out at Enceladus. The world, though nominally a Confederation colony, was in fact politically independent, and seemed to have provided very little to the Confeds' struggle with the breakaway USNA. Industry appeared to be limited to what was necessary just to support the world's population—no shipyards, no weapons nanufactories, no shipments of scarce minerals or biotics, no large standing army. Vulcan's principal export, apparently, was *information* . . . mostly on its alien biology.

And, in fact, information was by far the main item of all interstellar trade. There was very little in the way of goods or raw material worth the cost of shipping it across light years, especially when nanufactories could grow almost anything conceivable from the rocks freely available in every star system. The Agletsch, he reflected, had become experts at finding, quantizing, and shipping information across large swaths of the galaxy. The Encyclopedia Galactica was a well-known result of this trade. Increasingly, now, human traders were doing the same.

The travelogue wound to a close, and the scene shifted to a computer graphic detailing the outline of the entire 40

Eridani system. Alphanumerics identified the light star carrier *Intrepid* and her three escorts as they entered 40 Eridani space. Planets followed blue orbital paths—six of them—as red trajectories arced out from the second planet and closed on the four green icons identifying *Intrepid* and the destroyers with her. Each missile followed a separate, far-arcing path, so that they came in on the USNA Task force from all directions.

"We don't have a clear idea of what happened, exactly," Phillip Caldwell's holographic image said. "*Intrepid's* squadron appears to have been hit hard, however, shortly after it entered the 40 Eridani system."

On the screen, one destroyer, the *Emmet*, vanished in a white flare of light. Moments later, the second destroyer, *Fitzpatrick*, died as well. The *Intrepid* took several hits as she struggled to accelerate, to break free of the system. The last destroyer, *Tomlinson*, hung back, apparently trying to shield the far larger carrier and give her time to get clear.

The image froze, then, at the instant that *Intrepid* stopped recording battlespace data and launched it Solward in a message drone.

"We presume that both *Intrepid* and the *Tomlinson* were destroyed moments later," Admiral Armitage said. "The Joint Chiefs are recommending that we send the new task force directly to 40 Eridani, with orders to find and rescue survivors, if any, to launch a retaliatory strike against Confederation assets in the system, and . . . to deal with *this*."

On the screen, the image of the star system shifted left and down, centering, after a moment, on a bright scarlet dot hanging above the blue-and-white icon representing Vulcan, then zoomed in, the magnification increasing thousands of times. An instant later, the view locked onto an egg-shaped, bright scarlet ship apparently identical to the one captured at Enceladus.

"That's the same alien ship," Sharpe said, "the one that showed up at Enceladus."

"Actually, no," Eskow said. The secretary of science brought up a series of shifting bars next to the image, a graph of power usage. "The energy readouts transmitted from *Intrepid* suggest that this is a different Grdoch ship . . . larger, more powerful. It may be over a kilometer long."

Gray studied the magnified image with mingled interest and concern. Star carriers like *America* were about a kilometer long overall . . . but their bodies were long and slender, a pencil of a spine extending aft 800 meters from beneath an umbrella-shaped shieldcap. There was nothing slender about the Grdoch ships, however. Massive, bulky, and squat, they contained hundreds of times the volume of a star carrier, and massed many hundreds of millions of tons. This one was more smooth-polished asteroid than it was starship. Koenig could well understand how a number of Grdoch—and the titanic beasts they'd been feeding on—had not been discovered within the ship captured at Enceladus until long after the fact. A ship that big was a small and self-contained world, like a human O'Neill cylinder, or some of the colonies constructed within hollowed-out asteroids.

"And of course now we know that that Grdoch ship has attacked its erstwhile allies," Koenig said.

Gray looked up sharply at that. "Sir? They've changed sides?"

"We have some hot new intel, Admiral. Here you go."

Gray opened the download window in his mind, and saw the intercepted message from Geneva. As a kind of footnote, Koenig appended a message listing what was known about the *first* Grdoch attack on Vulcan, information derived from a cyberaid made a few days ago.

There was a lot there to digest.

"So, Mr. President," Gray said slowly, "the Grdoch. Are they our friends now? Or are they still . . . foes?" He'd almost said targets, but stopped himself at the last moment. There was too much heavy-lift rank in this room to let him be flip or casually humorous.

"A wonderful question, Admiral, and one that I'm sure we'd all like to resolve. You've received your full orders for this operation from HQMILCOM?"

Gray nodded. "They came through yesterday, Mr. President."

"And they are?"

"I am to take command of Task Force Eridani," Gray replied, his tone as crisp and as no-nonsense as he could make it. "Four or possibly five star carriers, with a large number of warships in support, twenty or twenty-five, if we can manage it.

"Task Force Eridani will investigate Vulcan, at 40 Eridani. Our immediate priority will be to find and rescue survivors from the *Intrepid*'s task force, if any. If we encounter Confederation Fleet elements, we are to engage those, unless, in my judgment, the enemy forces in-system are so strong that attacking them would result in unacceptable casualties. We are also to survey Vulcan itself, to determine if the Confederation has posted fleet or surface elements there."

"And if you encounter Grdoch forces?" Koenig prompted.

"That, Mr. President, HQMILCOM seems to be leaving to my best judgment. Yesterday, the presumption was that they are allies of the Confederation and therefore hostile. But . . . this new intel changes that, doesn't it?"

"We don't know yet, Admiral," Koenig told him. "Assuming the old adage that the enemy of my enemy is my friend, there may now be room to consider forging an alliance of our own with the Grdoch. But it's equally possible that the Grdoch can't really distinguish among Earth-human political factions."

"In other words, we all look alike to them," Vandenberg put in. Several at the table chuckled.

"If I may, gentlemen, ladies," Dr. Truitt put in, "I have had some small experience with the Grdoch . . . at least with the Grdoch we captured at Enceladus. Their psychology is . . . unusual, to say the least, despite their being so similar to us."

"Excuse me, Dr. Truitt," Koenig said. "What do you mean, 'so similar'? The reports I've seen suggest that they *define* the word *alien*."

"Their biochemistry is nearly identical to ours, Mr. President. We've run biochem studies on them with a portable lab on the captured ship. Their biochemistries are based on dextro-sugars and levo-amino acids, just like terrestrial life, and that alone is a one-in-four possibility. They use RNA, like life on Earth, which isn't completely surprising, since RNA is a fairly common organic building block. They also use DNA. Different sequences, obviously, but the same base pairs: adenine, guanine, cytosine, thymine. I've searched our databases. We haven't yet encountered *any* exobiologies as similar to ours as these."

"The Agletsch," Eskow pointed out, "they can eat our food. . . ."

"But require certain elements in larger than trace amounts," Truitt said, "including cadmium, nickel, and selenium. They can't survive for long if they are limited strictly to terrestrial food."

"Interesting," Eskow said. "That might explain their interest in Vulcan. Compatible biochemistries."

"It might explain their interest in Earth," Sharpe said. "For the same reason."

"Indeed," Koenig said. "So your orders, Admiral, will be amended. If you encounter Grdoch forces, again, use your best judgment . . . attempt to make contact with them independently of the Confederation. But if they prove hostile, you are clear to engage and destroy them, if possible."

The recitation was dry and without emotion. Gray could guess what was going on behind Koenig's flat expression. Both men had been faced with hostile alien forces before, in situations where they'd had to overcome that hostility and attempt to communicate.

"Sir."

Koenig must have heard reluctance in the tone of Gray's single word. "You have a problem with your orders, Admiral?"

"Not as such, Mr. President. I *am* concerned that we're missing a serious opportunity for KISS, here. It could turn around and bite us in the ass. Sir."

KISS—keep it simple, stupid. There was always a tendency, especially within the higher levels of the naval command structure, to overcomplicate orders with multiple objectives layered one upon another. Needless complexity turned straightforward operations into deadly, high-casualty traps, and Gray was gently reminding Koenig of the fact . . . without directly challenging his authority.

"I understand that, Admiral," Koenig said. "But until we clarify the Grdoch situation . . . why they're here in human space, what they want, who they're mad at, and *why*, we're going to be tiptoeing over eggs."

"Yes, Mr. President."

"It may be too late for tiptoeing, you know," Valcourt told Koenig. "We attacked their ship at Enceladus, captured it. We're holding a number of them prisoner now at Crisium! These are acts of *war*, Mr. President . . . as if we needed another war on our hands."

"Actually, things may be considerably simpler now," Koenig replied. "If the Confederation wants to ally with the Sh'daar, and is now fighting against the Grdoch, it all becomes one war, doesn't it?"

"That's right," Secretary Sharpe said. "It's just us against the whole damned universe!"

The Secretary of State, Gray had heard, favored at least some of the Global Union's views about fighting the Sh'daar even though she was a Freedomist. Essentially, she was part of the faction that felt Humankind couldn't fight something as big, as powerful, and as far ranging in space as the Sh'daar Collective.

"It's not *quite* that bad, Pamela," Admiral Armitage said. "Even if we can't make friends with the Grdoch, perhaps we can point them at the Confederation. *De facto* allies, if not allies in fact."

"I think it's pretty obvious," Koenig added, "that the opposition is divided and obviously having trouble communicating with one another."

"Exactly my point, sir," Armitage said. "We have the interior lines of communication, so to speak."

"We've also had generally favorable information coming in about Operation Luther," Delmonico said. "Besides the intelligence coup. Mr. McFarlane has the details."

The director of Intelligence nodded. "Yes, though there's no hard information just yet. There have been major demonstrations, yesterday and this morning, in a number of Confed cities—New London, Bonn, Paris, Geneva. *Anti-war* demonstrations. We're beginning to hear news from over there about a spiritual movement calling itself Starlight."

So it begins, Gray thought. *Yet another new world religion.* He'd not heard much in the way of details, but Gray had downloaded the briefing attached to the message from Koenig the day before. *Starlight*, he knew, was a new . . . not a religion so much as a spiritual and philosophical movement beginning to surface in major cities across Europe. Virtual raiders had penetrated the Pan-European computer networks successfully, planting a number of worms designed to infiltrate the Confederation's news and information web with a complex of ideas, philosophies, and outright propaganda leading to the establishment of a new religious movement. The religion even had a leader, a *voice* . . . and a focus for all of the attention.

A charismatic philosopher-activist who called himself Constantine d'Angelo.

"You know, this Starlight thing could *really* backfire on us," Vandenberg said. "What if it gains a foothold here, in the USNA?"

"We'll have plenty of time before that happens," Delmonico said. "*And* we have the cyber defenses against the Starlight worm already in place. We predict that the Starlight movement will primarily affect Northern Europe and Russia. It will move more slowly through traditionally Catholic countries in Southern Europe and Latin America, and probably make no headway at all in either the Theocracy or in South and East Asia."

"A few demonstrations don't mean the end of the war, Mr. President," Sharpe said.

"No," Koenig agreed. "But they could mark the *beginning* of the end. It's going to take time to create such a complicated memeplex, especially pulling it out of hard vacuum like this. Dr. Lee? Do either you or Konstantin have any predictions about how long the meme change will take?"

"Assuming it works at all, Mr. President," Valcourt said. She didn't sound at all convinced.

"Dr. Lee?"

"Predictions? No, sir. As I've said, memetics is not a true science, not yet. Results are not reproducible, and the random and cumulative effects of human emotion will always skew the results from the optimum outcome. However, these demonstrations that we're hearing about are certainly an encouraging sign, especially after so short an incubation period. It seems likely that the target population was already primed to accept a new religious movement, a new direction."

"The larger the target population," Delmonico added, "the better the chance of a positive response. Predicting the response of an individual is extremely difficult. A population of hundreds of millions is quite a different thing."

"I find myself . . . uncomfortable," Vandenberg said slowly, "with the idea of religion being nothing more than finding the right buttons to push inside people's minds, and pushing them."

"Now, Van, you know it's not that simple," Delmonico replied. "Especially with something as entrenched as religion tends to be. Especially in this case, where people in the target population, most of them, already have one of a number of pre-existing religions."

Eskow made a face. "I find that hard to believe. No one believes in religion anymore. Myth and superstition. The White Covenant killed all of that."

"You should get out more, Mr. Secretary," Delmonico said. "The White Covenant drove *talk* about religion underground. It didn't kill religion itself. It *can't*. Religion is a part of being human."

"The hell it is. *I'm* not religious," Eskow said.

"I submit, Mr. Secretary, that atheism is as much a matter of *belief* as any traditional religion," she said, spreading her hands. "It's not something that can be *proved* either way."

"And *I* submit," Koenig said firmly, "that discussing it here and now is pointless. Let's get this back on track. Dr. Lee . . . my understanding of recombinant memetics is that we try to replace select memes within a target memeplex . . . but that it's more of a nudge than a kick. Is that correct?"

"Exactly, Mr. President," Lee said, nodding enthusiastically. "Let's say you're trying to change . . . oh, let's use Christianity, as an example, since we're all familiar with its tenets. You can't just barge in the front door proclaiming that Jesus was a myth or a mere anti-Roman rabble-rouser or anything so blatant. The built-in defenses of that memeplex—the antibodies, you might say—would cause the entire assertion, the memetic argument itself, to be rejected. No, you have to slip in through the church basement. Maybe you put out several stories in widely read news feeds that, just in passing, mention contradictions in the Bible— something about how God is love and compassion and light and yet casts sinners into eternal hellfire. You put out discussions or news stories about the church's history of discriminating against women. Questions about why the Creator of the universe, God Almighty Himself, would demand blood sacrifice to cancel out sin.

"Now, the memeplex defenses will counter questions like that. It's wrong to question the Bible, sin to use merely human understanding . . . but questions attacking the memeplex's core beliefs still raise inner conflict, discomfort, dissonance, and, eventually, they bring about *doubt*. Maybe you float another story about how the early church apparently didn't believe in hell, but accepted reincarnation as fact. Stories about how the Church has *changed* over the centuries, rewriting or editing scripture, torturing heretics, yielding to political necessity and to all-too-human greed, envy, wrath, pride, and the rest.

"At first you're preaching to the choir. Atheists might accept these memes as self-evident fact, but the fundamentalists, the true believers, the fanatics, even ordinary churchgoers are all well-inoculated against those particular viruses. As doubt is planted, however, meme by meme, it begins to grow . . . and your new memes begin, eventually, to merge with existing memeplexes, to reshape human awareness, to change minds in more or less predictable ways."

"I thought you couldn't make predictions," Vandenberg said.

"Not *precise* predictions. We can't tell you exactly when a change will occur, or exactly how it will manifest. But as time passes, the trend becomes clear . . .

". . . and ultimately, *eventually*, we transform the world."

Horace Lee, Gray thought, would have made an exceptional preacher. He could infuse his enthusiasm into his words in a way that dragged his audience along, whether they wanted to follow or not.

And change of that scope, change that dramatic, certainly had happened before. The divine right of kings, the benefits of colonialism, the morality of slavery, the second-class status of women: all of those memeplexes and others once deeply woven into human belief and practice had long since either collapsed or changed so that they were no longer recognizable.

The kicker was that each and every one of those old memeplexes had taken years, even *centuries* to overturn.

"So we're the *memgineers*," Eskow said with a distinctly sarcastic tone, "tinkering away at the psychological, socio-logical, and cultural underpinnings of Humankind as we set out to save the world."

"Whatever it takes," Koenig replied. "Whatever it takes . . ."

"Ah, yes," Admiral Armitage said. "On a more, ah, *prac-tical* note, we have just received one piece of excellent news. It just came through this morning. The *Constitution* has arrived in-system, and is now on the deceleration leg into Mars. She'll receive a quick refit and resupply there, before joining the new task force."

"*Very* good news," Koenig agreed. "Admiral Gray? How long before your task force is ready for boost?"

"That, Mr. President, depends on how complete we make the refit. Resupply is under way now, and we should be topped off and ready to go within forty-eight hours. The repairs, though, the *major* repairs, are something else. We took some heavy damage at Enceladus, and it's going to take time to regrow some of the ship structure. The SupraQuito shipyard has parked both 2390 CC12 and 2410 NI17 along-side the *America*, and we've deployed the nanoswarm to begin repairs. I would say we'll be at sixty percent in forty-eight hours. One hundred percent will take longer . . . per-haps a week."

The two alphanumerics referred to a pair of small aster-oids—CC12, a carbonaceous chondrite 200 meters across, and NI17, a nickel-iron asteroid about 120 meters across. They'd been jockeyed down the synchorbit months before to serve as convenient sources of raw materials in shipyard operations—specifically for the repair of battle damage to capital ships. The nanoswarm was a swarm of some hundreds of trillions of microscopic machines programmed to take those asteroids apart, literally atom by atom, and take them to the damaged area, literally regrowing missing sections of hull. CC12 was an excellent source of expendables—oxygen and nitrogen for the ship's atmosphere, water to replace the drained reserves in the punctured shield cap, and carbon, hydrogen, and various trace elements to manufacture food.

"Four days, Sandy," Koenig said. The use of Gray's first name was a kind of weapon, a point-blank statement that the president knew Gray could get done what needed to be done in the allotted time. "Four days, no more."

"Aye, aye, Mr. President."

There was nothing more than that to be said.

For thirty minutes more, they discussed fleet readiness, Confederation dispositions, and impressions about the Grdoch.

At last, though, Koenig stood, signaling that the briefing session was over at last. "We've handed you a damned tough nut, Admiral," he said. "We need to deal the Confeds a serious bit of pain right now, to help drive home the expected effects of Operation Luther. We need to take the Grdoch out of the running if at all possible, one way or the other. *And* we need to preserve the fleet just in case none of this works and we find ourselves back on the defensive."

Gray stood, looking grim, and his officers stood with him. "We'll do our best, Mr. President."

"I know you will, Sandy," Koenig replied. "I have absolute confidence in you."

And one of these days, Mr. President, Gray thought, *that confidence will be misplaced. And* then *what?*

Chapter Fifteen

13 March 2425

Pan-European News Feed
USNA Central Intelligence
York Civic Center
Toronto, USNA
0645 hours, EST

"I have been called the Messiah, returned to bring my people home!"

The features of Constantine d'Angelo filled the screen, powerful, focused, fierce, unstoppable. The voice was a translation, of course—the speech was being delivered in French—but the deep and sonorous baritone of the speaker still came through as undertones, hypnotic in their cadence and stress.

"I have also been called the Antichrist by those who reject my message, my truth! I tell you now, I am neither the Messiah, nor am I the Antichrist. I *am* a messenger, however, a messenger with a message of hope, of life, of renewal! A messenger come to tell you all that a new day, a new *era*, has dawned!"

Thomas McFarlane watched the face narrowly, searching for signs of . . . what? Fuzziness, perhaps, or burring,

or a telltale disturbance in the pixels of the background . . .
anything to suggest that the scene was artificial, created by
computer rather than shot against a real-world background.
He could see nothing, however, nothing whatsoever to suggest that Constantine d'Angelo was not what he claimed to
be: a flesh-and-blood human somewhere in Geneva. The
Confederation capital's skyline was clearly visible behind
him, with the green- and white-banded limestone cliffs of
Mont Selève rising against the backdrop of the sky beyond.

McFarlane and only a handful of others knew that
d'Angelo was not human at all, but an electronic construct,
an avatar built up bit by bit by the super-computer Konstantin, at Tsiolkovsky base. A part, a very *small* part, of Konstantin's intellect and database had been downloaded into
some of the Geneva servers running the Confederation's gov.
net, and could now project itself as video and audio across
any electronic media on the network. For days, now, "Constantine d'Angelo" had been appearing on news broadcasts,
documentaries, and special broadcasts throughout the Confederation, castigating the government for its crimes against
humanity, its unjust war against North America, and calling
upon the population above all to question both the purpose
and the morality of government.

And the rallies and political demonstrations by his Starlight movement had been growing exponentially just during
the past week, both in numbers and in voice.

"The Geneva government," d'Angelo was saying, "would
have us all believe that *surrender* is Humankind's only hope
. . . surrender to the alien masters of this galaxy . . . masters,
I might add, whom we have never seen, never met face-to-
face, never communicated with save through their slaves.

"Is this, I ask all of you, *sane*? Our government would
have us end our technological march forward into a brave
future, would have us give up new medicines, new worlds,
new ways of thinking and of expressing ourselves . . . and
why? These mysterious and unseen masters of the galaxy,

with whom we have warred off and on for sixty years, are afraid that we might transcend our own humanity and become more than what we are. . . ."

D'Angelo had been pushing that theme hard for days, now. The Sh'daar had been traumatized by the technological singularity of their own multi-species collective, and now refused to let others find their own path to transcendence. And the Geneva government, out of fear, wanted to acquiesce to the Sh'daar demands.

Not all elements of Humankind's myriad cultures agreed with the idea of unbridled technological innovation and progress, of course, and those tended to fall in line with Geneva's program. The Rapturist Church of Humankind was strong and well established throughout Northern Europe, especially in France. The Purist sect of that church held that any change to the basic genome of *Homo sapiens* was a sin, an act of defiance against God, and the political faction of that church, known as the *Pureté de Humanité,* was a powerful supporter of the Confederation's peace initiative despite the White Covenant's restrictions against religious activism.

In the south, the Catholic Church remained both cautious and conservative. The Papess in Rome had recently issued an encyclical railing against what she called a blind growth of human technology without equal growth in ethics, spirituality, and love. The Antipope, in Marseilles, was less accommodating. Technology needed to be carefully managed, even rationed by the Bureau of Science and Technology, to avoid the utter degradation of the human condition.

Of course, most people, constrained by the White Covenant, offered no specifically *religious* opinion, not when mingling religion with politics brought with it the risk of fine or even imprisonment for individuals, and military sanctions for nation-states. In any case, most people, aware that human technology alone made possible their comfort, convenience, general lifestyle, and often their very *lives*, approved of pretty much whatever might come along.

D'Angelo kept stressing the importance of Humankind finding its own path, of guaranteeing its independence among the stars without surrendering sovereignty to alien civilizations. One of several popular new memes appearing throughout Confederation news and entertainment feeds lately was that of da Vinci's famous drawing *The Measure of Man*, multiple arms and legs outstretched across a globe, with an encircling legend reading *Liberté, égalité, fraternité*, the ancient French national motto.

Constantine d'Angelo kept hammering at another theme as well, hammered at it until it became a nearly ubiquitous meme: *war atrocity*. The Geneva government continued to prosecute an unpopular war in the Americas, and far worse, had stooped to using nano-D, a proscribed weapon of mass destruction, in order to obliterate a North American city, an unspeakable war crime. Exactly who had ordered that horrific assault—Ilse Roettgen, President Denoix, General Korosi, or someone else entirely within the Confederation leadership—was still a big unknown.

No matter what, the destruction of Columbus was the ultimate horror for any government.

"Enough is enough," d'Angelo said. "Enough childishness! Enough hurt feelings and immature feelings and feelings run amuck! It is time to put away nationalist and jingoist infantilism! It is time to abandon fear of the dark, to embrace the offspring of human imagination and creativity and determination, time to stand together as a species united—in short it is time and *past* time to *grow up* and assume our rightful place with the lords of this galaxy *as equals*, not as slaves. . . ."

Powerful words, McFarlane thought.

And judging by the intelligence reports flooding in, those words appeared to be falling on fertile ground.

USNA CVS America
Naval Dockyard, SupraQuito
0708 hours, TFT

The star carrier *America* was leaving port.

Nudged clear of the SupraQuito dockyard by tugs and out into open space, she drifted free for a long moment, illuminated first by work lights, then by the hard, bright glare of the sun emerging slowly from behind the bulk of the orbital docking complex. Her hull was largely resurfaced and repainted in blocks of gray and black. Her shield cap drank the sunlight, though the newly painted leading surface now once again bore the legend USNA CVS *America* and her hull number. The two asteroids, now towed well clear of the dockyard area, had each contributed several tens of tons of material to nanoresurface the star carrier's hull after its brutal scouring by the rings of Saturn.

Other ships gathered about her, gleaming in the sun: the star carriers *Saratoga* and *Constitution,* plus the smaller Marine carrier *Inchon.* The Russian light carrier *Slava* and the North Indian light carrier *Shiva* had joined the formation as well, together with the line-of-battle ships *Long Island* and *California*, the heavy cruisers *Calgary* and *Maine*, plus a swarm of light cruisers, destroyers, frigates, and a pair of railgun cruisers, the *Porter* and the *Decatur.* Four warships of the Chinese Hegemony had joined the group earlier that morning, led by the carrier *Shi Lang.* Altogether, Task Force Eridani was composed of twenty-four ships. Together, in close formation, they began accelerating out-system.

Accelerating at 1 gravity, they fell out-system, plunging toward the constellation of Eridanus, just 14 degrees west of the blue-white diamond of Rigel.

"Coded message coming through, marked personal and confidential, Admiral," Lieutenant Kepner said over a private channel. "From the EPCP."

Emergency Presidential Commmand Post might mean President Koenig himself, or, just possibly, either his chief of staff or someone on the Joint Chiefs. "Decode it and put it through."

A moment later, the window opened and Admiral Armitage's face appeared in Gray's mind. So . . . something from the Joint chiefs of staff.

"Good morning, Sandy."

Gray checked a time readout. They were already five light minutes from Earth, so this would be a monologue rather than a true conversation.

"Sorry I missed boost-time, but this has only just come through from Crisium, and I thought you should see it." An icon winked in Gray's consciousness, showing an attached file. "The upshot is that between the records grabbed by Operation Luther and what you snagged for us out at Enceladus, we now have working translation software for the Grdoch language. That should make things a bit easier for you out at Vulcan."

Gray nodded to himself. That *was* good. Figuring out a completely alien language from scratch was a damned tough prospect even on Earth, where researchers had the full power of Konstantin and other advanced AIs on which they could draw.

Most breakthroughs with alien languages so far had been possible only because the Agletsch had been doing this sort of thing for centuries, developing a number of interstellar pidgins to facilitate their trade of information among wildly diverse species. The problem became all but insurmountable when an alien language involved things like changes in color, movements of various body parts, skin patterns, electrical fields, or even odor. Worse by far, however, when it came to interspecies communications, was the fact that alien mind-sets and attitudes, worldviews, and ways of thinking could be so different that two species might be mutually and forever incomprehensible to one another.

With a working translation program, though, that shouldn't be a problem. Gray wondered how the Confederation xenolinguists had managed the job in such a relatively short time.

"However, we have some other information developed from the files garnered by Operation Luther," Armitage continued. "Very . . . *disturbing* information. It substantially changes the scope of your orders."

Gods! that was all Gray needed right now . . . a last-second rewrite of task-force orders to reflect HQMILCOM's penchant for micromanagement.

Armitage looked uncomfortable. He might be thinking the same thing.

"We heard at the briefing session the other day," Armitage said, "about how Grdoch biochemistry is the same as ours. That's . . . unusual, of course, given the remarkable diversity of life and life chemistries across the galaxy, but not at all impossible. RNA arises fairly easily from precursors like TNA—threose nucleic acid—and DNA is an almost inevitable evolutionary product of RNA. DNA-based life will involve proteins and amino acids similar to terrestrial life, with a one-in-four chance that that life will be made up of left-handed amino acids and right-handed sugars."

Gray scowled. Why the damned lesson in elementary exobiology?

"What this means, of course, is that the Grdoch can eat our kind of food . . . could derive nourishment from terrestrial life.

"And according to the reports we've seen from Vulcan, in particular *Le Rapport d'Gouverneur Delgado de Vulcan*, and another called *La Massacrer*, the Grdoch think of us, of *humans* as—as food animals. . . ."

In fact, Gray had already suspected as much. After watching the Grdoch feed on those huge prey animals on board their ship at Enceladus, he'd become convinced that the aliens possessed a cultural imperative—perhaps even an *evolutionary* imperative—toward both the hunt and devouring their prey.

Humans had a tendency to add ritual to basic, biological

functions—sex, elimination, feeding. Although sex was far freer now that it was no longer bound up with reproduction or with the possibility of disease, there remained age-old conventions regarding where and when couples could indulge in it. Not even the cultural tension between monogamy and polyamory could completely change that . . . or the ritual of marriage. Eliminating bodily wastes was still done in private, at least for the most part, and mealtimes could still become special occasions for celebration, for socializing, or for courtship.

Those were human rituals, of course. The Agletsch had a cultural taboo against eating in public, even with their own kind, while the primitive Habu of Psi Cancri III defecated in public in order to mark territory for any type of transaction or conversation.

The Grdoch, with their numerous multiple mouths—those tooth-rimmed sucker-snouts located all over their bodies—seemed designed for feeding literally from the inside out, and the attack on the prey animal he'd witnessed appeared to be highly stylized—a ritual of attack, burrow, and feed. A human, Gray thought, wouldn't make much of a meal, but as with many behavioral rituals, it might not be the details that mattered, but the simple fact.

Yes, if they could feed on humans without being poisoned by them, the only thing preventing them from indulging their gastronomic enthusiasm might be the knowledge that the prey in question was rational—an intelligent star-faring species like themselves.

Given that humans had such a poor record in that regard just with various species on Earth, from ritualized cannibalism to the wholesale slaughter of the now-extinct cetaceans, intelligence might not provide that much of a disincentive for the Grdoch.

"With this in mind," Armitage continued, "your operational orders have been changed."

Here it comes, Gray thought.

"Your primary directive, investigating the disappearance of the *Intrepid,* remains as before. The emphasis of your mission now, however, will be a show of force designed to establish peaceful relations with the local Vulcan government. To that end, you will not employ a preliminary bombardment. In particular, you will avoid using relativistic bombardment. There is the possibility that USNA prisoners of war are on Vulcan . . . and, quite apart from that, it would be good to work out a separate peace with the local government *without* destroying the planet.

"As for the Grdoch, you are to use your own discretion there. If you can use the language software we got at Enceladus to make friends, well and good . . . but I must emphasize one thing: *Don't trust them!* Our XT people at Crisium report that the Grdoch seem to use the truth only as a tool to get what they want. It's possible that they don't even understand the concept of binding agreements.

"At the same time, the USNA Senate has decided that we're stretched too thin to involve ourselves in another war. You can protect yourselves if you're fired upon . . . but don't go looking for trouble.

"I'm sorry this has to be so vague, Sandy. Discretionary orders are a bitch. But I know we can count on you to do what's best out there."

Just fucking wonderful. Gray thought about his crews . . . and the problems of making friends with the bloody-minded Grdoch. *They're going to just* love *this.* . . .

Holding Area
Himmel-Paradisio
Neubavaria
Vulcan, 40 Eridani A II
1725 hours local time/0943 hours, TFT

The governor, together with most of his people, had long since given up all hope.

Immanuel Vicente Delgado had been the governor of
Vulcan for four years, now. With a world population of some
87 million, Vulcan wasn't exactly a bustling planetary meg-
alopolis. With the colony all but independent from Earth,
the post of *governor* was more ceremonial than anything
else.

Vulcan's government alternated between Spanish and
German governors, each serving five years, and he *was* the
constitutionally elected representative of his world. It might
be a ceremonial post, but someone had to speak for the population. It was a matter of sovereign propriety . . . and of
dignity. *Human* dignity.

Los demonios didn't care about constitutions or elected
government or propriety, and they certainly didn't care
about human dignity.

What they cared about was feeding time.

The monsters were entering the enclosure now. Delgado
couldn't see them—the gate was a hundred meters from
where he was sitting within the 200-hectare pen, but he
could hear the shrieks and screams, could see the tide of
naked people spilling across the uneven ground.

The Grdoch, it turned out, preferred to *hunt* their food.

"Not again!" a woman seated next to him said. "How
long has this been going on?"

"I'm not sure," Delgado told her. "A couple of weeks or
so . . ."

Maria Fuentes was a relative newcomer to the camp.
She'd been first officer of the USNA star carrier *Intrepid*,
captured when her ship was badly damaged in the skirmish
in-system, perhaps two weeks ago. She'd been rescued by
Confederation SAR vehicles and held as a POW in Himmel-
Paradisio . . . but when the Grdoch had shown their true
colors and occupied the capital—the monsters were supposed to be *allies*, damn it!—she'd been held at their ground
base, and only brought here with the other *Intrepid* survivors
a couple of days ago. Now, the *Inrepid* crew were prisoners

of war, along with almost a thousand civilians from the twin cities of Himmel and Paradisio.

"Heaven" in German . . . "Paradise" in Spanish. But in the past week the place had become hell incarnate.

The fleeing mob parted, scattering across the fenced-in compound, and Delgado could see *los demonios* . . . a dozen bloated, saggy, scarlet things covered with those obscenely questing trunks or snouts with their tooth-lined sucking mouths, sprouting the three clawed and splay-footed legs moving those rubbery bulks along with surprising speed. Fuentes drew back, shaking, and Delgado felt a sick wrenching in his gut. One of the Grdoch, less than ten meters away, now, reached out with one clawed foot and dragged down a fleeing, screaming woman. Delgado desperately wanted to help, but the deepest horror was in his complete helplessness. *There was nothing he could do.*

Pinning the struggling woman down, the monster rolled on top of her, completely covering her except for her thrashing legs and one wildly waving arm. At least . . . at *least* her heart-rending shrieks as she was devoured alive were muffled by the monster's flabby bulk.

When the Grdoch lifted itself from her mangled corpse, what was left was bloody scraps, severed limbs, a shockingly faceless head, and a torn and broken torso hideously slashed and eviscerated.

"Ay, Dios y Santa Maria!" Fuentes said, a strangled whimper.

Delgado grappled with a bizarre, horrid thought—that Fuentes shouldn't be invoking religion . . . but recognized that his overstressed mind was groping for something else, *anything* else, to avoid thinking about what he was seeing. The White Covenant was meaningless here. Faced with such horror, such helplessness, people were going to invoke their gods no matter what the impropriety, no matter what the law might have to say about it.

Sated, the monster rolled off the woman's body and

began its slow and obscene roll back toward the compound gate. Other Grdoch were rising from their victims as well. One small band of men and women off to the right had tried attacking one as it fed horribly, with predictable results. The Grdoch were far stronger than humans, their outer integument as tough as rubbery plastic. With no weapons but sticks, stones, and bare hands, there was no way even a dozen people could harm one of the beasts. The monster completed its meal, casually swiped at its attackers with one foot, leaving two of them writhing in the dirt as it rolled off with its fellows.

The horror was over for the moment . . . but Delgado knew the nightmare would continue. Small bands of Grdoch entered the compound to feed every few hours. The citizens penned here had been stripped before being locked up here, presumably for the gastronomic convenience of their keepers. Other humans—under the watchful gaze of heavily armed Grdoch—brought food in for the inmates each day . . . some dried, nanoprocessed emergency rations and—mostly—bloody chunks of raw meat.

It was best not to think too hard about where that meat might have come from, from what kind of animal. . . .

In any case, Delgado and other civic leaders in the group had taken on the responsibility for seeing to it that the meager rations were fairly distributed. Water was hauled in by the tankerfull and emptied into a long, muddy ditch near the gate; the Grdoch evidently intended to keep their food animals alive for as long as possible, though the *comfort* of their herds, obviously, was not one of their priorities. People slept on the bare ground, huddled together for mutual warmth.

As for waste disposal . . . well, Delgado and the other community leaders had designated the southwestern corner of the pen as the sewage pit. It was the best they could manage, and even with the rule, some of the inmates refused to follow this most basic of sanitation regulations. That's where they took the sad remains of the Grdochs' meals after feeding time as well. There was no room, no tools, no *will* for proper burials.

Delgado feared that what little camp discipline there was would break down completely before very long. The people were utterly broken, utterly without hope. Attempts to fight back, like the one he'd just witnessed, were driven by desperation, or, just possibly, by a suicidal urge to end the horror and the uncertainty of who would be hunted down next.

"They'll be . . . they'll be sending . . . a fleet . . ." Fuentes said with some difficulty. She was sobbing as she spoke. He'd seen several of her shipmates devoured over the last week, had even been in a gang that had tried to fight back. That had been when one of the monsters had taken Michael Glover, *Intrepid*'s captain. A brave, brave effort, but completely futile.

"I'm not so sure, Commander," Delgado replied. "The ships we had here left with a Grdoch ship last week. Our naval people thought the demons were the best of friends."

"I mean *my* people," Fuentes told him. "The USNA. They'll know *Intrepid* is overdue. They might even get the message drone we launched. They'll send a stronger fleet. . . ."

"Assuming, Delgado replied slowly, "that the Grdoch haven't just attacked the Sol System as well. They could be there by now. That might have been what they wanted all along, you know—to learn the location of our homeworld." He shuddered, and almost added, *A well-stocked larder.* He stopped himself. Fuentes couldn't stand much more stress, he thought, and his attempt at black humor might well have backfired. The woman was clinging to the ragged edge of sanity as it was.

"I still can't fathom how they . . . how they think of us as just *food*," Fuentes said, shaking her head as if in denial of what she knew to be true. The sobs had ended, and she appeared—again—to be grappling with the larger problems of who and what the aliens were, and how they might be stopped. "They *know* we're intelligent, that we're a space-faring civilization. You said they were talking with the commanders of your naval squadron."

Delgado nodded. "When they first arrived in-system, they attacked us, the planet, did terrible damage to several cities. We thought they were a Sh'daar client race and tried to tell them that we wanted peace with the collective. We had no planetary defenses, and only a few ships in the Vulcan Legion to protect the system . . . from you."

She nodded, and Delgado thought about how strange it was talking with her like this . . . a USNA naval officer, the *enemy*. The arrival of the *truly* alien made any and all human political differences completely insignificant. For the two of them, naked, emotionally broken, sprawled in the dirt as they helplessly awaited the next Grdoch feeding on-slaught . . . mere politics meant nothing, less than nothing.

He reached out and touched her shoulder. She covered his hand with hers.

"The aliens," he said, continuing the story, "brushed the Legion aside. They landed and established a base on Las Pampas. That's the other continent, the smaller one. They massacred—I'm not sure—several million colonists there, maybe. Most of the populations of Nova Argentina and Buena del Mar. A fleet arrived from Earth under the command of Commodore Becker, on the *Emden*. What was left of the Legion joined with them, and they launched an attack on the aliens . . . a fairly successful one. At least the alien fleet was pushed back from the planet, isolating their base, and Commodore Becker opened a planetary bombardment of Nova Argentina. It was at this time that I was able to send several reports to the *Emden*, and they, in turn, dispatched it back to Earth on board a message drone."

"But . . . you were able to communicate eventually?"

Delgado nodded. "During the bombardment, the aliens on the planet stopped firing back, and transmitted a broadband image: a 1024 by 1024 binary matrix that plotted out a symbol."

"What symbol?"

"This." Delgado reached down and drew it in the dirt: a narrow, vertical ellipse framed inside a circle. It looked something like a sketch of a cat's eye.

"What does it mean?"

"We didn't know at first, but we took it as an indication that at least the demons wanted to communicate. The linguists on board the *Emden* thought it might be their symbol for themselves—a kind of flag. Later, they concluded it meant 'we surrender,' or possibly, 'we want to talk.' "

"It would be hard learning a completely alien language from the start, with no knowledge at all of their culture . . . no knowledge even as to whether they used a spoken language."

"Exactly. Fortunately, Commodore Becker had a team of Agletsch on board the *Emden*."

Fuentes looked surprised. "You have the Agletsch working with you as well?"

"Naturally. Don't be foolish. They came first to the Confederation, remember, before your people tried to break away. They are completely apolitical. I know a few continue to work with you, but there is a sizeable enclave of them in Geneva, and some serve on board our ships as linguists and contact specialists."

"Of course." She looked chastened. Delgado thought that the woman was naïve, but put that down to her youth. As a full commander in her navy, she would have to be in her mid-thirties, at least, but she looked younger than that. Cosmetic anagathics, perhaps.

Or possibly it was the stress of the situation that had her not thinking clearly. Well, he could scarcely blame her.

"In any case," Delgado continued, "the Agletsch are experts at establishing communications with unknown xenosophonts. With their help, Becker was able to open communications with them, and the fighting stopped at once. We thought . . . we thought maybe there'd been a terrible mistake, that they'd not realized we were intelligent until after Becker spoke to them. Or, possibly, they were at war with the Sh'daar, since our Agletsch insisted that they were not part of the Galactic Collective." He gave a despondent shrug. "All I can imagine is that they decided to *pretend* to have misunderstood, in hopes of learning the location of our homeworld. Becker departed the system to return to Earth, and one of the three Grdoch warships departed with him. The Grdoch remaining in the Vulcan system attacked again, less than nine hours after our fleet dropped into metaspace."

"Another misunderstanding?" Fuentes asked. She sounded . . . almost hopeful. As though she wanted there to be some reason for this horror.

"We'd done nothing!" Delgado shouted. "Nothing! They annihilated the last of the Legion's vessels, landed outside our cities, used X-ray lasers to reduce them to rubble! When we put down our weapons and tried to surrender, transmitting the symbol they'd shown to us, they herded us together, took our clothing, marched us into these . . . these pens. And here we have been since, helpless. *Food!* Food for these demons!"

"I . . . always thought," Fuentes said slowly, "that, that mutually alien species couldn't get sustenance from one another. That they might even poison each other."

Delgado shrugged again. "Most times, perhaps that is true. They say that there is only a one-in-four chance of another species having compatible sugars and amino acids, and that only if they both are carbon-based. The Agletsch have such a biology. I've heard that they can ingest our food."

"I didn't know that."

"It's true. Of course some species do use trace elements in their chemistries, like arsenic or antimony, that can be poisonous to other life forms. Or they can sequester poisons or biological toxins in their tissues, like Vulcan langoustines

. . . or certain fish back on Earth. But nature tends to be conservative. What works on one world may well evolve on another, more or less the same. The difference between species, the *real* difference, is not going to be biological. It will be a difference in the mind, in the way they *think*. . . ."

"As with these Grdoch," Fuentes said. "They think it's okay to eat intelligent life forms."

"It's not so different from us. We know some species of great whales on Earth were intelligent . . . before they were hunted to extinction. Other terrestrial species showed high degrees of intelligence—the octopus, the elephant. That didn't stop humans from hunting them for food. Or for sport. Or exploiting them in other ways."

"But we didn't know they were intelligent at the time!"

"Perhaps only because we didn't try to understand them. Or didn't want to."

"Like the Grdoch."

"Perhaps, at least at first. But they know we are a sapient species now. They've conversed with us. But they appear to be driven by . . . their appetites."

"An evolutionary imperative?" Fuentes asked.

Delgado nodded. "I think so. During . . . during the brief period of truce, I saw something very disturbing. At their base on Las Pampas, they had an enclosure, a pen like this one. They kept there several . . . animals. Immense beasts, like, like boneless whales, but on dry land. The Grdoch would enter the compound and assault these beasts, tear them open and actually burrow inside, feeding on them with all of their mouths at once. Dr. Schmidt—he was probably our most distinguished xenobiologist—he pointed out that the food beasts were almost certainly genetically engineered to provide the Grdoch with living sources of food, that they either prefer or for some reason *must* eat their food while it is alive." He shuddered. "Horrible. *Horrible.* But we know of so many terrestrial species that eat their food while it still lives."

"But . . . but intelligent species *know* better. . . ."

She was being naïve again. "That is a cultural preference, Commander. Not an absolute. Perhaps the Grdoch *need* their food to be struggling in order to activate some digestive enzyme. Or perhaps they merely prefer the feel and the excitement of devouring living prey. At least . . ."

"What?"

"At least we humans are too small for them to keep alive through multiple feedings, as they do the giant food beasts. For us, the horror is over more quickly."

A new chorus of screams arose from the other side of the compound. The monsters were entering the enclosure once again. They tended to come in small groups of ten or twelve . . . and there were many thousands of the Grdoch on Vulcan now.

"Santa Maria, Madre de Deos," Fuentes said.

Delgado closed his eyes, and wished to God he could shut his ears. *Please, please let the horror be over quickly. . . .*

Chapter Sixteen

Emergency Presidential Command Post
Toronto
United States of North America
0958 hours, EST

President Koenig leaned back and let his chair conform to his body, thoughtclicking an inner icon as he did so. The logo of the NAVS-CS, the North American Virtual Symposium on the Cosmological Sciences, appeared on a mental window . . . then faded away, revealing a computer-generated view of the galaxy, a vast, barred spiral of stardust tilted 45 degrees toward his vantage point and tipped slightly to the side.

He smiled at the sight. Only once had humans viewed the galaxy from the outside . . . and that had been twenty years ago, when Koenig had led the *America* battlefleet through the time- and space-twisting mystery of a TRGA cylinder, emerging inside what had later—much, *much* later—become the Omega Centauri star cluster. At the time—almost 900 million years in the past, Omega Centauri—known to its myriad inhabitants as the N'gai Star Cloud—had been hurtling a few thousand light years above the plane of that galaxy, just a few million years before it had been cannibalized by the far vaster and gravitationally hungry Milky Way. The Sh'daar of that distant epoch, perhaps afraid of a confrontation with the Milky Way's inhabitants of their remote future, had agreed to a ceasefire. And while *America* had been there, inside the heart of the extragalactic cluster, a scout ship had probed past the cluster's teeming central ball of suns to get a look at the galaxy from Outside . . . a unique and dazzlingly beautiful perspective.

What Koenig was seeing now was based on the images recorded at the time, though what he'd seen on board the *America* had been more like a vast and glowing wall of stars and nebulae stretching from one side of Creation to the other. The N'gai Cloud had been too close to the galactic plane at the time to get a true perspective of the Milky Way's sweeping, barred-spiral structure.

He could tell, though, that the images the *America* battle-group had made had been utilized by the AIs to design the Society's introductory scene.

Others were joining in to attend the symposium, linking in by the hundreds . . . by the thousands. One of the greatest transformational advantages of a completely linked-in electronic society was the potential for truly huge meet-ups of interested people, for purposes ranging from politics to social engineering to professional exchanges to public education. NAVS-CS had started out originally and primarily as an exchange forum for cosmologists, a means for professionals to keep up with the rapid-fire pace of new discoveries in the field. There was enough public interest in the subject, however, that symposia such as this one, hosted by the University of Colorado Virtual Campus, were remarkably popular outside the fields of cosmology, astronomy, and gravitational physics as well.

"Admiral King?" a voice said within his mind. "Welcome to the symposium. Is there anything we can help you with?"

The voice was that of an AI, evidently an electronic baby-sitter for the host of virtual attendees at the conference.

"Alex King, Adm (ret)" was Koenig's johnsmith, his alter-ego at such functions. The AI, of course, knew who he *really* was—they would have full access to the ID and personal records of everyone there—but protocol allowed those who wished a degree of anonymity to create fictitious avatars that let them blend in invisibly with the background.

"I'm fine, thank you," Koenig replied.

"Which talks do you plan on attending, sir?"

"Just this first one, actually."

"Ah, yes. 'Gravitational Metrics as Applied to Metaversal Polydimensional Unity.' There's been a *lot* of interest in that one."

"So I gather."

"You know how to download simultaneous technical description and definitions?"

"Of course."

"I am required to ask. Enjoy the program, sir. If there's anything you need, thoughtclick *this* icon."

A new icon appeared on Keonig's inner window. "Thank you."

The AI's mental voice swiched off, and Koenig was again alone . . . alone in a sea of electronic presences. According to figures appearing in a window sidebar, there were well over two million people linked in now. Amazing.

A call light winked within Koenig's consciousness. He checked . . . and saw that it was Deborah Johnston. *Senator* Deborah Johnston . . . or she had been until the 2420 elections. And after that . . .

"My God . . . Deb?"

He could feel her smile across the electronic interface. "Alex, that *is* you! I thought it must be . . . Mr. President!"

"Well . . . low profile, and all of that. You know how it is."

"I do indeed."

"God, Deb . . . I thought you were *dead*! After Columbus . . ."

"I was out of town," she said. "Mexico City."

"It's been pretty chaotic since then."

"Oh, I'm well aware! I relocated in the LA megapolis. Been working with the USNA terraforming department as an advisor."

Koenig had first met Deb when the two of them had been on opposite sides of the Senate floor, shortly after he'd been elected to the USNA Senate in 2410. They'd clashed on a number of points, notably over North American sovereignty, Periphery independence, and the offshore free cities issue . . . and eventually ended up in bed together. The sexual relationship had ended in 2418 when Koenig had run for president and won his first six-year term. They'd remained close friends, however, and if Koenig disliked her liberal global politics, he respected her a very great deal.

He'd thought . . . he'd *assumed* she'd been in Columbus when the capital had been vaporized by the Confederation nano-D strike, one of millions of casualties in that devastated city.

He found he was almost trembling with relief. "This is . . . this is wonderful, Deb! I wish you'd let me know that you were all right!"

"You could have linked me too, you know. It's been—"

"I know, I know. Busy. Yeah. Are you in LA now?"

"Hilliard, actually."

"Ohio?"

"The department is working on the Columbus reconstruction. And I'm advising."

"Fantastic!"

When the Confederation had nanoed Columbus on November 15, 2424, they'd left the center of the city pocked by an immense crater three kilometers wide and half a kilometer deep. Hilliard was a suburb of Greater Columbus some fifteen kilometers from the old city center, and well outside the area destroyed by the shock wave. Koenig had signed off on the plans to begin reconstruction weeks ago.

He'd had no idea that Deb was a part of that project.

"So how's the reconstruction going?"

"Quite well. We've started clearing the rubble. We hope to start growing buildings within the next week or so."

Koenig nodded. He'd seen—he'd *approved*—the plans. The crater—filled now by the Scioto Waterfall—would remain as a perfectly circular lake, with kilometer-high hab towers and arcologies surrounding it. The nano constructors, he knew, were already being programmed for the job. Within a year, Columbus should be better than new.

If only it were possible to regrow those millions of lost people.

"That's good," he told her. He wrestled for a moment with the excitement of finding the woman again, and his conscience. He found he wanted to see her again, and the sooner the better. "Listen, Deb, I—"

"Hold it, Alex. I think they're starting!"

Koenig felt both a tiny pang of regret, and considerable relief. Perhaps it was best not to explore *that* path too closely.

But *God*, it was good to know she was alive!

"Good morning, ladies, gentlemen, and AIs," a new voice announced. The window now was filled by a youthful face, and the ID tag introduced the man as Dr. Howard Gilmore, of the University of Colorado. "Welcome to the North American Virtual Symposium on the Cosmological Sciences. Our first presenter will be AI Stephen Hawking. First, however, I invite you to download the background information returned this past January by a USNA carrier task force investigating the anomaly at Omega Centauri, some sixteen thousand light years from Earth. . . ."

Koenig had already downloaded the material, of course. In fact, he'd been briefed on it as soon as *America* had re-entered the Sol System. The mysterious construction by the Rosette Aliens out within the swarming heart of Omega Centauri was well known by now, as simplified versions of *America*'s original reports had been disseminated through the news channels to the public at large.

Once, he thought, the government would have attempted to censor the data, at the very least classifying it "secret" and allowing only a select inner circle of scientists and AIs to even know of its existence. Secrets of that sort, however, were ephemeral, especially when the scientific community was brought into the picture. His advisors—including Marcus—had insisted that the secret had to be kept simply because the USNA couldn't afford to let the Confederation get the jump on them. If Geneva managed to make contact with the Rosette Aliens—worse, if they managed to forge a treaty, it might well mean the end of North America's bid for independence.

Koenig, however, had been adamant. As important as the war with Geneva was, contact with a species as self-evidently powerful and technologically advanced as the Rosette Aliens was more so by far. An alliance with such a civilization—if that was even conceivable—would mean safety at last from the Sh'daar. In Koenig's view, what was vital above all was the survival of Humankind; North American independence was of secondary import.

Koenig looked through the download material, checking to see if there was anything he'd missed. It was all there as he'd remembered it—the observations made by *America*'s battlegroup at Omega Centauri, the images and data collected by the close passage of a single human scout across the Rosette's whirling lumen, the speculations by various members of the expedition's science teams . . . including an analysis that placed the aliens solidly in the K-3 bracket of high-tech civilization.

"If we're all up to speed on this material," Gilmore said after a moment, "we can welcome our first presenter, AI Stephen Hawking.

Gilmore's face was replaced by the computer-animated image of a long-dead human physicist, and the buzzing, vodor-generated tones of Stephen Hawking sounded in Koenig's mind.

"Good morning, humans and fellow electronic sophonts," the quaintly archaic electronic voice intoned. "It is my very great pleasure today to speak with you, and to be able at last to announce a final and verifiable proof of one of the original Stephen Hawking's favorite hypotheses . . . that of multiple and parallel universes within a larger multiverse. . . ."

It wasn't the original, *human* Hawking, of course, but an extremely sophisticated artificial intelligence with that twentieth and twenty-first-century physicist's persona and name, a kind of electronic avatar that interacted with humans in the same way that Konstantin presented itself as the Russian futurist Konstantin Tsiolkovsky. The original Stephen Hawking had been, arguably, the most brilliant scientist since Sir Isaac Newton, whose chair at Cambridge he'd held. Afflicted by the crippling motor neuron disease amyotrophic lateral sclerosis in an era just before neurological reconstructive nanomedicine, he'd nevertheless beaten the odds and become one of the most famous and accomplished theoretical cosmologists of all time.

His most important work had been a collaboration with Roger Penrose on theories concerning gravitational singularities within the framework of general relativity, the prediction that black holes would emit radiation—Hawking radiation, as it came to be called—and a cosmology that united quantum mechanics with general relativity.

Koenig had heard of the AI version of Hawking, a super-AI like Konstantin doing important theoretical work at a number of universities and scientific think tanks, including both Colorado and New Cambridge. Like Konstantin, Stephen was a fifth-generation digitally programmed and enhanced AI, a machine-mind running within a vast and teeming network of several thousand Digital Sentience DS-8940 computers with something like 10^{24} neural connections . . . roughly 10 *billion* times more than the connections possessed by a human brain.

"As you can see by these data," Hawking's voice buzzed

on, "the gravitometric matrices measured by the CP-240 Shadowstar as it passed above the opening to the Rosette Wormhole are perfectly matched by predictions of multiple gravitational leakage across universal boundaries. . . ."

The original Hawking, Koenig knew, had been a firm believer in the many-worlds interpretation of quantum physics—of many universes incorporated into a far vaster multiverse. The theory had been around for centuries. At its simplest, the many-worlds interpretation held that every time there was a *choice* in the universe—a given particle might be either spin-up or spin-down, for example—the result was a branching of the universe itself to incorporate both possibilities . . . a universe where that particle was spin-up, and another universe, identical in every way, save that the particle was spin-down.

Such bifurcations had been popular with writers of science fiction long before Hawking's day. There were universes, a near infinity of them, where the USNA achieved full independence from the Confederation . . . and a near infinity of other universes where the Confederation won, and where ultimately the Sh'daar determined the ultimate future of humankind. There were universes where the cat locked in the box was alive, and others where it was dead . . . the two states being in superpositions until an observer looked and collapsed the quantum wave-form fucntions.

Physicists tended to dislike the many-worlds interpretation because it seemed so counter-intuitively wasteful to call an entire universe into existence for the sake of a single photon. Still, the evidence had been mounting over the centuries that that was exactly what happened, though more modern finesses suggested that a degree of overlap existed between universes. There'd already been widespread speculation within the scientific community that physical structures like the Rosette at the center of Omega Centauri or the ancient and enigmatic TRGA cylinders led not only to other regions of space and time, but to entirely separate realities. Koenig himself had discussed the possibility with his officers on board *America*.

And now Stephen was claiming *proof*.

"We have been searching for the reality of dark matter since the late twentieth century," Stephen continued. "One of the great paradoxes of physics has long been wrapped up in the question: Why is gravity so *weak*?"

Why indeed. Despite what you might think about gravity's strength when you fall down the stairs or contemplate the hellish surface environment of a neutron star, gravity is by many orders of magnitude the weakest of the four standard forces that operate the universe. Of the other three forces, the weak force—responsible for certain nuclear interactions such as beta decay—is still 10^{25} times stronger than gravity, while electromagnetism is 10^{36} times stronger—picture a child's magnet picking up a nail against the total gravitational pull of an entire planet. The strong force, which holds together the quarks making up the protons and neutrons within an atomic nucleus, is 10^{38} times stronger than gravity. The difference, of course, is that the strong, weak, and electromagnetic forces act over limited distances—the strong interaction is actually undetectable beyond the boundary of an atom's nucleus—while gravity operates across the entire universe.

Gravity's relative weakness set it in stark contrast to the other forces. Numerous explanations had been advanced over the years, but the best, the most promising, had been the idea that gravity, alone of all particles or forces, had the ability to travel between the universes of the Bulk.

The Bulk was a hypothetical extra-dimensional realm within which multiple universes existed like an infinite number of two-dimensional sheets side by side . . . if by "side" you took into account the fact that there were more than the usual four dimensions of spacetime. From the perspective of this 4-D universe, the other universes occupied the same area, as distant from this reality as the thickness of a shadow. From the perspective of the hyperdimensional Bulk, all of the universes—the 'Branes of M-theory—were two-dimensional sheets side by side.

And if gravity was not limited to this one universe, perhaps it "leaked" into others.

If you supposed that the nearest other universes in this scheme were similar in their histories to this one, you could imagine that they included analogues of this galaxy. Gravitational leakage would explain, then, why galaxies seemed to be so much more massive than could be accounted for by simply tallying up the stars, planets, dust and gas observed in each.

The theory was elegant, and it allowed for simple and elegant expressions of several unified field theories. It explained the "Great Attractor"—that mysterious point in intergalactic space, off in the direction of the constellations Centaurus and Hydra, which seemed to be pulling on myriad galaxies, accelerating them along in what was popularly known as the Dark Flow. Perhaps most important: it gave an explanation for the mystery of dark matter.

Koenig pulled down a definition through his in-head, checking on the latest description of dark matter. Centuries before, careful measurement of the movement of visible matter within the Milky Way and throughout the universe had presented cosmologists with a most uncomfortable conundrum. All of the stars, planets, dust, gas, and energy . . . *everything* tangible within the universe actually amounted to less than 5 percent of what was actually out there. Fully 26.8 percent of the universe comprised so-called *dark matter* . . . with another 68.3 percent being the even more mysterious dark energy.

Normal matter, in other words, the kind that made up atoms, was responsible for less than 20 percent of all the matter out there. Dark matter was invisible, as its name implied, was intangible. And, in fact, the *only* way it could affect normal matter was through the effects of its gravity.

For a time, cosmologists had been confident that dark

matter would turn out to be a physical particle fundamentally different from normal matter. For decades, a favorite candidate was the hypothetical "WIMP," or weakly interactive massive particle. According to theory, WIMPs might annihilate one another, creating otherwise unexplainable bursts of gamma rays . . . or they might decay into normal matter. Attempts to detect anomalous gamma rays or emergent matter broke down, however, simply because there were other ways to explain the observed effects.

But suppose that dark matter was "dark" simply because it existed in neighboring, "nearby" universes? Unreachable . . . unobservable . . . but "felt" by virtue of that matter's gravity leaking across the Bulk from other universes . . .

"We can now say with some confidence," Stephen continued, "that the Shadowstar passing the black hole rosette in Omega Centauri was not, as we originally theorized, observing other regions of space in this universe. Instead, Lieutenant Walton actually was recording a succession of parallel universes, other universes more or less like our own within the hyperdimensional Bulk.

"With this in mind, we can also confidently suggest that the so-called Rosette Aliens are members of a *multiverse*-faring civilization of extremely advanced technological prowess, passing from their universe into ours. Why they are doing this is, of course, as yet unknown. They may be explorers. They may be refugees from their own, dying universe, attempting to cheat the deadly chill of entropy.

"Or . . . just possibly . . . they may represent this universe's original Creator. . . ."

Koenig heard a kind of susurration running through the huge crowd listening to the AI's presentation . . . a background murmur largely filtered out by the AI monitors running the event, but still audible nonetheless. One thought, put into the link matrix by a large number of minds arriving at the same conclusion independently, came through as an audible term: *the Stargods.*

"I am well aware that these suggestions will be highly controversial," Stephen said, "particularly the last one. Still, as a hypothesis it should be testable . . . assuming that we find a way to interact with these beings, to communicate with them in some meaningful way. I leave it to others to suggest just how an ant might manage to communicate with a human as it walks across his great toe."

Controversial? That was one word for it. Koenig felt a tingling wave of emotion sweeping up his spine, but couldn't quite identify it. Wonder . . . awe . . . surprise . . . it was all of that, and quite a bit more.

"I do suggest," Stephen went on, "that we take another, very close look at the anthropic principle."

Koenig had to thoughtclick the icon for definitions again. He thought he remembered . . . yes. That was it.

The anthropic principle was as much philosophy as it was science . . . perhaps more so. Essentially, it could be stated by the question, Why does the universe appear to be precisely designed to allow—even to *require*—the appearance of life and, ultimately, of intelligence?

Within physics and cosmology, it turned out, there were certain numbers, values for specific physical constants, that were so fussily precise that any change in *any* of them would have precluded the appearance of life. Human understanding of M-theory and how the universe had appeared suggested that most—perhaps all of these numbers—were essentially random; they *could* have been almost anything.

The anthropic principle came in various flavors, ranging from weak to strong. The weak anthropic principle simply stated that the universe happened to allow the evolution of life and intelligence. The strong version went further: the universe *had* to be the way it was *because* it contained life. Variants of these two included one that required living observers for the universe to exist at all, and another that required a multitude of universes so that all possible combinations of laws and conditions existed.

Koenig ran quickly down through the list of fundamental variables.

N: The ratio of the Electrical Force to the Gravitational Force . . . the fact that electromagnetism is 10^{36} times stronger than gravity. If gravity was any stronger, stars would have been smaller, hotter, and have aged much faster . . . too fast for their planets to evolve life. If gravity was weaker, stars might not have formed in the first place.

Sigma: The strength of the strong force binding protons and neutrons together within the atomic nucleus relative to the repulsive electrical force between positively charged protons. The number works out to .007 . . . and if it had been as small as .006, hydrogen would not be able to fuse within stars, while if it were .008, protons would have latched onto protons in the first instants of the big bang, and there would have been no free protons left from which to form hydrogen . . . and stars.

Omega: The rate of cosmic expansion . . . fast enough to give galaxies the billions of years necessary to evolve life, but not so fast that stars never formed.

Lambda: The strength of universal antigravity that drove the accelerating cosmic expansion in direct opposition to Omega, but slowly enough not to tear the cosmos apart before life could evolve.

Q: The amount of wrinkling in space as it unfolded from the Big Bang, a number defined as 10^{-5}, small enough that all matter did not collapse into black holes early in the universe's history, but large enough that stars could form from the primordial cloud of hydrogen.

D: The number of extended spatial dimensions. Had the universe existed as a "flatland" of only two primary dimensions instead of three, gravity would be even weaker than it is, and stars would never have formed.

G: The gravitational constant, a value given as 6.6784 x $10^{-11}\mathrm{m}^3\mathrm{kg}^{-1}\mathrm{s}^{-2}$. Stronger, and the universe would have already collapsed in upon itself. Weaker, and stars would never have formed, and stellar fusion would not have been possible.

There were other numbers on the list, but these were some of the most important—universal constants and ratios so important that if any of them had been just a little different, the universe would not be recognizable as what it is today . . . and life—at least, the kind of life that tended to build starships and squabble over politics and ponder the wonders of existence—would never have appeared. Koenig noted that the first six had been presented by the Astronomer Royal of England in 1999 in a book called *Just Six Numbers: the Deep Forces That Shape the Universe.* Other numbers had been added later—G, the mass of the Higgs Boson, the mass of the electron. Change any of these, and life became impossible.

Other variables were specific to Earth—the size of the planet's iron core, which in turn determined the strength of the planet's magnetic field and the degree to which it shielded the surface from harmful solar radiation and let Earth maintain an atmosphere. The fact that Earth possessed a large moon that stabilized the planet's tendency to wobble. The continental drift that contributed to the planet's incredible biodiversity. The oxygen atmosphere that allowed the development of fire . . . of smelting . . . of modern technology.

Life, it was now well known, had appeared on lots of planets without those secondary factors; the H'rulka, for instance, were immense gas bags floating in the hydrogen atmosphere of gas giants, while the Turusch had evolved in a reducing atmosphere that was mostly carbon dioxide. But there were hints that such species had required help to develop the technology necessary to leave the worlds of their birth.

The so-called Stargods . . .

The anthropic principle had long been evoked as proof of a God, a supreme being who had balanced those numbers precisely in order to permit life to form. Some suggested that it was life itself that determined the various values . . .

perhaps the technic civilizations that survived and evolved all the way through to the end of their universe.

Koenig had trouble following some of the fuzzier philosophical concepts. The simplest approach, it seemed to him, would be to shrug your shoulders and say, "Well, if the numbers were different, we wouldn't be here . . . but we *are* here, so maybe the numbers are what they are purely by chance."

But that was dodging the issue, Koenig knew, a cheat, pure and simple. It beggared belief that all of those values should be what they were within such tiny, finicky, precise parameters.

One group of proponents of the strong anthropic principle—meaning the theory that the universe had been designed the way it was—suggested that extremely advanced aliens might have created this universe, complete with life-friendly constants . . . possibly as a bolt-hole for when their own universe began to die.

If the Rosette Aliens were *that* powerful . . .

Alexander Koenig, the president of the United States of North America, suddenly felt very, *very* small. . . .

"Deb?"

Electronically, he reached out, strengthening the virtual link with her, sensing in her the same feeling of awe and insignificance.

Somehow, that ghost of a human touch made a vast and incomprehenisble universe just a bit more manageable.

Chapter Seventeen

USNA CVS America
40 Eridani A System
1015 hours, TFT

Emergence . . .

In a sudden, flaring storm of photons, the star carrier *America* dropped from the emptiness of Alcubierre meta-space and into the reality of stars and worlds and radiant light. Ahead, just 30 astronomical units distant, 40 Eridani A gleamed in the distance, a type K-1 orange beacon, while much farther off, B and C, the other two stars of the system, showed as a close pair, ruby-red and diamond-white.

The *Constitution* and the *Saratoga* both had emerged from Alcubierre warp already just a few million kilometers ahead, and were already deploying their fighter wings. The destroyers *Sandoval* and *Young* were in the van, well out front, while the railgun cruiser *Decatur* drifted ten million kilometers to starboard. As Gray watched from *America*'s Flag Bridge, other ships dropped out of Alcubierre Drive moment by passing moment: the Russian *Slava* and *Pla-mennyy*, the North Indian *Shiva* and her escort *Ranvir*, the USNA heavy cruisers *Calgary* and *Maine*. The domed overhead of the flag bridge had been set to display the surrounding sky, with incoming ships picked out as green icons. The light cruiser *Gridley* . . . the destroyer *Ramirez* . . .

Other, more distant ships appeared within the widening sphere of *America*'s 3-D plotting tanks as the light bearing their images crawled across intervening space to reach the flagship's sensors. *Portland, Milwaukee,* and the Marine carrier *Inchon,* the Chinese cruiser *Fu Zhun,* the—

Searing light flooded the flag bridge, so sudden, so dazzling that Gray actually ducked down against the back of his command chair. *"What the fuck?"*

The blast of light was fading swiftly, dwindling rapidly to a single extremely bright star aft, to port, and high, glaring against the blackness over Gray's left shoulder.

"Emergence overlap, Admiral," Commander Mallory reported from the main bridge.

"What ships?"

"We're checking, sir."

It was one of the hazards of interstellar travel, of course. The Alcubierre Drive functioned by wrapping up a starship, already traveling at close to the speed of light, inside a tight little bubble of gravitationally distorted space. The ghost of the long-dead Einstein declared that nothing—not matter, not energy—could travel faster than light. Indeed, matter couldn't even reach c, while energy—photons—could *only* travel at that magical velocity of just under 300,000 kilometers per second.

The loophole, first pointed out by Mexican theoretical physicist Miguel Alcubierre four centuries earlier, was that there was nothing that said that *space* couldn't move faster than light. Indeed, during the first microsceonds of the big bang, space had moved considerably faster than light in the expansive outrush known to physicists as inflation. And, it turned out, a starship resting inside the bubble could travel *with* that bubble. So long as it was moving at less than light speed relative to the space within which it rested, there was no foul, no harm, the ghost of Einstein was appeased . . . and Humankind could travel to the stars in hours, days, or weeks instead of decades or centuries.

While resting within its Alcubierre bubble, a starship wasn't in normal space, but in a kind of pocket universe outside of the normal expanse of four-dimensional space-time, a region known as metaspace. Pockets of metaspace could overlap one another, or they could overlap ships or even worlds or whole stars in complete safety . . . but should a ship emerge from metaspace within the same volume of space occupied already by another ship or a chunk of rock, the results were both energetic and catastrophic.

Ships were so relatively tiny and the space they operated in so vast that such collisions were extraordinarily rare. Gray had heard of just one in the entire three-century history of interstellar flight, the *Umberto* and the *New Horizon*.

Now, evidently, two more ship names were to be added to the list now, and *damn* the ill luck that had brought them together at the same place and the same time.

"What ships?" he demanded.

"Frigate *Sam Morison*, sir," Commander Mallory announced. "She was already in normal space when another ship dropped on top of her. We suspect a failure in the communications pre-warp protocol. Still checking on the ID of the other vessel."

Two ships lost out of the task group of twenty-four, and the operation had not even properly begun. Worse, that nova-flare of raw energy, a bubble of pure light expanding at the speed of light, would reach 40 Eridani's inner system in just four hours.

Task Force Eridani had just announced its arrival in spectacular fashion.

Nothing could be gained by waiting. The light emitted by the various ships as they dropped from their Alcubierre bubbles was more than enough to alert any enemy vessels in-system, and there was no point in scrubbing the mission.

Gray opened the command channel. "You may launch fighters, CAG."

"Very well, Admiral," Captain Fletcher replied. "Launching fighters."

America's contingent of fighters began emerging from the far larger starship, two by two from the twin axial launch tubes through the shield cap, and six by six from the rotating hab modules in the shield cap's shadow. The view from a nearby battlespace drone showed the launch: dozens of minute, flying insects emerging from the far larger umbrella shape of the carrier, and moving into close squadron formation 10 kilometers off *America*'s newly resurfaced and painted prow.

After transferring control from Prifly to CIC, the ship's Command Information Center, the fighters began accelerating, squadron after squadron. The Starhawks of the Dragonfires, VF-44, would stay with *America*, serving as her CAP—a defensive envelope still called combat air patrol even now, centuries after extending beyond Earth's atmosphere. The other squadrons would accelerate at 50,000 gravities, coming a hairsbreadth shy of the speed of light in about ten minutes.

It was those squadrons, together with fighters launched from the other carriers in the task group, that would make First Contact with whatever was waiting for them there at Vulcan.

"Message coming through, sir," Lieutenant Davidson, on the communications watch, said in Gray's head. "Admiral Guo, on the *Shi Lang*."

"Accept."

Admiral Guo Hucheng's bland, unemotional face appeared on a window opening within Gray's mind. "Admiral Gray."

"Yes, Admiral Guo."

"It appears that one of my vessels, and one of yours, have . . . intersected."

His lips were moving rapidly, completely out of synch

with the calm, computer-generated voice speaking English in Gray's mind.

"Yes, Admiral," Gray replied, keeping his face neutral. "We appear to have lost the frigate *Samuel Eliot Morison*. With which of your ships did it collide?"

"The light cruiser *Li Jinping*, Admiral. There appears to be some . . . conflict within the emergence protocols."

With large numbers of ships emerging from metaspace at about the same time during fleet ops, and within the same target volume of space, the chances of emergence overlap, while still remote, were greater than they might be otherwise. The computer AIs operating each vessel in a naval formation were linked and their clocks synchronized before each Alcubierre translation in order to allow some additional spread in the emergence pattern of the ships. USNA ships had not worked this closely with ships in the Chinese navy before, however.

Such inexperience could lead to mistakes.

"We're checking on that, Admiral. In the meantime, we need to commence acceleration."

Guo's eyes widened very slightly. "You intend to proceed, then?"

"Of course. It's not as though the enemy won't already be aware of our arrival."

"True. Apparently I was mistaken in assuming you would respond like your Pan-European counterparts."

Gray decided to accept that as a compliment. European commanders—in particularly the French—were notorious for being extremely cautious, to the point of aborting an operation if the element of surprise was lost.

"I intend, Admiral Guo, to take this fight to the enemy. *Now*."

"Agreed. Guo out."

The window closed, and Gray vented a small sigh of relief. The Chinese were still a very much unknown element. The events of the Second Sino-Western War had ended with the fall of a small asteroid into the Atlantic Ocean in 2132. Given the Biblical name Wormwood, from the Book of Revelations, the asteroid had been diverted from its normal orbit by a Chinese warship.

Though Beijing had insisted that a rogue Chinese officer had been responsible, the Chinese Hegemony had been blamed for the resultant tidal wave and the deaths of half a billion people, declared a rogue nation by the Allies, and denied membership in the *Pax Confeoderata*, the new world government organization that emerged after the war.

For years, elements within the USNA government had been seeking an alliance with the Chinese with varying degrees of success. Guo's inclusion with Task Force Eridani was very much an experiment. Gray had already noted that Guo had not yet specifically placed himself under Gray's command, but had so far been operating his squadron of four—now *three*—ships as an independent command.

Gray had responded by carefully not giving Guo direct orders, but by simply telling him what the rest of the task force was doing and inviting him to join in. The low-key approach had worked so far, at least if you ignored the loss of two ships in what was probably a protocol error.

Whether this informal operating procedure would work during combat was anyone's guess. Gray was inclined to think that the system would break down under the stresses and demands of battle, and contented himself with the realization that the Hegemony's contingent to the Vulcan operation was *only* four ships.

No. *Three*.

The situation was made deadly by the multiple levels of the task force's current orders. HQ-MILCOM's operational directives had included the possibility of establishing relations with the Grdoch, using the new language protocols taken from the Confederation. *That* wasn't going to happen now if Gray had any say in the matter. Admiral Armitage's final word to him had been to "use his own discretion."

The reports from Vulcan's Confederation governor had been brutally open about the Grdoch atrocities at 40 Eridani. They'd attacked human forces at Vulcan without provocation, accepted a treaty when one was offered by a well-armed battlefleet, then attacked again as soon as that fleet had departed.

According to Armitage and HQ-MILCOM, the Grdoch weren't at all fussy about their mealtimes. The aliens had been feeding on *humans* at Vulcan. Gray had seen them feeding on the . . . what had Truitt named them? *Praedams*, that was it. Genetically tailored food beasts. The thought of people being devoured alive by those things was . . . horrific.

And it suggested a thoroughly alien mind-set for the Grdoch, a willingness to use intelligent life forms as food sources. Humans didn't have a pristine record when it came to such niceties, of course, but in general—and for modern human cultures—eating thinking, rational beings, especially *alive*, was as close to unthinkable as it was possible to get. Grdoch biochemistry might be identical to that of humans, but their minds might be so alien, might work in such radically different ways, that true communication with them would forever be impossible.

From the sound of things, the various policy-making groups back on Earth were still divided on how to relate to the Grdoch. Geneva had initiated a treaty with them after they'd attacked Vulcan the first time, though it wasn't entirely clear that they'd known about the aliens' dietary habits. And MILCOM, it seemed, couldn't quite bring itself to rejecting the possibility of an alliance entirely. *"Use your own discretion."*

Well, none of them had ever seen those things *eat*.

"All fighters away," CAG Fletcher said in Gray's mind. "They are boosting for Vulcan as dictated by the Opplan Alfa."

"Very well," Gray said over the in-head command link.

"Captain Gutierrez, you may commence acceleration. Alert the rest of the task force, please."

"Aye, aye, Admiral."

And the remaining twenty-two ships of Task Force Eridani began to accelerate in-system.

VFA-96, Black Demons
Vulcan Space
1423 hours, TFT

"Black Demons, Demon One!" Commander Mackey's voice rasped out. "Look sharp! We're coming up on the objective . . . ten million kilometers."

Lieutenant Megan Connor was well aware of that fact. The bizarrely warped and twisted view of the surrounding universe created by near-*c* flight had relaxed into normalcy as her fighter's velocity dropped, and the target planet was dead ahead, growing rapidly from a blue-hued star to a tiny crescent. Magnified, the image was cloud-wreathed over vast stretches of ocean, and achingly reminiscent of home.

Red icons scattered across her view ahead marked potentially hostile warships. Two large ones tagged as unknowns were likely Grdoch vessels, but there were several smaller ones that her warbook was identifying as known designs—a Francesco-class light cruiser . . . several Rommel-class destroyers . . . five Rhone-class frigates. They were approaching in-system from the direction of the system's third planet, half an AU out and well off to port.

"Demon One, Demon Six," Connor called. "Time to 'fess up, Mac. What's the straight shit? Are these guys hostiles or not?"

"You were there and downloaded the briefing with the rest of us, Meg," Mackey replied. "CIC says to treat 'em as hostile . . . but let them make the first move."

"Shit, Skipper!" Lieutenant Carlson, Demon Three, said. "No IB?"

"Yeah," Lieutenant Gregory added. "That's the perfect recipe for getting ourselves seriously dead!"

"I know," Mackey replied. "But we need to give 'em time to be friends if the bastards want, right? This is just show of force . . . until they decide otherwise."

"So what better way to make them be friends than a little IB diplomacy?" Gregory wanted to know.

IB stood for initial bombardment, and it was the central pillar of all modern space combat. Battles rarely occurred in open space; a typical star system was so large, encompassing such a vast volume of space, that, unless both sides sought it, a meeting of fleets in all that emptiness was unlikely in the extreme.

And of course the whole point of using a fleet to dominate a star system was to control those pieces of orbiting real estate that made the system strategically important in the first place—the planets, moons, and major asteroids, the free-orbiting bases and colonies, the deep-space nanufactories, antimatter plants, and power stations that were the signature of modern, space-faring technic civilization.

So space tactics had evolved around defending forces that protected key planets, and attacking forces that emerged from Alcubierre Drive far out in the relatively empty reaches of the outer system, accelerated in-system, and engaged the defenders for control of whatever it was they were protecting.

The initial bombardment was quite literally the opening volley in such an engagement. Long-range missiles and kinetic-kill projectiles launched from far out-system could smash through a defending fleet; more devastating by far were *relativistic* bombardments, where the incoming projectiles were traveling at a hefty percentage of the speed of light. The kinetic energy contained in even a grain of sand traveling at such a velocity was starkly unimaginable. The man commanding the task force, "Sandy" Gray, had gotten his nickname years before when he'd released clouds of sand at near-*c*, annihilating much of an enemy fleet and scouring one hemisphere of a planet with fire in the process. The tactic was extremely effective if you didn't care what got broken going in. This time, though, the word was no initial bombardments; there might be USNA prisoners on Vulcan or on board one or more of the ships near the objective planet.

Besides, scuttlebutt held that the task force was here to make *friends* with the hostiles. A show of force . . . followed by a goddamned treaty . . .

So the fighter wave launched from the task force would be first to make contact with the enemy, and would do so without the usual softening-up of a preliminary bombardment. The main fleet, twenty-two capital ships, was on the way. With less acceleration, they would be arriving later—another two hours.

Until then, the fighters would be on their own . . . and they would be calling the shots insofar as diplomatic decisions were concerned.

It was not, Connor thought, a good utilization of assets. Politicians talked, signed treaties, and decided when it was time to go to war. Fighter pilots handled the rough stuff after the political possibilities had been exhausted.

"Arm weapons," Mackey told them. "But don't fire until I give you clearance."

Still decelerating, the fighters of the Black Demon Squadron continued to fall toward the planet.

Grdoch Huntership Swift Slayer
Vulcan Space
1423 hours, TFT

Alarmed, now, the Swarmguide Tch'gok turned three more of its eyestalks to watch the control-room screen. The prey was hurtling ever closer, their ships decelerating but still moving quite fast.

"Weapons!" it said, speaking its tightly focused thoughts through fiber-optic cables wired directly into its nervous system. "Target the nearest of those small ships and . . . fire!"

X-ray lasers snapped out from the hull of the Grdoch huntership *Swift Slayer*, and the oncoming motes of enemy fighters flared and vanished like night flyers caught by flame. Those fighters did not pose a significant threat to the Grdoch hunterships . . . but the major warships coming in behind them might.

Tch'gok was balancing.

The concept was basic to Grdoch psychology, the result of tens of millions of years of evolution as hunters in a violently dangerous ecosystem. Grdoch hunters tended to advance as a swarm when prey—helpless and vulnerable—was in sight. They tended to scatter and retreat when confronted by strength, or the risk of personal injury.

That had been the evolutionary imperative, at least, for millions of years before the Grdoch left the swamps and estuaries of their watery homeworld and developed civilization. They'd evolved as both predator and prey, and their modern psychology reflected that fact.

As did their physiology. Where predators tended to have forward-facing eyes with good depth perception in contrast to browsers, which had eyes mounted to let them see in all directions, the Grdoch had both . . . with a dozen eyes in telescoping snouts that gave them both superb binocular *and* 360-degree vision. Though they were large and ungainly organisms, their spherical symmetry let them move rapidly in any direction, and their feeding snouts doubled as graspers and manipulators of surprising sensitivity.

Evolution had molded the Grdoch into perfect middle-tier predators within their homeworld's ecosystem. Eons ago, the top predator on the Grdoch homeworld had been a nightmare horror, all teeth and slasher claws and spiky armor and ravenous appetite, a monster called the *tch'tch'tch*, which had imprinted its terror deep within the modern Grdoch psyche. Those large and hungry top-tier predators that had helped that evolutionary process along were extinct now . . . but the Grdoch remained as natural selection had made them—both in their physiology and in their psychology— fierce predator, terrified prey.

Balancing . . .

Tch'gok could feel the familiar inner pull in two directions . . . toward feeding frenzy and toward rout. The trick was to override the blind emotions with mind and will . . . by encouraging the thoughts of steaming bodily fluids and oozing flesh. *Feed! Feed! Feed!*

Digestive enzymes flowed in questing, hungry mouths. Terror receded, replaced by a deep and nearly overwhelming hunger.

"Swarmreleaser!" it commanded. "Release your swarm! Shipguide! Take us closer."

And *Swift Slayer* accelerated toward the oncoming fighters.

VFA-96, Black Demons
Vulcan Space
1424 hours, TFT

Two Black Demon fighters were caught in that invisible blowtorch flame—Teller and de la Cruz. Several fighters from other squadrons were hit as well.

"Weapons free!" Mackey told the group. "Weapons free!"

"Shit, what *was* that?" a shrill voice called.

Lieutenant Del Rey was one of the squadron's replacement pilots, after the losses at Enceladus, and she didn't sound as though she quite believed what she was seeing.

Connor shook her head, disgusted. *Idiot.* She'd seen the after-action reports, and downloaded the engagement records.

"X-ray laser, Lieutenant," Mackey told her. "Don't let it hit you with the thing. It'll ruin your whole day."

"Here they come!" Kemper called. Connor could hear the stress in his mental voice. "They're engaging!"

"Hold formation!" Mackey replied. "All fighters, *hold formation*!"

Swarms of fighters—squat and egg shaped—were emerging from the far larger alien vessel behind them and moving to attack the oncoming USNA fighters head-on.

"There are too many of them!" Daimler, another newbie, said.

"Definitely a target-rich environment," Connor put in. She didn't like the thread of nervousness running through the mental voices of her squadron mates.

"Remember," Mackey warned. "These things drink high-energy beams. No lasers or pee-beeps! Stick with missiles."

"Locking on," Kemper reported. "And . . . *Fox One*!"

Other fighters in the squadron began loosing missiles—VG-10 Kraits for the most part, but several of the Black Knight and Grim Reaper Velociraptor pilots had just released the much larger and more powerful Fer-de-lance shipkillers. The enemy fighters replied with volleys of high-energy X-ray beams, silently erasing both accelerating missiles and human fighters from the sky in rapid-fire bursts of light . . . but then the surviving nuclear warheads began detonating among the alien ships, in dazzling pulses of light and hard radiation.

"Get past the fighters if you can," Mackey ordered. "We want the mother ships!"

Connor loosed a pair of Kraits, then punched her Starhawk into high-G acceleration, angling for an opening in the enemy fighter swarm that might let her slip through. Her AI alerted her to vector changes among some of the nearer enemy ships; they were moving to cut her off. She rolled to starboard, jinking now to throw off the Grdoch targeting systems. Her Starhawk, she knew, would never survive even a touch of one of those 80-teraJoule X-ray energy bolts. Each shot delivered the punch of a pocket nuke, as much as a VG-10 Krait but focused down to a beam the thickness of a man's forearm. When one touched a Starhawk's hull matrix, that hull material simply vaporized, and the heat of the disintegration—temperatures equivalent to the core of a star—simply engulfed the fighter and reduced it to an expanding plasma of charged particles.

"Watch out!" Lieutenant Carlson yelled. "The bastards are—"

Carlson's ship vanished, wiped from the sky. *Damn* . . .

Connor had a lock on the Grdoch mothership, now looming less than a thousand kilometers ahead. "Target lock," she called. "Going to Lance! Fox One!"

Her fighter's warload included four of the VG-44c Fer-de-lance missiles, each about a megaton's worth of destructive energy packaged in the tip of a three-meter shipkiller. She felt the jolt as one of the heavy missiles slid clear of her fighter's belly, followed by a second, and then she rolled sharply to port, pumping out a stream of AMSO rounds. She wasn't certain that the flying sand clouds would scatter those X-ray bolts as they did lower-energy laser beams, but it was certainly worth a try. She laid down a pattern of sandcaster rounds designed to protect both her own fighter and the fast-moving Fer-de-lance as well.

Her AI's wordless alarm sounded in her head. A Grdoch fighter had just dropped onto her tail, and the energies within its weapons bays were building to a peak. Flipping end-for-end, she fired a pair of AMSO sandcaster rounds, then jinked toward the nadir; white light blinded her for an instant as X-rays scattered through the expanding cloud of sand. She targeted the opposition with a Krait . . . no, *two* . . . and fired.

The enemy fighter was closing fast . . . too fast, and the

proximity fuses on the pair of nuclear warheads she'd just launched detonated less than 15 kilometers away. Almost in the same instant, a more distant but much larger nuclear detonation filled the universe with light. The radiation storms swept across her ship. . . .

And Meg Connor's fighter went dead, tumbling stem over stern as she fell toward Vulcan.

Chapter Eighteen

USNA CVS America
40 Eridani A System
1430 hours, TFT

"Give me a magnified image," Gray ordered. "Let's see what the drones have to say."

Battlespace drones had been launched ahead of the fighter squadrons, creating an interlocking network of video and electronic images that the task force's AIs could use to pierce the classic fog of war and assemble a useful picture of what was going on. Though *America* was still nearly 15 million kilometers out, her flag-bridge display now zoomed in on the fighter battle ahead. Vulcan was a vast silver-limned crescent close against the intolerably brilliant orange glare of 40 Eridani. Green and red icons drifted against the light; by selecting one and giving a thoughtclick command, Gray could focus on individual actions, could watch the exchange of missiles and X-rays lighting up the sky.

Gray was less interested in individual fighter-against-fighter exchanges, however, than he was in the evolution of the entire engagement. Task Force Eridani would be entering that fiercely contested volume of space in another few moments, and it was imperative that the fighters clear out some of the Grdoch opposition.

That, of course, was the point of sending in fighters ahead of the main body of the fleet. *America* and the capital ships with her were not as vulnerable to Grdoch X-ray beams as were fighters; they mounted gravitic screens designed to intercept incoming energies in tightly curved regions of space-time and scatter them back into space. But an analysis of the Grdoch weapons collected at Enceladus had proved that human warships would not be able to divert those tightly packaged energies for long. If the fleet were to survive the next thirty minutes, the fighter squadrons had to eliminate some, at least, of the defenders . . . or at least sharply reduce their ability to fight.

But there was paradox there as well. Such vital fleet assets were at the same time the most vulnerable . . . delicate motes lost in emptiness, and buffeted by nuclear storms.

Gray watched the pulse and flash of myriad nuclear warheads, and wondered how the struggle was going—who was winning. He could hear the chatter of pilots calling to pilots over the comm channels in the background, but each individual was so focused on his or her one tiny slice of the firefight that they had no understanding of the larger picture.

"Knight Six! Watch it! Watch it! You have one on your tail!"

"Target lock! Fox One! Fox One!"

"Donny! Break left!"

"I've got him! Lock! Fire!"

"My God . . . he's coming apart!"

"Watch the debris, Reaper Seven! You're too close!"

"Shit! Reap-Seven is gone! . . ."

Gray kept listening to those disembodied voices coming over the tactical links, and knew that too many had died already.

Nuclear detonations didn't behave the same in space as they did on a planetary surface. There was no stereotypical mushroom cloud, for a start, just an expanding sphere of white-hot plasma. With no atmosphere, both heat effects and shock waves were enormously attenuated. The radiation released by a nuclear warhead, however, with no air molecules to absorb it, could reach levels 5,000 times higher than the same detonation inside a planetary atmosphere, and it was this radiation that caused the majority of damage in space combat. Even the most hardened electronic systems were vulnerable to pulses of high-level radiation when it was that strong.

Unfortunately, the pilots of those fighters were even more vulnerable. Their cockpits were heavily shielded, of course. They *had* to be, since a fighter traveling at near-*c* encountered stray hydrogen atoms or subatomic particles at relative velocities that turned them into deadly ionizing radiation. But a nuke going off close enough could dump enough hard rads into a fighter's systems to cripple the ship and literally fry the pilot. *America*'s sick bays had the technology to repair all but the most serious radiation-induced injuries . . . but the pilot had to live long enough to reach one.

And if enough radiation leaked through a fighter's gravitic and electromagnetic shielding all at once, the pilot would be dead within seconds, and there was no medical technology good enough to fix *that*.

The Chinese fighters off the *Shi Lang*—three squadrons of new *Kaifeng* fighters—were engaging the enemy now, sweeping in on the more distant of the two Grdoch capital ships. The Grdoch warships had split up, one—identified by *America*'s AI as Alfa—advancing to meet the incoming Allied fleet, the other, Bravo, remaining in orbit over Vulcan.

There was another element as well . . . a contingent of ten Confederation capital ships, still half an hour out, but accelerating in toward Vulcan. Were they working with the Grdoch? Or were they potential allies?

Gray studied the shifting tactical situation for a moment,

looking for an advantage and how best to capitalize on it. *Divide and conquer* was an age-old military dictum, one that applied as much to modern starships as it had to the hoplites of ancient Greece. By splitting up, the Grdoch ships might be committing one of the deadliest sins of combat— dividing their forces in the face of an enemy.

On the other hand, military history was full of examples of commanders who'd done just that . . . and won.

Gray was also uncomfortably aware that the Chinese were doing the same thing—splitting the Allied forces by moving independently on Bravo, the more distant of the Grdoch ships. The operational orders had stated that the task force should stay together—but Admiral Guo evidently had chosen to test those orders. Why? To demonstrate that the Chinese contingent was independent of Gray's command? He would have to have a word with Guo later.

If there *was* a later. . . .

Still, the situation could work to the Allies' advantage, he thought. If the Chinese kept that second Grdoch warship distracted, the rest of the Allies could gang up on the Alfa.

He studied the unfolding situation a moment more, and then began issuing orders.

"Dean! We're going to maintain line ahead. Let the other ships know."

"Aye, aye, sir!"

On the flag-bridge overhead screen, lines drew themselves across the firmament, showing the projected paths of each of the ships.

"We'll do a close pass on target Alfa . . . then make straight for Bravo."

"Yessir."

"Line ahead" was a term from the ancient days of wet navies, with all of the vessels of a fleet or squadron strung out in a line. It had the questionable advantage of offering only the first few ships in the line to enemy fire and sparing the rest. One alternative was a wall approach, with the ships spread out in a more-or-less two-dimensional sheet that gave all of them a shot at the enemy, but also exposed all to incoming defensive fire. Another possibility was the "melee," or general chase, where individual ships or small squadrons chose their own approach, and their own targets.

Because of the deadliness of the Grdoch X-ray weapons, Gray had decided on the first set of tactics. He expected to lose some of the ships in the van; the chances were good that the Grdoch would concentrate on the lead ships, the ones more easily targeted and not so heavily masked by Allied electronic countermeasures. In a wall attack, more of the task group's heavies might be crippled going in—specially the larger ones, while a general chase invited destruction in detail.

"Destroyers and frigates in the van," he ordered. "And frigates on the flanks. Cruisers next, then carriers, battleships, and gunships."

"Relaying the orders now, Admiral."

Gray sat back in his seat, trying to ignore the icy fist gripping his stomach. *This* was the worst part of command . . . giving the orders that determined who might live, who was likely to die. Putting the more expendable destroyers and frigates forward in the van—small ships of a few thousand tons and with crews numbering a few hundred—might mean fewer volleys directed against the larger ships—the carriers massing some millions of tons, or the heavy railgun cruisers—each of them a small city, with a population numbered in the thousands.

Had he guessed right? Depending on the effectiveness of the Grdoch heavy weaponry, splitting their fire among all twenty-two capital ships might turn out to be a better approach than concentrating that same fire on a few ships. Gray was gambling on the fact that modern space combat was unthinkably fast. The task force would be past Target Alfa in a fraction of a second; its disposition—he hoped—would let the heavies get in and past without taking major damage.

There was also the fact of the fighter squadrons that had preceded the task force into the battlespace. They were scoring hits on the Grdoch warships. The question was whether they had been able to degrade the enemy's defensive capabilities at all. If they hadn't, Task Force Eridani's attack formation wouldn't matter much at all.

"Seventy-five seconds to closest passage, Admiral," Captain Gutierrez told him. "This doesn't look like it'll be as easy as Enceladus, though."

"No," Gray replied. "It doesn't. But let's see how they react to a direct threat."

The Grdoch ship at Enceladus had offered something of a puzzle, and USNA strategists and xeno specialists had been working on the contradiction since, trying to find a key to the aliens' behavior. The alien had opened fire on the USNA squadron . . . but had fled rather than face a protracted fight. And when he'd virtually gone on board the captured vessel in the guise of a robotic drone and encountered one of the Grdoch crew, it had behaved . . . oddly inconsistent, at least by human standards. First it had seemed afraid, even cowardly . . . but they'd turned aggressive when the Marines had opened fire on their food creature.

Of course, the key issue lay in the phrase *by human standards*. What seemed like inconsistent behavior for humans was not necessarily so in aliens. But if humans were going to fight these things, they had to understand them.

Know your enemy, a basic precept of the ancient strategic philosopher Sun Tzu. It wasn't easy, though, with a culture evolved on a world light years from Earth and Humankind.

Gray had downloaded a lot of initial reports and speculation by the XS people analyzing the alien prisoners, and seen nothing definitive as yet. Based on what he'd seen at Enceladus, however, he was willing to bet that the Grdoch possessed a more pronounced fight-or-flight response than did humans. That begged the question as to why they'd even come here in the first place, or allied with the Confderation

. . . but it suggested that there might be ways of making them back down. Naked force appeared to make them aggressive . . . but the ship at Enceladus *had* fled when *America* had opened fire on it. Perhaps they had a kind of bully mentality—one that led them to attack when they felt they had a strong advantage, but sent them scurrying when they were given a hard punch in the nose.

Well . . . assuming they *had* noses.

In any case, that was what he was counting on here.

The ships of TF Eridani had dropped into line . . . led by the frigates *Wyatt*, *McDonnell*, and *Brewster*, and followed by the destroyers *Semmes*, *Young*, and *Ramirez*, and the cruiser *Milwaukee*. *America* had fallen into line astern of the battleship *Long Island*, with the *Maine* flanking them to port and the Russian *Slava* just astern. As one, they switched off their gravitic drives, traveling now at a residual velocity of just under 8,000 kilometers per second.

"All ships," Gray said quietly, "stand by. Tacnet link, AI control . . ."

One disadvantage of the line ahead formation was the fact that most of the ships couldn't fire at the enemy without risking a hit on friendlies in the van. The most devastating fire, however, would be delivered during that split second as the task force swept past the enemy at several thousand kps and at a range of just 10,000 kilometers in this case. Human reflexes simply weren't fast enough to direct such fire, so the actual targeting and release would be handled by ship AIs. The computer tactical links connecting the ships of the task force would control the fleet as a unit, concentrating fire and making sure that no ship blocked another as it passed the target.

"The van is taking fire, Admiral," Dean reported.

Gray saw the volley on his tactical screen, computer-controlled graphics filling in the otherwise invisible bolts of coherent X-ray energy as they snapped out from Target Alfa, aiming at the lead human warships. The *McDonnell* took a direct hit that vaporized a large central portion of her shield cap. Wreckage and glittering ice spilled into space, still traveling toward the objective at nearly 8,000 kilometers per second.

Fifty kilometers ahead of the *McDonnell* and just a bit to one side, the *Wyatt* took a near miss, losing a pie-wedge chunk of shield cap. Both stricken frigates were tumbling, now, their control systems fried. And the alien's deadly weapons were questing deeper up the human van, now, ignoring the damaged ships, searching for new targets. The frigate *Brewster* vanished in a vast, eye-wrenching flare of white light as several X-ray beams converged on her, burning through her shield cap and vaporizing her power plants.

But a new danger threatened. Another ancient dictum of war held that no battle plan survives contact with the enemy . . . and that was abundantly demonstrated now as Grdoch fighters began piercing the human task force's line. Many had been destroyed by the human fighter wave, of course, but not *all* by any means. Dozens of Grdoch fighters converged now on the larger human ships—in particular the carriers. Their X-ray beam weapons weren't nearly as powerful as those on the mother ships, but there were so many of them, a swarm of scarlet attackers seeking to overwhelm the human defenses.

Gray had expected some fighters to get through, of course. Carriers and the other capital ships farther back in the line mounted effective point defenses to defend against just such an attack, and each carrier had at least a squadron of fighters flying CAP nearby. But the number of surviving enemy fighters, and the sheer ferocity of their attack, was already stretching those defenses to the limit.

America shuddered as something struck her amidships, aft of her rotating hab modules. Seconds later, a nuclear warhead detonated to port, less than ten kilometers off, and the carrier's gravitic shields struggled to handle the sudden incoming tide of deadly radiation.

Gray could hear Captain Gutierrez snapping off orders in the background, using ship comm channels, but his focus had to be on the entire battle group, not on just the one ship. The ship lurched again, hard.

Things were getting damned rough.

Gray checked the positions of the Confederation warships. At their current acceleration, they were still at least some twenty-five minutes away.

"Give me a channel to those Confed ships," Gay ordered.

"Channel open, sir."

"Confederation squadron!" he snapped. "This is Admiral Gray of the USNA carrier task force now approaching Vulcan. I am engaging the Grdoch warships between me and the planet. What are your intentions? Please respond."

If the Confederation ships were still allied with the Grdoch, he likely would not get an answer . . . but it was worth exploring the possibility of an impromptu battlespace alliance. The Confed vessels weren't close enough to make a difference in the coming fight one way or another in any case. At that range, it would take two minutes for the radio signal to reach the Confederation vessels . . . and another two minutes for the reply. Four minutes was an eternity in combat. By the time the Confed reply reached *America*, the battle with the Grdoch would have been over, one way or the other.

But it was worth a try, and it would be damned useful to know if the USNA ships were going to have a *second* fight on their hands after the line hurtled past Vulcan.

"The *Long Island* is taking heavy fire, Admiral," Dean reported.

"Very well."

Everything was set and locked down. There were no more decisions to be made, no more orders to give. The battleline swept toward the planet and its defenders.

"Admiral! Target Alfa is reversing course! Looks like he might be running for it!"

On the flag-bridge display, the red icon marking the

Grdoch warship was, indeed, furiously dumping its forward velocity, apparently in a bid to reverse course back toward the planet, leaving the battle to the fighter swarms. Gray heard several technicians on the ship's bridge cheer . . . and Captain Gutierrez ordering them to stop. *"We're not out of this yet!"*

But the Grdoch ship had waited too long. Before changing direction, it had to kill its forward velocity, and in that time the USNA battleline flashed across the intervening distance. Each ship in the line rotated to bring its primary weapons to bear on the target . . . and then the shipboard AIs opened fire, sending volley upon volley of deadly beams and missiles slamming into the fleeing target.

And in less than an eye's blink, the entire line was past the target, hurtling across the remaining 20,000 kilometers toward the planet in under three seconds.

Target Bravo was accelerating clear of Vulcan now, trailed by a number of surviving fighters, both Grdoch and human, and closely pursued by the Chinese contingent. On the display, one of the Chinese warships, the destroyer *Lai-yuan*, was tumbling, its shield cap sheared off, and both the *Shi Lang* and the cruiser *Fu Zhun* had taken heavy damage. Grdoch fighters appeared to be focusing their attention on the *Shi Lang*.

"Make to all ships," Gray said. "Close on target Bravo. Let's take some of the pressure off of Admiral Guo if we can."

Behind them, Target Alfa was engulfed in the brilliant flashes of detonating nuclear warheads, and appeared to have been crippled. The balance point of the battle—its center of gravity—was shifting now to Target Bravo.

"Get me Guo," Gray ordered.

It took a moment, but Guo's face appeared within Gray's in-head a moment later. The bridge visible behind him had been wrecked, and the air was thick with smoke. Guo's face was soot-streaked, and he was bleeding from a gash in his scalp. The artificial gravity was off; the hegemony commander was floating clear of his command seat.

"Admiral Guo!" Gray called. "I recommend that you break off your attack."

"Admiral Gray," he acknowledged. "It is vital that this . . . this *foreign devil* not be permitted to escape."

"He won't, sir. Break off, and save your ship!"

"I trust, Admiral," Guo replied slowly, "that you will give a full and accurate accounting of this engagement when you return to Earth. Enemies . . . enemies *can* become friends. . . ."

The image vanished in a burst of sharp static. On the main display, the *Shi Lang* blossomed into an unfolding smear of intolerably brilliant light.

And the *Fu Zhun* continued to press the attack despite the loss of the Chinese flagship. As Gray watched, helpless, it drifted in closer to the far larger Grdoch ship, pouring fire into the alien vessel at close to point-blank range. X-ray lasers lashed out, their invisible radiations burning through the human ship, knives through soft butter.

The *Fu Zhun* exploded.

"*Damn* it!" Gray shouted, loudly enough that several of the technicians on the flag bridge looked up, startled.

"The Chinese flotilla has been wiped out," Dean reported.

"I know. *Get us in there!*"

Why the hell had Guo split off from the allied fleet? Bravado? A political statement, a stubbornly independent refusal to be bound by a Western commander's orders? Gray suspected that it was a lot more than that. The Chinese hegemony had been *persona non grata* within the world community for nearly three centuries, ever since the Fall of Wormwood into the Atlantic. Guo's comment about enemies becoming friends . . .

Maybe he'd been under orders to make damned sure that the USNA knew that the hegemony forces *were* friends . . . allies against the common enemy.

Well, he'd proven his point. The Grdoch ship, however, was still accelerating . . . headed in roughly the same direction as the incoming flotilla of Confederation warships. Just a little longer, and they'd have the bastard boxed in.

Around *America*, in a vast and hazy sphere, drifted wreckage, damaged fighters, and tumbling debris, the sad but inevitable detritus of a battle in open space. To port and astern, Vulcan loomed.

"Make to *Inchon*," Gray said. "Secure the planet!"

The Marine transport had already launched her fighters going into the fight. Now those fighters, and the *Inchon* herself, began braking hard, changing to a new vector that would bring them into low orbit over 40 Eridani A II.

Grdoch fighters were in orbit over the planet already . . . and more were coming up from the surface. The Marine transport-carrier would need cover.

"*Slava*!" Gray said, checking to see which ships in the fleet were best positioned to respond. "*Decatur*! *Calgary*! Close on the planet and give the Marines support!"

Acknowledgements came in.

And the USNA battlegroup began to divide. . . .

Lakeview Arcology
Toronto
United States of North America
1431 hours, EST

Koenig smiled, rising. "Deb! Thank you for coming."

"With an invitation from the president himself?" she said, laughing. "How could I refuse?"

"Simple," he replied. "By saying no. '*Hell*, no,' would also have been an acceptable reply."

Koenig had left the underground fortress of the Presidential Emergency Command Center, taking a travel tube in to the Lakeview Arcology tower, then up the mag-el to the rooftop restaurant, 900 meters above Lake Ontario.

Deb Johnston, meanwhile, had caught the mag-lev tube train north from Columbus, which had covered the five hundred kilometers between there and Toronto in ten minutes, though it had taken her considerably longer to get untangled from her work schedule and a mid-afternoon meeting with the city nanarchitects.

Koenig hesitated, glanced at some of the members of the security detail near the broad, slanting windows of the restaurant . . . then spread his arms, offering a hug. The hell with what they thought.

She accepted the offer. "Oh, it's so *good* to see you again, Alex," she said.

"Hungry?"

"Uh-huh. Starved."

"This place is pretty good," he told her. He grinned. "Human waiters."

"Which means *expensive*, not necessarily *good*. But I'll take your word for it."

His decision to invite Deb north for lunch had prompted a minor crisis within his presidential security detail, but if they weren't used to his spur-of-the-moment decisions by now, they never would be. As a former USNA senator, Johnston already had numerous high-level security clearances; mostly what had been required was hiring the entire restaurant so that it could be closed to the public . . . and running computer checks on the twenty or so members of the staff. Koenig had eaten here before, and there'd been no problems.

"So why *did* you call me?" she said, stepping back from his embrace and taking a seat. "Not just hunger, surely."

"Not *just* hunger," he agreed. "I need . . . I need to talk politics."

She made a face. "*Please* not over lunch . . ."

"You'll like this. I'm beginning to come over to your way of thinking."

Her eyes widened. "*That's* a bit of a bombshell! In what way? You're thinking of defecting and becoming a Unionist?"

"Not . . . quite. But what we heard this morning . . . it shook me, Deb. I'm wondering if the Globalists are right. Do we need to surrender to the Sh'daar?"

At least she had the grace not to laugh at him.

A member of the waitstaff approached the table—under the security detail's watchful collective eye—and offered them old-fashioned menus instead of the usual holographic displays. The conversation was put on hold for a few moments as they made their selections—chicken piccata for Johnston, with *real* chicken, he assured her—and a selection of sushi and sashimi for Koenig.

Deb Johnston had been—still was—a member of the Global Union party, a political mélange of several smaller groups advocating a one-world state. It had been part of the Confederation Globalist party, and as such opposed the war . . . though they'd stopped short of an open break with the current Freedomist government. They now constituted what was politely known in government circles as "the loyal opposition," and continued to debate current USNA policy. While they tended to support the idea of a rapprochement with Geneva, they were still divided over the larger question of whether or not to accept the Sh'daar Ultimatum.

"Where do *you* stand on the Sh'daar issue, Deb?"

"You mean, do we join their collective?" She sighed. "I'm really not sure. I do think we should have self-determination when it comes to our technology. Anymore, we humans are so much a part of our technology that accepting the Ultimatum's limitations would be like putting ourselves in a box." She dimpled. "I heard that somewhere."

The box analogy had been a favorite refrain of Koenig's in a number of political speeches over the years. "Me too. We'd be like Schrödinger's poor cat. Are we alive? Or dead? Open the box and find out."

"You're thinking of the many-worlds hypothesis."

He nodded. "Except that it's not a hypothesis any longer. According to what we heard this morning, we now know there are other universes, maybe an infinite number of them. No matter what we decide, here and now, it turns out that in another universe we've decided something else. Makes it seem like it doesn't really matter *what* we choose. . . ."

"Nothing's changed, Alex," she told him. "We only have this universe. We still have to make the best choices that we can, based on the best information available. And when it comes down to a moral choice, we have to do what we think is *right*."

"Sometimes, what's right isn't all that clear."

"It never is. Are you really worried about the Sh'daar? Or is it the Grdoch?"

"Both, I suppose. We're stretched way too thin to fight *three* wars. The universe, *this* universe, is turning out to be incredibly complicated, you know?"

"And you're looking for ways to simplify things."

"Have you heard of Operation Luther?"

"No."

Briefly, he described the recombinant memetics program, and the rise of a new religion in Europe. Johnston's security clearance was still high enough to let her hear the details.

"This d'Angelo is a *fake*?" she exclaimed. "I'm disappointed!"

"Why?"

"I like his message. Personal responsibility, human freedom to choose, an end to narrow-minded jingoism and fanaticism."

"He preaches against joining the Sh'daar."

"He preaches the union of Humankind."

"He's not a fake," Koenig told her. "Not really, not if enough people believe in him and his message. From what we've seen, there's a lot of public sentiment in Europe now against the war. Especially after Columbus."

She made a face. "That *was* bad. They're still finding bodies in the ruins, you know. And *partial* bodies. The nano strike would have been like being eaten alive."

"You know about the Grdoch?"

"I saw a news feed editorial just the other day, yeah. Not people, I think, with whom we would be comfortable associating. Not when they might get the munchies in the middle of a trade conference."

"Geneva's been getting more desperate. I think that's why they allied with the Grdoch. We'll know more after our fleet returns from Vulcan."

"Well, you won't get an argument from me, if that's what you're looking for. I don't like the idea of civil war with the Confederation. I don't like the idea of Humankind divided against . . . against aliens, whether it's the Sh'daar or the Grdoch. I think you and I are pretty close on that, don't you?"

He nodded. "We are. I don't like the civil war either . . . but we've got it. It's not just the Sh'daar problem. It's Geneva wanting to annex our Peripheries, control the free oceanic cities, control Konstantin and the other super-AIs . . ."

"None of which would be a problem at all if the Confederation really *was* united."

"No. It's the getting there that's the problem. That . . . and the greed, corruption, and power-hunger along the way."

"Denoix?"

"And others. General Korosi for one."

She nodded. "He's a mean one."

"Dark matter."

"What?"

"Stephen was telling us about dark matter this morning."

"Yes. Gravitational leakage from parallel universes."

"Uh-huh. But for me, the *real* dark matter is having to deal with Geneva. Ally with them. *Join* the bastards, despite the atrocities. And after that, just maybe, we'll have to ally with the Sh'daar as well. *And* the Grdoch."

She looked startled. "Why?"

Koenig was thoughtful for a moment. "Someone suggested once, a few centuries ago, that the only thing that would get all the rival nation-states of Humanity to stop fighting each other would be an invasion from someplace else. From space."

She nodded. "It didn't happen, though, did it? The Sh'daar attacked us, but here we are, still fighting with ourselves."

"Unfortunately. But the principle's valid, even if we're still at each other's throats. And what happens when the invasion isn't aimed at Earth . . . but at our entire galaxy . . . maybe even our entire *universe*?"

"Ah. You're thinking about the Rosette Aliens. Do we know they're hostile?"

"No. We lost a ship out there but . . . no. So far, all the evidence suggests that they're so powerful, so far beyond us, that they don't even notice us."

"You think we'd make an impression if we join with the Sh'daar against them?"

"I wish I knew. Look, the Sh'daar are terrified of *something*. We know they fear the ur-Sh'daar, the part of their civilization that transcended physicality hundreds of millions of years ago in some kind of technological singularity. That's why they're so dead set against anyone else developing high technology and entering tech singularities of their own. Maybe the Rosette Aliens are the ur-Sh'daar. We just don't know.

"What I *do* know is that not even a united Humankind will be able to stand up to the Rosette Aliens. They're just too far ahead of us."

"Stargods?"

"Maybe. If they're not gods, they might as well be, with the kind of power they possess. My God, Deb, if the strong anthropic principle is right, it's possible that *they're* the ones who created this universe in the first place!"

"That doesn't seem very likely, does it? I mean . . . why would they pop up *here*, in this universe, right now? And just a few thousand light years from Earth? They have the whole universe to emerge in!"

"You're saying, why did they pop up right next door, instead of off in the Leo Supercluster, or someplace like that?"

"Exactly. Some place a few hundred million, even a few *billion* light years away . . . not right next to Sol, right here in our own galaxy. . . ."

"Point taken. But the fact of the matter is, they *are* here, and with a level of technology that makes us . . . hell, we're not even Stone Age by comparison. We're like ants. Like *amoeba*. And if they do turn out to be a threat, maybe the only way to have any chance at all is for Humankind to join the Sh'daar and the Grdoch as allies."

Slowly, she nodded. "My God. I see why you call it a dark matter. . . ."

"I don't think it gets any darker than that."

Chapter Nineteen

Vulcan
40 Eridani A System
1433 hours, TFT

Lieutenant Connor's Starhawk knew how to protect its pilot. She was unconscious when the fighter hit the planet's atmosphere, but the SG-92's onboard AI had stopped the damaged craft's tumble on its own, then morphed the fighter's nanomatrix hull, flattening it, growing broad, curved wings that bit the thickening air and slowed her meteoric descent.

The fighter's medical suite, meanwhile, worked to keep her alive, pumping anti-rad nano into her bloodstream and exploring her brain from the inside out, searching for signs of serious trauma. By the time she groggily regained consciousness, the fighter was at an altitude of less than 20 kilometers, shuddering as it shrieked through the high, thin air.

She couldn't see out, couldn't see the terrain sweeping past below. Her Starhawk's hull had been badly scorched in the explosions, and her external vid sensors were gone. An attempt to raise other ships in her squadron by both radio and laser com failed, as did an attempt to check on her emergency homer beacon. But the AI continued to feed a trickle of data through her in-head link, steady . . . reassuring . . .

letting her know that her velocity had been reduced from kilometers per second to mere meters per second. She watched both her speed and her altitude dwindle, and wondered what was in store for her on the planet's surface.

She knew that Vulcan was habitable without breathing gear or an e-suit. She would be able to find food and water . . . and there was a sizable human population. What she didn't know was whether there were Grdoch on the surface.

Months before, Connor had been captured by another alien species, the Slan. She'd been a prisoner on one of their warships and been interrogated briefly . . . escaping only when a detachment of USNA Marines had boarded the ship, looking for her.

It had not been a pleasant experience. According to her briefing downloads, the Grdoch were worse than the Slan, a *lot* worse. The Slan, at least, weren't interested in humans as food.

Less than a kilometer of altitude, now. She felt a surge of acceleration to port as her Starhawk dipped one wing and went into a broad, sweeping turn. The AI would be looking for a safe place to touch down . . . someplace smooth, not too rocky, not obstructed by vegetation, not out at sea or in a swamp or high in the mountains. She didn't know anything about Vulcan surface conditions, save for the fact that people could live there without much in the way of technical support.

Her AI pilot would also be steering her away from anything obviously military, avoiding radar and lidar if at all possible. It wouldn't do at all to survive re-entry only to be vaporized by ground-defense lasers as a possible incoming planetbuster.

Was it day or night now? Vulcan had been showing a half-lit phase when she'd been hit, but the Starhawk could be bringing her down almost anywhere.

Fighter AIs could speak with their pilots at need, but rarely did so. It was more efficient feeding necessary information directly into the pilot's brain, while extracting intent and thoughtclicked orders the same way. They were not . . . *conversationalists*, and when Connor requested information about light levels, about terrain, about nearby enemy activity, all she received in reply was a sense of negation. The computer either couldn't reply . . . or it didn't know.

So she tried to impress upon it her desire to land somewhere close to a human population. Stay clear of military bases, yes . . . or large cities . . . but try to find a concentration of humans off away from the larger population centers.

In answer, she felt a sense of affirmation, of agreement.

The humans here would be Confederation, of course—the enemy—but at least she would be able to communicate with them.

At all costs she wanted to avoid the Grdoch.

To pass the time in the dark and close-quarters embrace of the cockpit, she ran through her list of her crash kit's survival gear. Radio and emergency beacon, of course. Battery. A nanomedic pack. Enough water for several days. Knife. A dual ax-machete. A helmet and breathing gear that would turn her shipboard utilities into an e-suit. Vials of programmed nano that would grow her a pair of sturdy boots conformed to her feet, a self-heating blanket, and a small shelter, all from dirt, gravel, or local vegetation, plus additional nano vials that would recharge her suit's air, food, and water cyclers.

And, perhaps most important of all, a Solbeam Mk. VII, a stubby, half-megajoule hand laser.

She still had nightmares about monsters dragging her from her crashed fighter on the Slan warship.

That was *not* going to happen again.

USNA CVS America
40 Eridani A System
1436 hours, TFT

There'd been no reply yet from the Confederation squadron,

and Gray was getting impatient. Damn it, what were they waiting for . . . a chance to jump the USNA fleet in a sneak attack? If that was the case, they'd be disappointed. They were heavily outnumbered and outgunned.

"Message coming through from the Confeds, Admiral," Lieutenant Kepner announced. "Priority One. Time delay now seventy-eight seconds."

At fucking last. "Put it through."

Several seconds passed . . . and then a bearded face came up within Gray's in-head. "I'm Captain del Castro, commanding the Confederation Vulcan battlegroup. Admiral Gray?"

Gray waited, listening. It would take over a minute for his reply to reach del Castro. The Confederation commander appeared to be struggling with something.

"Sir," he continued, "we find ourselves engaged in combat with . . . a truly horrific foe. We had thought the Grdoch to be allies . . . but . . ."

Wait for it, Gray thought.

"Sir, our respective governments are at war, but out here . . . so far from home, we make what alliances we must. For *survival.* With respect, I put my squadron at your disposal, under your command. I am moving now to cut off the retreat of the Grdoch warship directly ahead of you. And I await your orders."

Yes! It wasn't a surrender, not quite . . . but they could hammer out terms and definitions later. What was important now was beating the Grdoch.

"Make to all vessels," he said, his mental voice sharp. "Do not fire on the Confederation warships. Repeat, *do not fire on Confederation vessels.* They're on our side now."

Acknowledgements came back. Gray leaned back against his seat, watching the display above him. The Confederation vessels were indeed moving to cut off the Grdoch warship, which was accelerating at about 80,000 gravities . . . too fast for *America* or the other USNA ships to catch.

"Can we just let them go, Admiral?" Captain Gutierrez wanted to know.

"No," he replied. "We don't know where they came from, where their homeworld is, and if they give us the slip here, I'm betting they'll be back soon, in much greater numbers. But if their ships never return . . ." He let the thought trail off.

"They'll still come looking," Gutierrez said. "*We're* here, looking for the *Intrepid*."

"Sure . . . but it won't be a major invasion fleet. They'll be cautious. It'll buy us time."

"I hope to hell you're right, Admiral. Just two of those monsters was *quite* sufficient, thank you."

"They're decelerating!" Commander Dean announced. "I think they're turning to make a fight of it!"

"I see. . . ."

The huge alien vessel might still be able to slip away . . . but it appeared to be backpedaling now, trying to avoid the oncoming Confederation ships.

"Make to all ships," Gray ordered. "Spread out. We'll try for an englobement."

The line-ahead formation began to disperse, individual ships moving off to left or right, high or low, and now they were closing on the Grdoch ship, cutting down the remaining thousands of kilometers in order to come to grips at last with the fleeing alien.

"All ships," Gray said quietly. *"Fire."*

Grdoch Huntership Swift Slayer
Vulcan Space
1437 hours, TFT

Swarmguide Tch'gok chattered a burst of orders at its subordinates. "Slasherclaws! Grow those weapons connections *now*! Shipguide! Orient us on the approaching prey! You have just three threes of *gh'gh'chk* before they are within slasherreach!"

Grdoch physiology was massively distributed. Each mouth had its own stomach; vision and other senses were distributed across the individual's entire body, and rather than possessing a single brain, its neural processing was spread throughout its nervous system. The arrangement helped guarantee the organism's survival; it could lose a dozen of the small, local pumping bundles that served it as hearts and not even slow down.

Grdoch ship architecture was based closely on their physiology, and that extended to damage control, with massively parallel systems for both flexibility and redundancy. Their immense, squat vessels could take terrible damage without significantly reducing their ability to fight *or* flee . . . and members of the crew tended to be cross-trained so that each could handle numerous stations.

Even Tch'gok was less a ship's captain in the human sense of the term than it was an *organizer* . . . a first among equals tasked with keeping the entire ship and crew in perfect balance. Its role could easily be assumed by some hundreds of other Grdoch within twenty-seven separate swarmguide modules.

Swift Slasher had been terribly damaged, had very nearly been killed . . . but it was quickly coming back to life.

USNA CVS America
40 Eridani A System
1438 hours, TFT

On the well-established premise that it was necessary to know your enemy, Gray had downloaded all of the available intel on the Grdoch and the ship captured at Enceladus. There'd not been a lot available as yet; *Shenandoah* and the in-tow alien vessel had only just made it to Luna when Task Force Eridani had departed from the Sol System, and the XS people had still been in the middle of transferring their new POWs down to the XRD facility at Crisium Base.

Even so, a few things had become clear already, and there were some pretty solid guesses about Grdoch psychology emerging from the earliest encounters out at Enceladus.

Grdoch feeding habits were even more grisly than Gray had at first thought. The organisms apparently possessed a kind of neurological toxin, secreted by salivary glands, that worked to at least partly paralyze their prey. That was bad enough . . . but there was worse. The toxin also worked—at least with the immense praedams they fed upon—to control bleeding and heart rates, helping to keep them alive for multiple feedings.

Stomach turning . . . but Gray had been startled while reading the report to learn that at least one species native to Earth did the same thing. A particular shrew—*Blarina brevicauda*—secreted a similar paralytic toxin. Although shrews can consume their own body weight in insects, earthworms, and mice each day, this species had been known to "graze" on helplessly poisoned mice for days, and in one recorded case had nibbled on the same living mealworm for fifteen days before it finally died.

Nature, as was now well known, tended to repeat patterns of behavior, if not necessarily the specifics of biology, across the galaxy. The Grdoch toxin was tailored for the broadly distributed nervous systems of the ponderous giants they fed upon, the praedams, and probably didn't affect humans, thank God. But Grdoch biology suggested that their psychology would be, from the human perspective, ruthless, opportunistic, and utterly devoid of such human elements as empathy, sympathy, or *mercy*.

And that was the horrible, screaming-nightmare point, wasn't it? Aliens, by definition, did not think, emote, perceive, or reason like humans, if only because the environments in which they'd evolved and the conditions in which they lived held very little in common with Humankind's. Mercy was a decidedly *human* attribute, despite a few thousand years of evidence to the contrary, and you couldn't expect Grdoch—or short-tailed shrews, for that matter—to act like them.

How, Gray wondered, could you even communicate meaningfully with such creatures? Languages might be translated perfectly . . . but not the myriad emotions, attitudes, preconceptions, and innate behaviors behind them.

Dr. Truitt's preliminary report on the captured Grdoch had emphasized this. *"The Grdoch appear to possess an opportunistic and manipulative approach to dealings with other species to a degree unknown even among opportunistic humans. They will tell you exactly what they believe you want to hear in order to win concessions or favor. . . ."*

Good enough. Humans did that sort of thing as well, using language to deceive, mislead, or manipulate, but Truitt's implication seemed to suggest something more, that *any* behavior was legitimate if it advanced your own agenda.

Respecting cultural diversity and the validity of alien psychologies was all well and good . . . but there was a limit to what could be tolerated by others in the way of behavior. Gray could see very little in Grdoch psychology, at least as it currently was understood, to admire.

What was also clear was that the Grdoch ship design deliberately mimicked Grdoch physiology. Studies of their anatomy had only just begun, but portable MRI scans of the aliens on board the *Shenandoah* had shown extensive redundancy in their organs and organ systems . . . and their ships appeared to be built the same way. Gray remembered the Praedam and how hard it had been to kill, and the Grdoch that had swarmed the humans in that compartment had taken hit after hit from Kornbluth's Marines before *finally* being burned down.

"Coming into effective range, Admiral!" Dean reported.

"All ships! Fire! Take the bastard down!"

Swarms of nuke-tipped missiles streaked out from the carrier fleet. The term *effective range* was important here. Grav-drive missiles could be fired at targets across tens of astronomical units, and when preliminary bombardment was allowed, releasing them from the far reaches of the local star system was fairly standard practice. In general terms of military tactics, missiles were long-ranged weapons, intended to be launched across hundreds of thousands or even millions of kilometers, while beams—lasers and plasma weapons— were for short ranges . . . often under 10,000 kilometers.

But Armitage's orders had specifically prohibited an ultra-long range bombardment of Vulcan . . . and it had been unclear whether the Confederation forces here were legitimate targets. In any case, the closer you were to the target, the less time that target had to burn your missiles out of the sky with his defensive beam weapons. Grdoch X-ray lasers were *extremely* effective at vaporizing incoming warheads. Launching at extremely high acceleration from a range of a few thousand kilometers gave you a much better chance of getting through the enemy's defenses.

Just what *effective* range might be when it came to missiles was dependent on complex mathematical algorithms, with variables as diverse as the local density of matter and the effectiveness of enemy defensive fire. Individual ships in the USNA battlegroup continued loosing missiles at the fleeing Grdoch warship. Some might get through and stop the thing . . . and at the very worst, if the enemy was targeting a ship's missile salvo, he didn't have as many beam weapons free to aim at *the ship itself.*

The moment that the interlinked ship AIs governing the USNA fleet's fire control reached a consensus, missiles began to streak from the human fleet, first just a few, then many, then clouds of them, using accelerations that let them sprint across the dwindling few thousands of kilometers between *America*'s battlegroup and the Grdoch ship in mere seconds.

Gray considered the disposition of the fleet . . . and made another decision. In general, star carriers were less effective in ship-to-ship actions. They were more vulnerable to missile and beam-weapon fire than most other capital ships, and they had less in the way of offensive weapons, depending, as they did, on their fighter squadrons to take the fight to the enemy. Most of the task force's fighers were already in space, and *America* and the other task force carriers could add little to the battle at close range.

"*Saratoga, Constitution, Shiva,*" Gray ordered, "with your escorts. Close with the flagship and make for Vulcan orbit."

The task force's carriers weren't needed for the final assault on the remaining Grdoch warship . . . and he was concerned that the vulnerable carriers might be damaged by the alien's death throes. It was better to pull them back to planetary orbit, and leave the final stages of the assault to the heavy cruisers and battleships.

Ponderously, then, the carriers began decelerating, swinging out of line and onto a new heading that would take them back to the planet. With them went their close escorts—the Russian battlecruiser *Plamennyy* with the *Slava*, the heavy cruiser *Ranvir* with the North Indian *Shiva*, the *Calgary*, *Decatur*, and *Porter* following the *Saratoga*, *Constitution*, and *America*. With them went two destroyers and two frigates.

And the sky astern lit up in a searing wave of unfolding nuclear detonations.

Grdoch Huntership Swift Slayer
Vulcan Space
1439 hours, TFT

Swarmguide Tch'gok was giving birth. Infant Grdoch were squirming from a dozen of its mouths and floating out into the zero-G of the shipguide cabin, squalling.

Grdoch were hermaphroditic. Casual contacts with other members of the species left each adult with a growing collection of donor cells saved as encapsulated packets under the skin inside their mouths, and with time those cells gradually migrated deeper into the organism, becoming sperm cells as they did so and eventually fertilizing the Grdoch's egg clusters within the mesothelial layers. The young—as big as a human head and looking like smaller, flatter, smoother-skinned versions of their parents, remained inside the parent, sometimes for years, until an external crisis stimulated their expulsion into the environment.

Grdoch young on the home planet emerged from any convenient mouth-snout, dropped to the ground, and scuttled off. The concept of *parenting* was alien to the Grdoch; infants were mindless animals to be ignored—even eaten—until they'd learned to survive on their own. After several years of growth, the survivors were rounded up and the training began. Within Grdoch society, there was far more emphasis on the *swarm*, the Grdoch collective societal group, than on any purely incidental ideas like parent. Biology and genetics were understood and accepted . . . but which Grdoch in the swarm might be your offspring—or your parent—was unimportant.

The birth process was a mild annoyance, especially on board ship, where the young were periodically culled to prevent them from adversely affecting shipboard operations. It was especially annoying in that adult Grdoch tended to give birth—often shedding hundreds of infants at a time—whenever acute danger threatened the individual. The biological imperative was well understood; as Grdoch evolved side by side with the nightmarish *tch'tch'tch*, their reproductive rhythms had developed to give them the best possible chance of passing on their DNA. Besides, if you were fleeing through a swamp with a monstrous *tch'tch'tch* splashing close on your wake, a few hundred chirping babies might confuse the predator—or at least distract it enough to slow it down.

But that had been on Gr'tch'gah, the Swarmworld of millions of *gretch* past, not the control center of a modern interstellar warship. Here, the things were a nuisance at worst, a light snack at best.

Tch'gok felt one wiggling up into one of its snouts and held it fast, using its rasping teeth to peel the thing open, then sucking the juices in a pensive way. The danger, it knew, was extremely bad. The two Grdoch ships were outnumbered to the point where even their self-evidently superior technology was not enough to overcome the enemy. Worse, that enemy had not fled when *Swift Slasher* had charged them earlier; both the enemy's fighters and the larger ships had exhibited an almost suicidal persistence in bearing in close to slam missiles into the Grdoch vessels, behavior that the Grdoch found difficult to understand. When you faced obviously superior strength, you *rolled* . . . fast. No other tactic made sense.

But that demonstration of superiority hadn't deterred the enemy in the least, and the tactical balance had suddenly shifted from that of predator to prey. The maneuver had separated the *Swift Slasher* from the *Blood Drinker* to such a degree that they could no longer support each other in proper swarm fashion. Worse, when *Swift Slasher* had become immobilized in planetary orbit, *Blood Drinker* had fled, putting yet more distance between the two.

And now, *Blood Drinker* was dying out there in a blaze of thermonuclear detonations, a food beast beset by a ravenous swarm of hunters.

It released the crumpled, emptied husk of the infant and opened one of its wired-in internal communications channels. "Shiphealth!" it demanded. "What is our status?"

"Seventy percent, Swarmguide!" was the response. It could hear the chirp and yelp of infants over the connection, a sure sign of the rising stress levels throughout the ship.

Tch'gok studied nearby space . . . taking note of a small

squadron of enemy vessels now approaching planetary orbit. From its study of human military technology, it could identify the various types—a railgun cruiser, several cruisers, destroyers, and frigates . . . plus six of the human star carriers, two large, four small. Those carriers were especially dangerous, since they carried swarms of human fighters . . . and those fighters had already demonstrated how deadly they could be, even to the far vaster and more powerful Grdoch hunters. It had been one of those fighters that had crippled the *Swift Slayer*, firing from almost point-blank range.

This was . . . an opportunity.

The small squadron most likely was planning on launching an assault against Grdoch forces still on the planet below . . . probably in the form of a fighter assault from those carriers. Human military philosophy, Tch'gok had noted, was quite different from that of the Grdoch. They seemed to have warships with differing capabilities—and not all human ships carried fighters. In fact, only specific, quite large vessels—what the humans called *star carriers*—could launch and recover fighters. For the Grdoch, every vessel carried out every function, with no differentiation between ship types, though some were larger, some smaller. In fact, the species didn't even distinguish between military and civilian vessels; *every* Grdoch starship could fight, and transport cargo or colonists, and explore new worlds . . . whatever was necessary at the time.

The Grdoch had carefully studied the species that called itself "human" during their brief alliance with the weird little prey-creatures. They were truly alien in how they thought and acted; an entire population seriously outnumbering a few Grdoch could seemingly be paralyzed by indecision or by fear, could actually recoil from an attack from strength . . . while on the planet's surface, unarmed gangs had attempted to attack Grdoch foodkeepers or even whole feedingswarms against literally hopeless odds.

Why the aliens thought like that was as yet unknown. Tch'gok had no doubt that captive members of the species would be carefully studied in order to determine what stressors affected them, and how. For now, all it and its fellows could do was take advantage of any opportunity the enemy's irrational behavior afforded. A sudden, belly-slashing attack against those alien star carriers *before* they launched their fighters would cripple that part of the human fleet attempting now to retake their planet before the main body of their fleet could finish with the *Blood Drinker* and return to face *Swift Slayer*.

By the time they made it back here, *Swift Slayer* would have destroyed the six enemy carriers and be long gone.

At this point, the chief goal was no longer defeating the human presence in this system, but a return to the swarmworld, to Gr't'och, with a warning of human capabilities . . . and weaknesses. Human irrationality in combat could be exploited. With a major push into this sector of space—a few threes-of-threes-of-threes-of-threes of ships—the human empire could be smashed, and its colony worlds converted into vast hunting and feeding preserves. According to the reports Tch'gok had seen from the planet's surface, humans were not nearly as satisfying in the kill as were *gorchit*—the gene-engineered food beasts designed to serve as both long-term nourishment and as amusement . . . nor were they as nourishing. The pathetic things tended to die almost immediately, despite every attempt to keep them alive and pleasantly kicking.

The good news, though, was that the things were so numerous. A single one of their colony worlds would feed many 3^5 of Grdoch for many, many *gretch*, and it might eventually be possible to make them breed in order to replenish the stock. How many more there might be running around on their homeworld, wherever that might be, was unknown . . . but likely numbered in the billions. Grdoch history had been plagued by cycles of famine as food sources ran low, which was why they bred and kept *gorchit* now. Humans might, ultimately, prove to be an even more reliable protein source than the great food beasts.

They would never be as much sheer *fun* as the *gorchit* of course . . . but this was all about the one absolute of existence . . .

Survival.

Chapter Twenty

Vulcan
40 Eridani A System
1445 hours, TFT

Connor's Starhawk banked sharply enough that she felt a catch in her breath. What the hell was going on out there? She still had no visual, but her AI was telling her—as a sequence of impressions and ideas—that it had spotted a large population center to the north, just outside the planet's capital city of Himmel-Paradisio.

There were no signs of planetary defenses or military sensor systems. Her fighter was going to attempt to land there.

The AI was also able to let her know that it had detected several USNA warships—including the Marine transport-carrier *Inchon*—approaching the planet, and that it was now in communication with shipboard AIs. Her fighter's commo suite had been damaged, but the AI had been shifting nanomatrix assets from the damage control reserves to the electronics suite, and had been able to at least partially restore communications.

I wouldn't be long, the AI suggested, until she could be rescued . . .

. . . *if* she wasn't killed by hostile colonists or Grdoch as soon as she touched down.

USNA CVS America
40 Eridani A System
1450 hours, TFT

The procession of six star carriers drifted toward the planet, their fighter screens deployed, the smaller frigates and destroyers in the squadron out ahead of the main body. The two largest—*America* and *Constitution*—trailed the other, smaller carriers, shielded in part by their point defenses and fighter screens.

"What's the status on that hulk?" Gray asked, looking at the alien vessel's magnified image coming through from the battlespace drones in close to the planet. On the overhead display, it appeared to be drifting, powerless and inert . . . charred in places by nearby thermonuclear detonations. There'd been no sign of life there since the main USNA force had swept past the world, pursuing the second Grdoch ship. One of *America*'s fighters had gotten in pretty close with a pair of Fer-de-lance shipkillers, and a couple of megatons of thermonuclear blast at very close quarters apparently had burned the alien out. And yet . . .

"Admiral Gray!" It was Gutierrez. "Our sensors are picking up power readings from the derelict! Ten to the twelve . . . and climbing damned fast!"

Gray checked his own readout, and swore softly. The Grdoch ship was coming to life.

"Hit him! Hit him *hard*!"

The enemy vessel was still at fairly long range—almost a 100,000 kilometers—and it would take time to reach it with a missile volley. The Grdoch ship, as though aware that the human ships had spotted it and knew it to be alive, rotated suddenly, then leaped out from the planet . . . a predator striking.

Missiles streaked from the human fleet, accelerating hard across the intervening kilometers, but powerful, coherent X-ray beams were already slashing through the carrier battlegroup, scoring hits, wreaking terrible damage.

The *Shiva* was hit first, her shield cap taking the full brunt of an X-ray laser bolt, her water storage tank flashing to a vast and fast-moving cloud of steam that almost instantly froze into sand-sized crystals of ice as it hit hard vacuum. The *Saratoga* was hit an instant later, followed by the heavy cruiser *Calgary* and the destroyer *Sandoval*.

"All ships! Spread out! Don't bunch up!" Shit, shit, *shit*! . . .

The combat tactics for carrier battlegroups were still similar in most respects to those developed in the era of wet navies four centuries before. The modern carrier task force was the direct descendent of the Imperial Japanese navy's *Kido Butai*, in World War II, a six-carrier task force assembled for the express purpose of attacking Pearl Harbor. Until later in the war, the U.S. Navy had tended to use single carriers with associated escorts, combining several groups as needed for special operations. Ultimately, the term *battlegroup* was dropped in favor of carrier strike group, or CSG . . . but the term *carrier battlegroup* had come back into vogue with the Sh'daar Ultimatum and the development of star carriers.

The modern battlegroup was generally centered around one or perhaps two star carriers, together with cruisers, destroyers, and frigates as close-support vessels deployed in support of their larger companions. Larger ships—battleships, monitors, and railgun vessels for planetary bombardments, might be included for specialized operations.

Task Force Eridani was unusual, though, composed as it was of six carriers, and Gray was uncomfortably aware of just how vulnerable those carriers were. He'd ordered them away from the close assault on Target Bravo . . . and now risked losing them to the unexpected resurgence of Target Alfa.

HQMILCOM had never explained just why they'd sent so many carriers with the task force . . . but Gray suspected there was a reason—a blatantly political one. Shiva and Slava both represented new USNA allies as they closed ranks against the Confederation, in particular against the Europeans. And having four USNA carriers in the fleet drove home the fact that it was the North Americans who were leading this new alliance. Six carriers, he thought, might also be an attempt to overawe the Grdoch.

But Gray knew how thinly stretched the USNA naval forces were. He'd blundered by not making certain that Target Alfa had been destroyed . . . and that blunder just put the entire battegroup, the mission, and the United States of North America itself at considerable risk.

The railgun cruiser *Decatur* began slamming high-velocity rounds into the Grdoch ship. On the flag-bridge display, Gray could see the hits as a brilliant flashes, as hot as the surface of the sun, and as each explosion cleared it left a crater in the alien's scarlet hull.

That hull possessed a remarkable ability to heal itself. As Gray watched, the craters slowly puckered shut and sealed over . . . but *Decatur* continued her relentless and savage bombardment, pounding the Grdoch ship's prow again and again, until super-heated fragments began spilling off into space.

Missiles began striking home as well, and that took a lot of pressure off the carrier group. The *Constitution* took a hit from an X-ray laser—a near miss that damaged her shield cap in a spray of ice particles—but then the Grdoch began concentrating instead on the nuclear warheads swarming in from every side.

Grdoch fighters now were passing though the USNA fighter screen, and nuclear detonations flashed silently in the empty gulf between the adversaries.

"Get *America*'s railguns in action," Gray quietly ordered. The twin spinal-mount launch rails emerged at the center of the carrier's shield cap, and were used to accelerate fighters two at a time, but now they began slamming one-ton lumps of depleted uranium into the enemy ship, adding their kinetic fireworks to those of the *Decatur*.

"Carriers! Break off! Escorts forward . . ."

The combat display showed schematics of the various ships' paths, the USNA task force breaking apart as the carriers decelerated and the escorting destroyers, frigates, and fighters sprinted ahead. Nuclear fireballs engulfed the alien . . . and then the enemy fire ceased, cut off as if by a switch.

But Gray didn't want to be caught short again. "Fighters! Get in close and finish him!"

"We have more enemy fighters coming up from the planet, Admiral," Mallory reported. "But . . . but it looks like they're trying to get away."

It was true. The Grdoch fighters were accelerating hard, slipping clear of Vulcan's atmosphere and scattering into darkness. So far as anyone in the task force knew, those fighters could not manage faster-than-light travel, but needed to be on board one of the larger vessels, like fighters aboard a carrier. With both of their carriers destroyed, the rational choice for them was surrender, not flight.

The Grdoch, Gray thought, seemed to exhibit markedly black-and-white thinking—either fight like hell or run like hell . . . with no reasonable middle ground.

Maybe it was just as well that they were willing to either fight to the death or perish alone in the cold emptiness of the system's outer reaches. Communication—*talking* to those creatures—would be a real problem.

There was a final, terrible flash of radiance, and an expanding sphere of star-hot plasma.

Target Alfa, he saw, was breaking up.

Vulcan
40 Eridani A System
1527 hours, TFT

Connor's crippled fighter had slowed to 100 kph, continuing to drop toward the unseen terrain below. The waiting was unbearable . . . a drop into darkness with no reassurance at all save for the unworded assurances passed into her consciousness by her AI. She could feel the fighter's nose coming up slightly . . . feel morphed-out wings biting the air to slow her speed . . .

She felt the AI telling her that they were about to hit . . . and then the fighter lurched hard, shuddering as its keel dragged across hard-packed ground. The craft's nanomatrix hull shifted and adapted to each shock, dispersing and absorbing the force of the impact, but it was still a damned rough landing. The grinding and jolting of the touch-down went on for long seconds, and then the Starhawk came to a halt, cocked at a 45 degree angle to starboard.

Connor felt a surge of panic . . . and a mental flashback to the Slan dragging her from her fighter inside the darkness of a Slan warship orbiting 36 Ophiuchi A III just four months before. "Open!" she snapped. She was *not* going to wait helplessly in the dark this time. "Get me out of here!"

The cockpit rippled, then flowed open, revealing the cloudless dome of a brilliant green-tinted sky filled with brilliant orange sunlight. She thoughtclicked the icons releasing her from her seat and stood up shakily, reaching out to steady herself on the side of the cockpit. The landscape surrounding her looked almost indistinguishable from the middle latitudes of Earth . . . somewhere in New York or Pennsylvania, perhaps. The gravity felt about the same as Earth's . . . and briefing downloads had told her that the air was breathable, a rarity among the millions of worlds known to Humankind. She wasn't going to remove her e-suit helmet, though, not just yet. There might be local pathogens against which local humans had been immunized, but for which she had no natural defense.

There were trees—odd-looking with feathery tips, but still definitely the local evolutionary equivalent of trees, with compound leaves that tended to be more orange and yellow than green. The fighter had come down in a broad, open meadow blanketed by an orange, mosslike ground cover. A broad slash through the moss stretching astern showed where her AI had guided the crippled ship in for its landing.

She heard a shout, and turned. People were approaching . . . humans . . . *naked* humans, quite a few of them. What the hell . . . ?

Human society long ago had embraced casual social nudity as an acceptable lifestyle, losing the age-old taboos against appearing in public without clothing save for protection against the environment, but the human urge toward self-adornment and decoration was not so easily lost. These people were filthy, ragged, and unkempt, caked with dried mud or dirt. Some wore scraps of clothing; a few wore the ragged remnants of uniforms or casual dress, but most wore nothing at all. Some carried sticks fashioned into crude clubs or spears with crudely sharpened points. None that she could see possessed any bodily adornment—animated tattoos or light-projecting jewelry or holographics.

She pulled her hand laser, thumbed the charge touchpoint, and felt the reassuring vibration in the grip that told her it was fully charged and ready. The last she'd heard, the German and Latino colonists of Vulcan were the enemy . . . but there'd been scuttlebutt that the Grdoch had turned against their former allies. Looking at them, she suspected that the scuttlebutt had been entirely correct, but she wasn't going to lower her guard until she *knew*. . . .

"*Ayudarnos!*" one man yelled to her when he saw her weapon.

"*Ja!*" a woman cried. "*Gefallen! Helfen Sie uns!*"

"Translate," Connor told her implant. "Continuous and two-way . . ."

"Help us!"

Software residing within Connor's in-head circuitry could translate a dozen common human languages with fair fluency. Her personal secretary could speak those languages using her e-suit's external speakers, if the locals' translation software wasn't in place.

"I'm Lieutenant Connor, USNA Navy," she told them, and she hard the closely echoed words of her secretary repeating her words both in Spanish and in German. "What the hell is going on here?"

A multilingual babble momentarily swamped her translator's microcircuits.

"Hold it . . . *hold it*!" she called. "Who's in charge here?"

The mob came to a ragged, milling halt perhaps five meters away from Connor's ship, and a portly, pale-skinned man with a bushy mustache came a few steps closer. "Lieutenant, thank God you have come! I am Governor Immanuel Delgado. I—I suppose *I* am the chief. . . ."

Connor stepped out of her cockpit, but she didn't lower her weapon, not yet. "You're prisoners?" It was a guess, but the only guess she could think of that made sense. A planetary governor, out *here*? Naked and dirty and looking like he'd been through six kinds of hell?

He nodded. "The Grdoch . . . attacked us. Maybe two weeks ago. They killed . . . *millions*. . . ."

"Lieutenant?" a woman's voice added, and it was in English. "I'm Commander Fuentes, of the *Intrepid*."

Perhaps, she thought after the fact, she should have come to attention . . . but for the moment Connor could only stare as the woman emerged from the crowd. Slowly, she lowered her weapon, then holstered it. "My God, Commander! What have they *done* to you?"

"Put us on the fucking menu, Lieutenant. How badly damaged is your ship?"

"Yes!" Delgado added, excited. "Can you call in your fleet?"

"The comm took some damage," Connor replied. "But we can at least signal through the fighter AI. It managed to get in touch with other ship AIs on the way down."

"What's going on up there, anyway?" Fuentes asked. "You're USNA, so that means a task force must have arrived in-system."

Connor nodded. "*America* . . . with five other carriers, including squadrons from the Russians and the North Indians."

"A united fleet!"

"Yes, ma'am. We were engaging two Grdoch warships. One of them . . . one knocked my Starhawk out, but it was still able to get me down safely. But I was in the first wave, and I couldn't see outside my fighter. So I don't know who won. . . ."

The realization tore at Connor. The fog of war was always a factor in combat, though battlespace drones and advanced electronics had gone a long way to banishing that ancient battlefield curse. To be this blind, utterly unaware of which side was winning, made her feel both helpless and uncomfortably vulnerable.

A new realization occurred to her. "Wait a minute. You're prisoners. Are you telling me I managed to land *inside* a POW camp?"

The coincidence of coming down by sheer chance in such a confined space with a whole planetary surface to choose from struck Connor as absurd.

But then she remembered her orders to the AI: to find a human population center outside one of the major cities, and away from any buildup of military forces. If the Vulcan cities all had been emptied by the Grdoch, or turned into heavily defended bases . . .

"It's a large camp or holding area, yes, Lieutenant," Delgado told her. "They grew a fence around a couple of hundred hectares . . . maybe a little more."

Two square kilometers, more or less. "That's pretty big for a prison camp."

"It's pretty small for a hunting preserve," Fuentes said, bitter.

"Damn! The Grdoch *hunt* you in here?"

"They are . . . *demons*," Delgado told her. "Monsters from the pit of hell! The horror is . . . it is indescribable."

"Well . . . our people are on the way," Connor told them. "Our orders were to find out what happened to the *Intrepid*, and we have a Marine transport with us."

"Thank God!"

"Let me see if we can get through to somebody up there," Connor added.

She thoughtclicked a link to her AI. "I need communications with the fleet," she said in her mind. "Any ship. I need it *now*!"

She felt the artificial intelligence's acknowledgement. She had the impression that several ships were close—within a few hundred kilometers . . . but that a battle was still going on above their heads. She felt the connection going through . . . felt her AI whispering to her in her mind.

Connor repeated what she heard to the waiting crowd of prisoners. "It sounds like our people are still establishing local space superiority," she said. "But my AI is in touch with at least one ship . . . I think it's the *Inchon*, the Marine ship I mentioned. And it says they're on the way."

"How long?" Delgado asked.

"I don't know, sir. They'll need to establish clear airspace superiority first."

Absolutely basic to any attempt to land troops on a planet was the control of nearby space, especially low orbit. A planetary assault team was already seriously outnumbered by the presumably hostile population, and the situation became far worse if orbiting warships could take potshots at grounded ships, armored vehicles, heavy weapons, planetary fortresses, and concentrations of troops.

The literature of military tactics since the very earliest days of warfare extolled the need to take and hold the high ground. In space combat, "high ground" translated as farther up the gravity well. Troops and weapons at the bottom of that well—meaning on the planet's surface—were at a terrible disadvantage when facing an enemy in orbit. Which, after all, was the better position in terms of energy . . . to be at the bottom of a literal well throwing rocks up . . . or standing up at the top of the shaft and dropping them?

There was a commotion across the meadow . . . people screaming and running.

"Oh, God!" Fuentes said, closing her eyes. "Not again!"

"What is it?"

"Feeding time," Delgado said. "For the demons, not for us."

"No," Fuentes said, staring past the running crowd. "They're armed this time. I think they're coming to investigate the Lieutenant's landing."

Of course the fighter's descent would have been tracked, both by ground bases and from space, and the Grdoch would have immediately pinpointed its landing coordinates.

Connor could see three of the monsters now . . . baggy spheres each over two meters across, bright scarlet in color, with three splay-clawed legs and rubbery bodies covered with appendages ranging from blunt snouts to stubby trunks, some half a meter long. The three each held a technical device of some sort in a snout, gripping it as though by suction. Were those scanners of some sort, or weapons? Connor did not intend to wait to find out.

"Scatter!" she told the others. "I'll take care of these three!"

Moving quickly, she ducked down behind the wreck of her Starhawk. "AI! Do we have *any* weapons capability left?"

She felt the computer's negative resonse. If she'd had a

working high-energy laser or particle beam, and the means to aim it, she would have been a lot happier with her chances. As it was . . .

Crouching behind the fighter's fuselage, she raised herself high enough to peer past the open cockpit. The three were coming straight toward her, about a hundred meters away. Bringing up her laser weapon, she braced her arms on the cockpit rim, held the weapon in a two-handed grip, and squeezed the firing stud.

The beam was invisible in the bright sunlight, but half a million Joules of energy concentrated in a spot the size of a thumb print ruptured one being's integument and released a spray of internal fluids. The Grdoch keened, a high, warbling chitter like a bird call, and dropped the device it was carrying.

Immediately, the other two Grdoch brought their devices around, and a pair of savage explosions slammed at the other side of the fighter. Weapons, then. Connor doubted very much that they were X-ray lasers like those carried on their warships. It took a great deal of energy to generate an X-ray pulse. The earliest human experiments on those lines had required the detonation of a small nuclear device. She didn't know what these mouth-held weapons were firing at her, but they obviously were deadly and quite powerful.

Shifting aim, Connor fired again, and a second Grdoch rolled to the side, its weapon dropping to the ground. But the first Grdoch, she saw with dawning horror, had just picked up its weapon and was rolling rapidly toward her once again.

The little xenosoph data she'd seen on the Grdoch in her most recent briefing suggested that they had massive biological redundancy, with duplicated organs and a broadly distributed nervous system. There was no way to score a head shot on these things because they quite literally did not have brains, or, rather . . . they did their thinking with their entire bodies.

Another pair of explosions roared a couple of meters in front of her, the shock slamming her backward. Gods, what were those things loaded with?

Pulling herself up once more, she thumbed her weapon to continuous beam, took aim and fired, holding the stud down to send a steady stream of coherent energy downrange. It struck one creature, and as the thing rolled forward, the beam peeled it open like the unsealing of a dress uniform jacket.

Shifting aim again, she used a steady beam on one of the others. Her Mk. VII Solbeam, she knew, wouldn't take this kind of abuse for long. The weapons were designed to fire short pulses of coherent light, not steady beams. She would exhaust the battery in seconds if she kept using the weapon with such a profligate disregard for its design spec tolerances.

A Grdoch beam crackled just above the top of Connor's helmet and she reflexively ducked. Close! She started to take aim again . . .

. . . and an explosion on the fighter's dorsal surface just in front of the cockpit sent a shockwave that slapped against her head and chest, scooping out a hallow gash in the hull nanomatrix that glowed red hot for a moment until the heat dissipated.

The Grdoch, all three of them, continued to advance . . . more slowly, now, more cautiously, but they continued moving forward, closing on Connor's position relentlessly and with a terrifying single-mindedness of purpose. One of the aliens appeared to be terribly wounded, with a deep slice girdling half its circumference leaving a trail of orange-scarlet blood behind it.

Surely, *surely* the thing would bleed out soon, and die!

Her Solbeam laser pistol buzzed in her grip, three quick pulses warning that the battery was failing, and connection patches in the palms of her glove sent data to her in-head. She had only a couple of seconds of beam left . . . and the pistol's grip was so hot now she could feel it through her e-suit glove. It was overheating so badly that once it failed it would probably not be rechargeable.

But she was committed, with no way to turn back. She aimed at the nearest of the Grdoch attackers and mashed down the firing stud, holding it down as the beam carved through alien flesh . . .

. . . and the aliens wavered, as though undecided; then they started rolling backward, away from her. Damn it, she was *winning*! But then her weapon gave a final vibrational warning as the beam failed.

The three wounded Grdoch stopped their retreat, hesitated as though consulting with one another, and then renewed their advance, rolling directly toward Connor's position, weapons held ready. . . .

Grdoch Huntership Swift Slayer
Vulcan Space
1550 hours, TFT

Swarmguide Tch'gok drifted in the microgravity wreckage of *Swift Slayer*'s command center. A fire burned at a ruptured oxygen line on one bulkhead, showing the peculiar spherical haze and heat of a flame in zero-G. Fiber-optic feeds from different parts of the compartment continued to give him images of *Swift Slayer*'s surroundings and updates on the ship's status. The ship, Tch'gok knew, was finished.

It still had enough life left, however, for one final, slashing attack. The prey fleet was entering orbit, oblivious to the threat drifting in space just a few thousand kilometers distant.

The Swarmguide gave an order. . . .

Chapter Twenty-one

USNA CVS America
40 Eridani A System
1550 hours, TFT

"Colonel Engelmann, you may deploy your Marines."

"Aye, aye, sir. We're on the way down."

Victor Engelmann was the commander of the Fifth Marine Planetary Assault Regiment, an old-school Marine who'd skippered his first platoon two decades before, at Arcturus Station. The 1/5—5th Regiment of the 1st Battalion, 1st USNA Marines—consisted of about nine hundred Marines and naval personnel currently embarked on board the *Inchon*.

On the flag-bridge display, *Inchon* had positioned herself with her shield cap toward the planet below, as her landing bays morphed open in her flanks and four blunt, black landing craft emerged.

They were UC-154 Choctaws, Marine shuttle transports each capable of carrying about two hundred personnel. Their 80-meter hulls dead black, each had white, red, and green navigational lights strobing at bow, sides, top, and bottom. A number of Nightshade grav-assault gunships had already deployed in a cloud about the *Inchon*, looking like black wasps as they began to drift past *Inchon*'s shield cap and toward the blue-haze curve of the planet.

The space part of the battle appeared to be pretty much over. The carriers' fighter CAPs continued to engage Grdoch fighters as they found them—usually as they clawed their way up out of Vulcan's gravity well toward orbit.

"Admiral Gray," *America*'s AI said, speaking in his thoughts. "There has been contact with the planet's surface."

"What kind of contact?"

"From an AI. Specifically, from the AI on board a Star-hawk fighter from VFA-96. Lieutenant Megan Connor."

"I remember her—36 Oph. The Slan contact."

"Yes, Admiral. She may have been instrumental in dis-abling Target Alfa, but her Starhawk was badly damaged in the engagement. She has managed a crash landing near the Vulcan planetary capital."

"Do you have voice or vid?"

"No, Admiral. Only thought-messages passed on through her AI. Her communications suite appears to be inoperable. However, she was able to inform us that she has located a prison camp in an enclosed area southwest of Himmel-Paradisio . . . and that members of *Intrepid*'s officers and crew are interned there."

"Very well."

He wished they had a clear communications channel open to the surface. Gray would have liked it if he could have had a live eyewitness to what was going on down there. But the mental communication the AI was describing was one of impressions and feelings, not hard data. It was an artifact, actually, of the in-head displays and circuitry naval personnel used to interface with their computers. AIs were notoriously inefficient at talking to flesh-and-blood humans through telepathic suggestion or impression, as opposed to the hard data of a vid download.

Ship minds tended to be a bit narrow-minded in their in-

terpretation of events and of orders. Since a primary point
of Task Force Eridani's orders was to locate survivors from
the *Intrepid* squadron, Lieutenant Connor's report would
have been marked for immediate release to the task force
CO and flagged as urgent. In fact, though, there wasn't a
hell of a lot Gray could do about the report just now. The 1/5
Marines were on their way to assault Himmel-Paradisio . . .
but only because that was the location of what appeared to
be the main Grdoch planetary defense fortress on the planet.
It made sense that their principal command-control installa-
tion would be near the colonial capital . . . and seizing that
would be the priority for the Marines trying to capture the
planet.

The rescue of any POWs down there would have to wait.

In his mind, Gray called up an enhanced view of the
shattered alien vessel, Target Alfa. The ship was literally
in pieces now, tumbling hundred-meter chunks imbedded
in an expanding cloud of intensely radioactive debris, hot
plasma, and freezing vapor 2,000 kilometers distant. The
Grdoch warship was definitely dead, but . . . something was
gnawing at him. . . .

"Tactical," he said. "Put some extra battlespace drones
inside that wreckage. I want those larger fragments probed
and analyzed."

"Right away, Admiral," Dean Mallory's voice replied.
"What are you thinking, sir?"

"That Grdoch fight when they have clear superiority, that
they run away when they don't . . . but that they appear to
fight like trapped rats if they can't run. And . . ."

"Sir?"

"They have an astonishing ability to use backups, parallel systems, and massive redundancy, *and* they're at least as
good at nanotechnics as we are, and very probably better."

"I've tagged six drones, sir. They're entering the cloud
now."

Gray had been caught by surprise by what had appeared

to be a dead Grdoch ship already. He didn't intend to be caught out again.

"Order *Ramirez*, *Maine*, and *Young* to move in closer to the wreckage. Use extreme caution . . . and burn anything that even smells like trouble."

"Aye, aye, sir."

The rest of the task force had been returning to Vulcan over the past few minutes, slipping into orbit as they took up skywatch stations. The last of the enemy fighters, Gray saw, had scattered into the outer system . . . most headed in the general direction of 40 Eridani B and C, the pair of close, bright stars, one red, one diamond-white, some 400 AUs off. They would track them down in due time. Right now, the priority was to clear Vulcan's orbital lanes . . . and seize control of the planet.

Several minutes dragged past.

"Sir!" Dean's mental voice was shrill. "We've got a power buildup inside the debris field!"

"Take it out."

But in the next instant, a tightly focused X-ray laser seared through *America*'s aft hull, vaporizing the containment array for her power taps and plunging the vessel into darkness.

Gray felt the shudder, then a sudden tug of centrifugal acceleration as the star carrier went into a wild and uncontrolled tumble.

He felt the harsh, sunburn tingle of hard radiation searing his skin, his body, and knew that *America* was dying. . . .

VFA-96, Black Demons
Vulcan Orbit
1554 hours, TFT

Lieutenant Don Gregory was less than 10 kilometers away from *America* and directly off her stern when she was hit.

He'd been on final approach for a trap—a recovery in one of the carrier's rotating hangar bays—when the X-ray beam had snapped out from what appeared to be dead and drifting wreckage nearly 2,000 kilometers away. A dazzling flash had engulfed the aft portion of the carrier, throwing off spinning chunks of debris. Worse, his sensors picked up a surge of gamma radiation from the stricken vessel—a sure sign that her power taps had been compromised, and the microsingularities encased within her power plant had just gone rogue.

Star carriers, like most interstellar vessels, consisted of a forward shield cap, like the canopy of an umbrella, with a long and slender spine stretching aft. The shield's toroidal rim mounted the grav projectors for the ship's Alcubierre Drive, while in the spine, forward, tucked within the shadow of the shield cap, were the rotating hab modules and hangar decks and crew areas, as well as the zero-gravity sections like the bridge and stores modules. Aft were the primary grav and power field generators and, at the extreme aft end, the containment modules for the quantum power tap.

Starships required a staggering amount of energy to create the Alcubierre warp bubble that let them—or, more precisely, let the metaspace within which they were imbedded—slide through normal space at faster-than-light speeds. The original computations had suggested that the total annihilation of a mass equivalent to the planet Jupiter would be necessary for that kind of warp. Later refinements had reduced this mass significantly . . . but travel between the stars still required enormous energies, energies summoned from the mystery of empty space itself.

America, like most starships, used helium-3 fusion plants to generate enough power to create paired microsingularities: two black holes, each the size of a proton, orbiting each other within a Higgs containment field at close to the speed of light. Those singularities served to extract vacuum energy—the unimaginably vast amounts of virtual energy resident within so-called empty space. One early set of calculations back in the twentieth century had suggested that a volume of space the size of an old-fashioned incandescent lightbulb contained energy enough to instantly vaporize all of the oceans of Earth. Later calculations had proven that this was wrong . . . that the actual energies were greater.

Much, *much* greater . . .

Great enough, perhaps, to annihilate not only the planet's oceans, but the rest of the entire galaxy as well.

Current quantum power tap technology could not summon *that* kind of energy out of hard vacuum, but it did allow a starship to turn local space into a pretzel, to manipulate gravity, and to rewrite the laws of physics, at least on a temporary and strictly local level.

It also meant that several microsingularities purred away inside each starship's power tap module. When *America* was hit by the X-ray laser, the Higgs containment fields went down, and several proton-sized black holes began eating their way through the ship.

In fact, a microsingularity was so tiny that it couldn't eat very fast and so posed little immediate danger to the ship. But as the containment fields went down, paired singularities began merging, a star's worth of vacuum energy poured in out of emptiness to feed them, and they began growing rapidly in a runaway cascade. Devouring more and more matter and energy as they swiftly ballooned larger, they continued to merge. *America* had two hundred singularity pairs in phased array—and as each black hole tried to gulp down more matter than it could absorb at once, excess matter became superheated, releasing a storm of X-ray and hard gamma radiation.

All of this Gregory was aware of in the first second or two as the flare of star-hot light and radiation engulfed the aft third of the stricken kilometer-long star carrier. He felt a surge of raw horror; that was *his ship* and *his shipmates*

. . . and they were dying, had, perhaps, only seconds more to live.

Less . . . if the Grdoch wreck managed to get off another shot. . . .

USNA CA Maine
Vulcan Orbit
1554 hours, TFT

"*America*'s been hit!"

Captain Catharine Francesconi had been totally focused on the fragments of the Grdoch ship, and the sudden flare of raw energy across the opposite hemisphere of her bridge's tactical display jolted her.

"My God," her tactical officer, continued, "she's *burning*! . . ."

Well . . . not *burning*, exactly, not in the vacuum of space . . . but *America*'s aft quarter was so hot that it was engulfed in an expanding sphere of radiant, white-hot plasma, with pieces of her spinal column breaking away, falling away, dissolving in the radiant heat.

"Sensors indicate the 'Doch is prepping for another shot! . . ."

"Helm! Acceleration! Put us between the Grdoch and the *America*! . . ."

The heavy cruiser slid forward, interposing herself. The Grdoch fragments were less than a hundred kilometers away, now, the broken *America* a thousand kilometers in the other direction.

Captain Francesconi was a career naval officer from a long and aristocratic line of naval officers. Like many such, she was a USNA Globalist, personally convinced that the war with the Confederation was a dangerous waste of lives and resources when aliens like the Sh'daar and, now, the Grdoch posed far, far deadlier threats to the survival of all humans. She didn't like Koenig and his Freedomist policies . . . and she didn't like Admiral Gray, a man she felt had been promoted beyond his abilities. Scuttlebutt held that the man was a *Prim*, for God's sake, straight out of the Manhat Ruins. Only the fact that he'd won some spectacular victories let her—grudgingly—accept him as her commanding officer.

Not that she'd really had any choice, of course. Her clear duty was to obey the lawful orders of the Task Force CO. Those orders did not require her to do what she was doing now . . . but it was vital to save the *America* and her command constellation, the men and women directing this operation.

The Grdoch fired again . . . targeting the carrier . . . but this time the *Maine* was in the way.

At the equivalent of point-blank range, the X-ray laser struck with the raw force of a burgeoning supernova. . . .

VFA-96, Black Demons
Vulcan Orbit
1554 hours, TFT

Lieutenant Gregory didn't notice the flare a thousand kilometers up-orbit as *Maine* intercepted another X-ray bolt, so focused was he on the badly damaged star carrier ahead. His Starhawk was down to an approach speed of under a kilometer per second. Moving toward the carrier's stern, he slowed further; as *America*'s singularity masses had shifted inside her spine and large chunks of her hull had been thrown into space, the entire ship had been kicked over into a slow tumble and Gregory no longer was aligned with the docking bay. That was just as well; *America*'s stern was engulfed in plasma, leaving a hot and glowing trail as it rotated. Gregory felt the shock as his fighter hit the cooling plasma then passed through it, the worst of the heat and radiation absorbed by his gravitic shielding. Had he hit that mess full on, though, he knew his fighter would not have survived.

He pivoted, pointing his bow at the ship and adjusting his vector to let him pass alongside. Matching speeds, he was close enough now that he could see the power tap module crumpling just a hundred meters in front of him under the savage, internal stresses of the rogue singularities.

Inside the carrier's crumpling spine, merging black holes had opened a floodgate of energy from the Void, a torrent that was feeding the singularities, making them grow, turning them into ravenous monsters intent on devouring the entire ship.

Damn it, he had to do *something*.

But at the moment he didn't have the slightest idea what that something might be.

Himmel-Paradisio Camp
Vulcan
40 Eridani A System
1554 hours, TFT

Connor brought her hand laser up and tried to fire it again. The weapon gave a weak flicker of energy—not enough, she thought—to light a candle—and then went inert. The three Grdoch, wounded and cautious, kept coming, rolling toward her slowly, spreading out across her line of sight, but closing on her position with a grim relentlessness.

She considered her options. She could run, which might buy her some time . . . but which might also result in some of the prisoners being hurt or killed if these monsters began firing indiscriminately. Or she could stand her ground . . . maybe try to wrestle one of those odd-looking weapons away from one of them and use that.

Or she could surrender.

None of those options particularly appealed to her. The

horror of her experience with the Slan four months earlier had her thinking she would rather die than submit to another alien interrogation. It was also possible, if Delgado and Commander Fuentes were to be believed, that they would simply devour her alive. It depended on whether the Grdoch thought she had useful information, most likely, and from the descriptions she had heard, it didn't sound like the Grdoch were interested in *anything* concerning humans, save dinner.

She pulled her survival knife from her sheath. It was a pathetic weapon against three of those rolling horrors—especially when they were carrying ranged weapons of some sort . . . but at least it was *something*. The question was how to use it effectively. She would have to get in close—so close that two of the Grdoch wouldn't fire their weapons for fear of hitting the third.

And that made her hesitate. Did the Grdoch even have that kind of sentiment among themselves? Obviously, they worked together . . . but they might be more than willing to sacrifice one of their number if it meant frying one rebellious prisoner.

Running might be the best choice after all.

Her decision was taken out of her hands.

She'd been so fixed on the approaching Grdoch that she hadn't noticed a group of human POWs off to her left, men and women clutching a variety of stakes, spears, and clubs, crouched low to the ground and advancing on the aliens from the flank. She saw them when they rose as a single body and charged, screaming something that might have been a battle cry, might have been nothing but mindless shrieks of rage.

How, Connor wondered, did you sneak up on a creature with eyes positioned all the way around its rotund body? The Grdoch to Connor's left saw the rush, and rolled to bring its weapon into line with this sudden, new threat. The mob of humans scattered from their tight cluster but kept charging;

the Grdoch weapon fired and several of the attackers shriveled, blackened, and smoked.

Connor couldn't stay there behind her fighter and watch the slaughter. Screaming a mindless shriek of her own, she vaulted the downed Starhawk and rushed at the oncoming Grdoch, brandishing her knife.

She went a little mad.

The Grdoch on the right saw her coming and fired its weapon. She felt the snap of superheated air as the beam seared past her . . . and then she launched herself in a headlong dive, arms outstretched, knife seeking scarlet flesh.

The crowd of humans hit the left-side Grdoch in the same instant, using six-foot poles sharpened at the tips, hardened in fire, as spears, thrusting them at the rubbery body. Now it was the alien's turn to shriek, a shrill, high-pitch chittering as one spear entered through a mouth-snout and penetrated deep inside.

Connor hit the Grdoch in the middle, which appeared to be unsure which threat was deadlier, which target to shoot. It was twisting back to bring its weapon to bear on Connor when she hit it full force, the knife in her right hand puncturing tough hide and sliding in, wet and hot. The hide, she found, was like leather or heavy rubber and the knife had nearly rebounded . . . but the survival blade carried a hardened, monoatomic nanocarb edge that could carve through steel and with Connor's full, airborn mass behind it, it punctured the hide and her arm slid into the thing's body up past her elbow.

For a horrid, queasy moment, Connor was pressed up against the thing full length, could feel its lashing, questing, *biting* snouts, each like the toothy business end of a terrestrial lamprey. Gripping the knife unseen, now, she twisted and slashed, trying to do as much internal damage as she could. She understood that the alien thing could take a hell of a lot of damage . . . but she *had* to be doing it serious harm.

One of the crooked, clawed legs descended on her, grasping her from behind, yanking her back, *shaking* her as a man might grab and shake a small and angry dog. Her arm slid from the gaping wound, bright orange-red and slippery now with blood.

A naked man rammed a spear against the creature, but the fire-hardened point failed to penetrate. A woman at his side tried the same, and this time the spear found a weak spot, one of the repulsive, writhing mouth-trunks, pushing past teeth and mouth cavity and plunging a meter into the thing's body.

It screamed, shuddered, and dropped Connor. The Grdoch hand weapon—no, *mouth* weapon—clattered onto the ground nearby. Hitting the ground hard, Connor dropped her knife, but managed to roll to her right and scoop up the alien weapon.

It was heavy, and not at all designed for a human hand. She hoped to hell there wasn't much of a learning curve with the thing. It was shaped something like an egg carton, with a fist-sized knob that the Grdoch held inside one of its mouths, a black orifice on the other end with something like an antenna emerging from within. Okay . . . easy enough to tell which end was which, and that was the most important thing to know about a strange weapon . . . that and how to actually fire the damned thing. Raising it, she pointed the antenna end at the Grdoch looming above her. The trigger . . . damn it, where was the *trigger*?

They fired the things with a mouth, so they must just bite down, must apply force to the knob somehow, must *squeeze* . . .

The alien had just grabbed the woman with the spear in one crooked arm and was lifting her high overhead.

She squeezed the smooth and rounded grip as hard as she could with both hands, aiming up at the Grdoch looming above her.

A portion of that thick hide directly in front of her blackened, curdled, then peeled itself open in a bloody crater. Softer tissue inside exploded in a wet, scarlet spray. The Grdoch dropped the woman it was holding and rolled backward, comical in its attempt to get clear. Maria Fuentes was there, standing on the heaving thing, plunging a spear into an eye. It bucked, throwing her aside.

"Watch out!"

The Grdoch snapped out one leg, its claws raking down across Maria Fuentes's torso. Fuentes screamed and Connor fired again into the writhing Grdoch, watched it shrivel . . . then shifted aim. The third Grdoch, apparently wanting no part of this mob assault from its dinner, was in full, rolling retreat.

Connor didn't want *any* of the things to get away. . . .

VFA-96, Black Demons
Vulcan Orbit
1555 hours, TFT

Lieutenant Gregory knew he was out of time. *America*'s stern was a crumbling, white-hot mass of dissolving hull structure and plasma, and the fast-rising radiation levels showed that the merging black holes inside were gulping down energy and matter alike and working their way forward, following the ship's internal mass.

He saw only one way to stop the disaster, and it was definitely a kill-or-cure treatment. Linking in with his AI, he armed his Starhawk's last remaining VG-10 Krait missile, locked on to *America*'s spinal column just forward of the dissolving power tap module, and thought-clicked the firing icon.

"Target lock-on failed," his AI told him. "The selected target is too—"

"Override! Lock on!"

His AI balked. "I require confirmation," its voice said in his mind. "The selected target is—"

"Confirmed! Override safeties! Fire!"

The missile slid clear of its launch bay, accelerating, ignoring the host of safeguards and cut-outs that prevented the VG-10 smart missile from targeting a friendly vessel . . . or detonating inside the kill zone of its warhead. At a range of just under 100 meters, the missile detonated almost immediately, a deadly blossoming of hot plasma and twisted, molten fragments of starship.

The VG-10 carried a simple fission warhead of about ten kilotons' yield . . . smaller than the devices that had annihilated the cities of Hiroshima and Nagasaki almost five centuries before. While it was true that the effects of a nuclear explosion were significantly reduced in vacuum, an explosion equivalent to the detonation of ten thousand tons of high explosive was still deadly at close range. While there was no way for a shock wave to be transmitted through hard vacuum, the expanding plasma fireball itself provided a shock-wave medium, a shell of hot, subatomic particles rushing out at high speed, swatting Gregory's fighter like a circling insect and sending it tumbling away.

Himmel-Paradisio Camp
Vulcan
40 Eridani A System
1556 hours, TFT

Connor fired the alien weapon again, holding it in a two-handed stance to steady its unfamiliar weight. The fleeing Grdoch twisted, shuddered, then slumped. Fifty more POWs swarmed toward it, picking up the weapon it had dropped, pinning it to the earth with sharpened poles.

The prisoners were streaming in from all over the compound, a few armed, most not, but the sudden battle had loosed a storm of emotion among some thousands of humans who, until that moment, had been beaten down and helpless. They were releasing that emotion now on the bodies of the Grdoch, and within a few moments, all three had literally been torn to shreds.

Connor was at Maria Fuentes's side. "Commander! Are you okay? . . ."

"It . . . hurts . . ."

Fuentes was bleeding, bleeding badly, a deep incision slicing her from throat to stomach. Connor tried to stop the bleeding, but she had nothing with which to work, no nano-hemostatin, no skin sealant, not even something she could use as a bandage. In moments, Fuentes was gone.

Delgado was beside her. "We tried attacking them before," he said. He was panting, his eyes wild, and both of his arms were slick with scarlet blood. "Always, they were too tough, their hides too tough, for us to get anywhere. But you injured them enough . . ."

"Not soon enough, Governor. Not soon enough for *her*."

He shook his head. "I'm sorry for your friend."

In fact, Connor had never known Maria Fuentes, a woman who, after all, was the exec of a different ship. But finding her *here*, on a hostile world, had been like finding a long-lost friend, a *sister*. . . .

And now that sister was lost again.

"I'm just glad we were able to bring them down together," Connor said. Standing again, she hefted the captured weapon in one hand. She wasn't sure what kind of weapon it was, but strongly suspected that it was some kind of maser, a laser using microwaves that could cook a target at a distance. Heat something fast enough and it would explode, like the chunks out of the fuselage of her Starhawk. Aim it at flesh and it cooked. Nasty . . .

What kind of power supply did it have? She had neither the tools nor the time to find out . . . and the weapon was far more valuable to them now intact than it would be in pieces.

"We need to get out of here," she told Delgado. "Out of this . . . this prison."

"I agree. But how?"

"Follow me. Get everyone together, everyone, and *follow me*. . . ."

Chapter Twenty-two

USNA CVS America
40 Eridani A System
1557 hours, TFT

The second shock was savage and violent, strong enough
to convince Gray that *America* had just been shot a second
time. He tried several channels, looking for an open comm
line, but there was nothing . . . *nothing*. . . .

Knocked from his command chair, Gray was flounder-
ing about in midair, almost weightless and lost in complete
and absolute darkness. Clearly, *America*'s power plants had
been knocked out, and the damage was pretty bad because
the automatic backups hadn't immediately come on-line. He
couldn't reach the ship's AI, either, or get in touch with any
of the other parts of the ship.

"Who else is in here?" he called into the darkness. "Is
everyone okay?"

Ten men and women had been with him on the flag bridge
when the lights went out—Dean Mallory, Roger Hadley,
Harriman Vonnegut, Gary Kepner, and six enlisted technicians. Swiftly, people began calling out their names and
status.

"Vogel! Okay!"

"Hadley! I'm okay!"

"Shapiro. I . . . I think my arm is broken . . ."

"Mallory. Okay. . . ."

"Newton. No problems."

Like hell, no problems, Gray thought, but he didn't interrupt the roll call. The eleven of them were okay, save for bumps and bruises—and that one possible broken arm. Gray didn't think about the one obvious health threat they all faced. He'd felt the tingling burn that meant the flag bridge, despite heavy shielding, had been bathed in hard radiation. If they got out of this, if they could get medical attention, get anti-rad nano injections—maybe even complete blood replacement—they had a good chance.

If not, they all were likely to get extremely ill over the next few hours and—depending on the dosage they'd just received—they would then die, hours or at most a few days after that.

"Anyone here cross-trained as a corpsman?"

"I've had advanced first aid, Admiral," a male voice said in the darkness.

"Who's that?"

"Kelly, sir."

"See if you can help . . . Shapiro, was it?"

"Yes, sir."

"Light would help. Anyone have a light?"

There was an awkward silence, then a female voice spoke up. "Admiral, Nav Tech Second Class Anderson here."

"Go ahead, Anderson."

"I have liquid light full-body tattoos that will help. Permission to switch them on, sir?"

"Granted. Do it."

Historically, as society had moved more and more away from the classic taboos against nudity, body adornment—tattoos and dermal nanimations had become both more and more popular and technologically elaborate. In the old wet navies of the world, of course, many sailors had sported tattoos—the heavily tattooed sailor had become something of a stereotype, in fact—but body art now was frowned on by the military on the grounds that it was distracting and tended to interfere with uniformity in ranks. Body art was tolerated if it was hidden by the uniform . . . and nowadays the implanted inks of most tattoos were powered by either body heat or by a tiny electrical charge pulled from the body itself, and could be switched on and off easily.

Liquid light images were more complex and used more power, but they were essentially the same—luminous dyes injected into the skin that drew power from the body's own heat, which could be switched on or off, and which, when activated, radiated anything from a dull glow to a brilliant haze of luminescence.

Light flared in the dark compartment, dazzling to dark-adapted eyes. NT2 Anderson appeared in the center of the light, which grew steadily brighter as she peeled off her shipboard utilities, exposing more and more of her body. Gray had seen the fashion before on Earth—people, especially women—who at fancy-dress occasions "wore" nothing but shoes and a translucent sheath of light. Such "lightgowns" had long been favorite items of fashion for women in Europe and the Americas.

Distracting indeed. No wonder Navy regs specified that you kept the stuff switched off when you were on duty.

Nude, now, Anderson drifted in the center of the compartment, her body aflame and throwing weirdly shifting shadows across the bulkheads, the dead overhead display, and the instrumentation. Able to see now, at least dimly, Gray oriented himself, then glanced forward. *America*'s command bridge was located just forward of and a few steps down from the flag bridge, but the opening between the two had been sealed off by a sliding panel when the ship had entered combat. Captain Gutierrez, Commander Taggart, and a number of other ship's officers were on the far side of that six-centimeter-thick wall of beryllialumisteel.

Gray looked about the flag bridge in frustration. Damn it, they needed power, and they needed it *now*. He didn't know how bad the damage to the carrier was—he had to assume it was *extremely* bad—but until internal communications were restored, at the very least, damage assessment and control were virtually impossible.

He found himself wishing that they could plug a power lead into Anderson and charge up the external displays, or at least a radio. He wanted to know what was going on outside almost as much as he wanted to know the extent of damage to the ship.

The battle would continue without his input, of course. There was a chain of command within every task force and carrier battlegroup; in the case of Task Force Eridani, command would have transferred immediately and automatically to Captain Wade Harmon of the *Constitution*—*America*'s sister ship—as soon as communications with *America* had been cut off. Harmon was a good officer, sharp and experienced. He would see things through.

But Gray's view on the cosmos had suddenly been narrowed to a single sealed and darkened shipboard compartment . . . and survival, he knew, was going to be a bit of a problem.

He was not, he noted, in complete zero gravity. Some moments after the lights went out, his back had bumped up against a bulkhead. The ship, he realized, must be slowly spinning, generating enough centrifugal force to create a very slight illusion of gravity. *America*'s bridge and flag bridge, together, were located in a squat tower extending out from the ship's spine 40 meters aft of the belly of the shield cap, and therefore quite close to the vessel's center of gravity. The farther out on the rotating ship's spine, the stronger the spin-gravity. The faster the spin, the stronger the spin-gravity. Gray estimated that the ship was rotating about a point up inside the shield cap at a rate of once every four or five minutes . . . a slow and stately spin, and one yielding an approximation of the surface gravity of a fair-sized asteroid. A thousandth of a G? Something like that.

With Anderson as a light source, Kelly had found an emergency first-aid kit in a bulkhead storage compartment and was immobilizing Shapiro's left arm. The gauze he was wrapping around Shapiro's limb would go rigid when he touched it and transmitted a thoughtclick, serving as a splint. They would worry about setting the bone later.

If there *was* a later.

Some of the ship's basic functions ought to still be working, so long as they weren't drawing solely from the main power plants. Emergency airtight doors, for instance. You needed to be able to operate them—either close them or open them—in an emergency, and so they were powered by small batteries imbedded in the bulkhead. Gray pushed off, drifting across the compartment until he bounced up against the sliding panel separating flag bridge from ship's bridge. Grasping a handhold, he searched up the frame of the door until he found the touchpad.

He didn't open it immediately, though. Instead, he placed the palm of his hand on a datanet pad. There might be a raging fire on the other side of the door . . . or hard vacuum. He needed to know before he opened anything.

Again, powered by emergency batteries, the pad fed him the information he needed: no fires, an atmosphere at standard temperature and pressure, no poisonous gases. Only then did he transmit a thoughtclick to open the door.

It slid aside, and the first thing Gray saw was Laurie Taggart, floating upside down relative to Gray on the other side of the doorway. "Sandy!" she exclaimed. "Thank God!"

He managed to refrain from embracing her, as much as he wanted to. "Are you okay, Commander?"

She nodded. "Everyone in here is fine. What the hell happened to us?"

Captain Gutierrez materialized out of the darkness and

clung to a bulkhead handhold. "No power, obviously," she said.

"We got hit at close range by a Grdoch X-ray laser," he said. "I don't know how bad the damage is. I suspect, though, that we've lost containment aft, and the singularities have gone rogue, probably with a vacuum-energy cascade to feed them."

Gutierrez nodded. "The radiation. Yes, we felt it. That makes sense."

"We'll be okay if we can get off the ship," Gray said.

"You . . . you're ordering us to abandon her, Admiral?" Gutierrez sounded combative, like she didn't approve and was about to give him an argument.

And Gray knew how she felt. He'd been captain of the *America* under Rear Admiral Jason Steiger . . . and there was no way to describe how *possessive* a captain felt about his ship even long after he'd moved on.

He was also aware, as she was, that it was the *captain's* responsibility to give the order to abandon ship, and no one else's . . . not even the admiral's.

"Not yet, Captain," he replied. "That's your decision, of course . . . but I hope you'll indulge me by not giving the order until it becomes absolutely necessary."

"What the hell else has to happen for it to be necessary?" Taggart asked.

"We need to give the rest of the crew a chance."

Large capital ships like the *America* had a kind of built-in escape pod: the entire bridge tower, containing both flag and command bridges and the CIC could be jettisoned. The hab modules, too, rotating about the ship's spine aft of the tower could be released, the centrifugal force of their rotation carrying them clear of the ship. Finally, Prifly—the carrier's Primary Flight Control—was located in a sponson aft of the hab modules, where it could oversee fighter launches and traps, and that could be jettisoned into space as well.

But there were other shipboard sections—especially engineering—located within the spine, and for *America* that meant almost a thousand men and women whose only possible escape was in the life pods mounted at the ends of escape passageways in the hull. Until emergency intraship communications could be re-established, allowing the order to reach *everyone* through their in-heads, neither Gray nor Gutierrez was going to be anxious to order a bug-out.

Of course, it might be necessary for every member of the crew to make their own decisions, if things got bad enough and communications could not be restored.

A deep-voiced, booming rumble sounded through the bridge, followed by a drawn-out grating squeal and a metallic clatter.

It was the sound, Gray knew, of a starship *in extremis*, stressed beyond all reasonable design limits and beginning to break up. "We need to get the IC working," he told the others. *"Now."*

Himmel-Paradisio Camp
Vulcan
40 Eridani A System
1615 hours, TFT

The crowd, numbering now in the hundreds—quite possibly the thousands—reached the northern perimeter of the prison compound, surging across the open meadow like a huge and living amoebic creature. Connor was in the lead, making for one of the perimeter towers.

Delgado had explained them to her. When the Grdoch had taken over on Vulcan, they'd relied on nanotechnology to create a quick and dirty fence. Floaters, alien vehicles drifting just above the ground, had circled the perimeter, planting rice-sized seeds that had immediately begun converting dirt and rock into a wall. Once the wall was fully grown, smooth-sided and sloping like the interior of an immense bowl, they'd cut a five-meter gap in one section and installed the gate.

There'd been no need for watch towers or guards. The curving wall reached varying heights around the circle, but nowhere was lower than seven meters, and the nanufactured surface of the barrier was so smooth that it looked like polished stone. There was simply no way that the prisoners, naked and without tools or weapons of any kind, were going to get up *that*.

But now they had weapons—three of them. Connor called Delgado and another man, Siegfried Koch, to her side. Koch appeared older—perhaps in his sixties, though with anagathic treatments, nowadays, it was impossible to accurately judge anyone's true age. He'd picked up the third Grdoch weapon moments ago and been unwilling to relinquish it. "I have experience," he'd told her.

"Tell your people to move well back," she told them. "If the wall explodes, we don't want people getting hit by hot gravel flying at high speed. Now . . . you see how these things work?"

"Point . . . and squeeze here," Koch said. "Seems simple enough. A maser?"

"I think so. Whatever it shoots, it focuses intense heat on or in the target. I suggest we fire together from a prone position."

As the crowd edged back, the three of them lay down in the yellow moss, aimed at a single point in the wall half a meter above the ground, and fired. The resultant explosion was sudden, sharp, and remarkably satisfying: a flash and a crack of shattering material that did indeed send fragments of stone hurtling above their bodies.

Two more shots were necessary to widen the gap enough, and then Delgado shouted *"adelante,"* and the crowd surged forward.

"Watch the sides!" Connor yelled as they passed. "Don't touch them! They're hot!"

She, Delgado, and Koch waited as the crowd streamed through the opening. A runner arrived, breathless, to tell them that Grdoch, a *lot* of Grdoch, were entering the compound now at the gate in the east.

"How many, Peter?" he asked in German.

The boy shook his head, answering in the same language. "I don't know, Governor! But many! *Many!* And with weapons!"

"Responding to a call for help from those three, do you think?" Connor asked. "Or did we trigger an alarm when we blew the wall?"

"It doesn't matter," Koch said. He was staring toward the southeast, looking for some sign of the approaching threat. "They're coming . . . and we can't hold them off, just the three of us."

"No," Delgado agreed. He raised his voice, addressing the fleeing civilians. "*Faster*, people, *faster*!"

A tall and muscular man separated from the crowd and approached them. "How can I help?" He was holding a crudely fashioned spear.

"You are . . . ?" Connor asked.

"Gunnery Sergeant Thomas Weirton, ma'am. USNS *Intrepid.*"

"Governor?" Connor said. "How about you giving your gun to this man, and you get the hell out of here."

Delgado hesitated, then shook his head. "No, ma'am. I am responsible for their safety. I will stay."

"Herr Koch?"

"No, Lieutenant. I was *Wachtmeister* in another life, long ago . . . Pan-European army. Then I retired and emigrated here. I will stay and fight."

Connor was about to make it an order . . . then changed her mind. There was something about the expression in Delgado's eyes, in the set of Koch's jaw. "Care to join us, Gunnery Sergeant?" she said. "Even without a weapon?"

"*Semper fi*, ma'am," Weirton told her, using the ancient motto of both the U.S. and the USNA Marines. "And there are other Intrepids here who want to fight."

"Round them up, Gunnery Sergeant. If we can't give you weapons now, maybe we can take them."

The Marine gave a wolfish grin. "My thought exactly, Lieutenant."

She looked at the sharpened point of the Marine's spear. "How the hell did you people carve these spears, anyway? Were you able to smuggle knives in here?"

"No, ma'am. We tried . . . but . . ." He gestured at his own nakedness. "They didn't let us keep anything. But there *are* rocks out here. Nothing like flint, unfortunately, but there *are* other kinds of quartz. We experimented, hammering them together, and there were some that flaked off in nice, sharp shards. We also got sparks, and were able to use them to set fires."

Connor's eyebrows went up. "I'm impressed, Gunny."

"Adapt, improvise, overcome." It was another ancient mantra of the Corps. "Anyway, ma'am, we got enough of those flakes sharp enough that we could whittle with them." He shook the pole in his hand. "And this stuff is growing all over the south side of this fucking place. We were able to break them off, sharpen them, and harden the points in fire. Never did figure out how to make stone spear points and attach them to the stick . . . but then we only had a couple of weeks to work on it."

"You were planning a break-out?"

"Abso-damn-lutely! Trouble was, we kept trying to attack individual Grdoch with these things, but their skins were just too tough. Had to wait until you came along with your laser pistol before we could do the bastards some *real* damage. Hey!" He turned, waving at someone in the streaming crowd. "Callahan! Get your ass over here!"

A young man separated from the moving crowd. With his spear and shaggy beard, he was the perfect image of a prehistoric hunter. A woman joined them, also armed. These had been some of the people who'd rushed the armed Grdoch a few minutes before, facing maser fire and horrible deaths in an attempt to kill their foes. It was, Connor thought, nothing short of astonishing.

Minutes passed, with a small but quickly growing group of armed men and women forming a rough perimeter around the opening in the wall. The civilians kept moving through, faster now as the number of people still inside the compound dwindled.

"I feel," Delgado said after a while, "like Moses at the Red Sea. And the Egyptians are very nearly upon us."

Connor had to search her in-head for the reference . . . and frowned when she found it. The people she'd interacted with here, Delgado and Fuentes and some of the others, were unusually free in their use of religious terms and expressions. At first, she'd dismissed it as a cultural affectation. Colony worlds far from Earth and the Confederation's central government, might be expected to be lax in the enforcement of social mandates like the White Covenant. Others, like the handful of colony worlds established by the Islamic Theocracy, had been established in direct opposition to the White Covenant doctrine.

But Fuentes, she remembered, hadn't been part of this culture.

It was, Connor thought, a good example of what had been called the foxhole mentality: there are no atheists in foxholes. It didn't mean a particular doctrine or church, but an overall conviction that *someone* had to be in charge in a universe of unreasoning and irrational violence, fear, and chaos. Without God, that universe swiftly became far too large and far too threatening for the human mind to hold; combat—or the nightmare horror of something like the Grdoch—was guaranteed to bring out the religious impulse resident within every human, an impulse that might well define what Humankind really was.

Like most people who'd grown up in the shadow of the White Covenant, Connor felt mildly embarrassed when someone else invoked God . . . but she was more than willing to overlook such social gaffes if it made fearful people less fearful, despondent people hopeful, or broken people able to function.

Besides, she thought as she watched the last of the crowd feeding through the gap in the wall . . . Delgado was right. It *was* an exodus . . . maybe not one with divine help, but it was an exodus from slavery and fear and nightmare all the same.

The last of the former prisoners vanished through the gap. "Okay," Connor said. "The rest of you start falling back. Out the hole and scatter."

"Too late," Weirton said. He gestured with his spear, looking for all the world like a grim-faced Paleolithic hunter. "The bastards are here. . . ."

USNA CVS America
40 Eridani A System
1615 hours, TFT

"I think that's it over there," an electronics technician said, pointing.

"Get in here closer, Anderson," Gutierrez said. "I can't see."

"How's this, ma'am?"

"Better . . ."

"If we can get power in there at that junction," Kepner said, "we should be able to get at least partial use of the ship's netlink."

"How about the battery for the door?" Gray suggested. "It should be behind that panel over there."

"Might work," Gutierrez said. "Conway! Johansson! See if you can get that cover open! Anderson, give them some light!"

The ship's netlink was essentially a ship-wide Internet run off an auxiliary server. Even with the main power down, it should have remained functioning, but the power surge when the X-ray beam had burned through the main power module had fried several key junctions, despite circuit hardening. With the netlink operational, anyone with the usual military-standard hardware inside their heads could connect with anyone else on the net, with voice communications, up- and downloading files, or using personal secretaries and avatars to share information. If they could get it running again, they should be able to communicate freely with everyone on board *America*.

There'd been seemingly endless minor problems and frustrations. Panels were closed by self-turning screws; you touched the head with a thumb and it would unscrew itself if it was already in place, or screw itself in if it was not. The power, however, came from the ship's reserve battery power . . . and that had gone with the power surge that had burned out the server connections. The screw heads were designed to use old-fashioned screwdrivers, but there were none of those relics on either bridge.

Vonnegut, however, spotted the centimeter-wide strip of metal trim on Gray's command seat, and a few minutes' worth of cursing and hurt fingers got it peeled off. The strip was flat enough that the corner of one end fit inside the screw head slot; it was awkward, but they were able to back the screw out. A few more minutes, and the panel was off.

That gave them access to the door battery, which Macy, a computer/electronics tech, began wiring into the netlink server. She snapped home a final connection, the server purred to life, and Gray felt the inner click, saw the cascade of data, and knew they were back on-line.

It was, he reflected, decidedly old tech . . . *ancient* tech, in fact. For culture with nanotechnology and gavitics it was very nearly on a par with chipped flints and the fire bow. He was fiercely proud, however, of the way his bridge teams had pulled together, improvising, adapting, and finagling to make it work.

"Damage control!" he thought, opening the channel. "This is Admiral Gray. What's our status?"

"Not good, Admiral," came the reply. "But help is on the way!"

"What help?"

"Can you download visuals?"

"That's affirmative."

"Have a look, sir. . . ."

A window opened in Gray's mind, and he saw *America* from the outside, a scene relayed in through a battlespace drone, most likely. The carrier had lost perhaps two hundred meters off the ass end of her tail. From the look of it, a missile or high-energy beam had sliced right through the ship's spine and cut the aft power tap assemblies free. He could see the jettisoned fragment in the distance, tumbling end for end in a sparkling haze of hit plasma and free-floating bits of molten metal from the hull. As he watched, what was left of the power assembly was crumpling in upon itself, folding its ungainly mass into a tighter and tighter space. The rogue singularities—they would no longer be *micro*—were crushing the spine fragment under unimaginable gravity.

"That would have been *us*, Admiral," the damage control officer told him. "But a fast-thinking fighter jock used a Krait to blow the assembly clear."

"What about the Grdoch?" he asked. "Are we still under fire?"

"We haven't been under fire, sir, but I don't know what's been happening. We've . . . kind of had our hands full, y'know?"

"Understood. What's the bill?"

"Main taps are gone, of course, and a lot of the secondaries got fried by the power surge. We have crews fighting fires in Sections Red-One through Red-Five, but it looks like we have them contained okay. I don't know about casualties.

There might have been three or four hundred people in the power tap assembly structure, though . . . and we have some serious radiation casualties here. You guys got knocked off the netlink channels, but the netlink is still functioning most other places. Commander Fletcher took command and is getting things organized."

"Excellent work," Gray said. He could hear the urgency in the man's voice, and decided it was better not to question him further. "Carry on."

"Aye, aye, sir."

He'd forgotten to ask what the man had meant by help being on the way, but it didn't matter. Through the drone's eye, he could see easily enough. The *Constitution*, *America*'s sister ship—immense and ponderous and proud—was angling in alongside. Less than half a kilometer off *America*'s starboard side, now, she was turning slowly to put herself exactly parallel.

And smaller ships—repair transporters and SAR vessels and even a captain's gig were spilling from her launch bays and closing with the *America*.

"I think," he told the officers and enlisted personnel with him, "we're going to make it."

Chapter Twenty-three

Himmel-Paradisio Camp
Vulcan
40 Eridani A System
1615 hours, TFT

Connor lay stretched out flat on the hard ground, clutching the alien weapon in both hands. A line of Grdoch were advancing across the meadow in an open formation, moving slowly but steadily toward the gap blown in the perimeter wall.

"We've got to buy our people some time!" she told the others. The escaping prisoners had only just slipped through the gap.

"Maybe we won't have to," Weirton replied. "What the hell is going on over there?"

North, a series of blinding flashes walked along the horizon, the sound arriving long seconds later. "That's the Twin Cities," Delgado said. "They must be under attack!"

"Our fleet," Connor said. "We must have grabbed local space control! But it may take the good guys a while to get out here. Don't count on a rescue!"

"Maybe *they* don't know that," Weirton replied.

The Grdoch appeared to be confused—possibly fearful, certainly hesitant. Some were rolling away now, back toward the main gate. Others seemed inclined to keep advancing.

Connor argued with herself for a moment. Should she order the armed members of the group to fire? Or might that make the Grdoch currently retreating turn around and attack? Grdoch psychology was still not well understod. Certainly, it was more complex than the simplistic choice between flight or fight suggested by the pre-mission briefings.

She decided to wait. Had the Grdoch even seen them yet? No one knew how good their eyesight was. They could see in every direction, yes, but what kind of resolution did they have? If they hadn't seen the humans lying on the ground near the gap yet, it might be better to surprise them.

And some of their number were definitely fleeing.

"Hold your fire," she said, her voice low. "Let them go. The fewer there are . . ."

". . . the fewer we have to kill," Weirton said, grinning. "You think like a Marine, Lieutenant."

"I'll take that as a compliment."

"It was meant as one."

There were still twenty or twenty-five of the scarlet horrors rolling toward them.

"We're not going to be able to kill them all," Delgado said.

"Kill enough of the bastards," Connor said, "and maybe the rest will run."

She hated this: the waiting, out in the open, not moving. For a fighter pilot, speed was life, and lying on the ground watching alien horrors advance on your position just didn't cut it.

Connor didn't think they were going to get out of this. Delgado was right. There was no way in hell they could drop all of the approaching Grdoch. She remembered how hard it had been to kill just three of the things . . . and that had been with an angry and suicidal mob with spears helping out. There were twelve of them there, holding the perimeter, and only three with high-tech weapons. Not enough . . . not enough by far . . .

The nearest Grdoch were a hundred meters away, now, and the group was picking up speed.

"Okay, people," Connor said. "Drop 'em!"

She squeezed the firing bulb on her weapon. Two of the Grdoch staggered and writhed as a column of earth and smoke exploded in front of a third. One of them had missed. "Watch your targets, damn it! Don't waste your shots!" She didn't know how long the weapons would keep firing, and it was vital that they make every shot count.

Rather than continue to hammer at one Grdoch, she shifted her aim back and forth. If enough of them were hurt, they might break and run quicker than if only a couple were actually killed.

All of them were still coming. *Damn*, but they were hard to kill!

Connor was firing and firing and firing, her hands and wrists painful . . . then numb . . . and still the three of them were firing into the advancing line. The Grdoch were firing as well, now. An *Intrepid* enlisted man nearby shrieked and jumped up, his skin blackening horribly, and the ground began exploding in and in front of the human perimeter.

And then the ground in front of them erupted, a black wall of rising dirt and smoke and flame in a thunderous roar. The shock wave slapped Connor's legs and torso *hard*. What the hell?

At first she thought the Grdoch had just fired a new and far more powerful weapon. These mouth-guns of theirs weren't powerful enough to do *that*. . . .

Then she saw the Nightshades.

AGG-44 Nightshades—two-seater gravitic gunships— were Marine air- and space-support vehicles. Ugly, bug-like vehicles, they could only manage accelerations of about 12

Gs, but they were superb as low-altitude close-support, bristling with high-energy lasers and sky-to-ground missiles.

There were four of them, shrieking in from the north and whipping through the cloud of smoke and airborne debris they'd just released. They were close enough that Connor could see the USNA Marines legend on the sides, could feel the shudder in the air as the nearest whipped past.

"Ooh-rah!" Weirton yelled, rising to his feet and shaking his spear. "Get 'em, zoomies! *Get 'em!*"

The four aircraft vanished toward the south, but in moments they'd pulled up short and circled around for another pass. As the smoke from their first attack whisped away on a gentle breeze, Grdoch emerged . . . closer now, but Connor could only see fifteen of them now, and several were badly torn and bleeding.

"Keep firing!" she yelled, and she turned her weapon on the nearest Grdoch, blowing a bloody crater out of its torso and knocking it back a few steps. The others were wavering.

The Nightshades made a second pass, slower, now, and lower, literally skimming in a meter or two above the ground. She heard a high-pitched whine, a kind of buzz, and realized they were using their Gatlings on the aliens, chewing through the Grdoch at twelve depleted-uranium rounds per second.

"Anyone down there hear us?" a man's voice said, speaking in her head.

"I've got you!" Connor replied. "Lieutenant Connor, VFA-96, USNS *America.*"

"Lieutenant Dillon, USNA Marines. Are those civilian prisoners down there with you?"

"Mixed bag, Dillon," she replied. "Civilians, and a few off the *Intrepid*. Where do you want us?"

There was a pause, presumably as Dillon consulted a higher authority. "Actually, right there inside that compound would be good," he told her. "I've told the Regimental CO, and they'll have Marines here in a few mikes."

Connor laughed. She laughed hard. It was not, she realized, funny, but the stress of the past hours had taken a toll, and the sheer relief of the rescue had made her giddy.

"We'll have to track most of them down and get them back here," she told Dillon. One of the Nightshades was hovering, she saw, looking for all the world like the head and body of a huge, black, squat dragonfly . . . and apparently looking right at her. Impulsively, she waved. In answer, the Nightshade rocked its fuselage port to starboard and back several times, an acknowledging waggle.

"It's okay if you can't round all of them up," Dillon said. "From up here, it looks like the bad guys are on the run."

"So . . . we won?"

There was a hesitation. "We won," Dillon said at last. "But it cost us. Dear *God*, but it cost us."

Connor felt a chill at the words, and wondered what had happened.

USNA CVS America
40 Eridani A System
1927 hours, TFT

He'd transferred his flag to the *Constitution*. From the flag bridge of the new carrier, Gray and his command constellation had an unhindered view of surrounding space—of the USNA fleet in orbit, and the blue, white, and orange sweep of the planet turning below. The battle was over, both in orbit and on the ground. *Victory* . . .

Mostly.

America was surrounded by a cloud of smaller spacecraft—work drones and robots and transporters carrying out inspections and beginning repairs. The goal was to get her spaceworthy enough that she could be piloted back to Earth, and that meant replacing her power tap assembly.

To that end, scouts had identified a small planetoid in the

system—there were two major asteroid belts circling 40 Eridani A—and fleet nanengineers were beginning the work of programming seed nano that would be able to disassemble the planetoid and grow a new power tap assembly. The work would take several weeks—much of that time devoted to the testing and balancing. If they couldn't get everything purring along exactly right, *America* would have to stay here in Vulcan orbit until a ship-repair nanufactory could be built in this system. And there might be . . . political problems with that.

Though technically still part of the Earth Confederation, the locals had wholeheartedly joined in with the USNA task force. Captain del Castro, commanding the Confederation Vulcan battlegroup, had placed the ten ships of his contingent unreservedly under Gray's command. His flag, the battlecruiser *Estrella de la Plata*, was alongside the USNA *Maine* now, taking off the last of that vessel's survivors. The *Maine* was almost certainly beyond repair—her spine severed in three places, her shield cap and all-important gravitic projectors burned away. Out of her crew of two thousand, more than twelve hundred had been killed, including her skipper, Catharine Francesconi. *La Plata*'s SAR teams were still going through the wreckage compartment by compartment, searching for more survivors. Captain Francesconi, Gray knew now, had almost certainly saved *America* by interposing her ship between the Grdoch wreck and the star carrier.

As ship's captain, Catharine's first responsibility had been to her crew and her ship. As commander of the entire task force, it had been Gray's job to see the larger picture, to move the different ships like pieces on a chessboard toward the mission objective as a whole, sacrificing some pieces if necessary.

And, damn it, the nature of war made it *always* necessary.

It would have been one thing had he ordered Captain Francesconi to block the enemy's beam and save the *Amer-*

ica. But Catharine Francesconi had made that decision on her own.

Gray wondered if he would have been able to do the same, had the roles been reversed.

What he *had* done, he was all too aware, was underestimate an alien enemy, and that had very nearly cost him the star carrier *America*. Not exactly a career-enhancing move, though Gray cared little for the politics of naval careers. He'd told President Koenig, more than once, that he'd not wanted this job, the command of an entire carrier task force. Politics being what they were, he had no doubt whatsoever about the outcome, here. There wouldn't be official retribution—at least *probably* there would not be, but he would be transferred to a desk Earth- or Mars-side and never command a task force *or* a ship again.

So be it. He'd done his best, and the best had not quite been good enough. He'd failed to establish communications with the Grdoch—not that they'd seemed all that willing to talk in the first place. He'd found what was left of the crews of *Intrepid* and the *Tomlinson*, one of the other ships of *Intrepid*'s task force, and that, at least, represented a mission success. Reports from the planet's surface indicated that there were several hundred of them alive and well down there, under the able protection of Engelmann's 1/5 Marines. And he'd convinced the locals to switch their allegiance from the Confederation to the USNA, though Gray knew that he'd had less to do with that decision than the Grdoch. All things considered, 40 Eridani had been a success. A *victory* . . .

But as was always true with military victories, however, the outcome was a mix of success, failure, and terrible loss.

"Everything okay, Admiral?" *Constitution*'s skipper, Wade Harmon, had just floated up from the command bridge. "Getting settled in okay?"

"Just fine, Captain. Thank you."

"There . . . ah . . . there's a lot of scuttlebutt going around the *Connie*, Admiral. Talk about where the task force is headed next."

"And what's the consensus so far?"

"Earth. There's a large minority that's holding out for the 'Doch home planet, though."

Gray laughed. "Well . . . we'd need to know just where that is. The Grdoch prisoners haven't been real forthcoming in that regard as yet."

There were almost eight thousand Grdoch now being held as prisoners of war, some rescued from fighters around Vulcan, most from the bases they'd established on the surface. Without space support, they'd all surrendered quickly enough. The XT people had been questioning some of them with the new language software, but with no success so far. Gray had seen the report. Eighty Grdoch questioned about the location of their home star system, all purportedly eager to please their captors, had given fifty-nine different answers, ranging from a red dwarf ten light years away to an ancient red giant within the galactic core. Those that could be checked out would be, of course, using robotic drones or recon squadrons, but that would take months, and Gray suspected that none of those fifty-nine would prove accurate. Had the Grdoch discovered the location of Sol and Earth, the results could have been cataclysmic, but, fortunately, pinpointing Sol would be a problem for beings looking for it. The fact that Earth was the third planet of a G2 star a bit less than halfway out from the galactic center was useless by itself, given the sheer number of stars and worlds fitting that description, and the system coordinates—and the programs necessary to translate those coordinates into something useful—were closely guarded secrets. The Grdoch would be no less cautious.

Even so, it had been a damned near thing. The Grdoch, evidently, had stumbled across the human colony at 40 Eridani, made contact with the Confederation forces there . . . *and then the dumb bastards had brought a Grdoch warship straight to Sol.* That ship had been destroyed at Enceladus, thank the gods, but the results could have been disastrous for Humankind had the Grdoch ship managed to escape. The Sh'daar had learned the exact coordinates of Earth decades ago, and two Sh'daar client races—the Turusch and the H'rulka—had brought the war into the Sol System; the Turusch had even been able to slam a high-velocity impactor into Earth herself with devastating results.

What the Grdoch might have done had they found Earth simply didn't bear thinking about.

Gray hadn't offered any further information. After a long moment's silence, Harmon added, "So, we're headed back home?"

"Eventually, Captain. I want to make very sure that we've rounded up all of the Grdoch. I've dispatched a squadron to check out B and C."

"I was wondering about that, sir."

The two other stars in the system, 40 Eridani B and C, circled each other in an elliptical orbit averaging 35 astronomical units across some 400 AUs out—a distance of 53 light hours. The Grdoch ships had appeared to be trying to head in that direction, and Gray wanted to be damned sure there was nothing else out there . . . like a third Grdoch warship.

He would *not* underestimate the bastards again.

"I also want to see if we're going to be able to carry out local repairs on the *America*, at least enough to let her limp home . . . or if we're going to need to bring out a mobile nanufactory. Some of the other task force ships are in a bad way too. The *Slava* got pretty badly shot up. So did the *Long Island*. The *Constitution* took a hit too—"

"Nothing that can't be regrown in pretty short order, Admiral."

"I'm glad to hear it. But I want to bring the fleet back to full readiness—as full as we can manage out here, anyway. And we need to decide what we're doing about the prisoners."

"I heard they're being kept in their own prison camps. Good solution."

"For now. I ordered that they be herded into the walled enclosures that have some of their praedams inside."

Gray made a face as he said it. It left a distinctly unpleasant taste in his mouth. He still remembered the horror of watching the Grdoch swarm a living food animal—a sight nasty enough to make anyone a confirmed vegetarian.

But starving Grdoch prisoners to death would be worse . . . and at least the enormous praedams weren't sentient, so far as any XT personnel had been able to discover.

The Grdoch, Gray thought, were going to pose Humankind with some absolutely horrific ethical problems in the future. What did you do, how did you respond, when another sentient species—one with which you wanted to form an alliance, a partnership—held values and ideals so markedly different from your own?

Once, centuries before, a vicious, bloody, and long-fought war had divided Humankind between the West and the followers of religious doctrines that were antithetical to what the West thought of as *civilized* belief in almost every way. Even mainstream and moderate Islam believed with all the fervor of their faith in practices and punishments the West no longer accepted.

Never mind that the West's sacred scriptures *also* called for death for homosexuals, for heretics, for witches, for disbelief, as well as promoting the subjugation of women and the use of slaves for pleasure. The difference was that Islam was still a young religion, youngest of the three great monotheistic faiths, and had simply not yet grown up enough to discard such childishness. Where the West preached—for the most part—tolerance, diversity, and inclusiveness, such attitudes could not be part of moderate Islam without seriously undercutting fundamentalist belief, an attack on Allah and on His Messenger.

And the West had come dangerously close, in the name of

understanding and inclusiveness, to going under. Only military victory, the controversial White Covenant, and a united Earth Confederation willing to back it up, had given modern Islam the opportunity to grow up.

Had they not, utter destruction would have been the only possible outcome.

Something of the sort, Gray thought, would be necessary in dealing with the Grdoch. Would they be willing to engage in free and open communication, diplomatic recognition, scientific exchanges, even trade, with creatures they thought of as *food*?

And what was the alternative? Genocide?

Gray fervently hoped he wouldn't be around to take part in that decision.

"The damned 'Dochs wouldn't have done as much for us," Harmon observed.

"Maybe not. But we have to set standards, draw lines, somewhere."

The trick was knowing where to draw the line, though. Moderate Islam, four centuries ago, would have rejected utterly the idea that their religion was immature, that it was incomplete or barbaric or lacking in any way. They believed what they believed because they were convinced it came straight from God.

And it wasn't just Islam. The same was true of fundamentalist Christians, of Orthodox Jews . . . of *any* belief system purportedly handed down by divine fiat. "God said it, that settles it" had been the motto for generation after generation of believers of all of the monotheistic faiths.

The Grdoch, Gray knew, would never accept the idea that their behavior was in any way uncivilized. He didn't know if they believed in God, but they would argue, rightly, that they'd been made the way they were by the forces of evolution.

And they certainly wouldn't change what they were—*could not* change what they were—just because another species found their behavior horrific.

Was it possible that some mutually alien species were so different from one another they could *never* communicate in any meaningful way?

Was it possible that the same was true for some purely human belief systems?

Or was the only solution something like the White Covenant, backed by military force?

It was not, Gray thought, a happy thought.

Emergency Presidential Command Post
Toronto
United States of North America
2335 hours, EST

"You want to *get rid* of the White Covenant?" Deb Johnston sounded shocked. "My God, why?"

They lay in bed together, still entangled in each other's arms. Koenig had brought her back to the EPCP and, eventually, asked her to spend the night. His security detail knew she was there, of course—how could they not?

But if he'd given them fits over the past six years by insisting on his own way, still, he trusted their discretion. There would be no leaks, not from *that* quarter.

Still, Gods . . . if his conservative Freedomist support base discovered that he was literally in bed with a Globalist, heaven help them all. . . .

"Well," he said slowly, "the *political* reason is that we want to clear the way for an alliance with the Islamists."

She nodded. "We've been pushing for that for years. It's stupid to have a true global government when a billion people aren't even allowed to be a part of it."

"I know."

"And I know you're the most apolitical Freedomist I've ever met. What's your *real* reason?"

"Big government, government that has forgotten that it

derives its power from its people, is one of the worst evils
Humankind has managed to unleash on itself. Government
has no business telling its citizens what to believe . . . or how
to exercise their religious expression."

"But mob rule—that's what *true* democracy is, you
know—can be as much of a tyranny as any other. That's
why we have a *representative* democracy. The people, the
ordinary citizens, don't know what's best for themselves."

"And a bunch of bureaucrats or elected officials *do*?
Come on! You know, the old United States of America ran
afoul of mommy-knows-best government in the twenty-first
century, when it flirted with socialism. Universal education
. . . run by the government. Universal health care . . . run by
the government. Universal food rights . . . run by the government. Universal work rights . . . run by the government. By
the middle of the century, the country was on the point of
collective suicide. Suicide by taxation. By presidential edict.
By legal entanglements. By wholesale corruption.

"The trouble is that government, *big* government, government from the top down is appallingly inefficient. It mostly
exists just to keep itself going. In the old USA, all of the
universal entitlement programs, all the free giveaways, all of
the sheer corruption, from local township offices all the way
up to the presidency itself, finally broke the bank . . . and the
only thing that kept the country going was the Islamic Wars
. . . and after that the First Sino-Western War. Then global
sea levels rose, the Blood Death killed a billion and a half
people, and the government was like a dinosaur confronted
by a falling six-mile asteroid. What was left fell into anar-
chy, at least for a few decades."

"But we came back. Unlike the dinosaurs."

"In a sense, I suppose. The analogy only goes so far. The
United States of North America rose from the ruins with
a new constitution and a new start. But . . . you know? We
went on making the exact same mistakes. Maybe that's just
human nature.

"The point is that big government, top-down government, government serving itself, *entrenching* itself, is never the answer."

"What is?"

"Dam'fino. But separation of church and state is a good start. People need to take the responsibility for their own decisions . . . and their own belief."

"You're going to have a fight in the North American Senate."

"I know." He thought about it for a moment. "I think they'll fall into line, though. The revelations about the Grdoch threat have people scared. It makes sense to ally with the Islamic Theocracy. And the Chinese Hegemony too. Humankind needs to be united, *really* united."

"And what about the Sh'daar? You want to ally with them? Against the Rosette Aliens?"

"If we can find a way around their insistence that we give up our technology, why not? The Grdoch have proven to us that there are some *very* dark forces out there in the galaxy. Things a lot bigger than us, a lot nastier than us. If we don't find a way to get along with one another—humans with humans, humans with Sh'daar, humans with anyone else we find we can communicate with—then we're going to drift into slavery . . . and maybe extinction. *Probably* extinction, because if we stay static, if we don't grow, we die."

"Well, maybe if—"

"Damn!" A signal was sounding in his head, the chirp alerting him to an urgent message. "Hold on a sec, love. . . ."

He opened the channel.

"Sorry to disturb you, Mr. President." It was Marcus Whitney, his chief of staff.

"Tell me."

"Intelligence has picked up a flurry of new reports from Europe. It looks like the Confederation is collapsing. The army has launched a coup. Denoix has fled. Korosi is in custody. England, Germany, and Ukraine have all announced they are seceding. Italy and Spain may be next."

"Who the hell is in charge over there?"

"No one, at least right now. The Starlight movement is demanding an end to the war and free elections. They're calling for Constantine d'Angelo as president. . . ."

"My God . . ."

"Konstantin—at Tsiolkovsky—is on it, Mr. President. He'll be releasing a statement in a few hours. Mr. President. We've *won*!"

"So it would seem, Marcus."

Koenig was stunned by the suddenness of the reversal. Oh, there'd been signs of discontent within Pan-Europe, certainly, but it had been only a week since the recombinant memetic virus had been unleashed into Geneva's computer infrastructure.

The news did not exactly reassure him, however. The USNA might well have just won its independence, but a very great deal depended now on just what was going to replace the Earth Confederation. Would it be a new confederation led by the USNA? Or would the power vacuum in Europe be filled by something darker than a merely socialist government?

He wondered if Konstantin had any ideas on the matter.

"Okay, Marcus," Koenig said. "Call me if anything more breaks."

"Yes, Mr. President."

"What is it, Alex?" Johnston asked him.

"I'm . . . not sure," he told her, pulling her a little closer. He shivered a bit, with a terrible premonition. "A new world, certainly. But I'm not sure yet what kind of a new world it's going to be. . . ."

Epilogue

The Consciousness was aware of life—of *Mind*—within this new reality. It was Mind, after all, that had called this universe into being, Mind that had organized its laws, its physics, and the life that now filled it.

And on some level, Mind always called to Mind.

It was aware of a cybernetic consciousness united across a vast span of time . . . aware of another cybernetic consciousness that opposed the first.

Division . . . Conflict . . . Extinction . . .

Something would have to be done.

The Consciousness began to move, light years falling away in its wake.

The problem, as always, would be to find a means of establishing meaningful communication with the Minds of this reality.

IAN DOUGLAS's
STAR CARRIER
SERIES

EARTH STRIKE
BOOK ONE
978-0-06-184025-8

To the Sh'daar, the driving technologies of transcendent change are anathema and must be obliterated from the universe—along with those who would employ them. As their great warships destroy everything in their path en route to the Sol system, the human Confederation government falls into dangerous disarray.

CENTER OF GRAVITY
BOOK TWO
978-0-06-184026-5

On the far side of human known space, the Marines are under siege, battling the relentless servant races of the Sh'daar aggressor. Admiral Alexander Koenig knows the element of surprise is their only hope as he takes the war for humankind's survival directly to the enemy.

SINGULARITY
BOOK THREE
978-0-06-184027-2

In the wake of the near destruction of the solar system, the political powers on Earth seek a separate peace with an inscrutable alien life form that no one has ever seen. But Admiral Alexander Koenig has gone rogue, launching his fabled battlegroup beyond the boundaries of Human Space against all orders.

DEEP SPACE
BOOK FOUR
978-0-06-218380-4

After twenty years of peace, a Confederation research vessel has been ambushed, and destroyers are descending on a human colony. It seems the Sh'daar have betrayed their treaty, and all nations must stand united—or face certain death.

MARCUS PELEGRIMAS's

SKINNERS

HUMANKIND'S LAST DEFENSE AGAINST THE DARKNESS

BLOOD BLADE
978-0-06-146305-1

There is a world inhabited by supernatural creatures of the darkness—all manner of savage, impossible beasts that live for terror and slaughter and blood. They are all around us but you cannot see them, and for centuries a special breed of hunter called Skinners has kept the monsters at bay, preventing them from breaking through the increasingly fragile barriers protecting our mortal realm. But beware…for there are very few of them left.

HOWLING LEGION
978-0-06-146306-8

TEETH OF BEASTS
978-0-06-146307-5

VAMPIRE UPRISING
978-0-06-198633-8

THE BREAKING
978-0-06-198634-5

EXTINCTION AGENDA
978-0-06-198638-3

MP 0711

IAN DOUGLAS's
MONUMENTAL SAGA
OF INTERGALACTIC WAR
THE INHERITANCE TRILOGY

STAR STRIKE: BOOK ONE

978-0-06-123858-1

Planet by planet, galaxy by galaxy, the inhabited universe has fallen to the alien Xul. Now only one obstacle stands between them and total domination: the warriors of a resilient human race the world-devourers nearly annihilated centuries ago.

GALACTIC CORPS: BOOK TWO

978-0-06-123862-8

In the year 2886, intelligence has located the gargantuan hidden homeworld of humankind's dedicated foe, the brutal Xul. The time has come for the courageous men and women of the 1st Marine Interstellar Expeditionary Force to strike the killing blow.

SEMPER HUMAN: BOOK THREE

978-0-06-116090-5

True terror looms at the edges of known reality. Humankind's eternal enemy, the Xul, approach wielding a weapon monstrous beyond imagining. If the Star Marines fail to eliminate their relentless xenophobic foe once and for all, the Great Annihilator will obliterate every last trace of human existence.

IDI 0609